Barcelona Calling

Other Titles by Jane Kirkpatrick

The Daughter's Walk

Portraits of the Heart Series
(two titles including *A Flickering Light*)

Change and Cherish Series
(three titles including *A Clearing in the Wild*)

Tender Ties Historical Series
(three titles including *A Name of her Own*)

Kinship and Courage Series
(three titles including *All Together in One Place*)

The Dreamcatcher Collection
(four titles including *A Sweetness to the Soul*)

A Land of Sheltered Promise

Nonfiction titles

Homestead

A Simple Gift of Comfort

Aurora:
An American Experience in Quilt, Community, and Craft

a novel

JANE KIRKPATRICK

ZONDERVAN®

ZONDERVAN.com/
AUTHORTRACKER
follow your favorite authors

ZONDERVAN

Barcelona Calling
Copyright © 2011 by Jane Kirkpatrick

This title is also available as a Zondervan ebook. Visit www.zondervan.com/ebooks.

This title is also available in a Zondervan audio edition. Visit www.zondervan.fm.

Requests for information should be addressed to:
Zondervan, *Grand Rapids, Michigan 49530*

Library of Congress Cataloging-in-Publication Data

Kirkpatrick, Jane, 1946–
    Barcelona calling / Jane Kirkpatrick.
      p. cm.
    ISBN 978-0-310-29364-4 (pbk.)
    I. Title.
  PS3561.I712B37 2011
  813'.54—dc22   2011005752

Published in association with Hartline Literary Agency, Pittsburgh, Pennsylvania 15235.

Cover design: *Extra Credit Projects*
Cover photography: *Getty Images®*
Interior design: *Beth Shagene*

Printed in the United States of America

11 12 13 14 15 16 /DCI/ 23 22 21 20 19 18 17 16 15 14 13 12 11 10 9 8 7 6 5 4 3 2 1

To the almost-famous everywhere

Cast of Characters

Annie Shaw — a writer

Annie's friends:

    Misty — a mom and former bodybuilder

    Bette — a cook at a senior residence

    Darlien — a police officer and Annie's sister

    Kari — a social worker and cousin to Annie and Darlien

Clint — Kari's husband

Randolph — Annie's agent

Mavis — Annie's hired publicist

Irving — Annie's editor

Stuart — Annie's ex-husband

John — Annie's cat

Ho-Bee — Annie's dog

If the only reward I obtain for my writing
is the writing itself, let it be sufficient.

Barry B. Longyear

◎

It is only when we believe that we are creating the soul that life has any meaning ... I have been over-concerned with the materialistic aspects of bringing out this novel, the dangerous hope that it become a best seller or that for once I might get a leg up on the critics ... and not have once more to see the work ... make its way, heart by heart, as it is discovered by a few people with all the excitement of a person who finds a wildflower in the woods that he has discovered on his own.

May Sarton, *Journal of Solitude*

◎

Fame, archaic: rumor;
to make famous by talking of ...

The American Heritage Dictionary
of the English Language

◎

I have seen all the works that are done under the sun;
and, behold, all is vanity and vexation of spirit.

Ecclesiastes 1:14 King James Version of the Bible

Chapter 1

I built a ship, a great large ship,
And Pride stood at the helm,
And steered for Fame…
W. H. Auden

Cathedral bells don't clang in Barcelona; they vibrate through the soul. No amount of ruckus or rescue in the heart of a big city can change the direction of love. Miranda knew this now. She'd never again mistake the meaning of this passionate journey nor let Jaime Garcia convince her that she had.

"The end," I read. "*Miranda of La Mancha* is finished." I turn over the last printed page and even out the stack and then lean back. I sit on the blue stuffed couch that takes up most of my Milwaukee flat living room, that and the coffee table I'd shipped back from Barcelona, a venture costing nearly as much as my ticket.

It's a huge couch with rounded arms that my grandmother gave to me, and when I curl into its corners I can feel her arms around me. I squirrel into the corner, needing all the nurture I can get while I wait for the critiques of my four closest confidants.

Bette blows her nose, wipes at her eyes, then holds her clasped hands to her heart. Misty polishes her nails and air-writes as she says, "Good job!" Darlien, my sister, looks thoughtful. "It's good, it is. But I don't like the character that plays Miranda's sister, the golfer. Is that supposed to be me, Annie? Because if it is, it doesn't ring true."

"It gets you right here," Bette says, her slender hand patting again at her heart. "It's excellent. I can't believe Miranda came to that decision at the end and yet, it was so perfectly orchestrated."

Kari, my cousin, sits up now. "It's grand, hon. All the while they traveled through Spain, with all those things happening to them, I thought, will she? Won't she? Then you ... well ... it's perfect tension. A very satisfying read. I love how you worked in actual events with the fiction."

Misty says, "It's so emotionally uplifting. Inspiring. Makes me want to celebrate." She rips open a second pack of baby carrots and passes the roasted red pepper hummus as she makes specific points about the story that she loved.

Relief settles on my shoulders. I know it'll be short-lived, but at least for the moment I have a sense of satisfaction. My friends approve, even my older sister.

Bette wipes at her nose again, then uses hand sanitizer before reaching for the carrots. "It's going to make you famous even without our help! You have to be pleased with it."

"I still think the sister is too pushy," Darlien insists. She has her long legs crossed at the ankle where lines mark her tanned legs. She wears those little socks golfers wear with pompoms attached to the heel. Her arms are crossed over her chest. She sneezes.

"You need to eat healthier, Darlien. Burritos are not part of the food pyramid."

"It's allergies," Darlien reports.

"You can tone down the sister, can't you, Annie, I mean if Darlien objects?" Bette says.

"The editor will have suggestions about my characters, lots of them," I say. "Truth is, he may not even want Darlien, I mean the sister, in the story."

"So it is me!" Darlien says sitting straight up in her chair.

"No, she's just a composite of policemen who are golfers, people you've talked about and ones that I met in Spain, too, remember. And of course a composite of older sisters I've known —and loved."

"Editors can do that, wipe someone out?" Misty asks. We all sit and crunch.

"If her presence doesn't move the story forward, they might suggest cutting her," I say. I sigh then share my deepest fear. "This could be the worst book I've ever written."

"What? Why would you think that?" Misty says.

"Honesty may be one of your strong points, Annie Shaw," Cousin Kari says. "But honesty without sensitivity is just plain rude. A person can be rude, even to herself, you know." I stare at her. Her voice softens. She crosses my living room to gently push loose strands of mousey brown hair behind my ears. Kari wears dangly earrings that one wouldn't want to wear around a baby. They look like teething rings. She's a social worker in Chicago, but we all get together often in Milwaukee where we grew up. Bette, Misty, and I attended the same Christian school. Darlien was a few years ahead.

"I didn't think I was being critical of myself," I say. "Truthful."

"This is novel number four, and still you thump yourself on the head about how terribly you write." Bette stands now and taps her fingers on my head. "Must be brain damage under those lovely brunette curls," she says. "From all that thumping."

"Mousey brown," I correct. "And yes, it is novel number four, but here's the thing: number one was a huge hi —"

"Because it was the story of you and Stuart. So romantic. I loved that book," Misty says.

Silence fills the room, looks exchanged.

"Oh, I'm sorry. I didn't mean —"

"It's all right," I tell her. "You're probably right. Anyway, the book after that tanked." Number three just came out, *The Long Bad Sentence*, and if it doesn't do well, Ardor Publishing might decide to bury Miranda's story before she ever arrives in Barcelona.

"Sales will pick up," Darlien says.

Bette thumps me again, playful, but her wrist knocks my glasses slightly ajar. I straighten them and stand, thinking I'll get us some lemonade.

"What ... what's wrong with your pants?" Darlien points.

"Nothing. Why?" I look down at my khaki capris.

"It's ... your stomach, it's pooched out funny."

I reach for the front and see a tag. — "Oh for heaven's sake! I've got them on backwards!"

"I thought you'd put on weight," Bette laughs. "But I didn't want to say anything in case you've been eating your anxiety about this book." Bette is two years younger than I am and the food freak of our group. She knows all the calories, carbs, and chocolate bars necessary for a nourishing life. She's also a part-time aerobics instructor for seniors. She hasn't introduced them yet to tai chi or yoga. Bette says the best instructors of those arts use Wii to prevent tangling one's toes with one's nose. Aerobics is a group sport, she tells us, and that's what her seniors really need. Her upbeat nature is one of her fine features and one of the reasons they love her as a cook at the We Care Senior Living Center.

"I guess I got nervous, knowing I'd be reading to you guys," I tell them.

"Us? We're harmless," Misty says.

They are, really. I sometimes think of us as a gaggle of geese who fly together, know where we're heading, and who remain loyal, no matter what.

"At what point will you stop being so hard on yourself?" Bette says. "You'd never say such unkind things to those kids you work with when they write their stories down. Why are you so critical about your own?"

I honestly didn't think I was being critical or whiney or discouraging — only objective.

Kari says, "If you want us to make this book a bestseller, you have to believe in it yourself first."

"We need to work on the plan," Bette says. She uses a low voice as though "the plan" is some deep dark secret out of Homeland Security. Her words take on a Stephen King feel, spoken through the algae-laced mask she put on as I started to read.

"I bet your publisher will love it. Best of all ... it's finished!" Kari says. She claps her hands. "Why don't you go twist your pants around and we'll get ready to celebrate! Want some lemonade?"

"I was going to do that for you," I say.

"Nope. This is our time to take care of you."

"Then I'll take hot tea." September in Milwaukee can be beastly humid, but I still prefer hot tea to cold lemonade. The ice hurts my teeth.

Everyone gives their orders, ranging from tea to power drinks to fruit juice. Darlien orders decaf coffee.

Bette and Kari pad barefoot to my kitchen, a room nearly as familiar to them as their own kitchens, while I hit my bedroom and turn my pants around. I wondered why they pulled funny. Sometimes, I need a keeper.

"If you can't tell your friends the truth, then who?" I shout to them down the hall. "Besides," I tell Darlien and Misty when I return to the living room, "it isn't really finished."

"It sounds finished to me. It's a great love story," Darlien says. At thirty-two, Darlien is two years my senior and she's had three unhappy marriages, I'm sad to say. She says it's an occupational hazard when cops marry each other, a lesson she didn't learn the first time. Now she says she'll be single for life. She returns to one of two wing-backed chairs from our childhood, curling her legs under her to keep my Persian blue cat, John, from leapfrogging over her. I've had both chairs reupholstered in bold reds and purples to go with the mauve couch. At the time, Darlien didn't want the chairs, but she always chooses one of them to sit in when she visits. She strokes the fabric that Misty helped me pick out.

A cupboard door closes. A tray scrapes along the tile counter. "Darlien and Misty, get in here," Kari calls. Misty stops me when I try to follow them into the kitchen, points me back toward John and my couch. I watch her walk on her heels, with orange rubber dividers between her freshly painted toes.

I hear them whispering. My friends prepare to pamper.

I stare out my window, checking on Lake Michigan's condition. A mere sliver of gray today, no waves surging against the shoreline. My view is the size of a crescent moon seen through the treetops and the roofs covering other Shorewood flats. I live in a second-floor flat with a view of the lake that today reflects the size of my confidence: small and gray. Not just because the book's future is so uncertain, but because I know it really isn't finished.

A book is never truly ended except when read, and then, if it's good, it lives on in a reader's mind maybe for years. But I'm speaking of the practical, physical side of a book, the one readers download onto their Kindle or Sony or buy at their local store. A book with paper pages and binding. Even during readings at little bookshops around Milwaukee's suburbs, holding the small paperback in my hands, I edit out a sentence or two, wondering why I kept that word or phrase in at all. Sometimes, I even suggest that in an additional printing of the book—if it goes to a second printing—a word or phrase be changed. Always perfecting, never complete, describes my books and my life.

I rub my fingers on the pile of manuscript papers. I always print out a copy to view the black on white. I still like to *see* the words march across the paper, how much white space there is, what short sentences might need to stand alone for emphasis. Reading it out loud helps me find glitches in rhythm too. At this stage, when the pages are clean and white and not yet in the mail, when a cyber copy pants, ready for attachment, waiting to be shot through space to an editor, I know it isn't even close to being finished, despite the words "the end."

My new editor hasn't seen the manuscript since I've made the recommended revisions of the *other* editor who went on maternity leave, so I know there'll be more changes to come. No, *Miranda of La Mancha* isn't finished, and Ardor Publishing and I are beginning a whole new relationship, one not at all romantically inclined.

What are those women doing in the kitchen?

One of the troubles with computer composition is that one never really knows how many "drafts" of a book they've written or which draft they're on when the editor finally says it's accepted. "It's accepted" is one more swish through that long and twisted waterslide of a publishing experience. A waterslide at an exclusive theme park, where writers risk being tossed and tumbled about, hoping to plunge into the deep pool of published, bestselling, famous authors. We all hope someone will notice if we sink, and that they'll want to pull us out; praying we'll surface to take the slide again.

"I write trash," I shout to my friends. "And someday soon, everyone is going to find out. Maybe they already have."

Laughter draws me toward the kitchen, but Bette stops me at the door and, hands on my shoulders, turns me around, back through the dining room to the living room, followed by the girls. I can hear their footsteps behind me on the hardwood floor, including Misty's distinctive heel-walk, her toes likely still wet with polish.

"Did you know that the top CEOs in the country list their number-two fear as getting up in front of people to speak?" Kari says as she sets a tray of drinks on the coffee table in front of the couch, the place Bette led me to and pushed me down.

"I'm pretty far below a CEO," I say. They're hiding something, a twinkle in each eye, hands behind their backs now as they form a half-circle in front of me.

"Because their number *one* fear, is that they'll be found out.

That someone will discover they don't really know what they're doing and that they shouldn't be at the top at all. That's you," Kari says.

"You're telling me this to make me feel better, right?"

"We're telling you so you'll stop being so critical of yourself," Bette says. "Everyone feels inadequate sometimes. It's part of life." She lists on her fingers the evidence that her assessment of my work is correct and mine isn't. "You get tons of hits on your website. People write you wonderful letters. You travel to exotic locations on trips you can deduct as research. You pay your bills without having a part-time job. You have a contract for more books. You have a good life. What more do you want?"

What more do I want?

"Ta-da!" Misty interrupts. "We have treasures."

From behind her back, Darlien pulls out a chocolate bar to rival the American Heritage Dictionary and braces it beside my teacup on the tray. It's wrapped in distinctive brown paper, and the blue lettering and oat colored string around it bring back memories of Barcelona. That city boasts the best dark chocolate in the world. Misty, Bette, and Kari then add their own packages: a See's chocolate bar, Rogers' finest dark chocolate, and Seattle Chocolate's Extreme Dark Chocolate. "I got the Rogers' at Nordstrom," Kari says when I raise an eyebrow at finding chocolate from British Columbia this side of the Rocky Mountains.

"Dwight Eisenhower loved that brand," I tell them. "He had it ordered in to the White House."

"You are full of the most amazing pieces of trivia," Misty laughs.

"I can rarely use them in a book so I have to abuse my friends with them," I say.

"Chocolate cures what doesn't ail you," Bette says. "And what shouldn't ail you is the future of this book. So let's celebrate with chocolate and then we'll help figure out how to make your latest release a bestseller."

"Make a note," Darlien says. "When you do the revisions in Miranda's book, change that sister character. Her bossiness really isn't realistic."

⟨⟨⟩⟩

"What makes a bestseller?" Darlien asks, a notepad in her hand. We're down to work now. She reminds me of the cops on old television shows where they actually took notes instead of speaking into smart phones. She's never had a bad hair day. Her soft waves look coiffed even when she first wakes up.

"You have to get *Publishers Weekly* and *Kirkus* to review them," I say, urging my friends to indulge in the chocolate bars. "Hardcovers get more reviews. At least that's what Stuart always said."

"Since when do you listen to your ex-husband's advice?" Darlien asks.

"He *is* a writer," I say, though he's never had a hardcover or any other kind of book published. Articles, though. In *Kite Magazine* and the *Milwaukee Journal*'s sports page.

"Getting one made into a movie, that would make a bestseller, wouldn't it?" Misty asks. She flexes her arm muscles as she sits on the window bench. It jiggles. "Or winning an award." She bites a small piece of the See's.

"I guess awards would help, but what really makes a bestseller is the story. It has to be full of such value that one day people will leave signed copies of the works in their wills or at least want to share it with a family member before they die. It has to make us care about the characters and find ourselves inside them, even the weird ones. It has to sweep us from our everyday into *their* everyday and hopefully, make us swoon and laugh and cry and hope."

"The kind of book that when someone mentions it you want to clasp your hands to your heart and say, 'Oh, yes, I loved that book!'" Bette says.

"Exactly," I say.

"The way you did, Bette, when Annie finished reading," Kari says.

"Here's what you need to know about my books, though: they're … kindling, I call them. Kindling for fires in remote cabins in the mountains rather than something people will leave behind, leather bound for an archive or sigh over, clasping their hands to their hearts. I'd love to write that kind of book, but my characters don't like to go that deep. They need therapy."

"The sister," Darlien reminds me. "Work on her." I notice she's munching on the Barcelona chocolate bar. I wish she'd chosen Seattle's because it would be easier to replace, but she is my older sister. I stare at the candy bar the way a younger sister can, and she carefully refolds the gold lining, puts the Barcelona bar back on the tray, and picks up a section of the See's. Eye-whining works with my big sister.

"At least they're intentionally mindless," Misty says. "I've read lots of books that were light that I was sure the authors thought were deep and profound but weren't. Mindless books are entertaining and make me forget the trials of my day, so they're not really without merit. I tell friends about them. Word of mouth. That makes a bestseller, doesn't it?"

"I don't have enough friends to get a bestseller that way," I say.

"But Facebook can help," Bette says. "We'll build a fan page for you. The We Care Senior Living Center has its own Facebook page. The residents love it!"

Misty says, "Getting your book picked by a book club like Literary Guild or Crossings would make you famous."

"Like that could happen," I say.

"We're brainstorming here, hon," Kari reminds me. "No throwing water on *any* idea tossed out."

"The bottom line is that *Miranda of La Mancha* is a terrific read," Bette continues. "Your fans will love it."

I groan and toss myself back onto the couch, nearly knocking over my tea and chocolate. " 'Her fans will love it.' That's what endorsers say when they dislike a book but they know it might sell to this select group of readers for whom there is no explanation for their devotion to a particular author." I take a deep breath. " 'Her fans will love it.' A kiss of death. That and 'luminous.' Makes me think of standing in front of the window at night with the lights on and undressing. When I get a rejection letter, it means someone was watching me and what they saw was so terrible *they* pulled the shade down."

"I've felt that way a time or two in my life," Misty says. "But you guys got me dressed and standing, with my head held high. That's where we'll get you too, Annie."

The horsehair of the couch scratches the back of my neck.

If reviewers are inundated with books to consider, maybe we could send something along with *The Long Bad Sentence* to make it stand out," Kari says.

"What's the theme of that book again?" Bette asks.

"It's the one set in the prison, a romance between a nurse and the guard. It's about romance happening in unlikely places and how we have to be ready to plunge."

"Right. I remember now. Strange ending, right?"

Was it? I hadn't thought so.

"Well, the boy doesn't always get the girl. Sometimes the romance wakes the person up to what could happen one day," I defend.

"I think in a romance novel though, the boy is supposed to get the girl or vice versa," Bette says. "Anyway, I could make little cookies that look like correctional facility badges. Or maybe a sponge cake cap with a little chocolate visor."

"I'd eat those," Darlien says.

"But would it make you want to review the book?" I say.

She shrugged. "It's worth a try."

I'm still reeling by her insight: only one of my novels has the girl and boy getting together at the end and that was *Sweet Charity's Rose*, my first one, the bestseller. "Oh my gosh, you guys. What Bette said, that's why my last book didn't go anywhere.

And now *The Long Bad Sentence* won't either. I write terrible books!"

"You're a kind person," Kari says. "If you think your writing is so bad, how can you perpetrate it onto the public?" She sips her lemonade and wipes at the perspiration on her forehead.

"I have a contract. I have to promote my latest and give the publisher something they can turn into a book they're willing to publish. It has almost nothing to do with me."

"How can you say that?" Darlien says.

"It's my experience," I say. "I write terrible books and if they do well it has to do with the editors and publisher and marketing and sales more than with—"

"There you are, demeaning yourself again," Kari says.

"Harpies," I tell her. "They tell me all the time that what I do isn't really worth the time it takes someone to read my books. They sit behind me while I write. They never leave me alone."

"My negative voices sound like Woody Allen," Darlien says. "I take a nine iron to them. Figuratively, of course. We all have to work to silence them."

"Mine told me I'd never pass that family law course," Kari said. "But I told them there wasn't any evidence for my failing, and I did what I knew to do, studied and passed. You'll do that too."

"My harpies are these shrouded actors who dance across the stage of Greek tragedies wearing black, keeping their faces hidden from the audience, such cowards. All hunched over, they point at the computer screen and cackle, 'This is drivel. Who told you you could write? Do you actually think people will give up cleaning their toilets to read this?' They're harbingers of doom and they know of what they speak."

The cat jumps onto the manuscript at that moment. He arches his back, kneading at the written words. "See? Even John knows it'll make better cat box fodder than reading material."

At that, my cat coughs up a bezoar, a fur ball. "Everyone's a reviewer." I pick up the bezoar, stand to throw it away.

Bette's straw slurps and she holds the frosted bottom of the glass to her temples. "*Sentence* was released last month, right?"

"Right. And *Miranda* will come out next June, or should. It depends on revisions and if they'll accept them or not. I have a new editor, recently assigned, which is not good, not right in the middle of things. It's like having surgery and asking a new doctor not only to close, but to take out the appendix while she's at it, when the first surgery was done to repair your heart. More possible infection sites, never a good idea. The editor's a man this time. I'm not sure how good men are at editing women's fiction — my kind of fiction, anyway."

My hands are warm and the chocolate melts softly on my fingertips. John shows up to lick them but I beat him to it.

"Ooh, a man," Darlien says. "That'll be interesting."

"Here's the truth," I confide. "I think they're trying to ease me out. They're sorry they signed me for four books. Unless I can make *Sentence* into a bestseller, they won't have to ease me — I'll tumble out. And Miranda will be relegated to the bay in Barcelona."

"Enough!" Darlien says, standing. "This is hard labor, you know, this cheering you up after each book completion."

"Do I go through this each time?" Her words genuinely surprise me.

"You only get twenty minutes to indulge your misery, and you're past that. Come on," Misty says. She pulls at me, the rest of them joining her. "Let's fast-walk around the block, get some ice cream, clear our heads so we can come up with the perfect way to make your latest release a bestseller."

"Pea pods. Let's get pea pods. They're better for you," Misty says.

"We need to change your brain chemistry," Kari says. "A good walk will do that. We'll come back in and really focus, but with the idea that this book is going to make you famous! You have to imagine the celebration ahead."

A gaggle of geese is successful because all the geese are on the same flight path, knowing where they're going, I suppose.

"Think of that quote you like from the guy who climbed Mount Everest: 'Whatever you can imagine, do it,'" Bette says.

"Or the Proverb: 'Commit to the Lord whatever you do, and he will establish your plans,'" Misty adds.

"Celebrating too early can jinx the final result," I say.

"You tell those kids you teach that celebrate means to fill up, over and over. So let's go fill up. We're all so proud of you, Annie," Misty says. She hugs me tight. "Your mom and dad, your sister, we all think you're grand. So take this moment in. Do it for us if not for you."

They're right. Not accepting their accolades for my book discounts their efforts, something I don't want to do. "I do need to celebrate this little stage along my publishing waterslide," I tell them. "I'll do it for you."

"Great," Bette says. We tap knuckles.

We're trundling down the steps and out the back door single file when Bette stops short and we all four bump into her like a column of cartoon characters brought to a halt at the edge of the cliff. Bette turns, her finger in the air as an announcement of brilliance, her auburn pony tail bobbing from side to side. "What will make you the kindling queen of fame and turn this book into a bestseller would be to get Oprah to mention your book."

"I agree," Misty says. "Pick the most famous person in the world and sidle up next to them and their fame will simply reflect right onto you. It's like the sun and the moon. Sort of."

"But that's what everyone says to writers. Last week the garbage man said, 'You know what you should do? You should get Oprah to pick your book for her book club.' They say it like it's never crossed a writer's mind or that it's easy. But it's not possible."

"Up until now it hasn't been possible," Misty says. "But we're your friends! Once we know the direction we're heading, we can accomplish anything. Yes, that should be the plan for making you famous this year, Annie. Getting Oprah to mention your book is just one of the many ways we're going to help make *The Long Bad Sentence* a bestseller; and if we get in a little mention of *Miranda*, well that's a good thing too."

Can it be possible? What will it take to make that happen?

"We didn't even have to jog around the block for our creative juices to flow. Just walking down the steps did it," Bette says. "I knew our prayers would be answered."

"Prayers and chocolate," Darlien notes. "And the promise of ice cream."

They're my best friends. They've prayed and stayed with me through whines and dines. Maybe Bette's right. Maybe this idea came as divine intervention just when I needed it to stop those harpies.

"All right," I agree. I'm now first in line and I stop short, causing a backup on the steps. "But what I need to do first is find duct tape."

"Duct tape?" Bette raises an eyebrow.

"To put over the mouth of those harpies singing about the impossible dream I've chosen to fly toward. I mean, how can a woman who puts her pants on backwards ever hope to meet Oprah?"

"Because you've got us behind you," Bette says.

It's an encouraging thought I decide to hang onto.

From: Website Contact Form
To: Annie Shaw
Name: Janis Jones
delirious@spotnet.net

I want to thank you for writing *Don't Kick Me*. I bought it at a garage sale and read it that same day. I'd just skipped two of my classes and then didn't go to my job as a pretzel maker because I was all bummed out by my boyfriend dumping me. Then I read your book! I'm so glad I read it because that's exactly what I do, stupid things that hurt me while I'm telling people to stop hurting me and blaming them. It isn't them like it wasn't for your character Emily. She must be real. I'm her! But she got smarter and so can I. Thanks so much for changing my life in St. Louis. Keep writing! Don't ever stop. Janis Jones. P.S. I haven't skipped a class since I read your book. And I'm still making pretzels too. The boyfriend — well that's another story.

Chapter 2

Dear Ms. Shaw,

Allow me to introduce myself. As we'll be working together on your latest manuscript, working title (fill in blank) <u>Barcelona Knight</u>, I wanted to introduce myself and let you know a bit about how I work and my expectations as an editor. I hope this will allow me to better extol your creative efforts to the editorial team and ultimately, the public. It is my privilege to be working with a writer of substance such as you have been represented to me to be. At the same time, it is my duty to provide the most insightful comments for this substantive edit and to assist you in addressing my concerns. I will be reading the manuscript over the next three weeks and will return it to you with red lines marking areas of concern along with related queries so you might better address them. I assume with all my writers that there will be concerns. We are all human, are we not? Perfection eludes us. Therefore, I plead with you not to take the suggestions personally but rather as a part of a team so that together, we might present the best book possible to marketing and production and publicity and sales for a successful publishing venture next year.

It's cool here in Denver today but lovely. I hope Milwaukee is likewise.

> *Very truly yours,*
> *Irving Stellar,*
> *Editorial Director*

"It's a form letter," my agent, Randolph, says when I call him a week later. Fear causes my voice to quiver and crack. I hold the email in my hand. Randolph's been my agent for six years and his primary work is to keep me from depression, though I doubt he'd accept that characterization of his job description. "Nothing to be alarmed about," he says. His voice soothes.

"My editor's using a form letter to communicate with me for the first time. He's used a title I didn't submit and he underlined it, like it was a fill-in-the-blank. It even says in front of it 'fill in the blank.' He sounds like a literary editor, Randolph. They want to edit real books, not kindling like mine. I knew I should have gotten a master's degree in creative writing."

"Now calm down, Annie. This is nothing to worry about. He even put in a little personal touch at the end."

"About the weather," I said then hurried on. "They're going to dump me, aren't they? You haven't told me but that's it, isn't it? The publisher is getting rid of me. That's why they've changed editors on me at the last minute. That's why they've sent me a form letter. Will they even promote *Sentence*?"

"Of course not."

"They won't promote my latest?"

"Yes. They will, though not as much as we hoped, since *Don't Kick Me* bombed." I wince. "I was responding to your worry that they're trying to get rid of you. They aren't. They have a lot of authors; you made them money with the first book. They're invested in you."

I sit on the floor in front of the fireplace, which harbors a dieffenbachia when it isn't winter. " 'Concerns,' " I read to Randolph. "He used that word more than once, didn't he?" I count. "At least three concerns."

"Maybe he's concerned about the, ah, sexual component."

"What sexual component?" I sit up.

"My point exactly. Your books rarely have steamy scenes,

Annie. Romances in this industry can hardly thrive without them. They're not called 'bodice rippers' for nothing."

"I write stories about people who fall in love, overcome obstacles, and who eat hope for breakfast, lunch, and dinner. I write inspiring stories about real life, leaving bedroom scenes to the imagination."

Randolph stays silent so I continue. "He says I was *represented to be* a fine writer, not that *he* thinks I am."

I can hear Randolph clear his throat over 1500 miles away in New York. "Why don't your characters have more sex in your books?"

"They do have sex," I defend. "Just not where you can see it. It's off the page. It's not gynecologically portrayed. I have an agreement with my characters: I will not reveal any of their personal sexual proclivities or idiosyncrasies, and they agree never to reveal any of mine."

"A little ... revelation might help your sales," he says.

"Randolph ..."

"All right, I know. You're not that kind of writer. But I've read Christian novels with murders and fires and death written right beside words of faith and hope, Scripture, and Jesus. So why not include another side of human nature ... lust."

"Did you just put lust and Jesus in the same paragraph?"

"Annie ..."

"Because I have my dignity," I say.

"Well, it's my job to keep presenting options to you, ways to take another look at what you do so that one of these days we have that break-out novel, one that hits the *New York Times* Best-Seller List. A little titillation couldn't hurt."

"I have something better to get a bestseller. My friends are behind me."

"They're a fine group of women, Annie, but sometimes friends aren't as forthright about your talent as an editor or your agent must be."

"No, I mean my friends are going to help me make *The Long*

Bad Sentence a bestseller. We're going to get Oprah to mention my book."

Saying it out loud sounds … doable.

"You and every other writer," he snorts.

Before he asks for details I don't yet have, I change the subject. "Have you heard anything specific about Irving Stellar, the new editor?"

"He's good. He's been around awhile. So lack of sexual content on certain pages in a romance might be worrying him. I'll try to get a handle on it for you."

"I do write about passion and betrayal, what Willa Cather says make up a good story. I don't need steamy sex for that."

"You write for *Ardor* Publishing. They publish romances."

"I write stories of the human heart—there's romance in that." I can hear my voice begin to rise and screech like an old escalator in Barcelona. "I have a reader following without the sexual stuff and if this new editor requires it of me, I'll be —"

"Calm down. I know this isn't a good time in the process for you."

"How is it that everyone else seems to know my *process* better than I do?"

"You're blinded by the trees and can't see the forest," he says. "Here's what I know about your new editor. They hired him away from HarperCollins. He and this woman, a high-powered editor there, were an item, or so I heard; and they broke up. People say he's good at what he does and he wanted to get out of New York. She's still here."

"He's in exile in Denver and they've assigned him to writers on the decline. I'm doomed, aren't I, Randolph? You haven't found a way to tell me."

"Maybe he's someone who knows what he likes, so he headed west. Maybe he's a terrific editor and they've assigned him to you because of your potential. They wouldn't want to waste him on a mediocre author. He'll be good for you, Annie. Bring a new dimension to your work. You have to look at the possibilities here, not just the problems."

"You're right, of course," I say. "I wish I could write like P. D. James."

"She writes mysteries, Annie."

"And really well too."

"Look. He's your new editor, and there's nothing you can do about that now. Look at the bright side of things. Here's someone who knew what he wanted, asked for it, and now has it. He didn't like the hustle and bustle of New York, let's say. He chose Denver instead. He's a man who knows his own mind."

"Do you think that means he won't listen to me, will want to do things his way? Will he push the marketing budget for *Sentence?*"

"Annie ..."

"Oh, Randolph, maybe they'll reject the book altogether this time. I've never had a book rejected."

"It happens to every author if they write long enough. You work it through. You rewrite. Anne Lamott had a book rejected once."

"But she's a real writer, with hardcover books, and she turned her rejection into a book *about* being rejected. Creative non-fiction. What chance is there that I can do that?"

"Start the next book; that's the thing to do. Or better yet, write up your ideas for marketing. That always sparks that creative spirit in you. You get clearer. That'll help when you talk to Irving. You know," he cajoles, "*Sweet Charity's Rose* did really well. It was the perfect romance. Boy meets girl; girl falls in love with boy; couple gets married. And the rose you sent to each reviewer tipped the scales."

Every time *Sweet Charity's Rose* is mentioned, my stomach hurts. That was my story with Stuart, written before I could see what my marriage was really all about.

"Maybe you should talk to Irving and see if he thinks a little more romance for Miranda might not be in order."

"Irving Stellar called it *Barcelona Knight*."

"I'm sure Irving is open to other ideas. Finish your marketing ideas, get your friends to go on Facebook, and talk up your title. Wait for Irving's recommended revisions, and then think creativity, Annie. It's part of the process. It'll take your mind off what you can't control."

But that leaves me everything to think about, because I don't control a thing.

From: Website Contact Form
To: Annie Shaw
Jerome Nathan
guardo@californiaprison.gov

Just finished *The Long Bad Sentence*. My girl gave it to me. I've never read a chick book before. I'm not much of a reader but a prisoner broke my shoulder so I was laid up for a few days and she gave me a stack to read including your book. Did you visit a lot of prisons before you wrote the book because it seems like you must have. You did pretty good research though I don't think you could exchange contact lenses very easily in the recreation area the way your one character did with his mother visiting. Still, it was inventive and I'll be watching for stuff like that. I didn't think anyone outside could educate someone working on the inside so that was new for me too. I hope you write more books but I don't know when I'll get to read them unless I break another shoulder. Can you send my girl a bookmark or something? Or maybe you don't talk to readers. Probably wise. Especially if they're affiliated with a prison.

Chapter 3

Be careful! Don't be led away from God by riches;
don't let much money turn you away.
Neither your wealth nor all your great strength
will keep you out of trouble.

Job 36:18–19

My ex's number shows up on caller ID. My stomach clutches. He's an energy vampire, and the reason why I'm reluctant to talk on the phone to anyone but my mom and my close friends.

"Hey," he says.

"Hey," I say. He has an oboe sort of voice, mellow but with a yearning in it that I've come to hear as "I want something."

"How's it going? How's John?"

"He's fine. I'm fine. Look, I'm in the middle of something and —"

"The car needs new tires."

"I imagine it does, but I haven't driven it for over a year, Stuart."

"Yeah, but you put a lot of miles on those tires doing research and traveling to book signings, so I think you might pay for a percentage of the tread, you know, based on how much tread was there when we separated."

"You know how much tread was there?"

"Sure. I had it measured. A guy doesn't want to be taken advantage of."

I should have known. He was a stickler for details that might benefit him, making sure my paycheck went as far as it could for his needs.

"No thank you." I sound pretty firm.

"You wouldn't want to be responsible if I had an accident when a tire blew, would you?"

I practiced a phrase Kari said I should use with people who tried to guilt me into an action I might later regret. "To take care of myself, Stuart, I have to say no."

"I can't believe you'd leave me without wheels! You always did put yourself first."

"I know you don't agree, but that's my decision."

"Well, how about you buy two and I'll buy two? That's only fair."

What are some of the other sentences?

I take a deep breath. "You can set money aside each month from your paycheck, Stuart, and eventually you'll have enough to buy your tires." I knew it was a mistake as soon as I said it.

"I don't need you to tell me how to fix it," he said. "I need you to loan me some money. Can't you at least do that? I mean, you had a bestseller. You couldn't have gone through all that cash. Oh well, you did quit your job even though I asked you not to."

By now my heart is pounding and I can't remember any of the other phrases Kari told me to say. I do what I do when I'm scared: ignore my instincts. "I'll send you a check for two tires, Stuart. Now good-bye."

"Hey, I don't want to inconvenience you. I'll come by later this week and pick up the cash."

⟲

"Ok. Darlien, did you go on Oprah's website?" This is Misty, following up on one of the items we have on our to-do list. It's later in the week of Irving's letter and Stuart's demand. Kari's returned to Chicago, so the rest of us are on our own, having lunch after Bette's served her people at the We Care assisted living facility.

"Yes. And on the page where you can mention books you really like, I put down *Sweet Charity's Rose* and *The Long Bad Sentence*. That should get some notice."

Bette says, "I think you have to do more than just mention a book. You have to say how it touched your life, you know, what the moments were that helped you find your inner you with it."

"I did that," Darlien says.

"We should all join the book club," Misty says. "Not just Darlien. And actually read what people write about the Oprah picks they've read. Then we can add better insights. The more people who post something on the site to mention Annie's books, the more likely she'll be noticed. Awareness is the first step toward success. Didn't Kari say that?"

"Isn't that somewhat ... false though?" I ask.

"Why? We've read the books. We like them. We want to promote them," Bette says.

"What I noticed," Misty says, "is that lots of Oprah picks have animals in them. Dogs, especially."

"Oprah is a dog lover," Darlien says. "I read that in *Notoriety*."

"She talks about them all the time on her show," Misty says.

"You watch her network?"

"Well, of course. How else will we figure out how to get her to mention your book? Maybe you could put a dog in Miranda's story, Annie."

"The entire story takes place in Spain, the protagonist is a tourist at the International Police and Firemen Games. She wouldn't have her dog with her," I say.

"Maybe you could change the location, or like, give her a dog she misses or something. Or I know, she finds a stray dog and he leads her to Jaime and —"

"Bette, please," Misty says. She pokes the needle through the shirt she's embroidering, stands, then stretches left and right as she talks, shifting at her waist, elbows out. Misty was once in a body-building competition, pre-Norton. Norton, her four-year-old, is in preschool until three o'clock, so this is a break for her.

"The location is rather critical to the story," I remind them. "Miranda's in Barcelona for a reason, and the atmosphere there works toward the romance between her and Jaime."

"Think about dogs, though, Annie," Darlien encourages. "It would be great to work in a comment about animals when we visit the web site and connect it to your name." She sneezes.

"I keep telling you, it's how you eat." Bette wags a finger at Darlien.

"Allergies," Darlien says.

"I've never had a dog," I say.

"Might be time to get one. Research. You love research!" Bette reminds me.

"We're supposed to mention the *Sentence* book. We want Oprah to say something about *that* book," I say.

"It has cats in it, right?" Misty asks. "How about if I make little mice that we fill with catnip and you can send them to the TV and radio stations in the region, along with the book and your card? We could even suggest an interview."

"I like the idea of the little mice. John loves catnip." On cue John saunters into the living room, finds the spot of sun, and rolls his back and belly into it.

"I'll get a list of the studio names," Bette says.

"That's great," I said. "I need people to go on Amazon too, and leave a review. A good review."

"You can do that," Darlien says.

"No, they'll see my email address and know I'm touting my own title. Not good."

"I don't want us to leave Oprah yet," Bette said. "Maybe she'd make prison reform her new cause. I saw a program with Oprah and Glenn Close talking about puppies in prison. Prisoners were training service dogs for returning soldiers. I cried through the whole thing. Your book would fit right in."

"*The Long Bad Sentence* isn't about prisoners training dogs," Misty says. "Is it Annie? I can't remember." I shake my head no. She touches her toes now, legs straight. Despite her weight gain, she's still as limber as her preschooler. Maybe having a preschooler does that for a person. "It's about finding your perfect mate in unlikely places."

"Like Barcelona," Darlien says. "So I'll go on line this week and mention the book as a good travel book. That's a legitimate link, isn't it? We referred to Rick Steve's travel books every day we were in Spain."

"We're promoting *The Long Bad Sentence*," I remind them. "Besides, it would take a lot more than mention of travel tips once a week on Oprah's website to have someone notice." For the first time since our decision to push toward fame with Oprah's help, I wasn't all that confident in our planning.

"Which is why you ought to consider adding a dog to the story," Bette says. "Besides, this is only the beginning."

Everyone's an editor I thought but didn't say.

"Oh, oh, I've got an idea," Misty says. "Take copies of the books and drop them off at the television studios, leave them with producers. That would work, wouldn't it?"

"Not really. You have to be buzzed in, and they check your name against a list of people they're expecting."

John starts to purr.

"Well what if you were to go there dressed as a cleaning person and say you were called to fix a broken toilet?" Bette says. "You could wear one of the custodian's shirts from We Care."

"I don't know ..."

"Sure. You'd leave a book with your card in the green room on the coffee table, and hand one to anyone you encounter. Give them a brochure and, voila! Come back out. They'll think you're really inventive."

"I'll think about it," I say.

"Good. We've got an entire range of activities to pursue," Misty says. "Kari is checking on the production schedule for

Oprah's show in Chicago, where we'll take books and give them away to people in the line and hopefully, to Oprah herself."

"I have to buy these books to give away," I say. "The publisher only gives me ten."

"Invest to succeed," Misty says. "My husband's always saying stuff like that."

"Reviewing copies of O costs nothing," I say. "I'll look for themes that my book might link with. I've scanned the 2010 issues at the library already, and my doctor had several from 2009 in her waiting room."

"Any themes?" Misty asks.

"Many. Inspirational things. Her 'Pay It Forward Challenge' uses money to leverage more money for good causes. My book doesn't have anything to do with that, though."

"I love that part of Oprah's show," Misty says. "It's the Golden Rule, sort of."

"Could you write an article for O maybe?" Darlien asks. "The magazine has short pieces, and there are places on the web site where you can make comments, not just shout out your book."

"I've really got to focus on the revisions, don't forget," I say. I don't tell them that I've never written a non-fiction piece. That was Stuart's skill. "I have to concentrate on the revisions when my editor gets them to me."

"It would be great if you could write something about making good choices," Misty says. "That fits with Sentence and with young moms who watch Oprah's show. Put in how the people in Sentence didn't make good decisions, how they ended up there, and how it affected their families."

I wasn't sure how deep my characters were for such a serious subject.

"I guess I could write an article about ... something I know, like the kids I teach writing to."

"Oprah loves kids! We'll work on research; you work on revisions and maybe an article idea for O" Bette summarizes.

"I'll send out badge cookies and Misty will make catnip mice. Next weekend we'll do an update," she tells us. "It'll be like planning a crime."

⑥

The morning turns cool, with a swift breeze off the lake. I fix a cup of tea, thinking about an article while I wait for the water to boil.

When I wrote *Miranda of La Mancha* with Barcelona as a backdrop, I had such rich images in my mind. Set during the International Games, an unmarried policewoman heads to Barcelona to compete on the golf team. She invites her sister, Miranda, along. Miranda falls in love with a policeman named Jaime, from Barcelona. Miranda then has to decide whether to follow her heart and stay in Barcelona or return to her predictable, mundane life in the States.

Miranda has a profession—she works in a child care facility—so people depend on her. Little people await her presence. And to simply give all that up for what might be a miscalculation fed by the romance of Barcelona would be the risk of her life. I'd already messed up on that sort of scenario once. Miranda has her struggles cut out for her. Will she leap or won't she? Is this the risk of her life or the edge of possibility? That's what the reader has to decide, if they care enough about Miranda. If I've written about her well enough to make them care. It's all up to me whether Miranda finds happiness or not. The responsibility is weighty.

The responsibility makes me hungry.

I rummage through my cupboards, looking for something to eat, and John eases his way around my legs, swishing his tail. I notice the sign I hung on the refrigerator after reading a Geneen Roth book about filling up on life instead of food. The sign reads: *IT'S NOT IN HERE*—a reminder that it's not healthy to use food to avoid the pain of living.

37

I don't eat anything and instead write a check to Stuart for his tires. Maybe this time he'll really drive out of my life.

Looking for a stamp, I encounter what's left of the Barcelona chocolate in the bottom drawer of my desk. What I'm looking for is in there: the soothing slice of chocolate to remind me that I can write, that I am worthy. Back in the kitchen, I pop a couple of slices of bread into the toaster but not before I've cleaned out the crumbs. I've needed to do that for some time now.

The toaster finally pops. I've burned the toast so I scrape the black into the wastepaper basket. John meows his displeasure as I soften the cream cheese in the microwave, spread it on the toast, and lay one on the tile counter for him. "The man in my life." I salute the cat. "Write about what you know," I crunch. "I know about love lost, being a volunteer for the Reading Ready program, and cats. Hard to build a writing career on that."

And yet I have. God's been good. My name isn't a household word. Still, I'm able to call myself a full-time writer—something Stuart didn't support. He liked my steady paycheck. People count on me. Randolph counts on me. He has kids in college. My publisher has people committed to the production of my books that can only occur if I meet my deadlines. My cat relies on me; he's become accustomed to having canned cat food on special occasions. I count on me to put my fears aside and write and participate in the other side of the literary life.

Oh, and the kids in the Reading Ready program rely on me too. I check my watch. I finish my toast, check on John's water, then I'm on my way.

⑥

Oakdale Elementary is a yellow stone building not far from my flat. I volunteer once a week to listen to a child read. It's a joy of my life, and I sometimes feel guilty that I have such a good time. The kids pick out books they like—some which I bring in from my own collection of children's books—and at the end of the session, they get to take them home. We hope their interest in reading will make Reading Ready readers out of their parents too. Lots of kids who are aspiring readers (I prefer aspiring to slow) don't have stacks of books on their bedroom shelves. Some of those kids don't even have bedroom shelves, as they're living in shelters or sharing a room with one or more sisters or brothers. So a book is a treasure that is made all the richer because they can read it themselves.

Buster saunters in, wearing an oversized Spider-Man T-shirt on his stocky eight-year-old body. He picks *Flotsam*, a Caldecott Medal winner picture book about a nerdy sort of boy who researches things that wash up on shore.

"I like that word," he tells me. "Flooooootsaaaam. Have you ever looked into stuff washed up on the lake?"

"I never have," I tell him. "I don't seem to have the time. But I like to walk along Lake Michigan."

"Look at what that boy found." Buster points to the words as he reads each one. "I'd like to go to the lake. Maybe a big dinosaur will wash in."

I'm about to suggest that isn't likely, but then honoring the dream seems like a good thing, so I tell him to imagine what other kinds of flotsam might show up there.

"Me," he says after a thought.

"You? You're not flotsam." I bump my shoulder into his. "Nowhere near flotsam."

"Flotsam's what no one wants," he tells me. "I'm a foster kid because nobody wanted me."

"Your foster parents did," I say, wishing Kari was here to ask for advice about how to talk to a troubled child. Who would have thought a book about flotsam would bring tears to a child's eyes? "And look how much the boy in the book learned by spending a little time with what others might not notice."

"Like you spending time with me?" Buster asks.

I'd like to hug him but the school doesn't recommend it. "Like you teaching me," I say, "You're so much more than not forgotten."

He smiles then and asks if we can read the book again, and I'm reminded of how much a writer can touch one life. Maybe that's what I should have as my goal, to simply touch one person's life with every story I write.

⑥

Marketing, Randolph's told me more than once, is just another way of storytelling. I think of that as I consider my tasks for marketing *Sentence*. We're all salesmen of a sort in this business, and what every salesman wants in a book she can sell is first a quality product. It was Randolph who taught me about the second quality a salesman wants in what they have to sell whether it's widgets or wedding rings

"A good story?" I asked Randolph.

"Yup. Everyone likes a story, Annie. If it's a good product, they can buy it anywhere but they'll buy it from you if they remember the story attached to it."

So I have to think of promoting this new book too, (before it's even finished) as though I'm telling its story. I sit in front of the computer, John curls at my feet. An empty screen stares back at me, as foreboding as an empty toilet paper dispenser when you need it most.

Maybe I'll think about my next book instead. This distraction fails because I don't have an idea for my next book. Not yet. Ideas have always been like children in a TAG class, raising their little hands in the front row, shouting, "Choose me, choose me!" and all I've had to do was pick one. The Barcelona story popped into my head when Darlien first told me about the games. Once I'd made the trip and experienced life unfolding across Spain, my fiction wove into reality and the story took shape.

A quote framed in my office/guest bedroom are words of physicist John Wheeler, who was asked if he had any advice for young people interested in physics. "Tell them to find something strange and thoroughly explore it." Sort of a flotsam idea, when

I think of it now. That's what my stories are about: something strange I explore. It's as close to physics as I'll ever come.

I must look for the unanswered question, that "something strange" that needs to be explored inside my prison story. But *Miranda of La Mancha* took more out of me than planned. I'd been more creative before Barcelona, before my publisher changed editors, before my second book bombed. If I listen to one of those new book ideas and Irving doesn't like it, I'll be sunk. I have to wait to see what Irving has in mind for revisions of *Miranda* before I get into some other whole new set of characters who move into my head, haunt my dreams at night, and give me out-of-body experiences without my ever having to leave my flat.

I need to focus. Work on the O magazine idea.

I head to the kitchen to get lemonade but notice that the tile grout really needs to be cleaned. The tile is a feature of the flat I truly love, making me think of old world Europe. Built in the 1920s, the building adds to the Shorewood neighborhood's character. I rent the upstairs. A graduate student in microbiology and his medical intern wife rent the downstairs. I rarely see them, but there is something comforting about knowing that someone else breathes in a proximal space; someone you might rarely talk to but who could be there in a crisis. Stuart thought a crisis was an opportunity to leave.

There's little grout cleaner left, so I decide to walk to the store to get some. I pick up a few other items too. Climbing up the stairs, I notice cobwebs in the corners. That's not a good thing. A broom with a towel wrapped around it takes away the webs, and then I decide the rest of the stairs could use a good sweeping. That causes me to cough, which drives me to the medicine cabinet that really does need cleaning out. Goodness, what if someone needed an aspirin or something and they went looking in there?

By now two hours have passed, and I remember I never did clean out John's litter box. Finished with litter duty—fortunately

John is a fixed male, so I won't actually ever deal with litters—I fix a chicken sandwich for lunch and look out my bay window. It overlooks the tree-lined street where young children skateboard around elderly people taking their daily constitutionals. Many senior walkers are retired professors who like being around students and the hustle and bustle of a neighborhood. It's an active world. I don't really participate.

Supporting myself as a full-time writer means making financial sacrifices. I use busses. I don't own a car—anymore. No insurance to pay, no fuel costs. Just the occasional tire. I don't have an iPod, and I rarely use my cell phone except to call friends. This is my life. Predictable. Controllable. Safe, except for the vagaries of publishing.

My tongue works at a piece of chicken stuck in my teeth, so I return to the medicine cabinet for floss. I try to pull the floss forward. It won't budge. I pull up. Nothing. A tweezers yank doesn't work. The white thread hangs out over my lower lip like a shoe lace. The phone rings.

"Have you heard from your editor?" Bette asks. It's been over a week since his letter arrived.

I describe the silence from the West and tell her of my marketing constipation, my brain not being available for new ideas. "I'm cleaning so I won't think about how my savings is disappearing," I tell her. "Irving has to accept this manuscript soon so I can get the second half of my advance. Otherwise, I'll have to adopt John out and I'll be scratching at your door or the nearest shelter for sustenance instead of a mere emotional shot in the arm."

"What's wrong with your mouth? You sound funny."

"I've got dental floss stuck between my teeth."

"Oh. Well, why don't you just call him? After you get unstuck."

"He might think I'm too anxious or be annoyed that I've bothered him before he's ready to talk about the manuscript."

"Well then, I guess we need to keep focusing our bestseller plans. Are you still reviewing *O* magazine articles?"

"I think the puppies in prison might have an angle. Turning tragedy into triumph is something Oprah knows for sure. She has a page of things she knows for sure."

"We ought to do that sometime," Bette says. "Make a list of what we know for sure. What would you put on it?"

"That stories touch lives." I tell her of Buster's flotsam.

"Write an article about that," Bette suggests.

"It's not about women," I remind her. There's a pause while I saw back and forth on the floss.

"The nurse in *Sentence* wasn't sure if she could trust her feelings. *O* magazine always has articles about how women make choices — what they desire and how they're really stronger than they think."

"Sometimes about how we sabotage ourselves," I said.

"So you know for sure that smart women can make dumb choices?" Bette says.

"I guess." I think about Stuart's check I mailed.

"Nothing new there. But maybe exploring the why, that might be intriguing for Oprah. Too bad your book's not a memoir. Real life would add appeal for Oprah."

I stay silent.

"It's not a memoir, is it, Annie? *You* aren't the characters in your books, are you?"

I swallow. There is a lot of me in *Miranda* but I don't want to tell that even to one of my best friends. "It's the prison setting that's real. The Games are real. Barcelona is too. But you make me think my kinds of books won't appeal to her. They're not, well, weighty, and I like a hopeful ending. Not happy, necessarily, but I hate books that say life is tough and then you die."

"She picked *Jewell* awhile back, and that was one of my favorites. It has a happy ending. And your book does too. Did you get the floss out yet?"

"No."

"Oprah's always saying to put our wishes into the universe and see what wonderful things return."

" 'Give and you'll receive.' I'll give the universe a great book and I'll receive a bestseller. Oprah will mention my book. Oprah will mention my book." I laugh.

"It shouldn't be what *will* happen but should be stated in the present. 'Oprah *mentions* my book. Oprah mentions my book.' " She sings the phrase like a ghostly mantra meant to raise the muses.

"Magic isn't what that verse is about. It's about generosity and faith, acting before receiving. You know, Bette, much as I know everyone has my best interest at heart, I've been thinking I should wait until I write a really good book before I try to get Oprah to mention it."

"Remember the midwives in Exodus," Bette says. "They defied the pharaoh together. That's what we'll do for you: together we'll defy the pharaohs of fear and unworthiness and even guilt that you haven't written the world's greatest novel. That's what friends are for. You just assume the position of a writer. That's what you're always saying you have control over. Show up and be creative. I have confidence in you. Oh gosh," she says. "Look at the time. I've got to get back to work or the unemployment counselor will know my name."

⑥

"I've never had this happen before," the dentist says, staring into my mouth. "An emergency floss extraction. Maybe you should have those bottom teeth fixed."

He puts the suction tube in my mouth and begins tugging, then picks up a tool that looks like a crochet hook. *I should have asked Misty if she had a crochet hook so I wouldn't be humiliating myself in the dentist's chair.*

"Next time you floss, don't try to lift up; just pull through, ok? You make more headway that way."

He has kind eyes and I nod to assure him I've learned the lesson. He tugs away. "What do you do again?"

"Ahm ah wrahter?"

"What? Oh, a writer? Written anything I might know?"

"Ah wrat wombens bahcs."

"Women's books. My wife reads those. You know what you should do? You should get Oprah to mention your book. That would make you famous. Isn't that a good idea?"

"Ah huh," I say.

"There we are." He pulls the floss from my saliva-suctioned mouth. "Do you want to save it as a souvenir? Oh, hey, maybe I should keep it." He holds the string up in the air like a trophy fish. "This is the dental floss of that famous writer ... what did you say your name was again?"

Chapter 4

I would give my fame
for a pot of ale and safety.
William Shakespeare

"Harpo's Production schedule for the *Oprah Show* goes from August to November and then tapes again from January to April," Kari says. We're meeting during Bette's break at the assisted living site, where soft couches invite visitors who often don't come. The air conditioning blasts its way into the room. Each of us brought hoodies even though it's close to ninety degrees outside. Mrs. Johnson lift-rolls by with her walker. She waves at us, and the hot pink flag at the top of a stretched-out coat hanger bobs before her as she turns the corner.

"I just love Mrs. Johnson," Darlien says. "When I'm that old, I want to be that active too, walker or not."

"You'll have to eat more than burgers and fries," Bette says. "They're all pretty self-sufficient. And you wouldn't believe some of the things they've done in their lives. A former trapeze artist, teachers, policemen, bricklayers. It's a pretty cool place to work. If I were forty years older I'd have a ready-made matchmaking site for myself."

"You ought to sign up for a finance class or something," Darlien says. "You could meet men there."

"I meet men at church and some of the grandchildren of residents here, but there haven't been any bells and whistles."

"When the time is right," I tell her. "It'll happen."

"Some of these residents could be featured on one of Oprah's shows—they're that interesting. Speaking of which, we better sign up for tickets now," Bette says.

"What would be the value of being in Oprah's audience?" Misty asks. Misty's son, Norton, is with her today, and he's in deep discussion with a man as slender as a nail, with silver hair and arthritic knuckles. His fingers hold Norton's toy truck as though it's a human heart. Norton points out various parts to Silver Nail's interest. Children are so intensely attentive.

"We'll see how the show works and get inspired. Maybe during the commercial space we'll talk with a producer, give them *Sentence*, maybe link it quickly to the dog in prison program," Bette says. "Producers stand off to the side during cuts. I've seen them on camera sometimes when they slip back just as the program returns to live."

"I don't think what we see is live. They tape it, I'm sure," Misty says.

"Ambush a producer?" Darlien asks. "They must have security people. I bet they won't even let us out of our seats. Arrest us as we walk forward or remove us. I would."

"Why?"

"Have you looked at us in a mirror? We're pretty scary looking," Darlien says. "Even if we leave the algae mask at home."

"If you have to leave to go to the bathroom," Misty says, "I hear you can't come back in to the studio. And no photographs. They might even confiscate our cell phones."

"I don't see how they could do that," Bette says. She wipes her hands on her apron. It must be one of her mother's, with the little strawberry blossoms faded to pale pink. Or maybe one of the residents gave it to her. It's right out of the 1940s. "Imagine getting the right cell phones back to people at the end of the show. A nightmare!"

"Look," I tell them. "I've decided to go about this the same way I go about preparing to write a book. First I ask myself, what's this story about?"

"That's good," Bette says. "I ask myself a version of that whenever I try a new recipe. It's a good way to settle nerves from trying new things. So what is this whole affair with Oprah about would you say?"

"My intention is for Oprah to mention my book. It's not a personal thing. I don't really care if she knows who I am. I only want what her recognition of my story could do for the story and for the many readers who would be ... nurtured by my work. They'd be encouraged and uplifted by such a gift."

"Your intention is strictly selfless," Misty says.

"Benevolent," Bette agrees.

"I've written *The Long Bad Sentence* and *Miranda* as hopeful stories about love—sisterly love, young love, and the love of profession, which Miranda would have to leave behind if she chooses to remain with Jaime, in Barcelona. Can she trust him? He's a policeman, yes, a noble profession, true, but even rogues are attracted to the passion of rescuing and saving others. They too love the limelight, the risk of the moment. He might not be the kind of man a steady preschool teacher like Miranda could keep happy, not to mention whether she can be happy in a country where she barely speaks the language. Change would be Miranda's middle name if she stayed in Spain. Miranda isn't good at change. Oprah's readers understand a woman's struggle with decisions. She triumphs with her readers when a character comes to terms with life as she knows it when a love affair dies. *Miranda* would be good for her readers. How's that for a pitch?"

"I'm impressed," Misty says. "But you skipped right over *The Long Bad Sentence*."

"Right. Ok. It is my intention to get my latest book into Oprah's hands so she'll discover this wonderful story that could bring joy to her audiences. It's not a healing story of abuse and broken hearts that Oprah is so known for, but a story about taking risks for love. But not just the love of a lover, but the love of occupation, of oneself. I mean, even Oprah chose her profession over a love life."

"Yes!" High fives all around, our cheers wake a resident dozing by the window. He shouts, "Ice cream!"

"I'll get you some, Benny," Bette tells him.

"Both stories have happy endings, even if the boy doesn't get the girl. The nurse in *Long Bad* lives a good life, even if it isn't with the prison guard. And my story has a happy ending for Miranda, even if it isn't a traditional ending. I can't let Irving the Editor change Miranda's final decision."

"I'm glad we can help you with those revisions," Bette says. "You're sounding much firmer. You'll be able to negotiate better with your new editor now. I was able to ask for a raise a few weeks ago after I thought about what my job contributes to the health of the residents. I'm not just a cook. I'm a nutrition consultant, maybe even a queen, with important subjects who need my guidance to make their way through The Kingdom of the Elders."

"They accepted that argument?" Darlien asks.

"I didn't share the queen part or the part about the kingdom. Catchy sound though, don't you think, Annie? The Kingdom of the Elders. It could be the title to a book."

"A kid's book," I agree, imagining the lovely illustrations that could go with such a title. "But I'm not so sure about the content."

"Believing in the importance of what I'm doing made it much easier for me to make my request," Bette said. "They didn't grant the raise, but they said they'd consider it at my next evaluation, so I made progress. That's all we really have control over, right? What we put forward?"

"And our attitude," I add.

One of the assisted living center's small dogs trots through the reception area, a red bow hanging askew from her little Pekinese neck. "We need to tell Kari to get tickets for the five of us, right?" Misty says. We nod agreement. "Okay. And Kari's also thought of another plan. It has to do with dogs, Annie."

"'I will not go there,' says the cat. 'I will not go there, that is that,'" I say in my best Dr. Seuss voice.

"Live with risk," Darlien opines.

"Dogs are always so busy huffing about and sniffing," I say. "And John won't like it. He'll cough up more bezoars."

As though prompted, the Pekinese trots over to me and puts her little paws up on my thighs. I stroke her fur. It reminds me of something ... someone. Ah, Jaime's mustache. The dog's fur is as soft and dark as my Spanish paramour's.

"I will not go there," says the cat, "I will not go there, that is that."

"It means you need to go to Chicago now," Misty says.

"Bette's still got time on her break."

She nods, looking at the big clock on the wall. I wonder who here besides the staff cares about the time.

"Not right this minute, but by the end of the week," Darlien says.

"I thought we'd all go down together for the show," I say.

"That's too long to wait. Kari's got an idea that you can do now," Bette says.

"Norton, please don't ride on Mr. Benton's wheelchair," Misty says. "You can take the ball into the courtyard if you want, or you and he can read together. You decide." Norton chooses Mr. Benton time. "Good job," his mother tells him.

Good kid.

"Kari knows someone who works for someone who used to live next door to the artist who has painted portraits of all of Oprah's dogs. The artist knows her former groomer, who has his own salon now. Oprah sometimes stops in there even though her current groomers come to her home. Kari says that's a perfect way to meet up with Oprah ... with a dog. All you have to do is get a pup and bring it to Chicago," Darlien says.

They must have all been talking to Kari, since it didn't sound like news to any of them.

"You'll need a few days to get used to your dog, before you

appear at the groomer's. That's what Kari thinks," Darlien says. "You'll acclimate well to canines, Annie. Managing a dog will be good practice for when you marry again and have kids."

The Pekinese snaps at my fingers, unwilling to be the canine I rent for Chicago.

"Oh, I almost forgot," Bette says. "Here's the We Care maintenance shirt. You can use my ID tag too — you'll look more official."

"For what?"

"For your foray into TMJ4 studios. The TV station. Remember? You've been called to fix a leaky toilet."

⑥

I may as well get it over with before I have time to consider all the consequences. I'll pretend I'm a fictional character with my blue shirt plus badge and black pants. I'll return Bette's lavaliere and ID when I'm done. I hope the receptionist is like me and rarely looks at the picture on the ID or the name, for that matter.

Darlien drives me to the studio but won't come in with me. "I think it's illegal for a cop to impersonate someone else," she says, "unless they're undercover. And maybe a little stupid." When my eyes get large she says, "But I'll come rescue you if they hit the alarm."

"Right," I say, picking up the pail with plunger and scrub brush that Bette loaned me. I have five paperback copies of *The Long Bad Sentence* in the bucket too.

I press the buzzer near the door and, instead of a voice asking me who I am and who I'm there to see, the door opens, and I approach the reception desk that's surrounded by another set of locked half-doors, which makes the receptionist look like she's sitting behind a jury box. I notice a man with a white cane tap-tapping his way to leather lounge chairs, talking with a friend. They apparently just signed in. I do that too.

"I'm here in response to a call about a broken toilet?" I say in my perfect up-end voice.

"Oh? Gosh, I guess I didn't get that call. But go ahead. It must be the one at the end of the hall. It's always giving us trouble." She presses another buzzer and the gate opens and I walk through.

I can't believe I'm in! It's so easy. Two people in front of me chat as the one who appears to be a guide tells the other, "Here's the green room. They come and mic you before you're on." I slow my walk down the corridor lined with signed photographs of the famous people and the news anchors and the hosts of *Positively Milwaukee*. I open that door on the left where guests wait to go on the air, smile at the waiting guest. I wipe down the coffee table with a rag, listen to the programming on the small television, and leave a book behind. The waiting guest doesn't seem to notice me. A man rushes past me, introduces himself to the guests, and tells them the procedures and when they'll be "miked" and on the air as I make my way down the hall to the next door. I'll leave another book. Since I'm supposed to be fixing a toilet, I locate one and decide to use it.

⑥

"Hey," a male voice says. "This is a pretty snazzy outhouse."

"How's that?" his comrade says. I hear a strange tapping and then the stall next to mine opens up. I lift my feet and sit as undisturbed as an empty toilet paper roll in a bachelor's loft.

"All they've got is stalls. No urinals in sight. Feel that? Doors on 'em. Privacy all the way. Here, let me help you with that." Some clunking sounds, then, "Just hang it on the door."

The second man thanks him amidst the clunking.

"Not the same as urinals," he tells his friend. "I'll be next door here."

He pushes against my door held shut with both a latch and my raised feet. "Humph. Stuck." He moves to a stall on the other side of his friend.

I'm in the men's bathroom!

"When you can't see a dang thing, everything's an adventure."

"Have to go see my doc when I get back home," the voice coming from the stall on the other side says. "Check out my waterworks."

This is what men talk about in the bathroom? Who knew?

I'm finished but I don't dare move. Nor can I step out now and admit that I was in the wrong bathroom and that I'd been in here this whole time, eavesdropping. I can only hope they'll hurry so I can get back out, leave the rest of my books and brochures, and disappear.

"Who do you see then? Doc Hutchins?"

"Naw. His associate. That new guy doesn't look old enough to drive, but they say he's good." He starts to hum.

Will they be in here all day?

"Finished?" Clunking sounds again. "Let me help you out there. Oops." I hear banging. Flushing sounds. A door opening and then action at the sink. "They got big mirrors and nice sinks in here too. Kohler faucets. Have you seen those commercials? Oh, sorry."

"I listen to 'em. Don't always get the point though, unless someone tells me. But I hear there's one with a blind guy in it kind of massaging the fixtures."

"You ready to head back? You'll be going on the air soon."

I hear them open the door to the hallway and sigh in relief. I stand to finish up, then hear a woman's voice, strident. "What are you two doing in here? This is the women's bathroom."

"It is? Well, I'll be. No wonder it smelled so good," one of the men says.

"So that's why there were no urinals. Should have figured," the other man says and they laugh.

"I can't believe you didn't figure that out," the woman says. "Can you find your way back to the green room?"

"Oh yes," they say. They're still laughing while the woman takes the stall next to mine.

Again I lift my feet, squatting on the seat now so she won't know I'm here because then she'll know that I've been here the whole time while the men tended to their business! What would she think of me? I have to wait until she's finished.

"Mom? It's me, Ruth. Yes." Pause. "Ok." Pause. She's on her cell phone! "Well, let me tell you. It's quite a story. It started on Saturday."

She might be in here forever. I have no choice.

"Maintenance!" I shout, flushing the toilet and making as much noise as I can. Then I slam through the door, spray water over my hands, run back into the stall to grab my bucket, and tear out of the restroom, where I run headfirst into an official-looking man in a beige shirt and dark, pressed slacks.

"Oh good," he says. "I was looking for you."

"You were? Did you see my book? I'm Annie Shaw."

"Book? No. I need you in the men's room. There's a plugged toilet in there."

I trail him to another men's room, knowing I shouldn't be allowed out on my own and definitely not in pursuit of a bestseller.

⑥

Darlien's asleep in the car when I finally come out—toilet unplugged. I tell her what happened and she agrees that maybe it's not a good idea to try the other stations in town, just send them a book and brochure instead. "You need to focus on getting to Chicago now anyway, to follow up on Kari's connections."

I return my costume and Bette's ID and spend the rest of the day recovering from my bathroom repair work, writing down ideas that sink, don't swim. I wonder if I should call Irving. I go on Facebook, then torture myself by reading the Amazon reviews of my books. I waste an hour.

My call to the Sunday school director telling her I have to be away for awhile leaves me feeling sad. "You'll be so hard to replace," she tells me. "The children really love you."

"I love them back," I say, and I try to think who I can ask to step in for me. Bette usually works on weekends; Darlien does too. Misty, maybe. "I'll see what I can do about getting someone to take my place," I tell her.

I call the school where I volunteer to tell them I'll be gone for several weeks and write a letter to Buster, assuring him I'll be back. I arrange when I can be in classrooms to help with writing projects once I return. It looks like the second half of the year will work best for them.

I call the site coordinator for the Reading Ready program.

"You always bring in such interesting children's books," Gracie tells me. "Your suggestions have certainly expanded our library collection. Some of the parents have asked for your recommended reading list."

"Really? That's nice."

"You have a good eye for stories," she says. "But I suppose that's why you're a writer. Maybe you ought to write a children's book."

She has no idea how difficult that would be.

I talk to my neighbor when I put the garbage out, and I pay my monthly bills. Through it all, Gracie's words filter into my scattered brain, sticking tight as dental floss. *A children's book. It's just another distraction.*

John arches his back beneath my fingers as I sit once again before my computer. His purr soothes as he drapes across my lap. Tiny cat hairs lift into the afternoon sun.

I'll miss those kids too. Even more than getting emails from happy readers, those children make me glad that I'm someone who loves words and books and wants to share them. I just couldn't make Jaime understand. My Jaime, the real Jaime of *Miranda of La Mancha*. Maybe I should have used another name for him as the character in my book but somehow he will always be Jaime, the man I fell in love with and almost changed my life for.

It's said that a publisher knows if a book will become a

bestseller before it's even released. This influences the size of the press run and how a publisher decides to promote that title ahead of time. Is it fate or happenstance or good writing that characterize the books that Oprah picks? "Maybe I should research all the past Oprah picks and see what they have in common," I tell John. "You don't think that's a grand idea? No? I guess you're right. I'm procrastinating. I'm being slothful. It will get me nowhere."

John leaps from my lap and hunches over on the floor, coughing up yet another bezoar.

"I see you agree."

From: Website Contact Form
To: Annie Shaw
From: Jessie Bennet
Wildman220@AmalgaU.edu

Dear Miss Shaw. I recently discovered your books on a cross-country flight. I'd finished the tome I'd brought along, re-read the scholarly journal I'd packed at last minute and, eschewing the in-flight movie, noticed instead what the woman sitting next to me was reading. It was *Sweet Charity's Rose*. She laughed, cried, and smiled a lot. So when she finished it, saying, "Now that was a satisfying and fun read," I asked if I could borrow it. Fortunately, I knew no one else on the flight so didn't have to be embarrassed reading a woman's novel. Much to my surprise, I loved the book. Moreover, my seat companion and I discussed the book and your clever use of gardening metaphors and we discovered a mutual interest in botanical things. We also commented on the number of other people reading your book in the airport and on the plane, which is certainly good publicity for you. I hope the book continues to do well. We'll look for others. Oh, and my seatmate and I are now seeing each other on a steady basis, so you see where your fine literary piece has taken us.

With gratitude,
Jessie Bennet, Associate Professor

Chapter 5

I call Misty about teaching Sunday school and she reminds me that she's already teaching at the Community Church down the road. "Why not ask Bette? She needs to be around younger people."

"But she works most weekends."

"Maybe she'd be able to come in earlier and leave for that hour. Give her a chance to say no, Annie." I agree.

I hear the ca-chink of the brass mail slot, one of the archaic delights of an old flat, followed by the doorbell. I race downstairs, to see the mail flutter to the floor. All the oversized sales stuff doesn't fit, so Henrietta, the post woman, rolls them into an old two-pound coffee can set in the foyer I share with my downstairs neighbors. We peruse the coffee can at our leisure, and I consider it a spam filter for snail mail, developed long before the electronic kind.

"Not much for ya today," Henrietta says when I open the door. She's still puffing from the three steps up from the street to the foyer, and I realize she rang the bell so I can sign a delivery receipt. She wears her summer uniform and her tanned knees look like the rings of cut trees announcing their age. "Looks like a letter from Spain, though. That's kind of interestin'. Not one you sent yourself is it, to get the postage stamps you like?" She turns the letter over in her hand.

"Not from Barcelona," I say picking up the pieces of mail she dropped through the slot.

She waits. I know she hopes I'll elaborate but I don't.

Henrietta knows a lot about me, but she doesn't need to know everything.

"Oh, and here's this big envelope from Denver. Someone with 'AP,' " she says. "Need your signature." I comply. "I guess I coulda put it in the spam can, right?" She grins.

I snatch it from her. "No, I'll take it. The rest too," I say. "Got a little time, so I'll look through the second-class junk that pays your salary. How does it feel to be a kept woman?"

Henrietta laughs. "All righty, then. Have a good day, and don't be zipping off to Barcelona without taking me with you, like you did last time."

"No chance of that," I say. I hold the letter as though it's charged with electricity. "No chance of that at all."

Heading upstairs, I decide not to let myself read either the Barcelona letter or the packet from the publisher until I finish what I'm working on. My intention statement is a little long. I need something I can say to a stranger on a plane sitting beside me when they ask, "What are you working on?" right after I've been asked what I do. Lots of times they follow my reply with "I've always wanted to write a book." Do neurosurgeons get that response when they share their occupation? "I've always wanted to be a neurosurgeon" isn't what you'd expect a person to say.

But everyone does have a story, I know that. It's what I tell the kids I work with on their writing projects, that to call themselves a writer just requires that they write, not that they get published or become famous. "And whatever has happened to you is worth writing down, even if no one else ever reads it," I tell them, adding how amazed they'll be learning about themselves just by writing their stories. Like a crime scene investigator of my own flotsam, I discover with each book that the story I've chosen to tell turns out to be something different at the end. The story tells itself to me. I learn something about me I wouldn't have known if I hadn't written that story down.

In *The Long Bad Sentence* I learned that love can be found

in unlikely places. In *Don't Kick Me* I discovered how often I did just the opposite of what I said I wanted to do. And with *Sweet Charity's Rose* I mined the treasure that some good marriages are made in heaven. I didn't learn until later that my marriage wasn't.

Perhaps I'm a slow learner, but kids aren't. At the preschool where I worked up until *Sweet Charity* gave me a successful novel, I'd write their words down when they arrived in the morning, two or three sentences, always finished with "The End."

"My mom put a plastic cup on the end of her fist and snaked our toilet." (I wish I'd remembered that tip at TMJ4!) There'd be an illustration request. "She had to go to the snake store where they had all kinds of toys and sinks and she fixed it! My dad says we have to stop giving our dog pig's ears to chew on so he won't drop them in the toilet. The End." They'd stuff the pages in their cubbies and loved pulling them out and having me read them again a day or a week later. I could almost see them discovering how words hold memories so they could have room for more imagination to bloom.

Only one percent of anyone, old or young, who says they want to write a book, ever does. Their harpies get too loud, I guess. My hope with the kids I work with is to silence the voices that might get in their way, so they can be what they were created to be: uniquely loved for who they are.

On airplanes or in waiting rooms where the subject of becoming a writer arises, I always smile and encourage the would-be scribes who make their living as real estate investment counselors or ballet teachers. I hope my encouragement doesn't suggest that how I've chosen to make my living can be easily done by any Dawn, Dick, or Mary. But I believe that any Dawn, Dick, or Mary can write a story if they persist, if they have courage, if they have enough duct tape.

"I'm writing a story set in Spain about a woman who falls in love during the International Police and Firemen Games and who wants to do the right thing for herself and the man she loves," I tell John. There. I have my intention statement. I'm inspired. Now I can read my letters.

I open the letter from Spain, knowing it's from the real Jaime. He's the only person from Spain who has my address. My hands shake. The stationery is tan and the script is beautiful, almost calligraphy. But it's written in Spanish. I can't read a word! I'm relieved. I don't have to deal with this, at least not now. I'll take it with me to Chicago. Kari speaks a little Spanish and will surely know someone who can read it.

I'm giddy with relief so with confidence take on the publisher packet. The large envelope from Denver lies in wait on the small end table, an old baby carriage wheel with Plexiglas over it so I can see to the hardwood floors. It's the only antique I won in the coin toss between my ex-husband and me over the special items we both claimed. How can I be both unlucky falling into love and then falling out of love as well? My ex got the antique wooden duck, the refinished secretary, the parson's desk, even the sugar jar that held salt during the Civil War. Well, Stuart has to live with the memories all those antiques would bring him. I only have the Victorian baby carriage wheel table to remind me of the cost of falling in love, an impulsive marriage, an efficient and sad divorce. If only he hadn't been so charming at that writer's conference where we met. He talked such a good game and sounded excited for me that I had a contract to write a romance novel, even though he wrote "serious pieces." I learned later those pieces were seriously flawed and his paychecks rare. But he made me feel wonderful, brought me flowers. My parents loved him. Darlien was a bit standoffish but she was recently divorced and a bit jaded about love. I'd been dreaming of marriage; of kids and a house and a life like Misty had with her sweet husband and child. It turned out to be a nightmare, and I was glad I was awake this time, with Barcelona calling. I wasn't sleepwalking into love.

I flip open the envelope. I wonder if Irving will be talking about *Barcelona Knight* or the title I chose. Is he trying to tell me in a subtle way that he's ultimately in control? Randolph says publishing is a team activity, but every team has star performers who ultimately call the plays. John kneads against my thighs, keeping me in the here and now.

Time to attack the edits.

The doorbell rings. It's Stuart.

"Hey, babe," he says.

"Hey, Stu."

"Thanks for helping me out." He's wearing a new-to-me Tommy Hilfiger shirt and pressed khaki pants.

"You learned how to iron," I say.

"Huh?" I point to his slacks. "Nah. Dry cleaner presses them."

"You take your laundry to the dry cleaner?"

"You got the washer and dryer."

"And you got the car. Can I count on you to help repair the washer if it fails? After all, you used it too."

"Don't be selfish, Annie. Do you have the cash or not?"

What are those phrases again? *Thank you but I think I'll pass.* It's too late for that. He's sucked the energy from my soul. I hand him the three hundred dollars deciding I'll stop payment on the check I sent and open the door so he'll leave.

"I wish we could be friends," he says.

"Friends don't keep asking for money," I tell him.

"Hey," he says and squats down to pet John, who has curled around his legs.

Traitor, I think, but then Stuart was always good to John. Maybe I should have him watch him while I'm in Chicago. No. He'd want to stay here and we'd have to talk and I'd end up sending him money for more than cat food.

"I've got work to do," I tell him.

"Yeah. Me too," he says. I don't believe him but he leaves and I sink onto the couch, relieved.

I suppose it's a mark of my creativity that I wrote about our romance in such a way that *Sweet Charity's Rose* did well.

Looking back, our relationship was filled with more thorns than roses. I'd created the ideal romance novel for AP. That's fiction for you.

I head for the refrigerator.

IT'S NOT IN HERE stares at me, my sign below the light. Maybe it's true that when I seek my fridge even though I'm not hungry, it's to soothe self-criticism. What have I just been telling myself? Oh yes, about my lackluster book, my editorial dither, a failed marriage, and Jaime's letter bringing up old issues I hope are long passed.

I close the refrigerator, pick up the letter. The stamp brings back memories of making a trip to the ornate old post office by the port of Barcelona. Even mailing a postcard was an adventure. Spain is a lovely country. But that alone won't be enough of a reason for someone to invite Miranda into their lives. I have to work on Irving's concerns.

The pages of my edited manuscript bleed red. I scan his comments, tears coming to my eyes even with the occasional compliment he's written in the margins. How can I be so far from what he thinks will make a good story? I'm so not in tune with my life, so how can I make beautiful music with words?

I'll wait until I'm on the bus to Chicago and think about it then.

@

I call Kari about getting the tickets for the five of us and to suggest that I give myself two months max to accomplish getting the books into Oprah's hands. I've already thought of a couple more things I can do in Chicago in addition to Kari's dog plan. Each will take time. "Are you up for a house guest for a month or so?"

"Not a problem, hon. It'll be fun to have you. It's not every day we have a celebrity to share our condo with."

"I'm not really a celebrity," I tell her.

"Sure you are."

"Maybe a little fish in a big, big pool," I say, remembering the dentist.

"You're in the pool," Kari says. "That's what matters."

"So tell me about the dog thing."

"When you get here, we'll go to the pound and get a dog that you can take to this groomer who used to work for Oprah. It was such a quirk that I even got his name, but it must have been for a reason. Everything happens for a reason, right?"

"I'm not exactly sure my landlord allows dogs. A cat is okay, but he was even a little reluctant about John until he met him." I stroke my cat's back and gently tug at his arched tail.

She hesitates. "We own the condo, so having a dog isn't a problem. That'll give you time to convince your landlord before you return. About the tickets? I think they only let you ask for four at a time."

"I'll stay home," I laugh.

"Don't be silly. Misty might not want to be away from Norton for a weekend. Or Ed," she added. "I'll check to make sure all the girls can all come. We can ask for two of us as one party and the other three as another. We'll work it out. We have to remember to bring IDs."

"Really, like we're going in to Canada?"

"A driver's license will do. Or your passport. It's for security."

How hard it must be to have security needs like that surrounding your every move. I feel a little sorry for Oprah. Maybe fame isn't all it's cracked up to be.

That portion of the plan settled, I ask Bette if she might take over my Sunday school class. "Boy. I'm not sure I can get off. But I'll ask. It would be fun to be around kiddos. Sometimes I feel pretty isolated here," she tells me. "I love the residents, but kids and other people ... I mean guys my own age, are really rare in this place. I'll check. And hey, I'm sorry about your maintenance thing."

"I did place my books and brochures in a bunch of offices. And I got to tell someone my name and that I wrote a book. I don't think he took me seriously though, when I could also fix the toilet."

"Kari's plan with the dog will work better," she said. "And I've sent off the police cap sponge cakes and cookies that look like badges. I made this really delicious chocolate frosting and wrote *The Long Bad Sentence* around the edge of the badge, just like the names of correctional facilities. I wrote it on the bill of the police cap. I took photos and we'll post them on Facebook. You should be hearing any day now from reviewers saying they'll review your book."

"You're more successful than I am of late."

I arrange for Bette to care for John, take in the paper, and check the mail. I stop by Misty's to say a firsthand good-bye; I pack my necessities, buy my bus ticket online.

"I'll drive you," Darlien tells me when I call to say good-bye. I can picture her. She stands nearly six feet tall. A dragonfly tattoo flies up over her back and nuzzles her attractive neck. I'm too terrified to have a tattoo and nearly fainted watching Darlien get hers. She wears contacts of various colors. My amber eyes change only by looking larger behind my thick glasses. Darlien moonlights as security for the Packer games when they play exhibition football games in Milwaukee Stadium. That's where she met all three of her husbands. She loves the moonlighting best, though she claims it's for other reasons than meeting potential husbands, like getting to watch Packer games for free. "Even when we lose," she told me once, assuming first-person status the way all Packer fans do, "the fans act more orderly than most of the guests at my wedding receptions did." She's munching on potato chips. How she can stay so thin and eat so much junk food is beyond me.

"Was it your second reception where the paper reported 'among the injured were'?"

"Very funny." Her tone inspires me to get up to clean John's litter box, holding the phone with my chin.

"I won't be able to take you until after the weekend, though.

The Pack's playing an exhibition game, and I'll want to be there for that."

"I'm taking the bus," I tell her. "You can drive the girls once we get the tickets arranged."

"Really," Darlien said, "there's no need for you to take the bus—sometimes unsavory people —"

"Unsavory? Just because we don't care to stand in line at the airport for hours or take off our shoes for total strangers doesn't mean there's a thing wrong with us bus travelers," I said. "I like bus travel. I can read, relax —"

"You can't take John with you very well."

"Plot, plan, even work on revisions." I ignore her interruption. One has to learn this if one intends to survive an older sister. "Bus transportation is very supportive of writers."

"Yeah. They provide villainous characters of remarkable originality."

"My books don't have villains," I say.

"Maybe that's why they don't sell so well."

Her words sting.

"They have conflict and they struggle about the meaning of life. That's just as good."

"Hey, I'm just telling you what you're always telling me."

"I can say it. I don't expect my sister to. Besides, John isn't coming along. My downstairs neighbors said he can have the run of the entire two stories, and Bette said she'd come by with food and keep the litter box clean. I'll only be gone a month, so John'll be all right until I get back. It's better not to disrupt his environment."

"Did you ever dream you could just go off for a month to write? I've been thinking about our goal for you. Maybe we're off the mark here. You have a good life. You don't need to be famous or produce a bestseller. Why not just enjoy being able to do what you love?"

"Getting into this makes me assess the value of my work. And besides, dreams change. It's good to have a new goal."

"Have you heard from your editor yet?"

"It's too complicated to go into. Let's talk about mom and dad."

Our parents are farmers in western Wisconsin, where my dad still milks cows. Sometimes he works as a trucker hauling fertilizer to fields. That means mom takes over the milking while he's away. It's what they do, adapt. I've watched my mom change tires, fix fences, sew up wounded cows. She always finds a way to get it done. Maybe that's how I managed to get my characters out of predicaments. Farming is good fodder for the writing life.

"Mom was asking about the Spain trip," Darlien says. "She wondered if you'd met anyone there."

"What'd you tell her?" I clean the litter box while I listen. The white puffs of scent-robber that tickle my nose sometimes smell worse than John's gifts.

"That you'd met this one guy, Jaime, and spent a fair amount of time with him. But I didn't know if anything had come of it. I mean, I don't really know if anything has. So I didn't want to mislead her." She hesitates. "Has anything come of it? Besides inspiration for the book I mean?"

"His English wasn't very good and my Spanish is even worse. So we just ... we were just ... are just, friends. You can tell her that."

"I don't know why you're being so secretive if nothing came of it."

My hands feel sweaty and I have trouble closing the bag containing John's ejects while still holding the phone with my chin. I dump the remains in the garbage, head to the bathroom to wash my hands.

"What did you do, Annie?" Darlien persists. "Before we flew back home?"

"There's nothing to tell. We went to Florence, visited Lisbon, came back. Jaime's happy as a policeman in Spain. He was, is, a good guy. That's it."

"So you've heard from him?" Darlien asks. "You haven't let this one slip away. I'm just asking for Mom. Has he written to you?" She clears her throat. I don't want to answer. "Well, just so you know, he wrote to Mom and Dad."

I drop my sister via cell phone into the toilet, right where my love life lives.

Chapter 6

I take Jaime's letter and the package from Irving with me on the bus, sitting midway back, where I can catch the driver's eyes now and then in the mirror. I like knowing he's aware of what happens behind him. Today, mostly, people doze or chatter to each other. One couple plays cards; a woman reads softly to the man beside her. I read my editor's letter over for the fourth time. This is the manuscript I sent him, the one my friends love but I can see that Irving doesn't.

> *Ms. Shaw. There is much to like in this manuscript; much, however remains to address. Let us begin with the scene on the Barcelona Metro. The Blue Line, I believe you called it. It seems highly unlikely to me that Gypsies or Moroccans would all dress in black pants and blue shirts.*

Odd, that was my maintenance garb as well.

> *This sets the scene up immediately as unbelievable, and thus you require your readers to make leaps of faith too early in the story. They will not make the leap. I myself would not have continued past this point if I was not required to. There is also the matter of being politically correct in the matter of Gypsies and/or Moroccans. Perhaps we should just say "locals."*

My heart sinks lower than an old pair of panty hose. My own editor confesses that even he wouldn't read the whole book, wouldn't give me even the smallest arena of goodwill based on my previous works, trusting that I can bring everything together. I always bring everything together.

But Irving doesn't know that—nor me, not at all.

That comment about being politically correct bothers me too. Isn't naming the culprits Gypsies or Moroccans, just as the police did, a way of distinguishing them, providing readers with the detail necessary to feel they're a part of the experience? Isn't it just a way of providing depth to a story, depth that lives inside details?

The worst part of reading Irving's comments about that scene in the metro is that it really happened that way and yet I didn't make the truth believable. Irving wants fiction, and I gave him unbelievable facts instead.

Maybe I can change the color of the thieves' clothing to make it more authentic, though the fact that the men looked so similar was part of their scam. One stole Miranda's sunglasses and gave them to another, who handed them to Miranda as though she'd dropped them. That interchange allowed the third member of the team to steal Miranda's wallet between the Jaumel metro stop and Placa de Catayuna. If they hadn't been dressed alike they couldn't have confused poor Miranda, alone, without her sister, on the underground big city scary metro.

Jaime had come into Miranda's life at that moment of vulnerability. He'd detected the scam, and in seconds, had prevented the three from departing the subway. Of course, others on the train assisted once he flashed his badge and even applauded that the culprits had been caught.

I flashed to the day the theft happened, the day I met the real Jaime. In broken English, Jaime explained who he was, asking me to remain with him so I could file a report against the three. I'd been both frightened and intrigued. The badge looked real and those on the train who spoke English assured me he was legitimate, but Jaime didn't look like any policeman I'd ever seen or imagined. He wasn't in uniform because he'd been competing at the games. He had eyes as dark as Barcelona chocolate, lips that slid into a lazy smile that belied the intensity of his energy holding the three at bay. But if I stayed on the train past my station, I wasn't sure if I could find my way back. My sister would be worried and so would I.

When Jaime removed his hat later, I saw he was completely bald, a feature that only made him more alluring. I'd been totally torn about what to do.

I sit up, spread Irving's letter on my lap. I've written about Miranda's journey, not mine; but mine is tied into it, and I've made it sound unreal.

My heart pounds for reasons other than romantic passion. Irving likes things tidy. He hasn't even folded the letter — one of the reasons why he uses the large white envelope. He obviously likes his stories tidy too. Well, life isn't always neatly packaged — I'd found that out with Stuart and again in Barcelona.

Someone coughs and I look around the bus. Most of the passengers on the Greyhound are old people, or older, I guess I should say, traveling in pairs, like Siamese twins. The few apparently single travelers that might be closer to my age sleep with their mouths open (I'm guessing students); or wear wild expressions in their eyes. A furtive-eyed guy sits in front of me, across the aisle, and he turns periodically to stare. Maybe he's glowering at the child sitting next to me or her mother and little brother in the seats in front of us. His one eye twists off to the side so I can't really tell who he stares at. A woman knitting looks up periodically, halting the needle midair as though it's a stun gun, then continuing her stitching. Another of Generation Now hugs his knapsack, hoarding whatever treasures he stores. I suspect some of the riders are from either the county mental hospital in Milwaukee heading to the Windy City or new parolees from the regional prisons; the latter distinguished by their hopeful looks, crisply cut hair, and new polished shoes.

Prisoners make me think of policemen and that makes me think of Jaime, the real one.

I can't believe he's written to my mother! Who could have given him my parents' address? My sister. She must have spent more time with him than I'd realized. They both competed in the golf events, so out on the fairway, while I'd been cruising museums and the chocolate and candle shops, my sister and Jaime conspired. What had she told him about me? What had he written in this letter? I pull it out just to look at the lovely penmanship. I'm anxious now for Kari to translate it.

"May I sit next to the window?" The child beside me has been silent for an hour and I realize suddenly she's staring at me. Dark, straight hair hangs below her ears and she wears a red flower barrette above a tightly coiled braid drawing back from her wise eyes. "You're not looking at the sky," she says. "You're reading." She must have been about ten years old and I detect a slight Spanish lilt to her speech.

"I guess I could exchange seats with you."

"Is she bothering you?" This from the woman in the seat in front of me.

"No. It's nice to see a child politely ask for what she wants," I say. She stands up in the aisle and I slide across the cloth seat, letting her hop in toward the window.

"What?" I say as she continues to stare.

"My name is Juanita," she says. "What's yours?"

"Annie," I tell her.

"That's a nice name."

I nod. "So is Juanita."

"I saw your letter," she says.

"You were eavesdropping? That's not polite," I say, but I smile.

"Eavesdropping is listening," she tells me. "I snooped."

"Oh, right."

I start to put Jaime's letter away. "It's in Spanish," she says. "Do you speak Spanish?"

"No. Actually, I don't read Spanish either."

"Do you know what the letter says?" I shake my head. "Why would your friend write to you in words you can't read?"

"It's the only language he knows. He's from Spain."

"I can tell you what he said."

I hesitate. What if what he wrote is something steamy? I tap Juanita's mother on the shoulder. "Excuse me. Juanita has offered to read a letter from a friend, in Spanish. He's a former boyfriend, and I wouldn't want to, well, in case there's something —"

"Let me look." She scans the letter. "It's okay. He pines for you but the sheets are clean."

"He talks about linen?"

"No, no. What he writes on the sheets of paper is clean."

"Oh. Good."

"Let me," Juanita says. I hand her the letter. She speed-reads. "Okay. He says you have nothing in common, but he misses your face in the morning. He says he doesn't understand why you left him without saying good-bye and that he wishes that was different. It's rude to leave and not say good-bye." She looks at me. "My friend Alice says it's really rude to leave a teeter-totter without saying you're going to."

"Painful too," I say. "One of you can get hurt that way."

She agrees. I guess Jaime and I were on a bit of a teeter-totter.

"He talks about his nieces and nephews. They say hello to you, his mother too."

"His mother?"

"And he wants to see you again."

"Lunch stop!" shouts the driver to us. "Half an hour here."

People begin to hustle out, stretch in the aisles.

"I gotta go," Juanita says. She hands me the letter and asks if she can please step over me now.

"Is that all he said?" I ask as her waif-body slips past me, a warm scent of flowers coming from her skin.

"I think your friend misses you." She heads down the aisle then turns back. "Do you miss him?"

72

I don't know how to answer. Juanita's mother rescues me and leads her daughter away.

I put Jaime's letter back into the envelope and give Irving's first concern one more look before putting it away and heading off the bus for lunch. Maybe Irving is on to something. The truth can be stranger than fiction, and perhaps a writer does have to make reality more fictional in order for a reader to believe it could happen. I mustn't discount him. Maybe I could change that scene a little and have leverage later, holding out for the really big scenes I don't want him to mess with at all.

Except that pickpocket scene with Miranda lifted of her wallet really is one of the big scenes in the book. It drives the whole story forward. Something has to happen to bring Miranda and her policeman together early in the story, and it has to be an event with a tinge of fear to it, of orchestrated tension that can become frenzied in strange locales. Miranda is a fish out of water, a pig without a pen, a cat without her purr when she arrives in Spain, her first journey to Europe. She's a woman afraid, thinking the worst and then, within hours of her arrival, the worst happens: she's robbed.

Miranda's vulnerability is intensified with her being "right." She'd told her sister bad things would happen in Barcelona; that she never should have agreed to come at the last minute, and on and on. But her reluctance to enter the scary possibilities in a European trip makes Jaime's rescue all the more endearing; makes Miranda's openness to his charms all the more believable, her hesitation in accepting his gifts all the more ... poignant.

Except that I don't really want poignant in this story. I want Miranda to be a strong woman who chooses her own destiny, even if it isn't what her sister wants for her or her parents or anyone else.

"Better head in to lunch, miss," the driver says. "You can leave your things on the bus. They'll be safe."

I step down; the diesel smell lifts to my nose by the breeze on this hot, late September afternoon in Elgin, Illinois. Like people heading to our last meal, we follow single file beneath a big swooping fish and a sign over the doorway announcing Chuck's Greek Isle Restaurant. The décor is more Chuck than Greek. Juanita joins her mother and brother, heading first to the restrooms. I figure I'll do that just before we leave so I won't have to use the tiny bathroom on the bus. I used it once and it makes me feel like a toothbrush being put into a holder.

Three women already seated motion me to join them. I prefer to eat alone so I can eavesdrop without notice, a typical writer ploy. But seating is scarce, and the three look safer than the furtive-eyed guy or the possible parolee with the new shoes or the grandmother with the stun gun knitting needle, so I join the women.

We sit beneath a ceiling fan that feels almost cold despite the eighty-five plus degrees outside.

"Would you like a sweater?" the waitress asks the woman sitting across from me. She nods yes.

A *sweater*? Why don't they just turn the fan down? And how do they have so many sizes of sweaters to offer? And who takes them home to wash them, the poor waitress? And what about head lice? I mean, I volunteer in schools for reader programs, I've taught in preschools. I know about head lice and how it can rage through a school like termites in an old townhouse. You can't have that many people stopping for lunch, sharing sweaters, without head lice.

"What about you, dearie?" the waitress says, turning to me. She has an apple face and lipstick too big for her mouth.

"What did you ask her?" I say. I vow to watch the waitress's mouth.

"Would you like ice water?"

"Ice water! It sure sounded like 'a sweater' to me," I told them as the women laugh. "I'm pleased to not have to worry about the head lice in shared sweaters, but now I think my hearing might be going."

"Oh, that's what we all worry about," one of the women says.

"We're falling apart bit by bit. That's why we travel together. That way one of us is sure to get what the others miss, and we can be the glue for each other, putting each of us back together."

Just like my gaggle of friends.

I decide against ordering my basic BLT and try something new. Might as well learn to live with a little risk, considering the goal I'd set for myself. The women chatter among themselves. They could be my mother and her sisters, with their round faces and brazen sleeveless tank tops that say they don't care if their arms jiggle enough to knock a soul out if they try to hug a grandchild too enthusiastically. Weapons of mass destruction. I feel the niggling of loose flesh on the back of my own arms twinge with the expectation of aging.

They ask what I do and I tell them. "I'm a writer."

"My granddaughter always wanted to do that," one woman says. "But she decided to be an engineer instead."

"I don't believe I've read anything of yours," a second says when I give her my name.

"You're in a select group of millions who have never read my work." The women all laugh.

"Have you written anything famous?" the third asks. "I love true crime. I just think they're the best books. That Ann Rule, well, she's something."

"My latest is a romance set in a prison. Does that qualify as true crime?"

"It might." I give them each a copy of my book from my backpack hoping they'll read it and tell their friends.

"This might be the perfect gift for my neighbor's grandson who's in jail. He loves true crime a little too much." This gets the three of them chattering about their favorite books—of which none are mine—and frees me up to "go internal" after I add a couple of cents to the conversation.

The Mexican salad, special of the day, tastes fairly good, the feta cheese, Chuck's apparent nod to his Greek roots. I eavesdrop, as a good writer should. My ex used to complain, "You're not listening to me, are you?" as my eyes glazed and my ears twitched to hear snippets of potential dialogue I could use in a future book. Sometimes amazingly profound things get said in restaurants or in movie theaters before the trailers begin.

Truth is, I listened to Stuart more than he did to me. He'd already been published when I met him. *Sweet Charity*'s success took us by surprise and after that Stuart became tone deaf to anything I had to say about writing.

"Oh, maybe we'll be in your book someday," one of the women says to me. "What did you say your name was again?"

"Annie Shaw." I say. "I write kindling books that build a fire in your heart."

"That's so sweet. And you write under that name?" I nod. "We'll look for more of your books, we will. And we'll read this one before we put it in a garage sale."

"Oh, well, maybe you could tell people about it. I mean if you like it." I wished I'd only given one to them if they were just going to sell them!

"Oh, we'll tell people that we know you."

"You know what you should do?"

Here it comes.

"You should get Oprah to read your book. That would be good, wouldn't it?" One of the sisters—as I'd come to think of them—says. Her white hair looks like an uncropped poodle's.

"It would," I tell her.

"I'm not so sure," the middle sister says. "Some of her books are well, pretty lustful. Are your books lustful?"

"Not really."

"Well, you wouldn't want people thinking they were filled with that sort of thing then. You'd lose your faithful readers."

"All those millions," the oldest sister interjects and we all laugh.

"I don't think Oprah's books are bad," says one of the women. "They're full of life and love and all that goes with it. You girls are getting prudish in your old age."

"Not me," poodle perm says. "I've always been prudish."

The driver calls the all aboard and I bundle up my backpack and follow the sisters, heading for the line at the ladies' room. There is no line for the men's room. At the airport in Barcelona, Darlien and I commandeered the men's room because they were cleaning the ladies' room just as all the people deplaned. But I don't suggest we take over the men's room. What happened in Barcelona must stay in Barcelona. From now on.

Chapter 7

He who would acquire fame
must not show himself afraid of censure.
The dread of censure is the death of genius.
William G. Simms (1806 – 1878)

"Do you actually know when Oprah's dog visits a groomer?" my mother says into the phone. I'm on the bus, and corn fields whiz by, broken up by clusters of houses as Chicago's suburbs creep out into the farmlands. I'll be in the city before long. "Doesn't Oprah have more than one dog? I'd have thought she'd have the groomer come to her estates in Chicago and California and wherever else she has a home." I let my eyes gaze over the head of Juanita, up into the blue sky.

"Oprah likes to frequent places that are known for their kindnesses to animals, give them a little boost in business, help their 'canine consulting' work."

"Don't you think this scheme is a little … far-fetched, dear? I've never heard of any other writer having to go to such extremes to sell books. Your other books have done well. I wish you'd rethink this."

"Only one book did well, Mom. And it's not me I want her to notice, honestly. It's my book. I'm just helping the publisher out here. It's just part of a marketing plan."

"The only markets I wish you'd be interested in sell wedding rings and baby foods and little toys. Did you know grocery chains sell toys now, so people don't have to go all over the place to get things for their kids? What does that tell you? People are getting married, that's what. They're having babies. Their needs are being met everywhere, even at Tomkins Market here in West Bend. Aren't you worried about your organic clock?"

"Biological clock, Mom. That's what it's called."

"Well, yes, but aren't you worried? You already have pigeon toes, dear."

I look at my feet. They're swollen from the bus sitting but they don't turn in. "No I don't. And what would my feet have to do with my biological clock anyway?"

"You do too have pigeon toes. There's no sense denying it. They're quite pronounced in that photo your young man sent me from Spain."

Now I'm totally confused. "What picture?" Darlien snapped a photo of Jaime and me at dinner one evening in an outside café in Barcelona where they charged more for eating outdoors under a tent awning than inside in air conditioning. Even the menus were different for outside. I remember that. But no full-length shots of us where our toes show.

"Mom. What photo did you get?"

"Of the two of you. At a restaurant with a lovely old Roman-looking wall in the background. And I can see those little pigeon toes running from your eyes. Maybe if your glasses weren't so thick. They magnify them I guess. You should get contacts like Darlien. People are usually old before they have that many pigeon toes."

"Crow's feet, Mom. They're called crow's feet and I don't have that many. I don't." I have all I can do to not pull out my makeup mirror and look, just to be sure there aren't small toes somehow stomping across my face.

"Oh right, crow's feet. He looks nice, your friend."

"Did he ... write to you or just send a photo?"

"Oh, he wrote. I can't read a word of it though. Except 'Mom.' He put that in English. Isn't that sweet?"

"Mom? He called you Mom?" I shiver.

79

"Maybe it's a term of endearment for all older women in Spain," she says. "I'll know more in a couple of days when I get the translation. Such a nice-looking young man. But it was sure a surprise."

I could add my "Amen" to that.

⟨⟨⟨

Kari picks me up at the Chicago bus station. Our fathers are brothers, and Kari inherited the family's long legs, while I ended up with the high forehead that everyone says means intelligence but for me is no more than a larger canvas for acne to splay out on when I get nervous. Even at the age of thirty I find myself watching the acne-reducing infomercials, hoping to end up as one of the pubescent "after" faces if I just buy and use enough of those magic elixirs. Lately though, the legal ads scare me: "If you or someone you love or someone you used to know or someone who is a neighbor to someone you used to know has been injured by standing next to someone who has used this product, you may have a claim...." Imagine, acne bringing in cash.

"You're the only person in our family without a driver's license," Kari says. Her sunglasses dangle from her neck and poke me as her slender arms wrap around me in a welcoming embrace.

"I do have a license," I say. "I just don't drive. And I prefer the bus. I can't afford to rent a plane to fly down here."

"Earning your pilot's license is a sign that you once took the bull by the horns and did something with a little finesse to it. I just wish I'd gone up with you once before that crash."

"Not many did." I try to think who had. "Dad did."

Kari laughs. "Your dad always was known for his high-risk behavior."

"That's social work talk," I tell her as we wait for my luggage to be rolled out from the bus's lower cargo bins.

"That's family talk. My dad always says his brother sashayed up to danger like he was courting porcupines."

"I guess that explains how he ended up with my mom."

"Your mom's a hoot, all right," Kari says. "Have you had anything to eat? I planned to stop at Johnny's. Clint said he'd meet us there. They're serving ribs. We could even stay for the square dancing if you're not too tired."

Kari doesn't look the country western square dancing type but she is. Two or three nights a week she and Clint put the stress of the day into their feet and let the music dance them away, pigeon toes and all. So much exercise probably accounts for her size-four body and a pink complexion that make her look about twenty-five instead of ten years older.

She maneuvers her way through the Chicago traffic and points out some highlights as she drives, no easy feat with eight lanes of whizzing cars. She takes the exit intended, turns left, then a few rights, then left, and with one hand pulls into a parking lot with neon signs that flash even in the afternoon. She doesn't have a GPS app on her mobile.

"So tomorrow we go to the pound, right?" Kari says after she shuts the engine off in the restaurant parking lot and turns to face me. "I believe things happen for a purpose, and there I was talking to the butcher who says something about Oprah —everyone talks about her around here as though they were personal friends—and he tells me about this other person. I called her and she referred me to another woman who knew someone else who knew Oprah's former dog groomer and then it just happens that he lets it slip that she's coming by sometime next week! To support his salon. Unannounced, so there won't be a crowd, but he can advertize it later. All you have to do is get your new dog an appointment there, maybe check out the appointment book to see when there's a huge block of time not filled. And plan to introduce yourself when Oprah steps in, tell her about your romance."

"My romance? Oh, right, you mean *The Long Bad Sentence*."

"Maybe you can slip in the Barcelona book too. Oprah likes books with a European flavor."

"It's a positive book, filled with courtship and relationships and overcoming hurdles to true happiness and everyone lives happily ever after."

"That sounds good and rehearsed."

"I've been working on it. Maybe I can talk with her about the puppy prison idea since I don't have dogs or cats in the book. Might be more interesting than the correctional facility part."

"Maybe Oprah will think it's a fantasy," Kari muses.

"Oh don't say that." I pause. "Sometimes I wonder if this really is the best approach to getting a bestseller. It doesn't feel authentic to push the book this way. My mom has questions about it too. Part of me doesn't think this is very smart at all."

"If you think of intelligence as being represented on a clock face," Kari says, "then 'really, really smart' would be twelve o'clock, right?" She forms her hands into a circle resembling a clock.

"Okaaaay," I agree.

"I read about this once," she continues. "Then a quarter past the hour would be 'smart' and six o'clock, 'average.' Then nine o'clock would be 'dumb,' right? And eleven fifty-nine would be 'really, really dumb.' So that means that 'really, really dumb' is right next to 'really, really smart' and sometimes you can't tell which is which. Who's to say that something that looks dumb really is? This could be the smartest thing you've ever tried to do. Do we ever really know until afterwards whether the choices we make were smart or dumb? It's only in reflection that we figure that out."

I stare at her. "Really, really dumb right next to really, really smart?"

"I mean, especially if you're listening to an inner voice, a calling. Then it can be really hard to explain to someone that you're acting smart and not dumb, because they can't see what's holding you up."

"I'm digital," I say, showing her my watch.

"Digital is good, but a round analog clock is more like the

world. Good things come in circles," she says. "Like wedding rings and dog collars."

◎

After stuffing ourselves with ribs and introducing me to a few of their friends who stopped by our table, my relatives postpone their square dancing until later in the week. We drive back and settle into their condo on the eleventh floor of a fifteen-story building that is forty years old but was recently refurbished. It's close to Kari's office and Clint can catch the 'L' within a block. They've lived in the building so long they have a parking space for their new Volt underneath the building. It stays there most of the time, as Kari usually chooses to walk the eight blocks to work, even in the dead of winter.

I lay out my marketing plan on her glass-topped coffee table. She reviews it, shakes her head as I mumble something that sounds like "really, really, dumb."

"Going to the pound is first," she says, patting my back.

"Unless one of your country friends has a hound they'd lend me for an afternoon or two."

Clint says, "You know, the pound vets potential owners. You'd better be prepared for an interview and to have a dog forever after if they let you adopt one."

"I figured I'd take the dog with me to set up the appointment at the doggy spa or Canine Cotillion or whatever it's called. They'll want to appraise the dog, be sure it's worthy of their work. It'll give me a chance to case the place, maybe peer into the schedule book, I hope. They might even have a photo saying 'Oprah visited here.' I know I would if she stopped by my shop."

"That's your whole point, I take it," Clint says. "For you to put 'Oprah knows about this book' inside your book?"

"That's one way of putting it." It sounds pitiful put that way.

"I hear that Oprah's pretty rabid about animals and how they're treated. If she thinks you're using a dog just to get to her —"

"I didn't know you paid attention to Oprah gossip," Kari teases him.

"It's on sometimes in the break room," he defends. "And now her new network, too. I don't have the remote."

"I should have brought John, but Oprah doesn't have cats, I don't think. It has to be a dog to attract her attention."

"Maybe you could go without a dog the first time, to get a better feel for the spa," Clint offers. "You'll reduce your risk if you do a bit of study first." Clint's investment broker voice is talking about risk.

"I don't have that much time. I've got to plunge right in, get a dog, have it for a day or so until we're comfortable with each other, visit the spa, hope for the best, and then return him to another pound."

"I've never known any day traders to actually have much success, especially over time," Clint says.

"A good dog will do it for me. I'll get one that's really, really smart. But one that's user friendly too, placid and laid back." If I speak out loud with confidence, I hope it will convince my brain.

"A dog that's really, really smart? How will you know?"

"There's this intelligence test," I say. "You put a towel over the dog's head and count the seconds until they toss it off. A really, really smart dog will do it in under three seconds. A not-so-smart one might take a minute or more."

Kari tosses a napkin onto my head. "I'm counting," she says with a laugh.

"It doesn't count unless my eyes are covered," I say.

"I'd say you're in a time trap, hon, stuck at eleven fifty-nine."

⑥

I've never been to a pound before. This one smells of sweet lavender, a scent I've read warms the cockles of a woman's heart. I didn't think they'd need that here. Seeing all these orphaned animals behind their cage displays, barking, their tongues lolling, big brown eyes pleading. Their wagging tails would melt anyone's resistance. Some lunge at the gate of their metal crates, barking their anxiety; others whine, big eyes nearly weeping as I walk by listening to the attendant, who tells me what she can about each of their personalities.

"We keep them for a certain number of days, you know, hoping they'll be claimed and if not, adopted out. Some have been brought here by their owners, of course, when they're unable to care for them. We've had a lot of that lately. A few have become … unruly." The attendant can't be more than twenty and she wears a black Metallica T-shirt that exposes a sliver of pink skin between it and her hip-hugger jeans where her cell phone is hooked at the belt. I pull at my knit top and feel old.

"There aren't any who are … dangerous, are there?" I ask her.

She shakes her head. "If there's any chance a dog might be out of control, you know, bite someone, it's sent to the dog therapist. We have an 'always alive' policy here. But if a dog is returned it's because we didn't match them well to their owners. Maybe the original owners got them as puppies and they grew into huge dogs asked to live inside tiny apartments. Do you work out of your home? That's always great for a dog."

"I'm a writer," I say.

"Are you?" She perks up, even more intrigued than with the dogs. "What do you write? I've always wanted to write a book about my experiences here."

"I hope you do," I say. I mean it.

She stares at me. "Oh, I write novels. Uplifting romances, really."

"Have I heard of you?"

"I don't know. My name is Annie Shaw."

"Nope," she says. "I'm into graphic novels. I like the pictures."

Graphic novels. Maybe Miranda's story should be a graphic novel!

She continues with the tour. "You know, it can just bore a dog to death to be home alone all day, and then they almost attack their owners when they step through the door. They'll jump and bark, want attention and their walk. You have to take them on walks, preferably twice a day for forty-five minutes each. Actually, the dogs adjust better than the owners but they still like it best when an owner stays at home with them." She sticks her fingers through the wire cage to a quiet dog lying at the back of the crate. He crawls forward on his belly and licks her fingers.

"The livelier ones find new homes first, of course, but all of them have been treated and inoculated for basic canine diseases."

"Has that one?" I ask.

She nods. "If I didn't have five cats and two dogs already I'd take him home in a minute," she says. "He's just the sweetest thing. His owner brought him in, saying he was too passive, that he lacked the personality of the breed."

"Not true to his brand," I say.

"Huh?" She says.

"A writer's footnote," I say.

"Oh. Well, I think he's just been depressed. He's so docile, wants to please. All he needs is for someone to take a chance on him."

Another being affected by risk, I think, and take my little soul mate home.

⑥

"So how do you like your dog?" Bette says when she calls that evening and I tell her of my progress.

I look at the Jack Russell terrier I've adopted. He lies sleeping on the floor, beside my feet. He really hasn't moved all that much since I brought him to Kari and Clint's apartment. "He reminds me of a Holstein cow," I say. "He's black and white and just lies around chewing his cud, so to speak. I guess it must be a pretty mellow breed."

"A Jack Russell? Mellow?" Her skepticism races across the phone lines. "I think you'd better go online and do a little research. Great personalities, but mellow would not be the word I'd use to describe a Jack Russell. We had one here at We Care, and he redecorated the woman's apartment with his antics."

"He's previously owned, as they say in the used-car business," I tell her. "Supposedly he wasn't true to the Jack Russell nature, which is fine for my purposes. He's small, won't take up much room here, and he'll be easy to find another home for when I come back to Wisconsin. I guess they don't like it much if you take the dog and then try to return it too soon."

"You'll fall in love," Bette says. "So you may as well get used to having him around."

"No. He's just for marketing, just for the goal of getting me that bestseller," I say. "Nothing personal," I tell the dog when he raises one black eyebrow to look at me, still keeping his face on his two front paws. "I'm not getting involved."

"Like you didn't get involved in Spain," Bette says.

"They sent along a bunch of pills for him. The vet says the dog's been pretty stressed and thin but he's healthy now. Just to give him the pills until they're gone. They're anti-depressants, I think. The vet thought having him groomed would be good. Clean his teeth and all, though they do that sort of thing before they adopt them out. It'll impress the groomer anyway. I had no idea they cleaned dog's teeth." I run my tongue over my own, glad I didn't forget my toothbrush at home.

"When's the appointment?"

"Well, first I do a trial run, just to interview the salon, so they know I'm a serious dog owner and wouldn't bring my pet to just any puppy groomer."

"Don't take the dog with you when you do that, all right, that scouting trip?"

"What's that about? Clint doesn't want me to take the dog along either."

"We just want you to succeed. It's pure luck that Kari found the groomer."

"She thinks it's divine intervention," I say. "Like if she hadn't talked to the butcher, we'd never have found this out, even though the library has all the old *People* and *US* magazine copies as well as *O* back issues. Maybe I'd have discovered the groomer eventually. People want to know everything about this woman, it's so amazing. What linens she likes, what foods, even what kinds of candle scent she prefers. Anyway, it makes for a good first salvo, discovering that Oprah did at one time take her dogs out to a salon. It's so kind of her to make a splash for this groomer, it just needs to be unannounced. Security and all that."

"I heard once that if she does pick your book for the club that you can't tell anyone, not a soul. Only the publisher contact and the author get to know, and if it leaks out before she announces it, they'll renege on the deal."

"Yes, it's all really hush-hush. Top secret."

"I wonder if she'll show up at the groomers then, since this leaked out?" Bette says.

I'm worried now too.

"Who else besides me would know? It was just a quirk that Kari got the scoop. When I called, the receptionist was pretty snooty on the phone. But when I said I wanted to come in and 'assess' their quality, she apologized and explained that they had to be very careful about serious clients since so many just want to see if Oprah might show up one day, as the owner had once been her dog groomer. I told them I did want a place that catered to the stars."

"Did you tell them you're an author?"

"I didn't want them thinking I was using them to meet Oprah."

Bette stayed silent.

"Okay, so I am, but I'm also advancing the cause of good stories everywhere, stories about women, strong women, urging them to take risks for love. That's what *Miranda of La Mancha* is all about."

"We're right beside you," Bette says. "Hey, while you're there you should check into cooking classes with Oprah's former chefs. They mention classes on the website. You could get new recipes I can make for my seniors and maybe drop the name of your book with the chef. I'm sure he keeps in touch with Oprah."

"That's a good idea," I tell her. I hear John meow in the background. "How's John? He hasn't bitten you, has he?"

"He's lounging on the couch. Besides, he's too smart to bite the hand that feeds him." Bette laughs. "You might consider that, Annie. And give Irving a call about the revisions he wants."

"I wish I'd never told you I hadn't called him back yet," I say.

"You didn't have to. He's called here and left messages. Avoiding the problem won't make it go away, you know."

Now I'm silent.

"Oh. I also heard back from some of the reviewers who got the cookies I sent."

"You did? That's wonderful!"

"Well, so far they've only asked for the cookie recipe. But I know they'll want to review the book, I just know it."

Everyone needs a cheerleader, even if the score is ninety-nine to nothing.

We say our good-byes and I hang up the phone, staring at my dog. Kari and Clint will be home soon. We haven't talked about tending the dog when I'm out and whether leaving him alone might be a wise idea. I'll have to invest in some dog equipment: a kennel, toys, dog food, a dish, grooming supplies.... I have a credit card yet to max out, and I don't really want to impose on Kari and Clint any longer than necessary. I might have to leave the dog alone in the condo while following up on my marketing ideas. Kari and Clint will be sure to understand. They're behind me all the way. The dog looks so innocent. I'm sure it'll be fine.

Chapter 8

"Your salon professional today will be Leonard, pronounced Len-ard, with accent on second syllable."

"From France?" I ask.

"Élan-Canine Salon originated in Quebec," the receptionist says. He wrinkles his nose at my naiveté. "You do not know theze?" I wonder where the woman receptionist is I'd talked with on the phone. "Len-ard began the salons a long time ago." He looks down at the appointment book on his desk as if it will explain my faux pas. "Fox paws" is the phrase that comes to mind. It's what my mother always calls those social mistakes one makes. I bite my lip to keep from saying it out loud. Why do I always want to start giggling in the middle of anxiety?

"*Mais, oui,*" I say instead. "I remember now seeing one of your salons while I was there last year at the film festival."

"You are a film producer?" he says, cocking his head and twirling his single earring now, his elbow close to the waistline of his skintight spandex shirt. His long, tapered fingernails are painted black and dotted with gold leopard spots. In the mirror behind him, I see pillows covered with an African motif dotting the perimeter of the walls and a woman dressed in a white uniform brushing dog hair into a leather bag. The hair provides the only indication that dogs are more popular here than people. It's an elegant salon fit for, well, Oprah.

"I'm only involved in film production. Writing, et cetera, et cetera," I say, casually brushing his awe away with my hands and swallowing my stretched truth. I did once try my hand at writing a script. I feel like a character in one of my novels. What has Irving done, forcing me to tell tales just to get recognition for my writing?

"My appointment is right there," I say, pointing to my name written with a calligraphy pen inside the leather-bound book. I lean over, then ease my way around the desk as though to better point out my name. He lurches back like I've touched him with the H1N1 virus. "I'm here to review the quality of the salon before I bring in my dog."

"Oh, oui, Mimi said someone called to assess our salon," he says. He squints up at me and leans away as though I'm dripping mayo on his expensive slacks. "Sometimes Mimi is a little rigid with the rules," he says conspiratorially.

"If you have other openings that would work better for you, I could reschedule," I say. I'm an accommodating patron. I don't think they have many of those—openings, that is—but it lets me look again at the schedule book.

"If you have the master with you—it is a male dog, oui?" I nod. "Good. You could be seen this afternoon. We have a cancellation."

How accommodating do I want to be? "It will take me a little time to retrieve him from … his day care," I improvise. "They're having naptime now and —"

"Of course. Just bring him when he awakens. In two hours?"

I agree and make my way back home on the elevated train. I'll have just enough time to retrieve the dog and return. Another stroke of good luck, as I'm sure I saw Oprah's name in tiny, tiny script at the bottom of the schedule, right after the cancellation spot I've been granted.

6

Holstein is lying where I left him, locked in the guest room at the condo. I wake him up, hook the leash I've purchased for him, and make my way to the salon. This is happening faster than I like. I've only known this dog for twenty-four hours, and here I am entering a salon, patting a dog that begins to squirm a bit beneath my arms, roused by the sounds of pooch pampering emanating from beyond the tapestry dividers. Soft music plays. I'm sure I hear a water fountain cascading serenely behind one of the African décor screens.

"Pardon, Madam," Andre says, lifting the schedule book and moving it on the other side of the wicker desk I'd slipped behind when I came in. He hadn't worn his nametag before. It reads "Canine Ambassador." He frowns at my invasion of his space. "Now is your appointment?" I nod agreement, point again. "Élan-Canine Salon welcomes you and your ..." He frowns at my dog, still underneath my arm. "He is a registered breed?"

"Oh, I'm sure," I say.

"His name is?" He tries to read the generic tag on my dog's cheap collar that I haven't yet replaced, so if he sees it, he'll have to call him Model 217.

"Ho," I finish for him. "His name is Ho-Ho-Ho."

"Thez is a strange name," Andre says as he taps the pencil on the appointment book.

"No, no. It's Ho, short for Holstein, see, his coloring? Black and white. We're originally from Wisconsin. The cows. Like the Cows on Parade you had around Chicago. Remember? Your city's very famous Warhol-like cows that people fell in love with. Wisconsin has lots of Holsteins."

"He is like a little cow? Yes. The Holstein sculpture cow was named Kari. It would be a better name for your dog."

"That's my cousin's name. I don't want to confuse them." I try to remember the other cow sculptures I'd seen on the streets and in the parks of Chicago. One of the red-spotted cows was named Brian. It stood in front of Mrs. Park's Tavern. Would the canine ambassador think better of me if I called him Brian or would he think me fickle for changing my dog's name at the first raised eyebrow of the day? "His name is Ho-Bee, a blend of Holstein and Brian, actually," I improvise. "He's well-trained," I say. "See how quiet he is?"

Andre hesitates, then picks Ho-Bee up and cuddles him under his arm. The dog warms to him and squirms a little to be closer to Andre's chin. The dog gently licks him. It's the most animated I've seen Ho-Bee be. Even on the elevated train he'd barely raised his head to watch the streets of Chicago lumber by. "Come this way ... Ho-Bee," Andre says, putting the emphasis on the last syllable. They turn toward the back. I follow quietly before Andre knows I'm with them.

I thought they'd make me wait. But in the back, I'll be bound to hear some scuttlebutt about Oprah and when she might stop by, and all the while they groom Ho-Bee, I'll have time to drop her name and link it with mine. I might be able to dribble a hint or two about my novel that the canine consultant would be induced to pass along. Clearly, it isn't *what* one knows in marketing and publicity, but *who*. Maybe that's true for the puppy spa business too. I might even meet Oprah's dog handler face to face. We could converse about loving people and their pets, while easing into a discussion of my manuscript and Oprah and dogs and Oprah and—

"No, Madam. It is better that your little one is left alone with the master, *non*?" He touches a slender earpiece I hadn't noticed, just like FBI agents on TV, and starts to speak.

"Well, no," I say. "I mean, it's his first grooming —"

"His first?" Len-ard's voice raises a pitch, a tone that addles Ho-Bee's squirming in the consultant's arms. "But he is a mature dog. What have you been doing to theze one that he has had no grooming?"

"His first at Élan-Canine Salon," I recover.

Andre visibly relaxes. "Then it is better that you wait in the parental unit salon." He points toward the end of the room, where a ceiling to floor mirror reflects back the crystal stoppers and the African tapestries. "There is a two-way mirror there so you can see him, but it is better if he does not see your worry over him. It will only serve to distress him. You do not wish theze, for your little, what did you say his name was?"

"Ho-Bee. Could I at least meet his official groomer? I don't want to leave him with just anyone. You understand."

Andre hesitates. "You are to have Len-ard himself. And of course, I understand your desire. Follow me."

I wish I had more time to plan. I wish my friends were with me. One of them could be in the lobby when Oprah came while I cover the grooming site.

Len-ard stands about six feet six inches tall, wears a black shirt with classic black pants (minus a single dog hair as far as I can see), and soft leather shoes, no socks. His hair spikes up, moussed to Smurf-like peaks on top, shaved tight to his head behind his ears. I think the short hair might be desirable for bathing dogs. Dark eyes and a thin mustache highlight a serious face. "Bonjour, Monsieur," he says to Ho-Bee. Andre whispers something to Len-ard.

"He says 'good day' to you too," I say.

Len-ard ignores me while he arranges instruments on a tray the way a nurse would prep for surgery. "You are in the moo-vies?" He has the same accent as Andre.

"Oh, well, I write," I say.

"For the moo-vies?"

"I wrote a screenplay once. And I did go to the Montreal screenings one year." I clear my throat. "A shampoo is really all he needs."

"Then a teeth brushing, oui?"

"Oui," I say.

Len-ard says something in French then, and I merely nod as he lifts Ho-Bee from Andre's arms.

"Ho-Bee only understands English," I say.

"Let us go to the operating room," Len-ard says.

Operating?

His Gucci slacks flow long over his shoes and he touches

his Peruzzi Italian-leather grooming kit hooked to his belt as though it might be a holster. I see the edges of what must be tiny, folded hundred dollar bills.

Tips! I haven't even thought until this moment about the tip! How much does one tip a canine consultant? If Len-ard is the owner, will he be insulted if I tip him? Would he be insulted if I don't? I don't want another fox paw on my record.

Len-ard takes my dog under his arm and I watch his little tail (Ho-Bee's) wiggle as I follow behind. Andre the Ambassador carries the tray of items Len-ard has arranged and opens a glass door, setting the tray on a granite-covered table in the center of the room that gives birth to five doors with frosted glass windows that lead off from the main room. It's an elegant foyer. Each of the suite doors is engraved with a different breed of dog. Jack Russell's aren't one of them.

Andre slips out past me, somehow dismissed by his superior, without taking me with him. Divine intervention yet again!

Len-ard sets Ho-Bee on the gray granite table slab. At the end, on a silver tray, rest glass bottles with lotions and shampoos (I assume) with crystal stoppers. A Josh Groban CD filters soothing music into a room that smells better than a florist's shop. I see movement behind the frosted glass doors, but nothing that resembles the visage of Oprah or even any human.

Len-ard turns to me as I step closer. He stops my further entry. "No no, Madame. It is better that your little one is left alone with the master, non? Andre will take you out. Oh, he has left. I call him back." He touches a slender microphone. Calls Andre back then reaches to lift Ho-Bee up, with both hands around the dog's belly.

At that moment, Ho-Bee bursts to life.

@

Maybe Len-ard's hands are cold. Maybe he squeezes too hard. Whatever it is, the Jack Russell terror is now the latest contestant on *Survivor*, venturing into the wilds. Quick as a hair snip slipped from a squirmy dog, Ho-Bee squeezes out of Len-ard's hands and skids across the smooth table surface, knocking down bottles that smash like water bombs to the floor. Neither Len-ard nor I can stop him. From there the dog twists like a rawhide chew, his tongue hanging happily out as he explores. Ho-Bee is on his own now, the long tail that looks well out of proportion for him slapping at the granite counter, shattering bottles not meant to be disturbed that tipple off the wicker storage bins lining the wall, spilling fragrances that pool on the elegant tray Andre has so carefully carried in.

Now Ho-Bee shows us his leaping ability. His happy yaps propel him over the backs of chairs and beneath tapestries draped to the floor between each of the five frosted doors.

My mouth hangs open. The dog has done nothing but sleep the entire morning I've had him, and now he's a weapon of mass destruction, destroying the room like a cluster bomb, his barks like Uzi's echoing through the once-pristine room.

The frosted window doors open, first one then another, until all the little studio salon suites stand wide open, with a canine consultant peering out of each. Beneath their legs come forth dogs in various states of shampoos and froth and furminating fluff who now follow Ho-Bee, their African-motif aprons dragging behind them or torn in shreds by their front claws as they scamper and yap their delight. Their handlers shout in various languages in an effort to get them back.

The furminating consultant stands with a halo of white, his goggles drifted with snow left behind by the giant Samoyed who is now Ho-Bee's best friend.

"Here, Ho-Bee," I call, not at all sure the dog even knows the name I've given him and just recently changed. Ho-Bee turns, and I have a moment of hope when he heads back toward me, but when I squat to pick him up he leaps through my arms, propels himself up over my shoulder, and squeezes out like toothpaste from my hands, doing damage to the other end of the room and my sequined T-shirt bought for the occasion.

More voices join the shouts as the consultants attempt to intercept their charges. Owners have left the Parental Unit Viewing Room, entering through a door that forms a seamless part of the mirror. They rush in to control their children and make complaints to Len-ard in wails and finger-wagging and high-end whines as they twirl around, trying to intercept their pups.

The woman wearing the white uniform eases into the room and calmly begins sweeping up broken glass. Her form acts as a natural divider for the cadre of dogs that split along either side of her, as though she's a wagon in an old movie and the dogs are stampeding buffalo. Yaps and yelps and plunges against calves and over shoes mark the dog's delight, with leather leashes and shampoo tailing them like jet streamers. The Samoyed stops, shakes herself, and the room looks like a burst feather pillow. We all cough.

"Who belongs to that scoundrel dog?" one of the parents shouts, pointing at my Ho-Bee. The man grabs onto an apron/bib, slowing his malamute. Another uses the trick to latch her charge, the poodle's diamond-studded collar soon in her hand, but not on her dog. Half of the poodle's neck hair has been shaved in an irregular way. "That mongrel is responsible for this!"

Interrupting one of Ho-Bee's followers seems to slow the rest, until all are gathered up except for Ho-Bee, tongue hanging happily to one side. He pulls on a loose apron bib, snaps it into his mouth, and shakes it as though it's a deadly snake. His body twists twice as fast as the soothing piped-in music, and when he shoots between my legs this time, apron trailing from his mouth, I catch him and whisk him into my forearms and hold him there, all wiggle to his weight.

"Your mother must spend more time with you, making you a better behaved one, non?" Len-ard says, wiping his forehead. He glares at me. Sweat beads on his well-tanned brow and his eye twitches. His mustache is drooping on one side. He turns to the other consultants, who check their secured charges for cut pads and begin replacing their aprons and calming the parents.

"I'm so very sorry," I say to all of them, and I am. "Something must have set him off. He's usually so calm and well-behaved."

"We can only hope no one is injured," Len-ard says. "You." He points a long finger at me. "My attorney will call you within the hour." I lower my eyes and nod. "And what did you says your name was, please?"

I consider fibbing but don't. "Annie Shaw," I mumble and give him my card.

"Annie Shaw," he says, hooking a leash onto Ho-Be, holding it with a dead-man's grip. "Annie Shaw, a writer as your card reads. Annie Shaw the writer, you will leave now out theze side door so as not to disturb any more of theze quiet place. And to protect you from the parents of theze traumatized children who might destroy you. I will have no way to stop them, even if I wished to."

"But —"

"You will leave. Now, Annie Shaw. You and your ... Ho. Bee."

There's nothing left to do but leave. Ho-Bee wiggles but I hold him firm as we head toward the back exit Len-ard's directed us to. Then, just behind the African tapestry, I hear a familiar voice and a woman gasps at the disarray before her as she says, "Len-ard, is everything all right?"

The words cut through my mixture of grit and guilt. I'd know that voice anywhere! It's Oprah!

"Miss Winfrey —"

"Annie Shaw," Len-ard says, grabbing my elbow and turning me out to the oblivion I deserve without even a sighting of Oprah. "Take your Ho-Bee and go." He tugs on the faux leather leash and guides us with no uncertainty out the opposite door.

"Who is that?" I hear Oprah say as Len-ard swings the door at my back.

"No one you need to know," Len-ard says. "But a name I will not soon forget."

Chapter 9

To: Annie Shaw
From: Lura Striker, Editorial Production
lura.striker@ ap.net

Miranda of La Mancha is your number one title choice but as is our practice, we'd like at least ten to choose from. We'll be adding to the list ourselves, but please submit your alternate title choices as soon as possible.

Lura Striker, Editorial Assistant

The email from my publisher greets me back at my cousin's. Now I have two problems: Irving addressing my early plot point scene concerns and a marketing and editorial alert about what to name my baby. Then there's the issue of getting an attorney for Len-ard's potential suit. They've already called and told me what the repairs will be. It's more than my advance.

"So how did it go?" Kari asks when she arrives home.

"I have a dog and ... I've had my encounter at Élan-Canine Salon."

"And?"

"Let's just says it was memorable. At least Len-ard took my card and says he'll definitely remember my name." I swallow. I didn't even leave a copy of my book there for the parental units to read while they waited, a missed marketing opportunity.

"That's good, isn't it? Perhaps he'll tell Oprah."

"Maybe." I hesitate. "I did hear Oprah's voice."

She squeals. "You're kidding."

"No, she was there. But I didn't get to talk to her about my book or puppies for prisoners or the manuscript or anything like that."

"Why not? Wasn't that what it was all about? What a stroke of luck to actually run into Oprah! You are a fortunate person, Annie. Truly lucky."

"It wasn't exactly the best time," I say. "Maybe an 11:59 moment, if you really want the truth." Kari frowns. "Ah, and I'll need the name of a good attorney here in Chicago."

"Should I sit down?"

"Maybe. Yes. It seems my little Ho-Bee perked up after I got him to the salon and they asked me to come in today because of a cancellation and I saw Oprah's name on the book at the bottom in little tiny letters. She came in but the dog blasted the salon and a lot of other dog parents are a bit upset with the haircuts a few of their dogs got as they leapt from their tables and scampered around the room after Ho-Bee." She points to the dog now lying on my lap, still as a rolled-up towel. I nod. "If it wasn't so awful it would be funny. They all mutinied, if that's a word. Ho or Ho-Bee, which I added at the last minute, was the leader of the pack."

"You'd better pick one name for him or we'll have a multiple personality case on our hands."

"I think we already do."

"He is cute. That long tail."

"The breed is supposed to have bobbed tails. I think his long one makes him off balance. Maybe that's fitting, since his new owner appears to be off balance herself."

"No self-deprecation," Kari warns. "The spots are fun. He's a Jack Russell. They're really busy dogs and need lots of activity or they'll take over your house. He was so calm last night . . . and now." She reaches to stroke him gently.

"I guess I don't really need him anymore now, I mean with the salon goal implemented." The dog rolls over on my lap and

I scratch his belly. "But he's growing on me. He comes when I clap my hands and leaps into them, at least when he isn't distracted by a half-dozen poodles and what not. John would never do that."

Kari pets him too, and one back leg jerks as though we're tickling him.

We'll talk about the attorney when Clint gets home, and you can call the rest of the crew and fill them in too." She fills the watering bucket and goes out onto the balcony to nourish her tomatoes, zucchini, and lettuce still producing. She waters the geraniums spilling red out of an old boot she's made into a planter.

I get up and go to the computer. Ho-Bee settles in again on my lap. Why couldn't he have been so calm at the salon?

"Got mail?" Kari says as she comes back inside and looks over my shoulder. Ho-Bee still sleeps on my lap.

I read Kari the email from editorial and marketing about the title listings. "They don't like *Miranda of La Mancha*?" Kari says. "I think it's kind of cute. A little corny, maybe." She chews on a piece of beef jerky, a healthy habit Misty recommended.

"Marketing always has the last say," I tell her. "So I have to propose at least ten titles and hope the one I want will be their final choice. It's a bit of a gamble, not wanting to give them too many good choices and yet not giving them so many campy ones that they know what I'm up to. It's a constant battle," I say, back of my hand to forehead, à la Scarlett O'Hara.

"I thought you were a team, you and editorial and all that?"

"I'm the player," I say. "They're the owners, managers, and coaches."

"They've done pretty well for you with your other novels."

"Considering I set a romance in a prison, you mean? What was I thinking."

Kari laughs.

"I do wonder why *Sweet Charity* did so well and *Don't Kick Me* bombed. I hope I didn't do the bombing stuff in *The Long*

Bad Sentence. I hate not knowing what I did right or wrong. Brainstorm with me. Give me some titles."

"Clint would love this," Kari says. "He's great at Scrabble. Be sure to ask him, too, when he gets home."

We brainstorm several titles but none of them jumps out at me. I tell Kari that titles can't be copyrighted, so I could call it *Gone with the Wind*. Ho-Bee characterizes that title as he shoots out the door when Clint opens it; a dog in a wind tunnel. Fortunately Clint catches him before he scampers out the door and into the elevator. I can just imagine where he'd get off!

Back in the apartment, Clint and Kari chew on beef jerky and Clint adds a few title ideas. Ho-Bee nods his head to their jerky movements. He bounds toward Kari, who shows him her empty hands. The dog does his happy dance consisting of jumping straight up and down in front of her. Kari laughs. He can jump to the height of the fireplace mantle. He yips, and if I didn't see it with my own eyes, I'd guess he used a trampoline to spring himself that high.

"What do you think he wants?" Kari asks. "He can see my hands are empty."

"Attention," I say. "Some folks will do anything to be noticed."

Ho-Bee bounces toward the fireplace. He doesn't appear to be able to reach the items on the mantle even though they've become the objects of his attention. Kari's collection of glass and ceramic frogs with huge eyes perch above him, and a couple of them look real enough that Ho-Bee might think he could chase them. I consider pushing the glass collection back, just in case, but that might serve to stimulate the dog's interest and maybe also increase Kari's anxiety needlessly. His movements mesmerize. I blink. "I need to get him toys, I think."

"Maybe you could use those robbers in the title somehow. I liked their names," Kari says.

"The brothers Butane, Propane, and Acetylene."

"Those names are a gas," Clint notes.

Kari and I groan.

"Those were the pickpockets. Miranda called them that since she didn't know who they really were. I don't want them in the title at all."

"But it's so cute."

"How about *Fog and the Portuguese Fado?*" I offer.

"There's fog in the story? I don't remember that."

"Miranda's in a fog about what to do, whether to stay or go, whether to take a risk or not."

"But fado. It sounds too much like "Fido," which will make people think it's a story about a dog. Have you put a dog in there after all?"

"No. A cat. A ceramic cat. Fados are Portuguese love songs. I'll use it." I type it on my laptop. "I have to have ten to give marketing. Maybe they won't notice that fado says 'Portugal' to a European rather than 'Spain.'"

Clint says, "*Doing What's Right.* I heard an interview on the radio with the guy who holds the Guinness Record for most consecutive free throws. More than seventeen hundred. He just gets in this certain position, does what he knows works for him, and never even thinks about the hoop or the ball going through it, that big goal at the end. He does what he knows is right for him and the result is exactly what he wants."

"I should follow that as a writer," I say. "I get panicked thinking about the end I can't see when I'm in the middle. I just need to do what's right, what has worked for me."

Ho-Bee leaps ever higher and closer to the frog collection. I want to bottle his energy and his hopefulness. "How long do you think he can keep that up?"

"The jumping? Until his medication runs out, I suppose." I adjust my glasses.

"I had a supervisor like that once," Kari says. "You could tell when her medication thinned." The dog's repetition hypnotizes. Yet he doesn't seem any closer to damaging the frog collection. The act of jumping appears to be satisfying enough. He's so in-the-moment.

"What about *Está Aquí*?" Kari says, back on titles again.

"You are here?" It's one of the few phrases in Spanish I learned—from the kiosks with maps of the city and the trains. "What does that have to do with this story?"

"Whenever I'm lost in the mall, I always look for where I am on those big maps. It's reassuring to know where you are," Kari says. "In fact, you can't move forward until you discover where you are; whether it's in a bad relationship or parked farther from the mall store than you realized. Finding your way home requires admitting you're lost. Moving forward does too."

"*Está Aquí. You are here.* I like it," I say. "Would you add the English or just leave the Spanish?"

"Do both. It gives you two titles that way."

I type both titles into the file.

"What about *Don't Do It*?" Kari says. "It has a little athletic flair and it's exactly what Miranda does. She listens to the 'don't do it' message in her head and then she does it, right?"

"The story says she does, yes, at one point at least."

"The girls said they thought the ending really fit, that Miranda considers staying in Spain and marrying Jaime but then she does the right thing considering their age differences, language barriers and all that. She comes home, right?"

"I wrote two different endings," I whisper.

Kari stares, aghast. I've always wanted to use the word "aghast" in a novel. I imagine a lithe heroine lying on her side, looking up at her lover, aghast. But since I don't write steamy romances, I don't think I'll ever be able to use the word. Now Kari's face resembles a character in just that state of amazement.

"My editor tells me which ending is best."

"You actually let someone else decide that? Oh, Annie, I had no idea."

"Movie producers have been known to do that. *Thelma and Louise* had two different endings. The studios have focus groups rate them. Besides, it's not just 'someone else,'" I say, fidgeting. "It's my editor. Or at least my old editor always chose the ending."

"But doesn't the story write its own ending? Otherwise, isn't it just contrived?"

Her insight is a paper cut to my soul. She isn't even a writer and she can come up with that? It has taken me years to even consider that the story might write itself.

"I have to have an idea of how it will end, of course, but sometimes I just can't decide and then —"

"You let someone else ..."

I shrug my shoulders. "After the ending is decided, then I rewrite the story if I have to so that it fits the reader's expectation, so they'll be happy and satisfied at the end."

"Doesn't that make it too predictable?"

"Just consistent," I say.

Ho-Bee stops jumping and flops on the carpet for a power nap. He lies on his side, still as bone. I lean over my laptop to make sure he still breathes.

"I do write the endings. I just let the editor decide which one she, or now he, wants. It's a team thing."

Clint shakes his head, turns off his mobile unit where he's been getting emails, chewing jerky in between. "The outcome ought to be decided by the author, I'd say. Anything less is bogus."

"This review from an investment broker," I defend.

"At least my recommendations are as honest as I can make them, based on my best effort, and the outcome has as much of me in it as I can give. Much is left to chance, that's true, but I don't think I'm unrealistic in what I recommend. I stand behind my assessments," he says. "You should too. Why, I bet your editor would admire you for it."

His comments make me wonder if I should listen more to the story so I'll hear the ending, the only ending that makes it truthful, before I carve it up a certain way or let it get into the hands of 'someone else,' who might not care nearly as much as I do about what happens to it after it's published.

"Wasn't there some memorable moment, some occasion

when Miranda and Jaime felt very close?" Kari asks, unwilling to let the title discussion drop. "I like titles that allude to an important moment in the story. My favorite title of all time is *Terms of Endearment*, because it has three different meanings."

"He bought me a ceramic cat," I say.

"Who did?"

"I mean Jaime bought Miranda a cat." I hope she can't see how my warm cheeks might be turning red. "It was made of tiny colorful tile pieces. It was on the afternoon when Miranda knew she loved him despite how little time they'd had together. The shopkeeper urges him to buy it for Miranda, as she lingers by it for so long. '*Recuerdo Barcelona*,' he kept saying. It means 'Memories of Barcelona.'"

"Now that, I like," Kari says. "*Recuerdo Barcelona*. It's not a Spanish or even Portuguese word I'm familiar with but hey, you're always making up words, Annie. Might make people pick up the book just to find out what the title means." She's gotten more jerky strips and she gives one to Clint, who kisses her lightly on the nose. She points hers to me as a final answer.

"Maybe I could have Miranda ask the clerk to write the phrase down for her as I have Jaime buying the cat, so the reader will know what it's supposed to mean. Do you like that title better than my pick, *Miranda of La Mancha*?"

Kari's forehead wrinkles with uncertainty.

"I guess knowing the ending would make finding the right title easier," I say. They nod agreement.

I have to learn to say, *está aquí*, admit I have major changes to make, and proceed to find my way home. My head hurts.

"Maybe I should take the dog for a walk," I say. "He'll be cooped up in here for a while tomorrow while I enroll in Oprah's chef's class. It's clear across the loop, so I'm not sure when I'll be back, but probably not in time to exercise him."

Maybe it was the whiff of beef that wakes Ho-Bee. He jumps between us, taking Clint's jerky from his hand. Then like a circus dog soaring through a ring of fire, the dog leaps. He totally misses the glass frog collection at the fireplace but he hits the dining room table dead center, his nails forming craters in the cherry wood and his nose knocking over the crystal vase holding fresh cut flowers. I leap for the vase. Ho-Bee stops himself just before he falls over the far side of the table. He spins around three times, then stops so his tail wags just over the table edge, the jerky sticking out the side of his mouth like a cigar.

"Ho-Bee," I chide, replacing the vase and picking him up. The wound in the table top needs emergency care.

His ears perk up; he tosses the jerky into the air, then catches it in one gobble. Looking proud, he then squats over the end of the table and makes a liquid deposit.

Clint looks at his empty hand while Kari stares at the waterfall descending onto her white carpet. She looks aghast.

"Memories of Chicago," I say, wondering where I can rent a carpet cleaner and hoping Ho-Bee's nails haven't left enough damage that to repair will cost more than what Leonard's attorney says I owe.

Chapter 10

"Do you want me to read them out loud to you or forward them? Or wait until we drive down next weekend and bring them along?" Bette says from her cell phone.

"Go ahead and read one to me, if it's a happy one. I hate it when people say 'you could use someone with grammar skills to look over your work' or 'that story sure moved slowly. Not sure I liked the second half at all.' Right now, I don't need to know those reader views."

"Didn't you tell me once that at the first sign of a negative adjective in a letter you toss it out?"

"Those were reviews. I throw out good reviews too, but as one bestselling author said, 'I read good reviews all the way through before I throw them away.' I can handle criticism, I really can. Just not today. So pre-read them, ok?"

I hear the shuffle of paper. Silence.

"Can't you find a good one?" I ask.

"I'm still sorting," she says. "Looking for exotic postage stamps. Which reminds me, did you get the letter from Jaime translated yet?"

"Yes."

"And?"

"He wants to pursue the relationship."

"That's good, isn't it? I wish I had a relationship to pursue. My mom's worried I'll end up married to my work at We Care."

"There are worse things," I say.

"I know. You had such high hopes for you and Stu."

"Haven't you found a good letter yet?

"Ok. Here's one. 'A friend gave me *Sweet Charity's Rose* and I thought it was one of the best books I've ever read. I actually prayed for the characters even though I knew they weren't real and that whatever was going to happen to them had already happened and been published.' Isn't that sweet?" Bette says. She continues: " 'I don't think people understand how life can just throw a bomb at you when you least expect it. But the idea that love is enough to counter any bitter blast we're handed is really gratifying. I think having your writers meet at a writing conference was really cool. I'm a budding writer. I liked it that this one ended in a marriage in a library ... I think you should write a sequel. I want to know what happened after the E. coli outbreak at the wedding reception and who the injured really were. You're a good writer anyway. I'll read all your books, especially since they're stories about people overcoming their fears.' The postmark is from Cleveland."

"That's nice," I say. "Maybe I should write a sequel. Might surprise a lot of people if I did. I've never written a series." I couldn't write that those two writers soon divorced. That would be a terrible sequel.

"But first ... finish revising *Miranda of La Mancha*."

"We're working a list of new titles. Would you let Misty and Darlien know so they can be brainstorming too this weekend?"

"That sounds like fun! Do you want me to read more?"

"No, just bring the letters along. It'll be something to look forward to."

I knew it wasn't wise to let one nice letter make my day, because that meant I could also let a bad letter ruin my day. Writing is about balance, and responding to total strangers' goods and bads is like being on a teeter-totter. I thought my plan to make a bestseller would keep me in balance; but after the episode at the salon, my quest is more like a reality television show than finding a way to truly advance my career.

"Are you making progress in meeting Oprah?" Bette asks.

"I was close enough to hear her voice yesterday," I say.

"Wow, that's great in so short a time. You've only been there a few days!"

"Yup. I heard her voice just before I was asked to leave out the back door and never darken their African-motif pet salon again."

"That doesn't sound good."

"I sort of derailed our plan," I say.

"You're always saying that a challenge doesn't mean you've made a mistake or that it's a dead end. You have to recommit to the goal."

"That's what I'm worried about. The goal to have a best-seller by getting Oprah to know my name … maybe that's the problem."

"Is someone trying to call in?" Bette asks. "I hear clicking."

I look at my cell phone. "It's Randolph, my agent. I guess I better take this one." Rethinking my goals would have to wait.

＠

I carry the phone out through the living room of the condo. The main room wouldn't be a place for a child, not with the heavy wooden tables and the designer fabrics on the dining room chairs, but then Kari and Clint have never talked of having children, at least not when I was around. It seems a shame, as it is for Oprah, I think, when good, loving people with resources decide to forestall families. Still, I wouldn't be relaxing in such luxury if my cousins' children roamed the apartment. I wouldn't have a small dog keeping me company either. Maybe living with children leaves little room for accommodating visiting kin, though we girls have had plenty of sleepovers at Misty's without incident. Well, without disasters. Ho-Bee snores beneath a living room chair, his black-and-white belly pushing in and out like a puffer fish.

On Clint and Kari's small deck I pinch a dead geranium blossom, while leaving the others to act as guardians of red and white against the iron railing. Kari's brought up wooden planters shaped like children's wagons and spruced them up with red-and-white checkered bows. She's planting daisies and other flowers, bringing a country look to Chicago's grimy Cook County. Though the Fourth of July has long passed, a dozen tiny flags flutter in the wind amidst the blooms.

I call Randolph back, as I've missed his call. "How's progress on the bestseller trail?" he says.

"I've actually gotten close enough to hear Oprah's voice when I took my dog to her groomer's," I tell him.

"Thought you were a cat person."

"I am, but one needs to adapt to the occasion. I signed up to take a class with her former chef too. At his restaurant."

"You should just be writing. Let others take care of this promotion. This is why I've called. It will please you to know that I —drum roll please—can get you onto Oprah's show."

"As an author? Really?" I sit down crossways on a lounge chair. "She'll know about my book? You're a genius, Randolph. Yes!"

"Well ... not as an author, no. But as part of one of those loving reunions, where she flies people in to reconnect with family and friends."

"What?" My mind trips through the family rolodex and finds no one whom I haven't seen in years that I'd want to be reunited with on national television.

"You *might* find a way to mention the book and your work-in-progress," Randolph continues. "That'll be your part of the task. I think it's inspired." His words, just a moment before having such lift, now feel like bird droppings on my suntanned knees. They splatter me back to attention.

"Who would I be reunited with?" I say.

"Your long lost lover from Spain," Randolph says. "I've read the manuscript. It fits right in. Brilliant, righto?"

Have I lost my mind and told him about Jaime, my Jaime? I'm sure I haven't. Only my sister and Bette know about the real Jaime. Well, and my mother.

"It's a novel, Randolph. There isn't any Miranda pining for her Jaime," I insist.

"I know that. But the stories are all made up anyway, so all you have to do is take on the life of your character for a week or so. Live your fiction, so to speak. You have firsthand information about the International Federation of the World Police and Firemen Games—that sounds so prestigious, doesn't it? People are clueless about those games, and they'd find that interesting in itself. You could say you were reunited with an old childhood pen pal when you attended the Games last summer, a pen pal who is now a policeman in Spain putting all his money aside to help his mother, so he can't afford to come to America and marry you. Oprah will love it."

"But it wouldn't be true," I say.

"Neither is it true that you own a dog needing grooming or that you really want to be a chef of some kind. You've always said you can't cook a whit. But that isn't the reason you're taking the class. So my little idea is as honest as your efforts to get Oprah to know your name."

I wince.

"I didn't think agents booked events like this. AP's publicist might see this as meddling and —"

"It's publicist work, righto," Randolph says, "but you're a mid-list author if not low-list author." I must have choked. "I'm just telling you where we stand." *Está Aquí.* "We need something big, your gal pals are right about that. Why not try it? It could prove a huge payoff if you managed to slip in even one word about the manuscript and suggested it has 'autobiographical' implications. *Fun in the Sun in Spain.* You can use that for a title suggestion." Randolph knows the routine.

"*Fun in the Sun* sounds like a beach travel book," I say.

"Go with me a little, Annie."

I sigh. "All right. What kind of person would you get to play Jaime?"

"Antonio Banderas." I gasp. "I knew I could interest you."

"Antonio Banderas? You can get Antonio Banderas to play Jaime?"

"In a perfect world," he says. "No, Oprah would know for certain it's fiction then. They know each other. But there's a guy who works at a Mexican restaurant here in Manhattan. His Spanish is pretty good and girls flock around him. He could be a fireman or policeman. He works out. He'd do it for a little cash." Randolph coughs.

"Spaniards from Cataluña speak a Castilian Spanish," I say. "It has a very different sound. *Gra-see-us* in Mexican is *gra-thee-us* in Castilian. Surely Oprah's researchers would note that, not to mention it wouldn't be too hard to find out he's been shredding lettuce at a taco place in New York rather than fighting fires in Europe. I think her staffers are smarter than that."

"He'd have to fly in from Spain, of course," Randolph says. "So we'd have to get him to Spain first. You'll need to front the money for that."

"I'd pay for that?"

"Righto." He coughs. "You have to invest money to make money."

"I invest in cookies sent to reviewers or a web blog or giving my 10 free copies of books to strategic places."

"Like the bathrooms of TMJ4?" He can be so brutal. "Just as you have to invest time and energy long before your book comes out. You know the routine, Annie."

"You've got to quit smoking those cigars," I say as he coughs again.

"Don't change the subject. I'm just trying to do more for your career; work smarter, not harder. You focus on writing and I'll focus on making a big smash."

"I think that's splash," I say. "How did this all come about?"

"I ran into a producer at a party and we exchanged cards and I got all enthused about your book but I didn't tell her that. I told her about my poor lovesick friend and her lover in Spain, and *she* actually proposed the idea! Maybe I should write a romance novel."

"Maybe we should find real people trying to unite," I say. "Just find them and then prompt them about my book, so I wouldn't have to actually, you know, be there with my ... fiction. Or your fiction."

"Oprah might be so excited she might even cover the next world games or Skype the event. They'll be in Montreal next, righto?"

"In Ireland next."

"Marketing would be ecstatic. *Fun in the Sun in Spain* might have to be changed to something else, to take advantage of the Irish connection. Let's see, *Aflame in Ireland*. That's a good one."

"*Miranda of La Mancha*," I say. "That's the title."

"Whatever. It would sell, whatever you called it, even if Oprah didn't pick it as her book club book. People would want to read the rest of the story, how Miranda and Jaime walk into the future. Maybe even a reality show could come of it."

"Your scheme lacks the hopefulness of my gal pal ideas," I say. "And it's a whole lot more expensive." I'd have to use my credit card to buy a ticket to and from Spain, and I wouldn't even be the person on the plane!

"I'm not trying to get her to choose my book anymore, Randolph. I'm just trying to get a mention of *The Long Bad Sentence*, that's all I want." I might have stopped then, told myself the truth. *Está aquí.*

But Randolph says, "Oprah is a rain barrel for stories. We can fill that barrel with a good yarn full of love and tears and reconciliation. Everyone loves reunions, and with a little hype from the games and all those uniforms on muscled men, well, the possibilities are endless—they really are, Annie. It's just good publicity, and it has a better chance of promoting *The Long Bad Sentence* than your scheme to get her to know your name."

The uniforms did have a certain draw. "There are women competitors too."

"So you're willing to advance the airfare if I can work this out?"

"I'm a little short on cash, Randolph," I say.

"I was meaning to ask you. I haven't heard from Editorial saying they've accepted your revisions yet." Randolph receives all my checks, takes out his commission, then sends the remainder on to me.

"Ah, it's not officially accepted yet because I haven't sent them yet."

Silence. "You want my help with that?"

"No, no. It's editorial in nature, nothing contractual."

"Get them finished so we can claim the next portion of the advance, Annie. We don't want to be too far off schedule."

Randolph makes money when I do. Of course that also means Randolph, like my publishers, has an interest in my being successful. They want me to do well. They're dependent on my doing well. Randolph might have a dozen clients funding his kids' college funds, but that means a dozen writers' hands to hold, hearts to encourage, to support. I should be grateful he's thought of a way to promote my latest release.

I only have four little books to support my life, the last one not even yet accepted or published so *we* are living off of the advance for *Miranda*. My friends think I get the full seven dollars list price of the book, multiplied by the number sold. I wish.

Randolph keeps track of that sort of thing. I trust him completely. Then why was I struggling with his request that I put the airfare costs for his scheme on my credit card? We have like minds, Randolph and me, and I have my own notorious schemes to front.

"I'm working on the scene changes, I am."

"Righto."

"You'd have me waste money to bring a taco master from Spain over here?"

"Not waste, invest. Maybe you'll be lucky and your numbers for this half of the year will be up and the royalty statement will cover what we need and then some."

"I need that to live on, so I can write. I don't have a contract for more books unless *Sentence* and *Miranda* do well. Maybe not even *Miranda* if I don't get the revisions finished." Irving might well recommend against future books, and then I'd have to repay the signing advance for it and try to find another publisher for that story and start this revision and promotion process all over again.

"A little testy, are we? Have you started that next book yet, Annie?" Randolph says. "That always increases your confidence."

"I can't begin the next book until *Miranda* is put to bed. Laid to rest. Until *Miranda* is accepted," I say. "My editor has issues. He wants —"

"Victims," he says. "Oprah loves victim stories where the woman discovers she isn't really a victim at the end, that she can make things happen herself. You do know that you always have a couple of things you can do when you feel like a victim?" I wait for him to tell me. "You can get clear about what matters in your life and then have the courage to act on that." He's taken with his own advice. "Maybe I can work that angle in when I finalize with the producer. A poor, victimized woman writer abandons her Spanish lover so she can complete a novel that the publishing moguls won't accept. It just might fly."

He signs off, leaving me to wonder what I have to lose by his fictional ploy. My integrity, yes. This whole affair is like a pair of hairy legs being shaved with a dull razor: I get the feeling it's going nowhere in a very painful way.

⑥

A few of Randolph's words ring in my ears as I settle down to address Irving's latest "concerns." I don't think of myself as a victim. I choose my own stories, I make my own expenses, pay my own bills, and I owe no one anything that I can think of. Well, I'll be sanding down or hauling up a new cherry table for Kari and Clint and paying for the carpet to be cleaned; and Élan-Canine Salon's attorneys might be in my future for Post Traumatic Stress Disorder damages as a result of Ho-Bee's escapades. But beyond that, I feel pretty much in control of my life. I even remembered to cancel the check I wrote to Stuart since I gave him cash for the tires. A victim is someone taken advantage of, right? Oprah's chosen books, even if they involve characters as victims, still celebrate men and women who eventually triumph. Miranda triumphs. Even Jaime does, in a way.

Ho-Bee's up and carries morsels of food from our bedroom out to the deck where he eats each one, then makes a return trip. How is it he can be so well-behaved now but not when I had that moment so close to Oprah? I watch his steady crunching. At any moment he might jump up and begin spinning. He has no moderate speed; just intense or stop. When he cuddles close, I don't miss my little students left back in Milwaukee nearly as much.

I am not a victim. While the trip to Spain hadn't been my idea, once I decided to go, I found a certain pleasure in planning. One of Darlien's colleagues had gotten ill and couldn't compete, months before the event. When the time came, I took over her plane ticket and hotel accommodations. I'd roomed with Darlien, so except for a fear of the Atlantic crossing, I went willingly, proud of my impulse to do something out of the ordinary. I'd been writing a book about the games and a girl falling in love with a fire-fighter before we ever left. Darlien had told me about previous games in Sweden and New Zealand she'd gone to so I had a structure. Miranda wasn't even in it though. But once there, everything changed. It was my story now.

Well, ok, it wouldn't have been the vacation I'd have chosen for myself, spending all that time with athletes. I stumble over my exercise mat and as a teenager spent as much time in emergency rooms getting stitched up as I did dating.

Though older than me, Darlien is much more athletic and

outgoing. She is someone who loves an adoring audience, which I happily oblige her with. I made the trip for quality time with her. I hoped I could discover what it was in our family genetic code that made poor mate selection worse than random. Darlien's three marriages all began with such joy and then ended with acrimony. Still, once the divvying up of the season tickets for the Packer games was settled, all her husbands seemed to get along with her and each other quite well. They sit together at the games.

I had my own failed marriage to assess as well. I must have been in love when we married. I fell for Stuart's languid smile, his encouraging words when my first novel had been accepted. The aura of the conference, up-beat and happy, infused us both with hopefulness. He told me he was "too lazy to work and too nervous to steal" so he'd taken up writing.

"Isn't that the title of a book on writing?" I'd asked him.

"You caught me," he said and reached across the table to push my glasses up on my nose. His touch took my breath away. I'd caught him, and he'd caught me.

Sadly, I didn't learn until later that he was too lazy to work or write and even stealing would have taken too much energy. I supported us and then when *Sweet Charity* did well, I quit my preschool position to finish out the other books in the contract. I hoped that would inspire Stuart, but it only inspired him to carp and complain until I filed for our divorce. My mother said maybe getting married in the library with just a judge to officiate left out God, the most important ingredient in helping a marriage last. I intend to change that if I ever marry again.

Ho-Bee sleeps again and I reach down to pat his smooth body. Once he wakes up I'll head to the pet store with him to get a kennel and toys and then walk to the hardware store and buy sandpaper and varnish so I can fix Kari's table. I need an activity that has a beginning, middle, and an end, that isn't related to my writing life, where I feel like I'm constantly taking a leap of faith.

"What about *Leap of her Life*?" I ask Ho-Bee. He barks once in his sleep. I can add that to the title list, a story not of romance, but of tragedy instead. Maybe I can add a subtitle to that one: *His Dream, Her Nightmare.*

Neither Darlien nor I expected for *me* to meet someone in Spain, for *me* to fall in love. Darlien was the expert in that. Fearing the consequences of love and walking away, that was my story. Here, back in the states, my reasons for not staying behind with Jaime, for not taking the leap of my life, don't seem nearly as compelling. "Let's go Ho-Bee. I need to distract myself." It was what I did best.

Chapter 11

I reread the reworked opening night scene. Irving tells me to write it so it includes conflict, causation, conversation, and change, and won't be a section people skip over.

Queues of people — men, women, and children — disintegrated into clusters of celebrants joining their athletic relatives for the opening night ceremonies. This evening was one of the crazier things Miranda had ever done, being with a man she'd just met in a crowd of thousands. People behaved in an orderly manner, filling Barcelona's Placa Espanya with laughter and chatter. The close press of the crowd made Miranda take deep gulps of breath. Eleven thousand competitors! Who knew how many brought wives and brothers and children and friends to cheer them on in the grandstands. Mobs could get unruly.

Miranda swallowed. She was committed now. Jaime was with her. She stepped onto the crowded event-provided bus. She moved with baby steps toward the back. Her forward progress stopped while she was in the middle, and warm bodies and the smells of garlic and perfumes swirled around her.

Bus after bus pulled up beside the fountain. Athletes, dressed in golds and greens, in reds and mauves, blacks, yellows, all the colors of the rainbow and their countries, stepped on board. Hundreds more had begun walking to the Olympic stadium at Montjuic Park. An African team chanted words she didn't understand as they jogged past the busses and on up the hill, past the Olympic village and disappeared around the bend to the Estadi Olimpic. Miranda settled down and let herself feel filled with the joy on their faces, the haunting baritone beat they continued even as the hill became steeper.

Her bus groaned as it pulled out with people standing on the stairs of the open door, waving as though the walkers were neighbors. Traffic moved so slowly that people walked past them as the busses ached forward with their treasured weight.

"Move to the back, mate," an Australian said, sidling past her. She smiled at him. She smiled at anyone who spoke English, surprised at how much hearing her own language made her feel connected, safer.

Miranda realized that the real safety she felt came from Jaime, who stood behind her now. She could feel the heat of his body close to hers and the press of his arm lying protectively across her shoulder. She was actually in Spain with someone of the opposite gender standing remarkably close to her, by choice.

Just beyond the Presidential Palace she smelled a glorious scent through the open windows. She inhaled the sweetness. "What is that smell?" Miranda asked. Jaime lifted his dark eyebrows, shook his head.

She'd have to find the word for scent or smell or blossom in her English-to-Spanish dictionary and come back here with him, to see if he could name the source then. It was futile, anyway, trying to hear above the din of laughter and chatter of a dozen different languages.

The air warmed and beads of sweat formed at the back of her neck, in the crook of her elbow, and on the backside of her knees beneath her short skirt. Why couldn't she perspire in normal places like under her arms or under her nose? She didn't do anything "normally," not even falling in love.

Was that what she was doing? Falling in love? Miranda was much too sensible for that.

She felt giddy and girlish and relished the crush on the bus that forced Jaime to move closer to her, his arm raised over her, gripping the handhold while the other rested a little more protectively on her shoulder. Just enough pressure to reassure her of his presence, not too much to threaten invasion; none at all to suggest possession.

Her sister, Belle, ahead of her, almost to the back of the bus, talked to an ice hockey player, judging from the patch on his uniform, but Miranda couldn't see where he was from. Ice hockey. In July. In Spain. Now that was a hopeful competitor. Belle towered over the four players from Mexico she spoke with now and she shouted to a couple of Canadians, acting as though she'd known them her whole life. Maybe she had. They were golfers too. But Belle could do that, meet a stranger, and in minutes anyone observing would think they'd known each other for years. Belle was an extrovert's extrovert and Miranda a slowly blooming introvert. Blooming, because Jaime nurtured the soil she stood on, offered himself as a stake beside her to buffet against winds.

She shook her head. She'd been watching too many movies on Lifetime. Love didn't happen like this, not real love, not true love. Long-lasting love took time and tenderness. Just as with a flower, it was the lengthening days that brought the bloom. Those hothouse flowers that were forced just never lasted.

"Ah ... you like fountain?" Jaime said. He nodded with his head toward the water spewing in arcs into a pool in front of the palace as the bus eased past.

"Yes," Miranda said. "Oh, yes. It's beautiful."

"The water will change the colors later," he said. "With the lights." Miranda had heard about the fountains of Barcelona, and the one by the palace was supposed to be especially grand. "Pero ... we will be in stadium. We will miss tonight," he told her.

Did that mean he intended to have her see it another night? She was too shy to ask, but everything he said took on twice the meaning.

At the stadium, Jaime guided her toward the athletes and family entrance, where Belle caught up with them and her American golfing partner. Guards dressed in khaki checked Miranda's backpack and told her with gestures and Jaime's interpretation that she had either to drink her water in the plastic bottle and leave the cap there or just leave the whole bottle instead.

Belle led them up cement stairs. Many stairs. All the way to the top row of seats. "So you can have a great view of everything," she said.

"You will watch for me?" Jaime said.

"Yes," Miranda told him, holding his gaze.

He smiled at her then, as though he wanted to say something more. He made no effort to kiss her cheek or even touch her hand and yet the space between them, the small, aching space, sizzled with a thousand connections. Miranda remembered a physics theorem that said when two elementary particles merely brush against each other, they are each forever changed no matter how far apart in time or space they separate afterwards. She and Jaime were that theorem, now and forever.

Jaime brushed her hand.

Belle said, "You'll be fine here, Miranda. Meet us at the archway where we came in afterwards, all right? We might just walk back; it's such a beautiful evening, and the busses stop running after eleven anyway. That's all right with you?"

Miranda nodded though she looked at Jaime, wondering if the "we" might include him too. She didn't ask. She couldn't be as bold as that.

"I go now," he said. "You watch."

Miranda nodded but wished he'd said, "You wait."

He knew of her hotel because he'd helped her file the report of the theft, but would he remember? She didn't know what time or the venue of his competitions, so she couldn't just show up, especially without an invitation. So this might be it for the two of them, their last contact, forever. She started to say something but he'd already begun skipping down the long cement staircase to the area where thousands of contestants gathered for the Athlete's Parade.

She willed him to turn around and smile at her once more. He didn't.

She should run after him, just thank him again, see if there was something in his eyes to tell her that he welcomed her interest. Her legs felt heavy. What would he think if she pursued him? What would Belle say? Why did it matter so much what other people thought?

Jaime kept skipping down the steep stadium steps. Miranda merely watched him slip away. It was better this way.

⑥

It was a better scene. Asking me to work it over, give it more emotion, made it come alive. Irving might just have something here. I saved it and attached it to an email to Irving letting him know that more revisions would be coming just as he'd asked.

"What are you working on now?" Kari asks, leaning over my shoulder when she arrives home from work.

I jump a foot. "Wow, you didn't make a sound," I say. My eyes scan for Ho-Bee but he sleeps peacefully in his new kennel. "Scenes from the book," I say, laying my arm across the page.

"Still? I'd have thought you'd be working on a new book by now."

"Irving wants a new scene for the opening night ceremony." I create on the computer, but revisions must be done on hard copy. White paper. The printed word. So I can see whether or not to break up large blocks of narrative or add in the sense of taste or smell or touch to some action before the reader disappears into that proverbial pull of mowing their lawns or polishing their nails.

I resist when Kari tries to lift my hand off the page. "You don't want me to read it?" Kari says. "You want thousands to buy and read this book, and Oprah too, but not me? I'm … aghast." She steps in front of me, the back of her hand to her forehead in mock distress.

She reaches down for the pitcher of iced tea, pours a glass, then sits on the opposing lounger. Cars honk and engine noises rise from the streets below, but the geranium cocoon surrounding us buffers the sounds.

"So what happens in that scene? It's where they're at the ceremony, right?" Kari has read the original manuscript since I've been in Chicago so now all my pals are up to speed … except for the revisions.

"How romance sets in. Timing, interest, and opportunity have to match up for romance to happen and for marriage and all that. You know. True love happens when you least expect it." We hear a siren squeal through the streets. "Timing and opportunity seem to be what I miss. I love your story of meeting Clint at a nail salon."

"Yeah, I thought he must be pretty courageous to have a pedicure, even if it was a gift from his sister. And he wore cowboy boots! I thought to myself, 'This is mental health meeting the Marlboro Man.' When he asked me to dinner, could I do anything else but accept? The rest is history. We were married by Easter."

"Had there been others?"

"Oh, I don't know. The ones I wanted to marry didn't want to marry me, and the ones who did, well, they didn't light that little fire I figured a girl should have."

"They were kindling," I say.

"Kindling. I guess all the material was there for roaring fires but they just didn't catch. Until Clint. Besides, I had friends who married often enough to make up for my lack of commitment. More often than not, they ended up in divorce court."

"Like me," I say. "Though I was pretty young at twenty," I defended. "But old enough I should have known what I wanted."

"I think that's an ongoing quest," Kari says to comfort me.

"I did love Stuart, or thought I did. Now I just don't trust my instincts." I knew she'd be a good listener, but I wasn't ready to tell her about my own kindling and what it lacked to make my time in Spain with Jaime a blazing fire strong enough to burn a lifetime.

"I think Darlien enjoys herself as a single woman," I say to change the focus from me.

"She has way more experience being married to compare it with than most of us."

"Being single isn't so bad," I say. "It's certainly a better alternative than marrying the wrong man for the wrong reasons."

Clint bounds through the door then and Kari stands to greet him. They mumble together. I hear a laugh and, "Oh, right, like that would ever happen." Clint kisses her and they head for the kitchen. I feel a pang of something, I'm not sure what. Maybe I've left more than memories behind in Barcelona.

⑥

I've taken over cooking dinner both as preparation for my chef's class and to be helpful to Kari and Clint. Even in another locale, I've formed a routine of sorts. I walk Ho-Bee, buy up fresh produce at the neighborhood market, read *O* magazine, and surf for more research, watching Oprah's show every day at 4:00 p.m. I feel like a stalker and hope repeated efforts to encounter her won't trigger Homeland Security. I hadn't thought I could so easily shift my routines from Milwaukee to Chicago, adding people and a pup to it as well. Maybe I'm more adaptable than I'd thought. But I'd never be able to adapt to other people's schedules for a lifetime as I'd had these past weeks. That's what one does in a marriage.

After a meal of crab linguini with a wine cream sauce, we finish our coffees that night on the balcony deck. The evenings are starting to cool, a sign of fall setting in. Leaves will be changing soon and the breezes from Lake Michigan will bring new scents. I miss my own lake changes. I have to be back home by Thanksgiving, Christmas at the latest.

For dessert that evening, I bring out three crème brûlée from the frozen food section at Safeway while Ho-Bee does his spinning dance. I hand him a dog cracker, holding it above my shoulder to see if he can really jump that high. He can. He plops down and, using his long tail as ballast, begins to lick himself in a contortion that only another dog could find attractive.

"This is good," Clint volunteers. "You don't need to take a cooking class."

"Yes I do. This dessert comes in a package, the little ceramic cups included. I need the class. Besides, it's part of my Oprah connecting."

"Where are they holding it?"

"At a tapas bar," I say.

"A topless bar? You're going to a topless bar for a cooking class?" Clint nearly chokes on his crème brûlée.

I laugh. "Not topless. Tapas, as in those little Spanish restaurants where they serve bunches of little tasty dishes. They're all over Barcelona. The cuisine finally made it to the Midwest. But the image of a topless bar for a cooking class does have possibilities."

"Perish the thought," Kari says.

I set my dessert plate down so Ho-Bee can lick it clean. "I'm not so sure that's a good idea," Kari says. "Dogs carry germs, you know. And we all know where that little tongue has been."

"I'll wash it well," I say, getting up and going inside, setting the plate on their mauve counter. "There's another crème brûlée left," I shout. "Do either of you want it?"

"Why not?" Kari says. "I may as well be fat as the way I am."

The phone rings and I recognize my own number on the

caller ID. "It's Bette," I say when Kari comes into the room. "Letting me know about my John, I suspect."

When I've checked in with Bette and then hung up, Kari is already licking the spoon from the last piece of dessert. "You won't have to fake it to look like a good cook with Oprah's chef," she says.

"So why'd you name your character Jaime?" Clint asks. "I'm curious about how a writer's mind works." Kari lowers the dining room lights and we ease into the living room, watching the city flicker its way into night. I'm stuffing little mice with catnip. Misty's sent the fabric mice that when filled I'll send to bloggers who have indicated an interest in my *Long Bad Sentence* book, hoping they won't mistake the catnip for contraband, which is a part of *The Long Bad Sentence* too.

"Sometimes a name just sticks."

"Is it based on anyone you met?" Kari asks.

I clear my throat. "I guess I can tell you. Mom and Darlien and Betty know." I pick at my cuticle. "There was a guy I met there named Jaime. He's sort of the character in the book."

Kari raises one eyebrow and I know she'll want to talk later.

"Aren't you worried he'll recognize himself?" Clint asks.

"If Irving doesn't approve the manuscript, there won't be any book for him to recognize himself in. And besides, it'll be published in English. The only foreign language rights that have been sold with my previous books went to Finland and another to Germany. Spanish-speaking countries have apparently shown no interest in my 'passion-less' books — at least, that's what Randolph tells me."

"What does that say about the Germans and the Finns?" Clint ponders.

"Jaime won't ever read it." I liked using Jaime's name so I could attribute thoughts and feelings to him, emotions that in real life I'd wondered if he felt, but hadn't had the courage to ask. Miranda, my protagonist, could speculate, but the reader, seeing through Jaime's point of view, would know how he truly felt, what his motives really were, while Miranda could only guess. Fiction was so much simpler than real life.

"An interesting profession," Clint says. He rises, checks the door locks, dead bolts, and key locks while Kari secures the window blocks even though we're on the eleventh floor. Clint stands beside her, his arm over her shoulder. Neon lights outside sparkle across their faces. An ache grows inside me, missing a tender touch in my life.

"I'm quite a character, hon," Kari says turning from the lights. She's picked up Drac, the little rubber mascot of the Spanish games Darlien gave her from Barcelona. It looks like a blue and green baby dinosaur with stiff little ridges down its back.

"You ought to create a character based on Kari," Clint says and kisses her nose.

"What makes you think I haven't?" I say.

"Which one?" Kari says. She's smiling.

"You'll have to read everything I've written to find out."

"I have read everything you've written." I can see her making a mental list of all the books and characters. "It better not be that social worker in *The Long Bad Sentence*."

I smile. "Nope. But take another look at the prison guard. You might be amazed what you see reflected inside her."

"Didn't I read somewhere that all writers' characters are autobiographical in nature? Maybe I should try to figure out what each of those characters in your stories is saying about you." She twirls her Drac mascot and wiggles her eyebrows.

"That's one of the reasons writers write," I say. "To find out who we are. Editors help us sort out what part of the story is the character's journey and what part of it is the author's. Perhaps that's why I'm struggling so with the revisions of this book. I don't know which part is Miranda's journey and which part is really mine."

Chapter 12

What is fame?
The advantage of being known by people
of whom you yourself know nothing,
and for whom you care as little.
Lord Byron

I've set the alarm early, washed my hair and straightened the frizz, then put soft folds back in with the wide curling iron. I dress. I don Donald J. Pliner–designed sandals, purchased in Spain, to make my feet look elegant. It feels good to be taking the next step.

Spiky heels, straight legged jeans that could be designer but aren't, a grey silk top with a swoopy collar, and a Spanish shawl in purple and peach finish off my ensemble. I look pretty classy for Chicago on an October morning. But will Oprah's chef want "classy," or will he want "sizzling, evocative, distinctive," words that could describe qualities of character as well as food? Maybe he looks for "studious and intense."

I decide to stay with classy chic so he'll know I'm a professional, truly serious about cuisine but also appearing well-heeled enough in my Pliners that I might be worthy of remembering and maybe, just maybe, I'll catch a glance of Oprah in the studio next door. Ho-Bee's in his kennel for the day. I hate to leave him, but I head down the elevator. Wind whips my shawl as I hail a cab; the driver zips through morning rush hour to the front door of the tapas bar where the event is to be held. Chef Smith must own it.

It's locked and appears deserted, but it would be at this early hour. Restaurants in the morning always look sad to me. Things are all happy, happy holding at night, but daylight reveals a restaurant's true neediness. They're nothing without people to receive the culinary artistry the chef and waiters deliver.

I wait in the shade of the old brick building offering a chill dancing with the wind off the lake as it does. I check, then recheck the time I've written down. It seems like others should be showing up for a 9:00 a.m. class, yet I appear to be the only one present. I finally walk around to the back. Surely the day choppers and a supervising sous chef are already at work.

I knock on the door. A small Asian man looks out at me and points. I think he might not speak English. I show him the flyer.

"The class is not here," he says in the King's English, as British as he can be. "You must travel a distance to Harpo Studios. I advise a GPS system if one is available to you." He writes down the address in perfect calligraphy.

The show will be taped two days from now, in the studio next to where Oprah shoots her show. I've written the time down wrong and mixed it in with the chef's restaurant. Tickets are free, and those standing in line will form a pool to fill any empty spaces in the audience. My luck has returned! I vow to go home, get a good night's rest, and show up well before the show, lawn chair and Ho-Bee in hand. That little dog is such a charmer, no one can resist him. I've already taught him how to sit, jump up, and turn off the light with his nose, and when I ask him if he'd "rather be dead than be a Viking fan"—a question every Packer fan will answer without hesitating—he rolls over and plays dead. Surely, I'll be noticed with Ho-Bee in hand, and all I have to do then is convince them that one of those empty seats belongs to me. Maybe I can get my friends to come early and join me. Bette could get a few new recipes in the process.

Kari's left me a message saying I've had a call on her machine so I punch play to hear it. The male voice clears his throat and my heart skips a beat. Then he begins to speak. Whew. No Spanish accent. I've never heard this voice before.

"It troubles me that I have failed to properly introduce myself prior to our having to negotiate some difficulties in your man-uscript and for this I apologize, profusely." He's from Texas, maybe. Or Mississippi. "Perhaps not profusely enough, as I left several messages on your home phone before reaching your friend, Miss Bette Farmington, I believe she said her name was who gave me this number. So please, if you would, Miss Shaw, return my call. I have a few of your revisions, and in addition to the scene issues, marketing has made suggestions related to the title. It will be so much easier to confer about this over the phone than through the concise emails we've exchanged. This is Irving Stellar." He leaves his number, then ends with "Good day now."

So he isn't British, only formal. Except for that little 'signing off' thing at the end that's rather endearing in its way. Perhaps I'll mention something about the Oprah plan to him so he'll know how hard I'm working on making my books successful.

I take Ho-Bee for a walk before calling Irving back. He's on Mountain Time, in Denver, an hour earlier than central, where I am. I call at six p.m. my time, making it five p.m. there. He'll be wanting to head home to his family, so we won't have time to talk long.

I've gotten his voicemail. "Um, this is Annie Shaw. You left me a message and asked that I call. Um, it looks like I've called too late and you've already left. I do want to talk with you about the manuscript and things. My cell phone doesn't always work, so for a while this is the best number to reach me. I'll be here, um, a few more weeks. Doing some research and promoting. I appreciate your taking the time to call me, and I hope what you recommend won't require me to lose sleep. I get pretty cranky without my sleep." I laugh. "Well, I guess that's all. Thanks again for calling."

I hang up, surprised that I wished he'd actually been there.

"Where have you been, girl? You've got to approve these brochures you ordered so we can get them to printing or you won't have any for the book fair next month."

"Oh, Mavis, I completely forgot!" Mavis is a graphic arts designer turned independent publicist I've hired to help promote my books. Mostly we trade time and talent in addition to a little money. My books provide her with Christmas gifts for her family and friends. I usually have to pay her more than the books are worth, but at least it's a deductible expense from my taxes, assuming I have income to deduct expenses from. I'm one of her first clients as she broadens her business by handling publicity. I hope she won't think that by involving my friends so much I'm showing a lack of confidence in her ability to help promote me.

A-list authors get top billing from their publisher's publicity department, with someone dedicated year-round to booking them for tours and events. I figure I'm mid- to low-list, based on the quality of restaurant I got taken to by my publisher when I was in Denver the last time. Starbucks is not a good sign.

Low-list authors gratefully receive what time is allotted us from publisher publicity—a relationship that like a passionate romance, is intense the first three months after publication. Books that don't sell after a time end up "remaindered" and are sold really cheaply, in bulk, to bookstores. In the ultimate solution to unwanted publications, they are recycled into ... paper. All kinds of paper.

Unless, of course, one blows across the kindling with a remarkable publicity idea that fires book sales and takes the publishing world by storm. Like getting Oprah to mention your title.

I'd decided to print up materials to leave at bookstores or

for mailing out to book groups and Mavis helped me prepare a flashy brochure for all my titles. We plan to mail them out just before the release of *Miranda* as a reminder to fans to please call their bookstores and order my latest.

"While you're in Chicago, why don't you go over to an independent bookstore and see if you can do a reading," Mavis suggests. "I'd be happy to try to set one up for you."

"I think it's a little late for scheduling. I should have done that as soon as I knew I'd be coming to Chicago. I'm not so well-known that I can walk in and they'll work me in."

"Yeah, they have to have time to advertise. I don't want you sitting at a bookstore with no one coming in," she says.

"I give good directions to restrooms, though," I say. Mavis laughs. I realize it's not the best use of my funds to hire Mavis and then not give her enough lead time so she can promote my books. I used to be much better about planning, but Stuart's sniping has rubbed away my confidence like water dripping on a sugar cube. I have to get my *Sweet Charity* thinking back.

"We might get you into a mall store for the walk-in traffic."

"At least in the malls the kids come by after school and they talk about what's going on in their lives and sometimes even share the stuff they've written with me. Kind of sad they'd share those things with a total stranger. Or that they have nothing better to do than talk with me."

"Are there opportunities you'd like me to try and book?"

"Well, there's a correctional facilities conference in Minneapolis next spring. Maybe I could speak there, with my book set in a prison. They might like the change of pace from workshops about food safety and cell-block management."

"I'll see what I can do. What are you doing in Chicago anyway? And how long will you be there?"

"I'm trying to get my book into Oprah's hands so it'll be a bestseller."

"Wow. If you make that happen, you should be a publicist instead of me."

"I'm sorry I haven't included you. Maybe I'm protecting you from disaster," I joke.

"What about buying a trailer?"

"What would I use a trailer for? I don't even own a car."

She pauses. "A book trailer, Annie. A DVD or YouTube submission promoting your book. Maybe you can get footage from your Oprah excursion. Meanwhile, let me know as soon as the title for the next book is firm so I can have the brochures made up. I think you'll like them. They look sort of Gaudi-like, with sharp squares and angles all done in blue and green tiles, like that little mascot Drac you brought back from Barcelona. I even put him in the corner on the inside."

"I don't think you can do that. Drac's copyrighted or trademarked or something."

"Oh. Well maybe you could get permission to use it. Sure wouldn't want the International Police and Firemen to sue you, although I've heard that there really is no bad publicity."

I think of Élan-Canine Salon and wonder if that's true.

"Just fax me the proof as it is so I can look at the brochure as you have it now."

"It's going to run around nine hundred dollars for printing and design. We'll need the money up front. Oh, you know, we should wait to final this, so we can use the cover of your latest. When will they decide that?"

"Any day now," I say. "But I think we should go ahead. I need to promote *The Long Bad Sentence* if it's going to be a bestseller."

"All right. You know, Annie, I've been thinking about that mall thing with the kids you mentioned; that's really touching. You should get Oprah to know about that. You could tell her about those kids and how they share what they write with you. I bet that happens in malls everywhere. Those kids don't have jobs, and lots of them can't afford the after-school sports or clubs and may not have the latest X-Box to spend their time on. Writing is relatively inexpensive, so they do that. Oprah needs to know about these kids that hang out and talk to authors. It's sweet and sad at the same time. They all want to be noticed. There might be real talent hidden there and a way for your stories to reach out to those kids."

"I don't write children's books," I remind her.

"No, but Oprah's Angel Foundation might fund drop-in centers at the malls. Oprah uses her fame for really worthy things. Authors could come in and teach classes to them and it could be a creative arts after-school program. Would you like me to talk to a producer? I'd sure be willing to try to get Oprah to consider a show about that. I mean, how hard can it be?"

⑥

An orchestra warmed up. Then strings swelled with what the announcer said in both English and Spanish was the official hymn for the games. The day faded, with the sun setting over the city, a city with spires and castles and a sunset worthy of Picasso.

They'd arrived at 6:30 p.m., and yet the grand entry wouldn't begin until 8:30. Jaime might have waited instead of skipping off, Miranda thought.

Miranda watched the children with their parents in the stands as she listened to the languages she couldn't understand. Birds dipped above them so close she could hear their wings whisper in the wind.

The grand entry began. One competitor from each country carried a flag, followed by streams of their fellow athletes waving up to the crowd in the bleachers. They looked like little pieces of colored paper, they were so far below her. "Albania," boomed the announcer, repeating it in Spanish. Hundreds of people in different sections of the stands stood up to applaud as the Albanians walked by, followed by the Australians. It happened with every country. It would be a long wait before "The United States of America" was called.

Two huge screens on either side of the stage where

the orchestra played let the audience see close-ups of athletes. But it was watching the real thing that entertained Miranda for the next three hours, the flesh-and-blood men and women who'd been chosen to compete, to leave their cities where they put their lives on the line for others. This week they'd come together to compete, not against the fire or crime, but against each other. As a preschool teacher, she knew how important play was even if she didn't allow it very often for herself. Every day every child needs to feel safe, to feel respected, and to play. Those are basics of the learning environment.

She thought her heart would burst when the Americans came in and then the Spanish contingent, the host country, always coming in last, following so close behind. Was that Jaime she saw there? Was he a flag bearer? In front of her, a group of children, an elderly man, and an attractive woman stood to wave and shout the name: "Jaime! Jaime! Jaime!"

With a small set of binoculars she'd purchased for the trip, Miranda spied Belle and then Jaime. Miranda waved vigorously, her whole body swaying that he might see her. The family in front of her waved too, and Jaime waved up to their section of the grandstand. It might be they were his family, Miranda thought. She looked more closely at the woman and children.

She really knew nothing about him. He could be married or engaged. He could be just an ambassador of Spanish hospitality, helping out a naïve American in distress. Nothing more. These people in front of her, had they come after he'd left? Could this woman be his wife? She'd better find that out before she let her imagination take her to places that resulted in pain.

Miranda couldn't find Jaime any longer in the crowd below. He'd be sitting with the other athletes somewhere near where her sister was. Soon the entire center of the stadium was filled with firework pops like gunfire, followed by swirls of light and smoke so dense one could hardly see the performers that had entered from the four corners of the field.

A helicopter circled overhead and quickly, so no one would think fear or terror, a fireman rappelled down into a cherry picker, the extended box used to rescue people from high buildings during a fire. This time he held a torch carried all the way from Greece. As he lit the flame a cheer rose up, and then in the darkness, new fireworks with displays to dazzle Disney took over the sky, spraying them all with huge blasts that had Miranda's ears ringing while pieces of paper the size of fists drifted over the crowd.

Miranda couldn't stop crying. She would never have a night like this again. She was a part of this world, this place, these Germans and Americans, Australians and Spaniards and Africans. She might never see Jaime again and there was nothing she could do about it, nothing at all, but this night of being a part of something grand would be enough. She'd let this gift in and cherish it forever.

It was nearly midnight when the events finished and people began moving out of the stadium, orderly, as though policemen directed them, though no one told them what to do. Miranda made her way to the arch near the entrance where Belle told her to meet her. She hoped it was below the right sortida, exit, sign. She looked for the water-bottle police but they'd long since packed up their stations.

She watched, waited for her sister, but tried to remember what Jaime had last said to her. "Watch for me." She'd done that and he'd waved back but then she'd lost him in the athletic crowd, watched his eyes move toward that family below her.

"I'm here kiddo," Belle shouted in her big, Wisconsin voice. She had a pack of men with her and she made quick introductions with little one-liners like, "This is Bud. Golfer. Airline lost his clubs. This is Maurice. Swimmer. Competes first thing tomorrow." She gave no nationalities, expecting Miranda would discover that from their badges. "Want to walk back? At least to the metro? It's right through the park. All downhill, Sis."

"I guess," Miranda said. She looked back. No Jaime. She wondered if she should wait. No. They started down the hill.

"Hola," a man's voice said, breathless, coming up behind her. "Ah . . . surprise you?" Jaime said. His smile was an hors d'oeuvre promising a delectable meal.

"Yes, you did surprise me," Miranda told him. Her heart pounded and she felt perspiration bead on her forehead.

"But I tell you to watch. To wait. I climb up top to find you."

"Did you? I missed the waiting part," she says. He'd climbed all the way back to the top of the stadium, just to be with her! Or with his family.

"Did you find your . . . family?" she asked.

He furrowed his brows.

Here it came. She was right. He needed to know that she knew.

"Ah . . . my sister and her children. Si."

"Your sister? That was your sister and her children?"

Jaime nodded. "You see them?"

"Only from a distance," Miranda said. She was laughing.

Jaime took her hand and put his arm lightly around her shoulder. "We walk through the park and see the colon change the waters," he told her. "Colors," he corrected and flashed her that smile that gave her sweet shocks, starting at her lips and trembling to her toes. "Is a beginning night, yes?"

"Yes," Miranda says. "Oh, yes."

He might have meant "beautiful night" but for her it was the beginning of a night that would change her life.

⑥

I reread what I'd written. Does this scene have enough conflict? Is the conversation realistic? Is the character being developed by the obstacles she has to overcome? Will Irving be happy?

Why hadn't I let this romance last?

Chapter 13

Cello-like. His voice had the soft deep tones of a cello.

"Ms. Shaw?"

"Yes."

"I'm so pleased to have at last found you available to talk face-to-face, so to speak." The caller ID says Ardor Publishing.

"I haven't been avoiding you," I say. "Last evening I redid the scene where Miranda discovers that Jaime has a sister rather than a wife."

"Oh, good, though I had no intention of suggesting you were avoiding me," Irving says. "Or that you change that scene." Do I sound defensive? I'll have to watch that. I don't want to make him work any harder to deal with me than any of his other authors. "I'm just pleased to make your acquaintance," he says. "Such as the phone lines allow. And I wish to apologize. For my seemingly implacable demands."

"Well, um, it's your mission to turn the pumpkin into Cinderella," I say.

"Actually, the pumpkin became the coach," Irving corrects.

"Oh, right. Yes." *He must think me an absolute dolt!*

"Let's see if we can't deal with some of these issues over the phone, and that way I may not seem so troll-like," Irving continues. He has a nice chuckle, the kind that starts in the belly rather than in the throat. "I'm not trying to create the Billy Goats Gruff here," he continues. "I'm certainly not trying to keep you from getting to your destination."

Irving's accent is cultured, formal, as though the letters of his words are straight up and down in a Roman type rather than swirling cursive. With a voice that deep, he must stand six feet or more, with broad shoulders and dark hair. I'll have to look up to him when I meet him in person. If I ever meet him in person. Doing such intimate work under the influence of someone you've never met requires almost a spiritual connection. "Would this be a proper time for us to continue?"

"Yeah. Yes. Certainly. I'm all yours. Well, not exactly yours, but ..." I pick at the cuticle of my nail as I carry the phone to Kari's leather couch. Ho-Bee barks in the guest room and I open the door to let him out, think better of it, make kissing sounds to pull him back in, then pull the door closed behind me.

"Excuse me?"

The kissing sounds!

Kari and Clint will be home soon. I should have Irving call me back on the cell so I won't tie up her landline, but I've put him off so much he might think it's another ploy.

"Just trying to get my dog back into his kennel," I say.

"You're a dog person? Your books only have cats."

"You've read my books?"

"Of course. Let's begin with your first scene, shall we?"

"Scene by scene," I say without thinking.

A silence lopes across the miles. I imagine Irving pulling on his pinstriped vest and straightening himself to his full six feet.

"As we have time for," he says. "I've found this is the best format to get at the issues. This first scene pulls the reader into the story. A pickpocket, or several in this instance, places the protagonist at risk. Action. Adventure. Vulnerability."

"I thought you didn't like it," I say. "That's why I rewrote it. You like the revision I sent?"

"I object only to the narrative that separates this first scene from the police station scene where I think she should meet her first love. You've yet to write that scene," Irving says. "This first part is too long and leaves the reader wondering if this will be a story of a weak woman, taken advantage of. We need markers pointing to a strong protagonist."

"But readers do feel vulnerable and fear being taken advantage of in new settings, especially a woman. Our protagonist is in Barcelona for the first time and feeling vulnerable, and then her money is stolen on the very first day."

"Yes, yes, I do understand this. However, your causal scenes and motivation make her appear ... naïve, nearly stupid, though that's a word I abhor. No one wants to read about a foolish woman. I believe it takes too long, ten pages, before Miranda stops ruminating about her plight and then notices that Jaime has subdued the men. She must do more than merely notice. She must take responsibility for her behavior if readers are to emulate her. As you've written it, she appears too ... not sympathetic. We need to see more of her before she is put at risk, see her strength in coming to a strange place, traveling alone on the subway in a foreign city. And all of this must happen quickly. In fewer pages to engage and hold our attention. Pacing," Irving says. "It's all about pacing, much as a children's book must capture and move quickly toward resolution."

"It's not a children's book," I defend.

"No. Of course not. I didn't mean to suggest that it was, though children's books are quite difficult to write, you know. A child won't let you take 300 pages to make your point."

I can't tell Irving that what I've written is the way it happened and that he is describing the real me as unsympathetic. "She was frightened, that's all," I say. I hadn't meant to demean children's authors. "I want readers to see that some of her mistakes are made due to her fears."

After a pause he says, "What about if the thieves are successful and then she must report it to the police and she meets Jaime there?"

"In Barcelona, people rarely ever report pickpockets," I tell him. "Nothing is ever recovered. You just cancel your credit cards and hope they don't get tons of Euros or dollars and that you kept your passport locked up in the hotel safe, as I did."

"As you did? This is about you?"

"No! I mean as Miranda did. It's the way tourists are told to take care of their passports. Besides, wouldn't that make her more like a victim, having to go and report a crime?"

"There must be a way we can do this and still have the scene ring with realism. What you have written, my dear Miss Shaw, does not." Despite the critique of his words, they strum soothingly, like warm fingers rolled across each vertebrae of a bare back lying on a soft, warm, Barcelona beach. He hypnotizes with that voice. I'll find myself agreeing to anything he says that begins with "my dear Miss Shaw."

My own life isn't realistic; that's what he's saying.

"Though it may have seeds within a real experience, this is fiction, and imagination needs to fuel the flames here."

Maybe I do need to pull this scene from my creative mind instead of trying to reproduce it from reality. Which part of the brain am I using when I write? Left brain? Right brain? Bird brain? That's what it will be if I let him talk me into something that doesn't feel right. Where is my integrity in the storytelling? I'd already changed so much of what I'd written first that I'm not sure what's my original story and what isn't—except for what actually happened there in Spain. But maybe time has changed that memory too.

"Miss Shaw?"

"Well, let's say her sister tells Miranda not to bother reporting the pickpockets, and the hotel concierge tells her that too but Miranda does it anyway. She takes her life in her own hands *because* she goes to the police station. It's after the fact. The policeman—Jaime—has subdued them and it's not even worth filing charges but she does. It's her choosing to do that against her sister's advice, even though she feels foolish for having put the wallet in her backpack and then failing to zip it shut before slipping it around on her back. She goes to be the witness to the theft in a language she doesn't speak against everyone's advice that it'll be futile to press charges. Her action shows her strength, her drive, her desire." Could I write that scene? I'm not even sure. "And then she meets Jaime there, again."

"Coincidence," Irving says.

"But there are coincidences in life, there are." How else can I explain meeting Jaime, falling in love so quickly?

Silence. He hates me, he hates me, he hates me.

"If the coincidence happens fairly early in the story then yes, I think a reader will accept it as congruent. Especially if there are a few more later on. A coincidence can get a character into trouble. Just not get them out."

"There's the one where her seats in the stadium are so close to where Jaime's sister and family sit."

"Yes. Well. That will work then. We have a compromise of sorts. Let us move on."

"Wait! Does that mean I should rewrite it, not have our hero make the day on the metro but rather have them meet later, at the police station?"

"Yes," he says. "Let it be that she is robbed as you've described it, except no one comes to her rescue. I do think that will be more realistic. If we cut the time between the theft and her going to the police, she may not seem so weak and there'll be no coincidence because she'll meet Jaime at the police station. Now then, let us look at the hotel scene, where she tells her sister what has happened."

We'd be on the phone for hours. I won't have the energy to defend every scene. He'll work me down into a puddle he can easily mop up.

"Stop, stop!"

"Excuse me, Miss Shaw? Do you need to be relieved?" Irving says. "This is not meant to be a trying time for you but one where we work together. Miss Shaw?"

"Not you," I say. My dog has opened the door to his room and, bouncing on the couch, soars over the table with one leap for projection, then scurries behind the chair, dragging something dark behind him. In pursuit, I catch Ho-Bee standing triumphant at the back of Clint's leather chair, a black Spanx hanging from his mouth, the two leg tubes hanging like a Fu Manchu. He looks so noble. "Ho-Bee!" I scold.

"Excuse me?" Irving says.

Who knows what Ho-Bee has done to the rest of my suitcase?

"May I call you back in a few minutes?" I plead. "I need to tend to my lingerie."

I take Ho-Bee out for a walk. It isn't procrastinating … it's being responsible to my pet. That's what I tell myself.

Kari and Clint live in an older part of town with oak trees lining the streets. Like swatches of cloth waiting to be placed into a crazy quilt, fall leaves lay scattered on the sidewalk, in the streets, bunched up against a fire hydrant or a bicycle rack. Ho-Bee prances as we walk, marking every tree trunk, greeting every squirrel with a stare, happily nosing any other dogs we meet. I don't think of myself as extroverted, but people automatically talk to you when you have a dog on a leash. Too bad their first comment tends to be, "What kind of dog is that?"

"Unique," I tell them, and then we stand and speculate about his breed, moving on to speak of their dog if they have one. Somehow a bond gets formed, and I might meet the same person the next day and already know a little something about them so we can do more than nod and smile. It's not unlike my work at a book fair or signing where I'm hoping to discover what might interest a person in my work. But this is about meeting people who don't know I write. Outside of my gal pals, I don't have many friends. After a bad marriage, I don't trust meeting new people, fearing I'll meet someone special and then what? It might end up like Stuart and me or worse, like Jaime and me. Still, a few moments of conversation on the street while walking my dog is a nice respite in the midst of a bustling city and an agonizing rewrite.

I limit myself to a thirty-minute walk.

"Why do you suppose I'm avoiding these revisions?" I ask Ho-Bee back at the condo. He shakes a goose toy I've bought him, the squeaker box inside it making me think domestic duck rather than goose. I am avoiding *Miranda* and Irving too. Kari works with people with phobias and what not. She says she sometimes has her clients give a voice to the object they most fear or are avoiding. She makes them put the object in a chair and talk to them and lets the object talk back. I'm not really interested in chair-talking, but writing from another voice might work, allow the fear to talk back. I can give *Miranda* — the Story — a voice and find out what I most fear.

◎

This is your Story speaking. You're avoiding me. How do you think that makes me feel? I'm perfectly willing to wait you out for awhile yet, but Irving isn't. You have obligations to meet and frankly, your credit card has been talking with me, and she's a bit unnerved with your recent expenditures. Dog toys really are overpriced, and a dog you say you aren't going to keep doesn't really need his own basketful of stuffed geese or plastic ducks. Nor can you afford the time away from me, me, me, the Story. But that's Credit Card's issue and you can bet she'll be talking to you. As your Story, I'm finally glad to get a little of your attention.

I've been a little miffed that you keep referring to me as "kindling." Are you suggesting that I'm all smoke with no real fire? I'm a story with passion and intrigue, with luminous fibers reaching out to the landscapes of people's souls. I wish you wouldn't diminish me. I suspect it's because you think talking about me is crass, commercial, all about money; and you think if it's about money, it can't be worthy or worse, inspiring. You are a bit of an elitist, Annie Shaw. How do you think that makes me feel? I'm a good story, an inspiring story, and I can reach out with fibers to ground people too.

146

Here's my theory of why you're procrastinating. You're avoiding me because you're nervous about exposing yourself. Somehow you've decided I'm YOUR story, about your life and lost love, about your moments of risk and then falling flat on your face. It isn't about you, you know. It's my story, about Jaime and Miranda, and it can have a new ending, not the one you wrote with your life. That's what Irving is getting at, finding the right ending. I'm fiction (and rather proud of it myself). A few more flourishes here and there, mixed with the straight facts hanging on the spine of reality, never hurt anyone. Goodness, even Jesus used me to make his points. People can listen to stories when they're so wounded they can't hear anything else.

I'm fiction but I'm true nonetheless. I don't need to fit into a neat little box of your life. I can't breathe that way, the life sucked right out of me.

You're also worried about being humiliated if I don't pan out, if I don't make you a bestseller and make you famous. That isn't my goal. I want to be told in an honest, forthright manner. Should you become famous, it won't be because of Oprah. It'll be because of me, Story, and the Spirit behind me. Frankly, I'll feel fulfilled if you work with Irving to get me down in black and white and finished, having done the best you could.

Just write me. Revise me. Turn me in to Irving for my final massage. I'll promise you a few insights, I will. I don't have to be perfect. Perfection doesn't mean without errors or omissions; it means complete. So complete me and see how fulfilling I can be.

Your friend, Story.

⊚

I put my journaling down, a little shaken at what I've written. I didn't know I knew that. I call Irving back. "I'm ready to discuss those next scenes," I tell him. "I know I can make this a great story with your help." For the first time, I really believe it.

Chapter 14

The Milwaukee crew arrives in Darlien's hot-yellow Pontiac Firebird convertible. I know they've driven it with the top down when the girls step into the condo. Bette's auburn, blunt-cut hair looks like something out of a Smurf commercial, standing on end at the top of her head in spikes.

"What happened to your hair?" Kari asks.

Bette catches a glance of herself in the hall mirror. "Yowza! I look like I've been tasered!"

"My scalp feels all tingly," Misty says.

"You must have been in the back seat of the Firebird," I say. "Where's Darlien?"

"Looking for parking," Bette says.

Kari tells me of a lot not too far away, and I take the elevator and wait in front of the building until Darlien comes around again. I hop in and direct her, rather pleased at how well I've managed to get around the neighborhood. Darlien wears a visor over well-behaved hair.

"Oh good," I say as I pick up the moving pillowcase at my feet. "You brought John. I didn't want him left alone over the weekend."

"We're lucky the pet police didn't stop us for transporting a cat that way."

"The vet told me to move him using a pillowcase," I defend. "He doesn't meow in there, or get sick, and he hates a carrying cage. This way his world is all around him and he can feel it, so he's secure. He knows all the boundaries." I pat his back through the green and yellow Green Bay Packer pillowcase. "We're almost there," I reassure him. "It's comforting to know your limits, isn't it, John?"

Back upstairs, cat is out of the bag. Clint's picked up ribs for us all and Misty says nothing about their nutritional value but instead comments on how good the sauce smells.

"How long can you stay?" Kari asks.

"We only have this weekend," Bette says. "I got coverage for *our* class, Annie. The kids sure miss you."

I feel sad to have the kids bounced from teacher to teacher so I can get my face—and book in front of Oprah.

"I have to get back on Tuesday for my strip therapy class," Misty says.

"Woo hoo," Clint says. "I bet Ed likes that."

"Ed could care less," Misty says. "Why would you think that?"

"A striptease class? A way to build a little fire in the marriage? Yeah, I can see Ed liking that."

"It's a quilting class, Clint," Misty tells him with a sock to his arm. "You know, strips of cloth that make up the sides of a barn or the skyline with clouds in a quilt scene."

"Oh," Clint says, disappointed. "I think I'll play pool tonight."

"You'd better," Kari tells him with a grin.

"It is therapy for me though," Misty says. "It puts all the other irritations of my day away because I have to focus on the strips and getting them just so. With a preschooler, it's the only thing in my day I can control."

"We'll head back after the taping of the Oprah show Monday afternoon," Darlien says. Bette used a day of her vacation time to be here; Darlien has rearranged her work time with another cop—she might have to work the Thanksgiving holiday in return; Misty's husband is chief babysitter and cook for the next three days. Even Kari plans to take Monday off so we can go to the Oprah show together. They've given up so much to help me with this goal and yet I'm having second thoughts after my browbeating from my own Story. Just working to make it the best I can make it might be the better goal to pursue.

"My scalp feels like tiny little insects are lifting weights, pulling on every follicle," Bette says. She brushed down her spiky hair.

"That happens in the back seat," Darlien says. "Wind whips around and makes your hair weird."

"Think of it as a scalp massage with little dancing feet zinging through your hair," Misty says. "I'll sit in the back on the way home. I love that sense that something's alive on my head that isn't head lice. Not that we've had that episode yet this year in preschool!"

"Fortunately nothing is alive!" Darlien says. She sneezes three times.

"Allergies?" I ask. "Maybe it's John and Ho-Bee."

She shakes her head. "Probably Chicago air I'm not used to. Not to worry. Hey, where is this beast who has taken over your life?"

"I'll get him. Then we eat and have sustenance for whatever might happen between him and John." They ooh and ahh as Ho-Bee prances into the room, an immediate star who gets attention from them all, then turns around three times and lies down to take a nap.

"Very well behaved," Misty says.

"He can be," I say.

After finishing his ribs, Clint excuses himself to the local pub, leaving us planners to our devices.

"Let's recap," Bette says as we finish up our ribs. "You've made progress we hear."

"On the book, yes. I've finally talked with Irving. He sounds very … elegant," I say. "And I have a direction for revising, yet again. I had a little conversation with the Story, and I'm a little less nervous about completing the work."

"You talked to your story?" Kari says.

"Story talked, or rather wrote. I listened, and read."

"Are you going mental on us?" Bette asks.

"Good information always helps reduce anxiety," Kari says.

"I used your technique for dealing with phobias and fears and gave the Story its own voice. So no, I'm not going mental."

"What's it sound like?" Misty asked. "Your Story's voice."

"A very firm ... Dorothea Dix," I say.

"Who is she? Some new sitcom star?" Misty asks. She's gone into the kitchen and gotten wet paper towels for our hands, the ones in the carryout bag not being enough. She wipes her face with one, and after each of us cleans up like John licking his face, we settle into the living room, a little Adam Lambert blasting from the Bose.

"Dorothea Dix was a reformer in mental health in the 1800s," Kari says. "She was a little quirky, came from a very dysfunctional family, but I can't imagine the sound of her voice."

"She did a lot of good, right?" I say.

"You are going mental," Bette says.

"Because she brings to life a historical woman or one from a dysfunctional family?" Darlien asks.

"Dorothea took on the establishment all by herself and got laws changed," Kari says. She drinks her soda from a straw. "She improved treatment for people who were mentally ill, especially those in prisons. We could use a Dorothea Dix today."

"And I didn't channel her," I defend. "My story had firmness when it told me to stop procrastinating and write."

"But how did you know how she'd sound? She's been dead for like, years, right? You couldn't hear her," Bette says.

"Don't you ever hear the voices of characters who never even lived?" I ask. "I do."

"That's why you're a writer and I'm not," Bette laughs.

"OK, think Glenn Close then. You like her voice."

"I like your story," Misty says. "The more I've thought about Miranda, the more real she's become. And I've been filled in about, well, your Jaime." I wince as she continues. "And I have a new title proposal, one with action in it. That's what's missing in *Miranda of La Mancha,* Annie. It doesn't have movement."

She's right. "So what's your title?" Bette asks.

"Miranda Meets Her Match in La Mancha. What do you think?"

"I like it," Kari says.

"Me too," Darlien adds. "It's got the match word, like a competition, so that takes in the games."

"And it suggests a little challenge: what's the match and how does she meet it," I say. "It's great. I'll send it to Lura and Irving before I go to bed tonight. It's a good one. Story will like it too." I laugh. "It'll be easier to get the title out there for us to promote, too, with the 'match' word having a double meaning."

"That's the point, isn't it?" Darlien says. "Your story and Miranda's is a good one and our task is to get that title out there so people will want to buy it. And Oprah is our way to make that happen."

"What about the Oprah progress?" Misty asks.

"I got to hear Oprah's voice, in person," I say. "Remember?"

"It's a start."

I give them the details of my disastrous day with Ho-Bee, who currently lies across my knees like a slug, offering no evidence of his bipolar personality.

"You wouldn't think such a little dog could cause that much damage," Bette says.

"He's a cutie," Misty says. "And so firm a little body. Norton will love having time with him when you come back home. Assuming John ever approves."

The canine and feline worked out their status when I released Ho-Bee from his crate and John spilled out of the pillowcase, eyeing the dog from a corner of the room. Ho-Bee sniffed then ran circles around the end table, chasing a red porcupine toy I'd bought for him. John made a sound. Ho-Bee's ears perked up and he trotted over, dropped the toy at John's feet, and the cat yawned. Ho-Bee lay down in front of the cat, barked once.

John coughed up a bezoar.

Ho-Bee sniffed it and picked it up, racing around the room with it in his mouth. They've been fast friends ever since.

"I'm not sure my landlord will authorize a dog," I say. "Even a little one. Especially one who likes to redecorate." I look at the newly repaired dining room table. "And don't leave your suitcases open," I warn. "Unless you want your dirty laundry spread across the condo."

"Do you think they'll really sue you?" Darlien asks.

"I hope not. Clint's attorney is getting them to reconsider the amount they told me. Most of the damage was broken bottles of shampoo and oils. Shouldn't be much cost in replacing that."

"You'd be surprised. I watch that show of groomer competitions, and you could get a tummy tuck for what a few of those oils cost," Darlien says. "And people are sensitive about their dogs' grooming. The patrons might be more upset than the salon owner."

I'd been feeling better about my future with lawyers, but now I wasn't so sure.

"You should call and find out what's happening," Kari says.

"Isn't no news good news?" I say.

"Avoidance is never good," she says. I think of Irving. It was better when we actually talked.

"Well, I've made progress too," Misty says. "I went online to Oprah's web page. It's something I can do after Norton's in bed and Ed's watching the late news. She asks lots of questions about what you know for sure, about issues in your life, finding your way, seeking fulfillment. She asks for photos. I like the panels on Fridays where they talk about God and faith. Last night she had a conversation about not living your life on unexamined perceptions. I had to think about that one." She pauses. "I entered comments."

"Related to Annie's book?" Darlien says. She's wearing a pair of khaki slacks that let you zip off the legs to make shorts.

She's zipped on the lower portion, giving herself long pants over bare feet she curls up under her.

"I told her about our gal pals," Misty says.

"You did?" A unison surprise.

"What did you tell her?" I ask.

"She wants book clubs to write about their club and I said I was part of a group and what we do to support each other's dreams. And that we also read books. Your books, anyway, Annie."

"We're not really a book club," Darlien says, ever the one for accuracy. "I think Oprah wants book clubs that read her picks to send photos."

"We could read her picks," Bette says.

"But we do what book clubs do," Misty insists. "We support each other, talk about stories and what not."

"Book groups take trips together to visit places where books are set, and we've taken lots of trips together," Kari agrees.

"Quilting groups do that too. I'm going to the big Paducah show one day," Misty says. "Maybe that'll be my next goal, to submit a quilt for competition at Paducah or Houston or right here in Rosemont. We could all go!"

"Maybe after *Miranda* comes out, people will want to go to Spain," Kari says.

"Or Milwaukee," I say.

"Both exotic locales," Kari notes.

"Did anyone contact you from the show?" I ask. "Randolph says producers do that within an hour if they see something they like."

Misty shakes her head. "But I did read about this singer who rented a hall to perform a concert. He made a YouTube video and had a T-shirt printed with the seating arrangement on it and then stood on the street and asked people if they'd come to his performance and he showed them where he'd set aside seats for Oprah and Gayle."

"Did they come?" Darlien asks.

"Gayle came. Oprah was in Africa. But he got to sing on her show when she got back. I think she liked his inventiveness."

"I remember hearing about that singer but I can't remember his name," Kari says. "Isn't that odd?"

"Me neither," Misty says. The others shake their heads too.

"He got on the Oprah Show, sang, met his heart's desire, but none of us remember his name?" I groan. "Maybe that should tell us something. So did he get a recording made? Is he now famous and we're the last people in America who don't know who he is?"

"Haven't heard."

"We could google him."

"This doesn't bode well even if I do get Oprah to mention my book," I say. My Story's voice is sounding wiser.

Ho-Bee begins to fidget. I wonder if he senses my anxiety. Can dogs do that the way I've read that infants can?

"'Let's not go there,' says the cat. 'Let's not go there, that is that.' Isn't that what you're always saying, Annie?" Bette says as Ho-Bee launches himself toward her, then whips his long tail against her legs and scampers up her jeans onto her lap, licking her face.

"All right, all right," she laughs. "He's very affectionate."

"Just what Annie needs, an affectionate male," Darlien teases.

Kari slurps the bottom of her soda glass. "Let's see what else we have on our agenda. Don't think about that unnamed singer," she says.

"Tomorrow I've arranged for us to go to a chef class," I remind them. "If we can get tickets. We'll have to stand in line and wait."

"Like on Broadway," Bette says. "What? I went there once."

None of us knew.

"Then there's the taping on Monday. And my agent has this harebrained idea that I don't even want to mention ... yet."

"We have some other ideas too," Misty says. "We think you should apply to be Oprah's dog walker."

"She has one I'm sure."

"Maybe that walker needs a relief walker." Misty has taken out a round form and an armful of material. She's quilting.

"Rather than a dog walker, what about a puppy waste manager?" Kari says. "I saw a car with "Puppy Poo Removal" painted on the side this past week. It never occurred to me that you could get a job doing that. You might actually get several clients around here."

"What do they do exactly?" Misty asks.

"Go to people's yards and pick up the ... poo," Kari says. "They pay so much a ... collection or so much money per yard and how often people want their yard scanned."

"People actually hire other people to do that?" I say.

"It's legitimate work. It has dignity," Kari defends.

"But why don't people do it themselves?"

"Time, I suppose. Or maybe they're really famous and don't want the paparazzi photographing them doing such mundane things."

"I bet there's more turnover in that than walking Oprah's dogs," Misty says.

"And the walkers probably do puppy waste management at the same time. Let's let that one go," Kari says.

"I'm so glad we can brainstorm without anyone getting upset that their idea isn't picked up," I say.

"Like poo?" Bette says and we laugh.

"Here's my idea," Darlien says. "What about meeting up with her gardener at her California house? Maybe he offers a master gardener class or something. We could google that and find out."

"I can't afford to fly to California on a whim."

"You took a bus to Chicago on a whim, and it got you close enough to hear Oprah's voice," Darlien says. "I'd come with you to California."

"Not the same thing," I say.

"Then you won't like my husband's suggestion either," Misty

says. "He offered the use of his parents' time-share in Hawaii. It's on the same island as Oprah's house. It's a beautiful place, older and done all in antiques. Oprah's house. She featured it in her magazine a while back. You could walk ... what did you says your dog's name is?"

"Ho-Bee."

"Ho-Bee. You could walk Ho-Bee on that same street and you'd be sure to run into Oprah. Dogs are such a natural way to meet up with people."

"I'd run into Oprah's dog walker," I say. "Look, this isn't going anywhere. I'm not sure I'll even keep Ho-Bee, let alone take him to Hawaii."

"You have to keep the dog," Bette says. "He's adorable. Besides, as a writer, you're pretty isolated. If it wasn't for us, you might never get out doing things. You subscribe to ten magazines; did you know that? I take them in every day at your apartment. And the catalogs! You must be dreaming all the time! You have to live a little, girl."

"Hawaii," Darlien says. "Live there for a few weeks. That's a great place to research, and you'd need to take me along. It's almost a foreign country and I wouldn't want you to get lost like you did in Barcelona. Hawaii has great golf courses."

"I found my way back to the hotel," I defend. "And if I can't afford to go to the almost-foreign country of California, I surely can't afford to fly to Hawaii." My credit card is hyperventilating inside my purse, I can hear it.

"I've been thinking, Annie," Bette says. "Maybe you would be better off if you just work on your writing as an entree into the bestseller world? You know, write that piece for *O* magazine or the *New Yorker*. Build on your strengths. Maybe an essay about those kids you work with who write such neat stuff or how writers' real lives are often intermixed with their fiction. You could mention *Miranda* that way."

"I miss those kids," I say.

Kari says, "Instead of pushing yourself to do things you're

not accustomed to do, you could write about the visit to the salon and how it got you a little notoriety and close to a famous person but no fulfillment of your goal."

"But that's the point of a goal," Darlien says. "To push us beyond what we're used to doing. Let's not abandon the best-seller part of that yet. We've barely begun and already Annie's heard Oprah's voice."

"And I've heard a new attorney's voice," I say.

"Well, there's that," Darlien says.

"Magazine editors work six months out," I tell them. "Even though it's October, they're already working on their spring issues, so they wouldn't use anything I submit for issues before then anyway, even if they did accept it."

"The timing might be right," Bette says. "Has Irving told you when the *Miranda* book will be out yet? Is it ok if I give him a carrot?"

"Irving?"

"Ho-Bee." Bette trots to the kitchen for her snack bag, then calls my dog to her. He wags his tail as she hands him the carrot. He promptly turns toward me, and I swear he knows that he looks like he's smoking a cigar, with that carrot wagging as hard as his tail.

"Add a hat to that dog and he's Johnny Depp in a crime film," Darlien says.

"Oprah is in to healthy things. Maybe your book could include an exotic Spanish recipe," Bette says. "Could you work that into the story line? Maybe the recipe we'll get at the class tomorrow. Or one I make up. An original."

"Oh, I know," Misty says, clapping her hands. "Miranda has a major health problem, one of those rare diseases, and we could suggest that Oprah have a show about it."

"I don't like those rare-disease shows," I say. "I can't watch *House* because I always get the symptoms of those rare diseases. The next day."

"Yes, but could you write one into the story? And then we'd

offer you up as someone who has written about it in this amazing book. Maybe we could even find someone with the same disease as Miranda. Poor thing," Misty says. "And she was so hoping she could marry Jaime but then ... she gets this terminal disease and—she has to go to treatment or therapy. How awful! And she's so young too."

"It's only a story," Darlien reminds her.

"And not Miranda's story," I remind her.

"Oh, right." She returns to her quilting.

"I'm already writing in a dog and Irving wants me to change more scenes and now you want me to work in a recipe and a rare disease too? No, my story will surely resist such changes made for the sole purpose of getting Oprah interested."

"You make it sound like the story is the decider," Darlien says.

"In a way, she is."

"OK. Let's keep visiting Oprah's web site and answering her questions," Misty says. "I'm pretty sure that's how they pick people for the show. Bottom line is that your story is about good people, and making good choices. It fits right into her Your Best Life theme, no matter how you write the story down."

"Are we trying to get Annie invited to the show? Or to get Oprah to pick her book?" Darlien asks. "I'm confused. We need clarity."

"We want her to know Annie's name," Kari says.

"Not the book title?" I ask. "I thought ..." I didn't continue, but I knew that what I wanted was to get back to *Miranda* so I'd have a good reason to call Irving. I was liking talking to him.

Chapter 15

A lot of strange people hang out on Chicago streets and not just Bears and Bulls and Cubs fans. Street people point fingers of cardboard at us while we wait in line for the tickets that are going to take me on to fame. The finger sign reads "will eat for work," making me wonder if there are jobs where you get to eat as work. I might need to look into that.

Bette's purchased multi-colored goggles better worn by kids in wading pools on hot summer days than by twenty-something women edging into old-enough-to- know-better, but people who came really early as we did notice and smile. It was still dark when we formed the line with only two people in front of us. Ho-Bee and John remain at the condo. I hope my dog isn't cluster-bombing their apartment. I'm grateful he isn't tangled up, running circles around my ankles. It's been a chilly wait but we bought cups of coffee and now that the sun's up, someone will surely come soon to open the ticket booth. We're not the first in line so I hope we get in. The couple in front of us are friendly but they've brought lawn chairs to sit on and they doze.

Chef Art Smith is actually Oprah's former chef. It's such an ordinary name for such an important position. Everyone knows his name. I've prepared a few of the recipes included in O magazine that Chef Smith contributed. While I'm not much of a cook, this effort to research and know a little about Oprah's meal tastes has increased my interest and my skill. I fixed chicken breasts with lemon and carrots that I didn't overbake so that's promising. I wish I had a piece now.

Darlien has her arms crossed in her policewoman stance.

"What's that?" I ask Darlien, pointing to a black cylinder in her pocket.

"A toothbrush. The one British Airways gave us. Along with the eye patches so we could sleep. Remember?"

"You brought your toothbrush along?"

"I'll want to be sure I have fresh breath," Darlien says. "In case we get invited to the table."

"I brought mine too," Bette says.

"Really. I never would have thought of brushing my teeth."

"Does Oprah have a dentist?" Misty asks. "She must."

"Oh, I can see me trying to talk to Oprah's dentist about my book," I laugh.

"It's hard to talk to any dentist," Darlien says. "You can listen. But they put those things in your mouth and then ask you questions. It's crazy."

"As a profession, dentists have a high depression rate," Kari tells us.

"I'd be depressed too, if no one ever answered me."

"Think of how Irving must feel that you don't answer his phone calls," Bette reminds me.

"You think I'm responsible for my editor's depression? How much more responsibility can I handle?" Actually, it is possible I am or will be depressing my editor if he doesn't approve of my revisions. I really ought to be writing now instead of standing in line to get tickets for a class that has only marginal make-my-book-a-bestseller possibilities. At least we'll have something interesting to taste when it's over. And of course, we'll have another story if nothing else.

⑥

"You didn't bring a pet?" the man says, handing me five tickets for Chef Smith's afternoon taping. "Chef Smith is making canine cuisine today, dog biscuits and whatnot, so most of the guests who bought advance tickets will also bring their dogs today."

I look at my watch.

"Clint will bring him," Kari volunteers.

"Swell. Remember to have your IDs with you," the ticket master says. "Be back at two o'clock. Taping starts at three."

We call Clint, who says he'll bring Ho-Bee. Since we're down town, we decide to shop and I find myself buying both cat and dog toys. After all, Ho-Bee is so charming he may well attract special attention by Chef Smith. Clint meets us for lunch at a nearby tapas bar. I think he misses the fun we gal pals have together. He smiles, hanging around while girls talk of shopping, music, books, and parents.

Parents! I tell Darlien how Mom thought I'd met Jaime at a "topless bar."

"You have to enunciate with Mom," Darlien says. "Her hearing is going. And she's probably never heard of a tapas bar."

"What kind of a breed is that dog, anyway?" a pleasant-looking man at the table next to me asks. We sit outside under umbrellas sporting the names of fruit drinks served inside. Little bottles of scent effusions sit on each table and lavender floats over us.

"A Jack Russell," I say. "I think."

"Ah. With a long tail. Interesting."

Interesting. A word used when you don't have something kind to say.

"Do you have a dog?" Misty interjects, then slips right over into promoter mode. "This is Annie Shaw. She's a very successful writer."

I feel my face grow warm.

"Congratulations. I've always wanted —"

"To write a book," I say. "I know. I think you should. Everyone has a story worthy of telling." I really believe that.

He frowns. "I could never write a book. Way too hard. No, I've always wanted a dog. But I travel so much. It wouldn't be fair."

"Unless you had friends to look after him," Misty says. "Or a wife."

"I have the former, not the latter, but none who wish to look after a dog. I don't believe I've heard of your work, Miss Shaw, was it?"

Already embarrassed by my own poor listening skills, I say, "Don't feel badly if you haven't read anything I've written. That puts you in a select group of millions who have never read anything I've written." He laughs at my disarming line to help people feel comfortable for not knowing who I am.

"We're making that select group smaller though," Misty adds.

He laughs. "What kind of books do you write?"

For the first time I don't say "kindling books meant to build a fire in your heart." I say instead, "They're stories of the human heart in conflict with itself. William Faulkner said that's what a writer ought to give their blood and sweat and tears to, when he accepted the Pulitzer Prize in 1954."

"Give him your card," Darlien urges.

I feel embarrassed but hand him the card Mavis has made up with both *The Long Bad Sentence* and *Miranda of La Mancha* on it. He looks at it. "Thanks. I like to travel, so a story set in Spain appeals to me." Mavis says we have to promote the current release and the promised next one, too.

The man has deep blue eyes and a voice that sounds like an old Robert Pattison might, though I wasn't sure the Twilight vampire would ever grow old.

"That book isn't out yet," I say. "And we're not sure of the title but —"

"I'll look for it," he says as he stands to leave his tip.

"Wait, here's her latest," Darlien says handing him a book. He accepts it, looks at the title. "Is it about grammar?"

"No," I tell him. "See the correctional patch on the man's shirtsleeve?" I point it out. "It's a light romance, set in a prison."

"Interesting," he says. "Well, I'll take a look at it. Thanks. It's nice to meet you, Annie Shaw. I'll try to remember your name." He nods to us all and walks down the street.

"Don't do that, Misty," I hiss after he leaves.

"What? He asked about your dog, started the conversation. You don't have to be ashamed to talk about your books. Besides, he wasn't married; he likes to travel. You have to take advantage of these moments of connection."

"It feels so ... commercial," I say.

"If you don't love your story, who will?" sings Misty.

"Mom." I say. "Mom will love my story even if I don't. If and when I get a good review it means that someone besides my mom thought it was a good read. But I don't want to foist my books onto total strangers!"

"Of course you do! That's why they're published. You definitely want strangers, many, many strangers to know your work," Bette says. "Where's that confidence?"

That sounds like something my story would say to me, chastising me about my worries over being commercial and about how I demean my own writing.

"Success is when planning and opportunity meet up; that's what Oprah says. We're just looking for that invitation."

But I'm starting to think that the invitation that matters most comes from finding a true calling and not writing to chase the fleet-footed twins of fame and fortune.

@

The line moves quickly, with people at the door checking both our ID and our dogs. It's a suburbia zoo with every imaginable breed carried, leashed, and led. I don't see any poodles with bad trims or half-furminated dogs that I'd left at Élan-Canine Salon.

Bette's talking food but I don't think she's heard that the *only* recipes today will result in dog biscuits and treats, because she keeps saying she can hardly wait to see what the chef has on the menu that she might adapt for her residents. I don't see how I can work a dog recipe into Miranda's life — or how Bette would take that recipe back to her assisted living cherubs either.

"Wait here a moment," the ticket taker says when he sees my ticket. "You've got a labeled one. Means you'll get to sit up front at the counter where Chef Art will be teaching."

Misty squeals in delight. "That's wonderful! You'll get to eat what's served right away," she says.

"Ho-Bee will," I say. "I'm not eating the dog treats."

"Oh, they'll surely have something more than that," Darlien says. "I hope."

"There'll be at least a little conversation time during the commercial breaks," Bette says. "Who knows what connections an enterprising person like you can build that into? You have books to give away, right?" I nod and she gives me a hug. Ho-Bee fidgets against my chest as Misty shuffles quickly to her seat beside Darlien, Kari, and Misty. They sit around little tables with a single iris centered in a vase. Ho-Bee and I are directed to a lovely granite counter with what looks like hand-joined oak chair backs and seats that swivel.

Dog in arm, I maneuver around cords and electrical outlets and step in front of cameras. I wish my T-shirt had the book title on it. None of us is now wearing the brightly colored kids' sun glasses. But maybe when we're introduced on air I'll have the chance to turn toward the camera, say my name and occupation, and mention *The Long Bad Sentence*. Surely the producer will ask.

Chance. It's all about making my own chances and not being ashamed of my story.

A make-up assistant puts a tiny touch of powder on my nose to take the shine off, I guess. The production assistant introduces himself. He asks our names and occupations and cuts me off before I can say anything about my book. He makes notes, then tells us where to sit, seating us not at the granite counter but at a table. He places me beside a college student with eyebrows that run together. He wears a "UNLV" label on his shirt. His Boston bulldog wears a matching white shirt. *Good idea!* The UNLV guy nearly slobbers with a Pavlovian response to a girl with hair so flaming red it looks like it could combust, and a smile as charming as chocolate. She sits diagonally across from me. Her dog is a teacup poodle, pink as bath suds and smelling just as sweet.

Another assistant comes in and lights fragrant candles at each end of the counter.

The chef stands behind the granite along with his French briard, a dog weighing at least 100 pounds and wearing what could only be described as dreadlocks covering his entire frame. The chef introduces him as Bruno as the dog behaves beautifully, sitting at the end of the cooking area.

Chef Art shakes my hand when I answer his question with my name and Ho-Bee's. "And I'm an author," I add.

"Are you now," he says. My heart pounds.

"Yes I write —"

"Words to treasure I am sure," he says.

"I've written this book about —"

"I'm sure it's wonderful," he says, kissing my fingertips to the swoons of the crowd and the barks of the various audience dogs.

Thank goodness I've polished my nails. They look good with the glitter on the tips sparkling against the table candlelight.

"I write, myself," he says and holds up his own cookbook that the camera shifts to.

"Oh, I know," I gush. "I love your cookbook!"

"Which recipe is your favorite?" he asks, and I'm suddenly appalled at what I've said, because I've never even seen one of his cookbooks before. The presence of greatness has caused exaggeration-itis. If I actually did meet Oprah, what disorder would I contract to steal the rest of my integrity?

"I love them all," I respond, grateful that he's moved on to meet another of the labeled people getting to sit close to him.

Ho-Bee puts his paws on the table, which is allowed, because I see the poodle doing the same. The tablecloth shifts a bit. Ho-Bee's attention shifts when he hears a deep bark in the audience. His back feet launch against my slacks and his paws grab into my shoulders as he yips at a Jack Russell in the third row table behind us. His action pulls my T-shirt up a little further on my belly than even a passionate Ardor author should expose. I yank it back and nearly lose my hold on Ho.

Chef Art chatters to each of the other tablemates, gives his French herding dog the command to "stay," then steps behind the granite counter stove top, sizzling garlic into hot olive oil. He chatters as he works, mixing flour and milk into a roux, but I think he should be checking what's on the stove because it smells hot.

We pull up our chairs to watch the chef at work. Applause breaks out at various times, as he adds some new ingredient the audience approves of. "All organic," he keeps saying. "Your dog deserves the best. All ingredients properly grown without pesticides or chemicals. Green indeed. So safe you can eat it yourself."

He has little cookie cutters in various shapes, including bones and little birds. Something that he used smells like a hot sauce with cayenne pepper laced with jalapeno, but I've not seen those ingredients anywhere on his cooking space. Dogs do like intense tastes, I guess.

Chef Art fixes an entrée that smells of catfish, with colorful side dishes of okra and a fine fresh doggie salad he says will be served last, "as in France," all the while joking and even delighting me by using my name once or twice, then my dog's. "Ho-bee, Ho-Bee," he says. "Such an unusual name." The camera pans on me and I mouth, "I'm a writer," all shame vanished. But the camera stops on Ho-Bee. He's getting the attention. I wish then I'd flirted a little, with the camera man if not Chef Art.

"Such an unusual name," the UNLV T-shirt says to me at the break.

"He's named after Brian, one of the Chicago cows," I say. "And that he's so happy he makes me think of Santa laughing. 'Ho, ho, ho.'"

"You like unusual food?" Chef Art asks. "I'll fix for you and your little Brian."

"Ho-Bee," I remind him.

"Don't forget us," UNLV says. "Our pooches love your recipes. We do too. In fact, we're both culinary students."

Suck-up!

The chef brings a big spoon of okra-like food over and holds it for Ho-Bee to lick, saying my name again. He winks.

He's flirting! What do I do back?

It would double my chances to get a mention of my book if I have a relationship with Chef Art. Is he married? I haven't researched that! But to have more than a momentary glance, this is fate. I can see it now: He'll invite me to Oprah's for dinner he's prepared himself. I'll meet Stedman. Gayle will call me and ask for book recommendations. My life will—

"Taste," he orders. I steady the Chef's hand with my own, gaze at him, and smile. "Take a taste of the okra dish."

It's awful, organic or not. A texture of slugs mixed with slime. It must be what I smelled. Ho-Bee licks the okra from the spoon, devouring it as though it were yesterday's garbage. I hate okra, but Ho-Bee apparently loves it. My stomach convulses.

"You will make this dish for him again, won't you, Annie Shaw?" Chef Smith says. I'm impressed that he uses all our names as though he's known us forever. Maybe he wasn't flirting with just me. The Chef's gotten another spoon and now offers it to the teacup while the bulldog slobbers. The bulldog drops a blob onto our tablecloth, and Ho-Bee thinks it must be for him so catapults from my arms and scrambles across the table, laps up the blob, then leaps to the counter.

"He loves this dish, your dog," the chef says. The audience

applauds as my dog licks the spoon in the pan. "You will make this again, yes?" I nod agreement to the lie.

No. This is fiction. I swallow what I feel moving back up. "Of course. Whatever my little Ho-Bee wants."

Ho-Bee has hopped back onto our table. UNLV glares as Ho-Bee leaps up and down, four-footed. I give out a little groan, wanting to go to the green room because that's the color I know I am.

The audience gasps. *Did I say my wish out loud?*

I reach for the dog leash and tug. But I also pull the candle that tips precariously before catching the tablecloth on fire. My shirt feeds the flames and I bat at my stomach as the polyester melts. Ho-Bee chooses this moment to yank the leash from my hand and now takes the flame trails toward the counter. A smoldering smell morphs into smoke. I bat at the tablecloth while attempting to shorten the leash to pull Ho-Bee back, my belly stinging. Teacup Poodle Lady screams and points; UNLV grabs the pitcher of drinking water and douses my shirt, which smells like old ashtrays. But it's too late. With no more smoke than a toaster gone bad, my shirt and the tablecloth are apparently enough to turn on the sprinklers, which every dog in the place takes as a sign that they're loved since it's like being allowed to run in the rain and they squirm and bark to do just that.

"*Pardon, pardon,*" the chef shouts and flaps with his waist apron to shoo the smoke away while camera people rush to remove their equipment and someone shouts to get the sprinklers off. The blond girl squeals and backs away, holding her poodle, literally in a cup now. UNLV hisses at me. "Celebrity stalker," he says as he and Teacup's mother leave. This part will be cut from the tape, I'm sure.

I stand with a charred hole in my T-shirt, wet pants, and Ho-Bee lapping at my cheeks as an escort at my elbow leads me away to the green room, I suppose, to tend to my scorch and keep me from considering a lawsuit. Fortunately, they've shut the sprinklers off—but not before the audience was bathed.

"What is your name?" the producer asks me. I hang on to Ho-Bee, who lies still in my arms as though the okra is a sedative.

"Annie Shaw," I whisper. "I'm a writer."

"Aren't we all?" The producer writes something on his clipboard.

"Really, I'm fine. I'll be happy to join my friends."

In another room, a man blinking away water dripping from his hair paws through the show releases we all signed before they started taping. "Ah yes, here it is. Annie Shaw. Well, we won't need your release for this tape. We'll have to chuck this entire show."

"There might be a clip for KGW news," I suggest. "You have a hero who saved a writer and a young woman and their pets and kept the studio from being consumed by flames. People love hearing stories where animals are saved. We all survived a close call. No dogs were hurt. You might need the release. And here," I pull a copy of my book out from my back pocket and hand it to him. Bette would be proud.

He stares at the book, looks up at me. "Good idea." My heart soars. *I'd make it on the news! My book will be on the news!*

"Bob. Get the UNLV kid in here. We'll make him a hero for the five o'clock." To me he says, "Your stomach, where you're burned. Is it —"

"It's fine. I'm fine."

"Good. Make sure miss—what'd you say your name was again?"

"Annie Shaw. It's right there on the cover."

"Right. Make sure Miss Flaw here is seen by the physician for that burn." He's ripping up my release as he talks, put the pieces like little bookmarks into my tome, then sets it down in a puddle of water pooling at my feet. "Then get an interview on tape with the kid and the flashy redhead in the wet T-shirt. With their dogs. Good copy. Might make a nice lead-in for the chef ... clumsy woman rescued by a young student while dogs eat Italian cuisine. Yeah. People will love it."

"Won't you need my name ... and consent for that?" I ask.

"There was so much smoke no one will see your face. We'll call it even by providing you with medical care for your scorched belly and not asking you to repay us for the fire and sprinkler damages. Sound okay with you, Miss Flaw?"

"It's Shaw," I say as my gal pals appear at my side. "My name is Annie Shaw." But maybe I should think about writing under a pen name.

Back at Kari and Clint's we hover around the eleven o'clock news. We wait through national events, the weather, and the latest sports news, including NASCAR updates and pictures of cars with sponsoring brands written all over them.

"Maybe they won't cover it," Bette says.

"They always close with some light local news," Clint says. "Your escapade will likely be next."

"Shh, there's the building!" Misty says.

"Guests of Chef Art Smith's culinary class today had quite a surprise," chirps the perky announcer, "when they attended his downtown restaurant class. Canine cuisine was on the menu, with dogs of every stripe present to share in the excitement as Oprah's former chef prepared gourmet dog food for dozens of his furry friends. In the midst of the festivities, a rambunctious Jack Russell terror known as Ho-Bee—that's a strange name, isn't it, Bill—ruled."

"Jack Russells always rule, Monica." Bill smiles.

"This Jack Russell toppled a candle that caught a tablecloth and his owner's T-shirt on fire and apparently burned a bit of her belly, or so we heard."

"Ouch!" says Bill.

"But culinary student John Stevenson, of Las Vegas, Nevada, saved the day. He tossed ice water on the woman while her dog consumed the okra delight."

John Stevenson, NLV, smiles into the camera, with his bulldog slathering beside him. Laughter in the studio causes the announcer to catch her breath.

"How embarrassing," I say.

"Quiet. She's not finished," Darlien says.

"The fire set off the sprinklers at Harpo Studios. Unit 550 of the Chicago Fire Department responded to the call," the announcer continued. "Oprah is said to have sent her condolences for the smoke-filled studio and the unexpected bathing of all the audience dogs too. She'd planned to join her old friend as a surprise, but the fire department sent her away."

"What! Oprah was going to come?" I gasp.

"At least they didn't use the hero's dog's name," Kari says. "Ho-Bee got noticed."

"She was there!" I wail. "If only I could have kept control over my dog I might have met her! In the flesh."

"At least they didn't show your face, so we won't be stopped when we go to the taping of Oprah's show on Monday," Darlien says. "There's always a silver lining—even if it did get a little wet."

Chapter 16

*A good name
is rather to be chosen
than great riches.*
Proverbs 22:1 KJV

"Suffer little children, and forbid them not, to come unto me; for of such is the kingdom of heaven." Matthew 19:14 is the sermon Scripture on Sunday morning. Afterwards, Kari asks if I want to go to Urgent Care to have my stomach looked at. My belly still stings but not as much as my pride. It feels as though I've sunbathed on the shores of Lake Michigan with an SPF of minus-one. It isn't anything serious and won't leave a scar, but it will be tender to the touch and too hot and cold for some time after it heals. Bette suggests Vitamin A, bananas, and aloe rubs. Misty's trying to quilt a patch to cover the melted spot on the T-shirt. "Does it hurt a lot?" Misty asks.

"I'm fine," I tell her. Still thinking of the sermon, I suggest instead, "Could we go visit the Children's Museum? I think we need to play a little and forget about the books and marketing and making a bestseller. I need to be a kid again."

"I didn't know you liked kids so much," Kari says.

I shrug. "I miss my class."

"Maybe playing will make our creative juices flow," Bette says, "and we'll be able to come up with something else to make *Sentence* a bestseller."

I frown but don't speak up. I know they mean well, but I'm

beginning to see the futility of pushing fame when fame is really a river that flows more smoothly by itself.

After a quick lunch and a potty break for Ho-Bee we head out, Clint included, taking the Blue Line downtown to the Lincoln Park District where the 7,000 square-foot building blends learning with play. The trip reminds me a bit of Barcelona and Miranda's bandits that were actually my own.

"Do you mind hanging out with all these women?" Kari asks Clint as we buy tickets to go in.

"Naw," he tells her, squeezing her shoulder to him. "I like the odds."

At the museum that towers three stories into the skyline we read about the permanent exhibits and Misty says, "Oh look! They have an exhibit called *Play It Safe*."

"I needed that yesterday," I say, rubbing my aloe-greased stomach.

"They've got a Cubs exhibit?" Clint asks hopefully.

"A talking oven mitt tells kids what to do if there's a fire, so I don't think it's about the Chicago Cubs," Kari says, reading further.

"*Play It Safe* is about danger at home. The talking mitt game is called *Now You're Cooking*," Darlien reads.

"I needed that yesterday too," I say.

We split up and lose ourselves, surrounded by the chatter of children and their caregivers, parents mostly, since it's a Sunday afternoon. Every now and then I notice Clint and Kari in close conversation with a look of longing on Kari's face. I wonder if all this girl time and my staying so long in Chicago might be putting strain on their relationship.

In the *My Museum* section kids take pictures of themselves and plaster them up on a mural while others model with clay. A tongue pinched to the side of a would-be sculptor's mouth reminds me of the really active children I've had in my classroom who often bit their tongue as though doing so helped them sit still and concentrate. I wondered if Ho-Bee might benefit from that insight. Maybe a bone to bite would calm him. He's adjusted to being in his crate whenever I'm gone but once out, he tools around the house like a skateboarder who's been released from a year-long solitary confinement.

I meander deeper into the *My Museum* section. I see Misty at the far side. She waves and returns to her sculpting. The kiosk says the kids might work the clay into something that represents who they are at this time in their life, something that speaks to their uniqueness. I look at the sculptures kids have created and wonder what I'd mold to answer the question "Who are you?" I sit down at the long table, next to Misty, with a cherub wearing rosy cheeks on my other side. The little girl passes me a glob of clay, then returns to what looks like a ballerina. Not bad at all.

"What will you make?" Misty asks. "I'm working on Wonder Woman."

"You are that," I say. "I don't know what to create."

A chameleon.

The thought seems odd to me. Reptiles, though, are able to change colors to fit in. As self-defense. Maybe that is me, rarely taking a risk for love but lately, risking my dignity for ... what? Not for security. I take these humiliating risks for ... fulfillment. I've failed to commit to what I really want yet let myself think that my name "reflected" by a famous person will somehow make me famous. And happy. That wasn't the reason I wrote my first book and it isn't the reason I wrote *Miranda of La Mancha*.

I close my eyes and begin to shape the clay, remembering an email from a fan I read yesterday. It reminds me of why I didn't stay in Spain. My books, the woman said, bring joy to her and her daughter. I need to let my books bring a little joy to me too.

⑥

We stop for ice cream on the way home and back at the condo, Misty asks if I got the letter from Jaime translated. I guess they've been waiting for me to bring it up.

I get the letter out along with the notes I made while Juanita, my third-grade translator, told me what it said. John meanders over to inspect the letter, switches his tail at Ho-Bee who has assumed the throne of my lap. I hear John purr.

"Ok. Here it goes," I say.

"*Although we have nothing in agreement*—he probably means we have nothing in common," I say. "*—It is my wish to convey to you of my great missings of your face in the morning.*"

"Your face in the morning! You didn't ... did you?" Bette whispers.

"Of course not. Never. No. We met for a coffee in the morning, very early, as he had to go out of the city for the golfing competition, ride the train for an hour and a half to get there. The second day he took a cab and I rode with him. He played the same course as Darlien that day, but she started later so it was just the two of us, together."

"But you traveled across Spain on the train," Misty says. "Were you sleeping —"

"I told you, no. I didn't. We didn't. We were in the same berth but another man had gotten there before us. The man was brushing his teeth when Darlien, Jamie, and I came in. I demanded that the men get out of our berth. I didn't realize that Jaime's ticket said the same thing as ours." I remembered feeling both outrage and fear that they'd booked us like that, men and women in the same sleeping car.

"That's the way it's done in Europe," Darlien says.

"Well, that guy, who spoke no Spanish or English, lay all night on the top bunk with his arms across his chest as though prepared for burial. I don't think he moved all night. I know I didn't." I feel my eyes get teary. "I could actually hear Jaime breathing in his sleep in the bunk above me. It was so romantic."

"Until you've heard it for twenty years," Kari says. She laughs. Clint winks at her.

"I don't think I would mind," I say.

"Then why, for heaven's sake, did you come back without him?" Darlien says.

176

"What else does he say?" Kari asks, rescuing me.

Darlien sneezes, three times. "Allergies," she says.

"*I don't understandings why you left without sayings good-bye.*"

"You just left him?" Bette says. "You didn't say good-bye? Where were you?"

"Lisbon. I had to get back."

"Why?"

I consider saying, "Because my ticket home with Darlien flew me out of Spain," but I answer from my heart.

"The children," I say then wish I hadn't.

"Jaime has children? I had no idea," Darlien says.

"No ..." I hesitate, not ready to tell them how children and Jaime are mixed into the reason I came back alone. "The children ... Miranda knew would miss her if she didn't come back to teach them." That was true, too.

"Miranda had a good reason to come back, maybe. She was a teacher, right, hon?" Kari says. "But you don't have any kids, Annie. You aren't a teacher anymore. You're confusing life with art."

"I had my book to finish," I defend. "This book." I point to my manuscript. "They're like children, every one of them."

"Couldn't you have finished the book there?" Misty says. "Isn't that one of the advantages of being a writer, that you can write where you want, when you want, wearing what you want? I mean, you're working on it here in Chicago."

"I have certain rituals that help me focus. I read once that students should study for an exam in the clothes they're going to wear when they take the test, that it'll help them be in the right mind-set for when they take the exam. It's harder to do in a new place."

"But newness can be inspiring too," Kari says. "It can energize us when we can't follow our old routine."

"Stress us, you mean," I say.

"That too, but Orville and Wilbur Wright would never have

gotten off the ground if they hadn't been willing to see things in a new way," Kari adds.

"They got off the ground because their sister did all the cooking for them," Bette says.

"I guess what's most important in my rituals are things I could do anywhere," I say. "I read poetry before I begin and pray that I can 'enter and live my story' and that if I become wealthy because of my work that I'll remember to thank God for it, and if I never gain fame, well, that the work will be enough. But I had to leave Spain and come back home to say it."

"You could have adapted to Barcelona, created new rituals there," Bette says. "As you have here."

"No. I had writing, not just revisions to do."

Kari looks at me through a practiced squint. "There's something here you're not telling us," she says.

I nod agreement. "'I will not go there,' says the cat. 'I will not go there, that is that.'"

Kari harrumphs once, then picks up the letter from me, reads my translation notes made between the lines. "Here's the problem, hon. *I'm coming to America.*'"

"What?" I stand up. "He says he's coming here? I don't remember writing that!"

My heart pounds as I reach for the letter back.

Kari grins. "No, he didn't write that. I thought I'd give you a start. Worked, didn't it?" I calm down. "Here's how he actually finished it, according to Juanita. *I am sorrys I didn't not have chance to show you more of country I love, make you falls in love with it. I thinks you should write to me so we can plan for future.* I wonder if his English is this choppy or it's Juanita's translation."

"Or your own handwritten notes," Darlien says. "I can't read your handwriting half the time."

"Really? When I sign my books people usually comment on how pretty my penmanship is."

"That's because they're looking at it upside down."

"He wrote the letter in Spanish," I say, returning to the issue at hand. "I'm sure it's impeccably written."

"It's clear to me," Misty says, "that he wants a relationship with you of some kind. He wants to see if it will travel, go some place. "

Her words get too close, so I try to change the subject with a word discussion suggesting that "impeccable" has the same rhythm as the word "implacable," a word in Irving's letter. "Irving says he doesn't want to be implacable. I always thought that word meant stubborn."

"I think it means unforgiving. Unbending," Kari says. "That's good, that Irving doesn't want to be unbending. That should give you confidence."

"Except that each of our encounters leaves me thinking him more implacable than the time before. I'm making all the changes. He's saying he doesn't like this or that."

"So defend it," Kari says. "If you feel so strongly about what you've written, say so. Stand up for your story, your children, as you call them."

"You think so?"

"You left behind a true love and you're creating a fool of yourself trying to get Oprah to make your book a bestseller." Kari says.

An audible gasp follows her words. Darlien had said almost the same thing when I dressed up as the cleaning lady.

"You think it's foolish," I say. "You never said that before."

"It might be the smartest thing you've ever done, I have no idea. I only know that you're risking looking pretty crazy for a novel—or one of your children's futures—while at the same time you refuse to take a chance on seeing where a real relation-ship with a flesh and blood guy might actually take you in life. But you said earlier that maybe you should focus on the writing, something you have a little control over," Kari says.

"And we gave you a hard time about that," Misty says. She sounds contrite.

"I'm not putting my energy into the publishing team, the group who puts me into print and makes me what I am. I'm risking that entire relationship. How can I be risky with some things but then ... not?"

"You're stubborn. Implacable," Darlien says. "Just ask me. I'm your older sister. I know." Her smile reduced the sting.

"Did you write back to Jaime?" Misty says. Ever the romantic, she asks if Jaime sent his address.

"Long distance relationships go nowhere," I say. "They're too fatiguing, and one of us would have to make a major life change in order for it to go to the next step. This is an implacable relationship, and it's staying right where it is, one half in the Midwest and the other half in Spain."

"Maybe you ought to talk with a professional about this," Kari says.

"I'm a writer. I'm already in therapy." Kari looks skeptical. "Willa Cather says the stories that engage us as adults are based on experiences we had before we turned fifteen. Writers are always working out those childhood issues, and I thank you very much for buying my books so I can do that. Otherwise I'd have to make a therapy appointment three times a week and pay for it myself."

"We don't buy your books," Darlien says. "You give them to us."

"I don't know, hon. I think you might be making a mistake here. This guy sounds like he could be the real deal. So how does he close?"

"*I knows this is for reals as you Americans say. My sister and mothers knows. They wants me happy. I loves you. You consider again,* Si us plau, *Jaime.*"

He used the English version of "Please" but has left it as *Si us plau,* the Cataluña phrase for "please." In the English, it means a promise, "see us plan." I can hear Jaime saying it when we said goodnight in Lisbon. By the next morning, I was gone following a plan of my own.

Chapter 17

"You go without me," Darlien says on Monday morning. "I'm not feeling all that well. My sinuses are stuffed. Maybe coming down with a cold."

"Oprah has Dr. Oz on lots of times. Maybe today will be that day," Bette says flip-flopping through the kitchen in her robe. "Here, drink some orange juice. What did you have for breakfast?"

"Chocolate."

"Well, that explains a lot."

"Maybe we should all stay home. How valuable will that taping be anyway?" I say. "We'll be in the audience, and I don't think they'll let us get up and move around when they change segments. That would be the only time to hand out a book or say something, and we'd have to behave like protestors to get her attention and they'd surely escort us out."

"Yeah, after the chef fiasco I've been sort of wondering about that myself," Darlien says. She's pouffed her blond hair with her fingers and it looks like it was styled by a professional.

"I hate it that you all came so far and took time off work and away from family, but ..."

"You're not backing out, are you? I mean we've barely gotten started," Misty says. "I got discouraged with my weight training but you guys stood behind me and kept me going."

"I wasn't sure I'd qualify for the International games either," Darlien reminds me. "But you all cheered me on. That's what we do, remember?"

The phone rings then. "It's for you, Annie," Kari says. "Your agent, Randolph. Apparently you haven't been answering your cell phone calls to him or replying to his texts?"

"Hello Randolph. Do you have good news for me from Irving?"

"Not from Irving," he says. "But I've got the answer to our problems! I've got a guy, emigrated from Spain. Cataluña, no less. Isn't that the province of Spain you say your Jaime is from?"

"He's not my Jaime. It's fiction —"

"Yeah, yeah. Anyway, he's game for this." Randolph has pursued the lost boyfriend fiction? "We're going to suggest this reunion thing and I've got that producer hooked in. This guy will tell them of his longing to see you and how you reconnected after being pen pals for years and how at the games you realized you were in love and then he got cold feet and backed out. And now he's wishing he hadn't and you won't talk to him or write back and he's desperate. Isn't this a great plot?"

"It sounds like a *Dr. Phil* show, not something for Oprah. And it's not true, Randolph."

He paused. "That's a great idea, Annie. We could do two hits. Oprah gets him here with you for the reunion and then you tell about your book, how it's really your own story, and then Doctor Phil gets called in so he can do counseling to help you two get together. Shoot, you might even get to be married on television."

"And our divorce will be covered by Judge Judy."

We're creating a terror-vision program.

"All the guy wants is the airfare back to Spain, before the holidays, so he can see his family and stock up on chocolate." Randolph laughs. "Let's get him back there. Meanwhile, he'll write letters to Oprah and send them to his family, who will postmark them from Spain."

"Bette just got a postcard from Spain I mailed to her four months ago," I told him. "So I'm not sure you can count on the mail service supporting this charade with any time accuracy."

"We'll use email then. It'll work, Annie."

"He'll probably get a free trip at my expense and we'll never see him again."

"He left his fiancée there, so he's anxious to go back. And if we buy him a round trip ticket, he can afford to bring her back with him. Think of what we'll be doing for love, Annie. And right before the holidays. Hey, maybe we should target Christmas."

"Look, Randolph. I really need to focus on having a book that Oprah might actually want to endorse if I *do* get her interested. And I'm really trying to get *The Long Bad Sentence* noticed or there might not be a Miranda book at all."

"You have to be inventive, Annie." He sounds pouty.

"My friends have a few tricks up their sleeves that won't require a credit card blowout. The expense of sending this guy back there and back —"

"You just do your thing, Annie." Randolph has perked up. "I'll advance him the plane ticket and help him draft the first letters. We'll go from there. I mean, I've got Oprah's producer interested! We can't back away from that. Change of subject here, have they settled on the title yet? Have you seen the cover?"

"No. Much has yet to be settled, Randolph. That's what I'm trying to tell you. I don't want you to advance the ticket money. I can't afford to pay it back if this doesn't work."

"It'll work. You'll meet new people, have a new experience, what more could you ask for?"

"A bestseller?" I say.

"You have to have faith. Isn't that what you tell me?"

An agent/author relationship is like a marriage. I've only had one agent my entire writing career, which has lasted longer than my first marriage, but it does make me wonder about my ability to take on long-term commitments. Randolph is a good man, I know that. Creative and energetic. A little pushy, but one has to be in this business. He's never been this pushy with me, though, and it makes me a little nervous. Maybe he's losing faith in me too, getting desperate for one last effort before he looks for an author with greater potential. Sometimes I feel like I'm part of a stable of women of negotiable affections, selling my wares to the highest bidder ... agents, publishers. Maybe even readers!

"What does he have in mind?" Kari asks when I hang up.

"It's too bizarre," I say. "You don't want to know."

Neither did I.

⑥

Darlien decides she'll come despite her sneezing. All the way downtown to Harpo Studios where Oprah tapes her show, I think about Jaime's letter and Randolph's plan and where my life is going. Maybe we do need Dr. Phil to help us out; maybe I should fly Jaime here to see if we could make things work.

On the Blue Line I watch people reading books as the train rumbles along. A couple have Nooks or Kindles, and I realize for the first time that without a real book, I can't tell what other people are reading. The book buzz is missing on trains or in airports or on park benches when people read e-books. It's hard to start up a conversation about a title if you can't see what it is. No more romantic encounters on airlines over a shared book. Books hidden inside electronics will make it even harder for me to get the word out about my books.

Misty leans over and points to a black and red hardcover book. "Vampire books are big sellers. Maybe you could put a vampire in the plot somewhere ... make it be the reason Miranda doesn't stay in Spain ... she discovers that Jaime is ... eternal."

"You're kidding, right?"

"An Amish subplot would be better than a vampire," Bette says. "You could put Miranda with a bonnet on her head on the cover and I bet it would sell."

"Maybe I should write a book about an Amish vampire," I say. My friends laugh. "Those books sell because they're well-written," I continue.

"They sell because people talk about the books and tell their

184

friends, don't you think?" Misty says. "That's why you want the person with the most friends to be telling her friends ... and that's Oprah."

"It's the same principle, just with more friends," Darlien says. "Have you talked about the book on your Facebook page?"

Darlien sneezes then and I wonder if she ought to have stayed at home. Maybe all of us. "Will you be all right?" I ask.

She nods. "I should have taken another allergy pill this morning. I think it's that and not a cold."

"It's your terrible diet," Bette tells her.

"Thanks for coming anyway," I say. I squeeze her shoulder and look at her closely. She looks tired. I feel a closeness to her I haven't felt for awhile. Maybe I feel more compassionate when people are vulnerable. Maybe that's why I attach to children so much. Someday I want to talk with her seriously about what happened with her three marriages. Whenever I bring it up, she changes the subject. Avoidance must be a family strategy.

We walk a block from the subway exit and approach the studio.

"Okay," Bette says. "I have a surprise for you all. Close your eyes." We obey. "Put out your hands."

When we open our eyes, each of us is holding what looks like a paperback book with bright lettering that reads *Miranda of La Mancha*.

"It's your book!" Darlien says.

"Not really," Bette says. "I talked with Mavis when I gave her your number, Annie. She told me about the brochures and we decided we could create a cover so that on the elevated or on a bus, we can look like we're reading your book."

I turn the page. It's a Terri Blackstock novel and the new "cover" fits over her book nicely. "You can't open it up for anyone," she says. "It's strictly for promotion. But if the occasion arises, we can raise the books up together and Oprah will see them."

"But we have copies of *The Long Bad Sentence* too," I mention.

"Your Miranda book has more romance, Annie," Misty says. I try not to take that as a critique.

At the studio we show our IDs that have to match our tickets, just like on the airlines. We haven't brought big purses, and I hope if Oprah gives something away today it'll be small enough to fit in a fanny pack. A producer who doesn't look much older than me tells us to use the restroom before we go in to take a seat because if we have to leave during the taping we will not be allowed back in. I remember my last public restroom foray at the television studio, and this time I follow my friends into the aluminum room and no blind man follows us. "It's like being a kid again, going whether we have to or not," Misty says. "No wonder Norton dallies when I send him to go potty. It's on my schedule, not his."

Each booth has its own door all the way to the floor and I'm careful to watch how the lock goes because in Barcelona I couldn't get the lock to unlatch and I had to pound on the door calling for help until someone came to tell me how to unlock it.

We head back out and hear more instructions.

"No pictures," warns the producer with a sheriff-like voice. "Absolutely no photographs with a camera or a cell phone."

"Would we go to photographer jail?" Misty whispers then adds, "She looks too young to be a producer, don't you think?"

"Some people are successful at young ages," I say.

"Turn off all cell phones. No calling out during the show to friends, no texting to say 'I'm with Oprah!' or 'O is Hot!' Not that she isn't. No Twittering. We don't want any cell phone use during the program."

"Who's on the program today?" someone asks.

"Dr. Oz is visiting." A murmur of approval rises through the group. "And we have a few more surprise guests as well."

Darlien sneezes three short blasts the way she always does. "Allergies," she tells the producer and looks shy as she says it.

"Bless you," say a dozen people, including the producer who then says, "What's your name?"

"Darlien France," she says. "I'm not sick. Allergies."

"Get that under control," she tells Darlien, referring to her sneezing; or maybe she's asking her to control us as we're holding our books up with their bright red covers and black lettering.

Misty notices a woman in front of us turn and wave. "I know her," she says. "We competed together. Gosh, she still looks great. She must be in training." She skips ahead to talk to the woman, then heads back. "She's not in training for body building but for a Walk for the Cure. She says it keeps her in shape and gives back to the community. Wow, she looks wonderful."

"So do you," Bette tells her.

"Yeah, with my melting body armor." She rubs at her belly.

"No negative thoughts," I say.

"You're right. Okay but —" Before Misty can continue we move into the auditorium single file and find our seats based on the time of the ticket reservation.

The cavernous room feels warm with the bodies of enthusiasm, all here to see Oprah in person. I wonder how many of them hope to also get her to know their name, to recognize their new business, or to somehow prey on her fame. Darlien sneezes yet another round. Misty holds up her book. Bette settles in but puts the faux book on her lap for all to see.

"This whole idea is senseless," I say. "Darlien's half sick; all of you have been so good about making time to help me. Let's enjoy the show and forget about trying to corral Oprah. Put the books away."

"Don't think negatively, Annie," Darlien says. "Honestly, how you can be so positive with everyone else in your life and yet so down on yourself just amazes me."

"Isn't that the way it is?" A woman sitting in front of us turns to join in our conversation. She looks to be in her fifties, with perfect black hair cut into a gentle page, no flat spot in the back of her head like I always fight. "We can cheer on our friends but not ourselves."

"I guess we all need to be midwives," Bette says.

"I don't think I understand that," the woman says.

I think Bette will tell about the pharaoh's being challenged by the strength in numbers of the midwives but instead she says: "Midwives start cheering for the mother long before the delivery. And when she's shown the ultrasound pictures she doesn't say, 'I can't see a thing in there' or 'I'll wait until the baby is here before I celebrate with you.' No, she celebrates then and again and again at each step of the way."

"Celebrate does mean to do something over and over," I say.

"Yes," the woman says. "That's exactly how we need to be. Maybe Oprah will do a show on midwifing ourselves."

"I'm not sure that's actually a word," I say.

"But I know what you mean," another woman chimes in.

Total strangers are talking to one another like it's a class reunion and we all know each other but have just changed through the years. Darlien chats with a woman next to her. A few other strangers join in to discuss friends they know who are "like your sister," they say, referring to me. "They can't accept their own worthiness," says a grandmotherly type. *Therapy* in the audience.

"You always sweet-talked those preschoolers," Bette says as the woman turns back around. "I was there with you one time when the kids arrived, and you found something wonderful to say to every single child—how one girl fixed her hair so creatively or how one boy remembered to hang up his jacket. If I'd had that kind of cheerful loving experience to begin my day I'd be a grand chef now and not a woman cooking in an assisted living facility."

"I remember how some of those kids had parents who ranted at them all the time, telling them to get up, sit down, come here, don't touch. If the kids had actually listened to them, they might have been warped for life," I say. "Besides, I thought you liked what you do, Bette," I say. Her admission that she feels she is only a woman cooking for the elderly truly surprises me.

"I do. It's just that I thought I'd be a master baker or a master chef by the time I was thirty and that's fast approaching and the seed of my dream hasn't even sprouted."

"Yes it has. You love what you do and your work extends good cheer to others. Isn't that fulfilling enough?"

"Is it for you?"

The sheriff/producer steps on stage, puts her finger to her lips asking for quiet. The lights dim and a sign asks for applause as an announcer gets us settled down. Then Oprah enters, in the flesh, wearing festive sandals, black pants, and a bright red sweater set.

She welcomes us as though we are sitting in her living room, asks if we're cold. A few people say yes. I wonder if they'll turn up the heat for those few, but then several others say they're warm. When Darlien shouts, "Migrate to menopausal climate zones!" Oprah laughs louder than any of us. Her smile seems genuine to me and I think to myself that maybe she's like Albert Schweitzer, who gave up fame to do what he loved; and fame found her because she loves what she does.

"We have Dr. Oz with us today," Oprah says. "And he's brought a very special item he wants to show us to help us take care of ourselves. I need an audience volunteer —"

Fifty hands shoot up before she even finishes.

"Who has allergies." She looks at a card her producer hands her.

"Raise your hand, Darlien," I say. "Dr. Oz is good!"

Misty and Bette stand, Bette pointing at me, Misty at Darlien.

"Sit down," I hiss. "I don't have allergies. Oh, no, she's looking this way!"

"Darlien Finette?" Oprah says. The sheriff/producer has seen her, and when she points our way Darlien begins sneezing again. Oprah motions for Darlien to come up on stage.

"Go, go," I say.

"Take your book with you," Misty whispers.

"You go! This is your chance," Darlien says back to me.

The sheriff/producer is by her chair now, motioning, and

before Darlien can protest again, we push her out into the aisle and she begins to sneeze. "It's either come on up or leave," the producer says. Darlien looks back at me with pleading eyes.

"Better thee than me," I say and mean it.

Oprah chats with people, makes us laugh. Darlien's been taken backstage, we assume. They begin to tape, Dr. Oz enters, and there's a segment on heart disease, the physical kind and not the emotional one. They take a break and Oprah chats with other audience members. Then we see Darlien come on stage wearing a sweater that isn't hers. She isn't carrying any books. She must have been cold. A makeup artist pats Darlien's nose with powder, which only causes more sneezing.

Dr. Oz and Oprah talk as Darlien sits in a chair, her nose as red as Rudolph of reindeer fame.

"Here's our little treasure pot," Dr. Oz comments.

"Are they talking about Darlien?" Bette whispers.

"That thing, on the table. Maybe it's for boiling special herbs," Misty whispers to me.

I don't know what it is and neither does Oprah apparently, as she holds what looks like a genie's lamp. "Maybe Darlien will get to rub it and make a wish," I whisper back.

"Like 'I-wish-my-writer-friend-would-have-a-bestseller,'" Misty says in a zombie voice.

"We take care of our teeth, our hair, our hearts," Dr Oz continues. "This little item from Tibet helps us take care of our noses." Oprah wrinkles her nose at the audience and we laugh. I find myself watching the monitor rather than the real thing in front of me. Darlien sneezes again, two quick bursts. "It's called a neti pot. The poor nose is relegated to sniffing as its claim to fame when it does so much more for us. Our sense of smell gives us such pleasure. Food tastes better because of our noses. Our lives are richer, more fulfilled because of our noses."

Fulfillment as the goal of even noses?

"A good working nose can keep us from getting terrible colds and a number of other health-related problems by keeping our sinuses healthy and clean," Dr Oz continues.

"Do you think you have a cold, Darlien?" Oprah asks.

"No. It's allergies. My friends say I eat poorly," Darlien says.

"Poor nutrition can contribute to colds and stronger reactions to allergens. Let's do a nose cleansing and see if it helps."

The audience murmurs again as Dr. Oz puts a solution of salt and water into the pot and then directs Darlien to lean over a glass bowl on the table, turn her head to the side, and place the long narrow spout into the uppermost nostril. Oprah looks at the audience with that "I don't know about this" look and then we watch as Darlien lifts the pot, sticks the spout in her snout. A universal audience gasp rises when seconds later, like a miniature water fall, the solution pours out through the other nostril and into the bowl. "Eeeyou," Oprah says.

"Put something in one side and it comes out the other side, having done its work in between," Dr. Oz explains."How did it feel?" he asks Darlien.

Darlien straightens her head, sniffs. "Good," she says. "Really good. I had no idea."

"Dog dander is a terrible allergen," Oprah notes. "Do you have a dog, Darlien?"

"I have a dog staying with me this weekend," Darlien says. "I'm visiting my writer sister, Annie Shaw," she says it loudly and distinctly, "and she has a dog. She's written this book called —" She sneezes.

"Time to do it again," Dr. Oz says.

Darlien bends again to her task. She stands and sniffs. "Feels great," she says. "And it'll make food taste better, having sinuses cleaned out?"

"It very well can. See if that next shrimp and pasta salad you eat doesn't make you glad you're alive, with its rich flavor. Aromas will be better too. Your turn, Oprah," Dr. Oz directs then. Darlien looks at me with a shrug. She gave it her best shot. Oprah changes places with Darlien. Dr. Oz puts out a new neti pot. Oprah bends her head as Darlien had. The audience applauds as the solution goes in one side of Oprah's nose and comes out the other.

In and out, just as my name has done in Oprah's ears.

⊚

Everyone in the audience receives neti pots and a book called *The Nose Knows* with the subtitle *Finding Your True Self* written by an author whose name I can't remember. Oprah interviewed him during the second segment of the show and I came away with tons of trivia related to noses but nothing further to get Oprah interested in either my latest or my future title.

Darlien doesn't sneeze even once as we leave the studio and head back to the condo. "I think that thing works," she says.

Back at the condo I tell them of Randolph's plan.

"I think it's probably your best bet," Darlien says. "And revising the manuscript as well as you can."

"Mavis said you were thinking of making a book trailer," Bette says. She tells the others what that is.

"I'm not sure that a prison setting lends itself to a light romantic trailer," I say. "We'd need a cinematographer to convert a dank prison setting into an appealing trailer and frankly, I can't afford it."

"Maybe we'll come up with something else," Misty says. We're packing the neti pots plus their overnight things into Darlien's convertible as they prepare to return to Wisconsin. "Are you sure you don't want to ride back with us to Milwaukee now? You and Randolph can work on that strategy from Milwaukee as easily as Chicago."

"I guess I am imposing longer than I need to," I say. I have Ho-Bee on a leash and he's sniffing oil leaks on the parking garage floor.

"You're fine here as long as you want," Kari assures me. "Dog dander and all."

"I don't think that's what the sneezing was about," Darlien says.

"We've been thinking about getting a dog," Kari says. "It never occurred to me to think about allergies though. Good thing we've had time with Ho-Bee and John to test that out."

"There's no room for me in that car with all of you and John too."

"Well, we have a surprise for you anyway," Bette says. "Something you'll enjoy. You can come home after that. Kari will fill you in."

We say good-bye and wave them off. Ho-Bee barks. I think he's missing John already.

"Oprah heard your name at least," Kari says. She smiles, and we walk with arms around each other's waists back toward their condo, my pet trotting mannerly beside me.

"Didn't change anything though, did it? I'd better get the revisions finished." I bend down to scratch Ho-Bee's ears. "It may be the only way to keep me from having to do what Randolph wants."

"Revision is an interesting word," Kari says as we step off the elevator to her floor.

"You're right," I say, surprised I hadn't remembered that before. "It means 'seeing with new eyes.' That's exactly what I need to do."

Chapter 18

On Tuesday morning, Kari and Clint leave early, but I barely notice as I've been up since three. By noon I've finished four of the scene revisions Irving asked for doing it in a new way, online, and not insisting I have to put them on hard copy in order to work. I'm on a roll. Then I try to attach them to emails so I can get them out of my hair. I have trouble staying online —something that consistently seems to happen when I'm on a deadline. Randolph puts a lot of confidence in the cyber-nature of his scheme, having all those fake emails originate out of Spain, but I wonder. I pad to Kari's computer with my thumb drive, hoping her connection might be better.

I plug in the thumb and am whisked online. I'm composing my email to Irving when a drop-down menu I didn't order appears. Then the cursor floats off the screen like the eyes of a tackled football player right before he goes unconscious. I roll Kari's mouse, right clicking, left clicking. Nothing. The screen is frozen. I turn the computer off, restart it, and punch F10, the code for "if you're having computer problems don't call us …" The GoBack system she has on her computer isn't kicking in, and I can't even highlight one of the four choices for what to do next.

"Ho-Bee, why does this have to happen now, when I'm desperate?" He performs his usual jumping-without-a-trampoline scene when I speak his name, then chases a toy rabbit I toss around the apartment, squeaking it as he brings it to me. I toss it well beyond Kari's frog collection. He's in sight and nowhere near my lingerie or my computer cords, so I'm safe.

I call technical assistance and toss the toy while I'm on hold.

"This-is-Lester-Badge-Number – 3347," a monotone says. "How-can-I-help-you." It's more of a sigh than a question, but he's a real person to talk to and I'm happy. His words sound so flat he might have been speaking through a fast-food order microphone.

"My computer has suddenly started to do these really weird things and I think it might be a bad mouse."

"You-have-a-virus," the monotone sighs.

"I have a virus detector."

"Do-you-use-it."

"Yes. I do. It runs all the time. I'd like to describe the symptoms here and maybe you can tell me if it's the mouse or not." I proceed to tell him about the strange drop-down menus and the floating cursor, and he tells me to shut the computer off and restart it and then highlight number one when that choice comes up. "I've tried that. I can't highlight anything; that's what I'm trying to tell you."

"It-won't-highlight." He's incredulous.

"Right. Or right or left click or even do anything when I touch escape."

Lester-Badge-Number – 3347 remains silent for a minute, then says, "You-see-those-little-feet-on-your-keyboard." *Feet? On my keyboard?* I lift Kari's keyboard and look. I tell him I see them. "Push-them-under-so-your-key-board-is-flat." I do. "Now-stand-up," he says.

"Stand up?"

"Stand-up."

He's going to tell me to jump out the window. "Now-pick-up-the-keyboard." *He's going to have me throw it out the window.* "Hold-it-eighteen-inches-above-the-desk." Is this high tech or elevated tech?

Kari's desk is made of oak. Hard oak.

"Okay," I shout into the phone. I've put it on speaker and

laid it on Kari's desk. "I'm holding it a foot and a half above the desk."

"Now-drop-it."

"Drop it?" I ask, picking up the phone to be sure.

"Yes-drop-the-keyboard."

"All right. I'm going to lay the phone down now," I say.

Am I really this gullible? Is this one of those phone pranks where someone calls, pretending to be from the electric company, and asks if your refrigerator is running and when you check to say it is they laugh back with "well it ran by here a couple of hours ago and we wondered how far it got." *Click.* Yes, I am a victim. Maybe Miranda is really more me than I want to admit. Maybe I am really, really dumb, a raving eleven fifty-nine.

But I called him.

"Okay," I shout, loud enough for Lester-Badge-Number–3347 to hear. "I'm going to drop the keyboard now." I do.

Ho-Bee startles and bounds over to bark at the keyboard lying dead on the desk. I stare at the computer screen. The screen clears and the cursor reappears like an adolescent zipping into the living room when she realizes her parents have arrived home early. The mouse begins to do what I ask it to instead of drifting around as though it were looking for stale cheese.

"It worked!" I shout into the phone I grab. "It must have had a piece of dust in it or something, a bug or dog hair or whatever. You're a genius, Lester, an absolute genius!"

"Is-there-anything-more-I-can-do-for-you."

"No, this is terrific. You must love your work, getting to solve problems every day, helping people move forward with their lives!"

"Is-there-anything-else."

"What? No. I'm so grateful. Thank you so much."

"This-is-Lester-Badge-Number–3347-have-a-nice-day," he says and we are disconnected.

I finish sending the revisions via attachment, pick up my

other emails while I'm at it, and answer them, still chuckling about such a primitive response to such a technological break-through. A piece of dust, a dog hair, such a little thing to stall the complicated tech world. I guess I could have texted Kari and gotten her help, but who would have suggested dropping the keyboard as a way to unstick it?

"I don't know, Ho-Bee," I tell the dog as I pat him. "Here I am, trying to make something even less predictable than a com-puter work, get myself a bestseller." I shake my head. It's such a long shot. I push the "home" button to go back to the begin-ning of the document I'd written, and it reminds me of why I'm doing this. What was my intention, my attitude, my purpose in all this? On the screen "home" stares at me. In the drop-down file next to it is "refresh," where I get to go back without losing my place.

That's what I need to do to find my way home. I need to refresh. I just don't know how.

⑥

Kari arrives home with new first aid. She spreads bag balm on my still-red belly wound. "Now don't turn your nose up at my ministrations, hon," she says. "My mama swears by bag balm. Yours probably does too."

"She uses it as hand cream," I say. "I can't get the scent of a cow's udder from my nose when I smell that stuff."

"Ho-Bee likes it," Kari says. The dog sniffs, then does a little dance on his hind legs, runs back, sniffs, then dances again. I can almost see him in a little tutu wearing a cap; he keeps in such perfect rhythm to "Who Let the Dogs Out" blasting from the CD player. "Shoot, you could get him as a guest on Letter-man, he's that entertaining," Kari says.

"You think so? Should I try?"

"I'm kidding," she tells me. "I think we've figured out that getting connected to celebrities isn't that easy or worthwhile."

"But celebrity access feeds the fantasy that once one writes a book, all doors to fame and fortune will open. In reality, those doors are ten feet thick and can only be opened from the inside or by divine intervention," I say.

Kari grabs beef jerky Misty has left behind and begins to chew. "Clint's at a friend's watching NASCAR reruns tonight,"she says. "So this is a perfect time for us to sit and assess. I do have that surprise that Bette mentioned before they left." She wears hoop earrings that have gone out of style but she claims keep mosquitoes from her ears. Little clinks of metal fill the room as she curls herself up on the couch. "The girls located one of Oprah's favorite massage therapists," Kari says. "Got her address right here." She hands me a sticky note with an address on it. "We pitched in to pay for a massage. I've made an appointment for you for tomorrow afternoon. It's one more shot to get your name before Oprah, and if it doesn't work at least you'll have a relaxing afternoon." We watch a movie together, then I go to bed. Three o'clock in the morning will come early.

⑥

Chapter Twelve:
Miranda Meets Her Match in La Mancha

They danced the flamenco; or at least Jaime danced. Miranda clapped and couldn't keep her feet from tapping. All around them people moved as though consumed by the music, while Jaime danced with his sister, his body an art form, studied and true.

They'd spent four days together — nearly every hour when he wasn't in competition or they were sleeping, separately, though for only a few hours each night. They dined at one o'clock in the morning sometimes and never considered an evening meal before nine when Barcelona seemed to come alive. Hand in hand, they walked the famous Ramblas flower shops where paintings on sidewalks spoke of color and life, funny toys spun from tent awnings, and musicians entertained while mimes dressed like robots moved only with a coin dropped into a tin cup they held. Miranda laughed as she hadn't for weeks, months maybe. "The pick-pockets, they train here. I . . . ah . . . protect you," Jaime said, pulling her closer.

In the daytime, now that his competitions were completed, Jaime showed her the sites that mattered most to him. The old underground Roman city being restored. The oldest candle shop in Barcelona. The cathedrals.

At the oldest cathedral in the city, Miranda bought a shawl so her bare arms and her head would be covered in this sacred place. Incense and the scent of wax flooded over them as they strolled through the chambers and chapels, their feet shuffling on the tile floor. At the far end, a tiny elevator took them to the rooftop, where they stepped out to the serenade of pigeons' wings. They walked the catwalks while Miranda fanned herself against the heat with her black Spanish-lace fan. She took a photo of the guard asleep in his chair, with Jaime standing over him holding two fingers up over the back of his head. Pigeons cooed and waddled along the tiles and they looked out over the city, over the bay, the blue, blue Mediterranean Sea, and it was there while Miranda held the black lace fan, Jaime stilled her movements. He gazed into her eyes and said in practiced English, "As blue as the sea. I sink into your eyes." And then he kissed her.

Miranda disappeared in his embrace, her whole being lost definition. She thought that she might faint, a good sturdy girl from Wisconsin, who had never fainted in her life. She could have stayed within his kiss forever.

Around them, tourists applauded and cheered and she pushed back from him, lightly, embarrassed as she lowered her dark eyes. She straightened her blue tank top, yanked at the shawl that had slid to their feet, then "pulled herself together," never before realizing how descriptive that phrase could be.

"My family goes to Italy during August," Jaime told her.

"Much of Barcelona goes to Italy, to Florence. You ... goes with us this year, si?"

"I ... can't," Miranda told him as he led her back to await the elevator to take them down. Even the little bit of shade provided by the cornerstones helped cool her flushed face. "I ... have to get back."

"Your sister says you will stay another week. It is arranged, she says. You goes to Madrid and Lisbon. You goes with me to Florence instead, si?"

"No. I —"

"Give me one reasons why not?" Jaime said as the elevator disgorged eight more tourists and prepared to take another load down. In the presence of six others on the jerky elevator, Miranda had time to be still and to worry more about the safety of riding this old contraption than the risk of what this man had just offered. She needed more time to consider. His kiss befuddled. Now the heat of his hand at her back threatened to melt her.

Belle conspired against her. Her sister was a master of accommodation, urging her to go with him. "He'll have his sister and mother along. How much more chaperoned than that can you get?" Belle asked her back at the hotel. "Come back to Lisbon, and we'll fly home together from there."

All the words Miranda could think of sank in the memory of Jaime's eyes, the celestial quality of his kiss.

And so she'd gone, stepped out alone without her sister, and entered into a new family in Florence whose members danced the flamenco now while Miranda stood and watched. It was what she did best, she realized. Watch, rather than enter in.

⑥

"Miss Shaw." My mind is wandering as I reread what I've written.

"Please, call me Annie," I tell Irving. I've initiated the call this time about the last revision that had catapulted a "Not

Workable!" response from him by email. This whole business is getting so dicey that I'm considering flying out to Denver to work these issues out in person. I'm ready to take a job at Taco True so I'll have a life free of stress and a steady paycheck, however small it is. Maybe I can work at the microphone, where it won't matter if no one understands me, so long as I can understand them. There's an opening at a Taco True in Manhattan, according to Randolph, who insisted that I call Irving.

I have to bite the bull by the horns. Or something like that.

"I really want to work these details out and, um, find a way to feel as though I'm on the right track. It must be very frustrating for you," I add, remembering my class in negotiation I'd taken as research for an earlier book. For those who feel like victims because others complain they're too strong, too aggressive, too overbearing, well, they have two choices: to increase their curiosity about the other person making them crazy with their criticisms; or increase their compassion, both for that accuser and for themselves. I don't have much confidence in increasing compassion for myself, but I do want to feel better about Irving's implacable approach. Why is it that our interactions are so fractious?

"What must be frustrating for me?" Irving asks.

"Oh, moving to Denver and having new colleagues and new authors to deal with," I say. "I'm sorry to be adding to that frustration."

Surprisingly, he laughs. "There are a few frustrations, that's certain, but it's part of the job, Annie. No, my hope is that the rat studies about brain-cell growth are accurate."

"What studies are those?" I say. *Rat studies? He likes rat studies?*

"Even old rats, when they are given new mazes to learn, actually grow new brain cells."

"Even old rats. I like that idea. So there's hope for me."

He must be much closer to retirement than I realize. I resist the desire to ask how old he is, but I add ten years to him. He has to be close to sixty if he's worried about old rats. Has Irving told me that about himself, that he's old?

"My favorite rat study is the one on blood pressure," I hear myself say.

"I'm unfamiliar with that," he says, his voice curious, almost friendly.

"If a rat from the same genetic or familial line is placed into a cage with rats of that family, the first rat's blood pressure actually goes down."

"Remarkable."

"Rats from other genetic lines don't make any change at all in blood pressure. I think it might go up, all those strange rats running around."

"I wonder how they get the blood pressure cuffs on those little rat arms," Irving says, and we both laugh.

Maybe I don't need to fly out there to work this out.

"I'm glad you've called," he says, all serious now again. "I'm scheduled to call you about an editorial decision made here earlier this week." He clears his throat. "We've decided to delay the publication date of *Bells of Barcelona* —"

"You've finalized that title?"

"What? No. That's the working title. Different from yours, I know. That's one of the reasons why we've decided to delay. Sales is uncomfortable with the progress of the work. We won't be able to make reader copies available to the publisher's reps in time for pre-promotion, since we've gone past the production deadline. I should have pressed you more, but I thought we had some wiggle room in the calendar. We don't. So we're pushing it back to a January release ... a year from this January."

"But —"

"I realize January is not an author's most favorite time."

"Hello. Even bookstore buyers are on reading overload in January."

"Yes, but they're all on vacation in Hawaii and take a good book with them, so it's not such a bad time for a release. I'm sure it will work out. It'll give us more time to nip and tuck these editorial issues; perhaps allow you time to work with a book doctor."

My heart leaps up and down like Ho-Bee lunging for Kari's glass frogs. A book doctor! Is the manuscript as ill as that?

"I actually called to tell you that I'm coming to Denver next week," I blurt. "On other business," I add. I can't let him know how desperate I am. "I hoped you might fit me into your busy schedule so we could resolve these editorial issues face-to-face. Maybe I could even meet with Sales and Marketing and Design, to ease their worries and help move us forward."

"I don't know ... I have the time, but I think we might be a little too far down the track to turn the train back."

"On the other hand, I could use some new brain-cell growth," I say cheerfully, thinking of those challenged rats. "Couldn't you?"

He chuckles. "I've stress enough," he says, "that's certain. But it might just be a good way to address this challenge. Let me check the team's schedule and I'll get back to you."

I need a rat of my lineage to lower my blood pressure.

I'd better call my mother.

Chapter 19

*"Fame —
the perfume of heroic deeds."*
Plato

"How are you, Mom? How's Daddy?" I'm on my cell phone, walking Ho-Bee. Walking calms me down. Of late, Clint's been taking Ho-Bee for walks, says he likes the exercise as much as the dog, but I see how my walking him is good for me.

"Oh, just fine," my mom says. "Your father finally got a hearing aid."

"That's good news," I say, already glad I've called to talk about something other than my need for a book doctor.

"It surely is. Last week he finally embarrassed himself into getting a hearing check. He always said he could pretty well fake his way by watching people's mouths when they talk and responding on some little piece of information that he heard even if he didn't get it all. Sometimes people look at him strangely and then he knows he hasn't gotten it. On the phone, he really gets confused."

"So what did he mishear?"

"His friend Fred was telling him a joke. You know how your father loves jokes that make third-graders laugh. Anyway, he apparently asked Fred where he'd heard all those jokes and Fred said 'Joe Cosmosis.' 'Joe Cosmosis?' your father asks him. 'Who's that?' 'Who's who?' Fred says, and they go back and forth until I take the phone and find out he's not saying someone's name. He was saying he learned the jokes through 'joke osmosis.' Well, now when Fred calls, he asks for Joe Cosmosis, so your father has gotten hearing aids."

"I'm glad for us all," I say.

"Have you written back to that nice boy from Spain?" my mother says, changing the subject with the speed of a preschooler heading to the snack table after recess.

"He lives a very dangerous life, Mom. He never knows when he goes out to work what he'll encounter. He could easily die. It's such a high-risk profession, being a policeman."

"What's that got to do with your writing to him or not to see if you can work things out? I can hear that organic clock ticking from here. You should write to encourage a man with such a dangerous profession."

"Things are pretty stressed with my book right now," I say.

"Maybe you should set it aside for a time, pursue this interest with your Spanish fellow. Maybe the trouble with your writing is meant to be. I've never believed in coincidence."

"Success is planning and readiness meeting up with opportunity."

"I don't remember that Proverb. Where is it?"

"Oprah," I say. "What's this got to do with Dad's hearing? That's what we were talking about." I'm annoyed now. I can see why my dad prefers the subjects of fiber and flow: They keep the rest of us from talking about something more painful. "How's his fiber intake?" I decide to change the subject but my mother makes another connection.

"Oh, that's better. He uses stool softeners and his friend told him that they can help melt ear wax that will improve his hearing."

"Taking those pills will melt wax?" Who knew?

"Well, not taking them, silly," my mother says. "Breaking the pill and putting it in your ear will do that."

She goes on to fill me in on news about my aunts and uncles, then reminds me once more of her current concern. "You write to that boy. You've wasted time enough. I never will be a grand-mother at this rate."

⑥

My Visa is maxed out with the plane fare to Denver. I try to pay my cards at the end of each month to avoid interest rates to match Argentina's, but that's all slipped away with my Bestseller Challenge. Customer service will be calling soon asking if the card is still in my possession since my "spending habits" have recently changed. I'm stealing my own identity, spending money like I have some.

But today, I'm looking forward to the gift of a massage. I've promised Kari I'll relax and not feel I've failed if nothing Oprah comes my way as a result of the massage. I can use the rest. The plane fare to Denver and repaying Randolph to bring his Jaime in from Spain weigh heavily. I put the brochure printing costs on the card too, and I'll have to take a cash advance to put into my checking account so I can make a payment on the Visa and pay the damages to the pet salon. I'm robbing Annie to pay for *Miranda*'s voracious appetite.

I drive Kari and Clint's car on the side streets to the spa, avoiding the Dan Ryan Expressway. I haven't driven much in the past few years, but, like milking a cow, driving a car is difficult to forget. It's early afternoon but already the rush hour traffic threatens. On impulse, I pull into a station with a car wash and client-operated car vacuums. Ho-Bee's presence in the car from time to time has changed Kari's "new car" scent. A good wash couldn't hurt, parked next to the Lexuses and Corvettes I expect to find in the spa lot, and it will be a nice treat for my cousin.

After the wash, I vacuum. Up under the seat I find a broken pen, a grocery receipt, and a surprise. Kari is apparently willing to take a risk. I put the unopened pregnancy test back under the seat, and then with my four last quarters, pick out "sweet raspberry" aroma from the scent wand choices. The directions say to place the wand under the car seat and spray.

I do.

Sweet raspberry in that concentration brings a funeral home to mind with all those sweet-smelling flowers. I pull the scent wand back. It catches under the car seat, breaking off. Plumes of scent roll out, along with liquid that soaks like blood into the carpet while I look for an emergency shutoff button. There is none. I pull the pregnancy test out so it won't be ruined. By the time I get the scent wand to stop spraying, the smell is worse than if Ho-Bee had eaten sweet raspberry and then chucked it up. If Kari does get pregnant, she'll have morning sickness even at night when she steps into this car.

I smell like regurgitated formaldehyde myself. No heroic deeds, no perfume.

I inform the attendant of the damage and he says it isn't my fault! Perhaps my luck is changing. He replaces the nozzle and steps away from me and my car, covering his nose. All is well. For him.

I wish I'd picked lemon or even new-car scent, which was one of the choices. I roll the windows down and I drive toward the spa, appreciating the big-city smells of diesel and hot tar and dirt that can only be found in the heart of Chicago.

There must be something I can do to reduce this scent dripping on me before I enter the pricey spa.

Coffee grounds! My mother's told me that freshly ground coffee beans can cancel out any bad car smell made by a dog's deposit or driving over roadkill. I swing into a grocery store, run to the coffee section, ignoring the wrinkled noses I leave behind, and buy a bag of coffee beans and grind them. Back in the car, I open it and inhale like the oxygen masks have just dropped down in an airplane. Breathe deep. I set it on the console between the seats, back out, and promptly knock the bag over with my elbow.

I'll need to vacuum again after my massage before heading back to Kari and Clint's. "Miss Klutz," I say to the ground beans, some of which I notice are soaking up sweet raspberry in

207

the carpet. With me around to spill things, Kari and Clint have a built-in training school for the presence of infants. Considering that pregnancy test, children might be Kari's next goal. I feel an ache, wishing it might be mine.

⑥

Oprah has her own personal massage therapist now, but once upon a time this woman spread oils and scents on Oprah's back. Now she's gone on to have her own spa. Oprah's spun off a lot of independent business people. She doesn't hoard her influence, which is nice, I think.

I arrive in a high-design reception room decorated in beiges and whites and sand tones with several ergonomic non-gravity chairs placed in a semi-circle around a steaming pool. The hostess wears a puzzled frown as she sniffs the air.

"The latest fragrance from France," I suggest. Coffee mixed with strawberry.

"Distinctive," she says.

Candles burn on a Chippendale table where two women dressed in white hover behind the scheduling altar. They speak in hushed tones, find my name, and suggest I wait in one of the far chairs.

I feel dizzy and nearly trip over a padded stool and wonder if the heavy car wash scent causes vertigo. I settle into the comfortable chair and put a copy of *Sentence* on the smoked-glass end table covered with magazines about spas. Another hostess enters and says, "Oh, is this your book? Better take it with you." She hands it to me before I can protest, then offers a brief orientation. I follow her into a suite with a massage table and small stool on wheels parked beside a dressing room. It isn't all that different from Élan-Canine's décor. *This must be so expensive.*

"Your therapist is Clare," the hostess says. "She'll be in shortly, but you have a book to read while you wait." She tips her head to read the title. "I've never heard of that author. Is she any good?"

"I'm her," I say.

"Really? How much did you have to pay to get it published?"

"Well, actually, the publisher paid me."

"Really. I thought they only did that for celebrities. I've always wanted to write a book, but I thought I'd have to be famous for anyone to pay attention. Huh!" she says. She wiggles her nose. "I'll have to ask Clare to tone down that raspberry scent. It's a little strong, don't you think?" She leaves before I can answer.

Floor-to-ceiling windows line the outside walls and overlook Lake Michigan, an absolutely stunning blue on this October afternoon as viewed from the seventeenth floor. Following written directions, I strip down, take a quick shower in a stainless steel tube in the corner, then wrap the thick white Turkish towel around me and lay on the table, stomach down, face pushed into the oval face hole. My tummy stings a bit, but I listen to the music and wish I could relax enough to fall asleep, forget about all things Oprah and bestselling.

"Annie Shaw!"

I startle up to see a woman with a name tag reading "Clare" who has a voice like a drill sergeant and close-cropped hair that smoothes around her head like the rubber bathing cap I've seen my mother wear in old photos. According to her silver badge, Clare's Croatian. She must have worked for a cruise spa at one time.

"I give you eternal face and body massage therapy today. Yes." I have to listen carefully to what she tells me, with her thick inflection applied to American speech and my tendency to make up words on my own. She shoots her words like bullets.

"Yes," I agree, nodding my head. *Anything she says I'll agree to.*

"Every day," she says as she oils my feet, my calves, my buttocks, and back. "Use every day. Don' wait until needed. Use every day." The oil smells divine.

She has wide hands, strong fingers, and she rubs the cellulite lotion into my foot calluses as she swathes my feet in oil.

The scent of pine and rosemary and lavender wafts through the room, taking out the sick car scent I brought in.

She has me turn over, soft Egyptian cotton sheet still discreetly covering my tender mid-section, while I imagine some kind of entrée into the Oprah subject.

"You use Botox? Yes?" She pulls at the flesh of my forehead now, taps my plump lower lip.

"No," I say. "Never Botox injections." I can imagine some unhappy man at a marketing meeting asking, "What could we tell women that would make them willing to shoot poison into their systems? Oh, I have it; let's tell them they'll be more beautiful!" Or I wonder about that other oddity of science: they can invent a telescope that can see into galaxies a million miles away, but are still unable to design an x-ray machine that can see through the density of a woman's breast without squeezing it to the thickness of a toothpick during a mammogram."

Clare stops massaging and stares. Perhaps I've rambled on.

"Use this oil." She points to the blue bottle brand. "Every day." She reaches for my arm, lifts it, and her eyes shift to the extra skin hanging like pancakes but still attached to my arms. "Don' wait," she says. "Use every day. Here too." She proceeds to put oil on my swaying underarm flab.

"Does Oprah use that oil?" I ask.

She turns silent and stiff. "You quiet now while I give massage. No more talk."

The next hour is all music, muscle, and oil as Clare occasionally sits on the wheeled chair, sliding around to massage my scalp, each arm and fingers, legs and heels. She gives special attention to my heels.

I take in the nurture and imagine a life where such massages are frequent and I have enough money to pay for them myself after paying for my children's shoes, dental appointments, and pediatrician appointments. A memory of the last argument between Stuart and me before I filed for divorce floats up. He'd spent what we'd been saving for a visit to a fertility specialist on a series of massages for his sciatica. "You wouldn't want me to be in pain, would you?" he'd said. "We can keep trying things on our own for the … other. We can save enough up to go to that doctor later if we need to. It's not like you're in pain."

Stuart has no idea what pain looks like on someone other than himself.

At the end of the massage, Clare talks again. She talks about the oils and lotions and whatnots that I really ought to invest in. She rolls on that little stool and picks up different jars as she speaks.

"I understand you are Oprah's favorite therapist," I say. "Does she use these? Do you ever —"

"Buy," she says, pushing the brochure at me. "Good for you. No more Oprah talk."

Oprah certainly inspires loyalty, even when people no longer work for her. I buy milk bath ($55), refreshing gel ($47), body scrub ($35), stress-free body oil ($65), and a back brush made in Germany of cactus spine. I wonder what part of Germany produces cacti.

"Includes spray for bristles," Clare says when I choke at the price of the brush moisturizer ($17.50). "Very good deal. Very good. Spray once a week with this to keep bristles soft," she says. "Once a week." She uses the spray bottle as her power pointer. "Use brush every day on dry skin, before shower. Every day. Don —"

"I know," I say. "Don't wait until I need it."

Clare smiles. Her voice softens. "You deserve good things for your body. Take away stress."

This visit has added to my stress with my consumption of lotions. My friends must have spent nearly two hundred dollars to get this woman's time. I've added another one hundred fifty before the tip, and I have yet to make any sort of link with Oprah or suggest my book lying there on the shelf might be of interest to either woman. Maybe my friends just wanted me to relax.

"Your tension stays in your feet," Clare says.

"Really?"

"You do foot soaks. Every day now."

"I have a little tension in my life," I say.

She pats her thighs. "We have program for you. Oprah likes this program. Good for cellulite. Ionithermie algae-detox."

Oprah in detox? No, her cellulite is in detox!

"Oprah likes it? She comes here for treatments?" I say, as casually as I can.

She scowls as though she knows she shouldn't have said Oprah's name. "Breaks down toxins," Clare says. She pats her hips, thighs, and abdomen. "All covered in algae mask with electrodes. Very good, very good. I show you video, how it works."

"And Oprah does this . . . here? Might I know when?" I hand her a fifty-dollar bill. I feel like slime, treading on this woman's loyalty. I have to take the chance. My friends have invested in me.

Clare looks at the money. "I cannot say when."

"Can you get me in?" I say. "Maybe on the treatment bed next to hers?" I tip her wildly as I say it, add a second fifty, barely able to hang onto my purse, as oiled as my skin is. I'm holding my towel up with my arm across my chest. "All you'd have to do is call me when she's scheduled." I hand her my oil-smudged card.

Clare takes my card but lets the cash sit at the end of the table. She stares at me and I can tell that she's considering my request. She steps toward the appointment altar, and just before she opens the door she says, "You dress. I see what I can do."

Why her words make me giddy with excitement, I don't know. I'm broke, so broke. I'll probably have to find a day job within weeks, my book deal is nearly shipwrecked on the sharp rocks of editorial, and my love life has an anchor I'm pulling at to set myself adrift.

But maybe this time next week I'll be lying next to Oprah, on a massage table, being detoxed of cellulite. Surely in that hour and a half I can tell Oprah about my prison romance or Miranda's plight.

I toss the towel so I can dress while my mind does happy dancing with my anticipated success. The view is still glorious through the full-length windows as I reach for the stool Clare used to glide around my table while she worked on my pores.

But my well-oiled bottom doesn't stick well to the chair. Before I square myself on the stool it squirts out from under me like a plastic donut float at the swimming pool. I land with a hard thump on my bottom and hear the stool go into orbit like an airborne skateboard. Twisting like a quarterback to see if the pass has been caught, I see the stool's still flying.

In slow motion, I watch as it soars toward the window.

I hear the shattering sound as the floor-to-ceiling window suddenly resembles snowflakes held together but stuck around one fat chair impaled within them.

I'll be hearing from the massage therapist, I'm sure. And another insurance company. They'll know my name. I kiss any cellulite detox time with fame good-bye.

From: Website Contact Form
To: Annie Shaw
Name: Mrs. Sylvia Cruces
SCruces@wecleanwell.net

My son, Salvador, came with me when I work at Capital Centre Shopping Center in Shorewood last summer. He is eight and not much interested in school. But he visits your book table at the Books in a Barrel bookstore and you listen to him. He tells you stories and you help him write them down. I know you were busy signing many books you've written but you took time to listen to him. I write to tell you how grateful I am. He tells me that passion means to feel deep and then he has me write that he is passionate about his dog, his bicycle, his little sister, and his family. He tells me that if we have to move that he will take with him the smell of his dog after he's been swimming in Lake Michigan. He now writes stories at home with my help about his day. His father is learning English and he helps him write stories too. I am United States citizen and my husband takes classes. Salvador has more interest in school and he makes up stories of what he will be when he grows up. I don't let him read your books but I read them. I like *The Long Bad Sentence* because it reminds me to work hard and to help my family gain education so they never end up on such a place, even if the nurse and the guard find romance there. Thank you for taking time with my son. We are so proud of him and how he wants to be a writer like you. Thank you.

Sincerely, Mrs. Sylvia Cruces

Chapter 20

Northwest Airlines flies nonstop to Denver, and I book it even though American Airlines is the "official airline of the Oprah Winfrey Show." I plan to leave on Thursday. I check my list. Have I done all I'm willing to do to make my latest book a bestseller? Maybe I can pretend to be a linen representative. Bette says when Oprah finally realized her wealth she surrounded herself with lush linens from around the world. She's passionate about them. But she probably already has what she needs and I couldn't afford to buy any to use as my "stock" to pitch her with anyway. Riding a bicycle through the hallways of her studio shouting, "telegram for Miss Winfrey" and handing her my book in a box wrapped like high-end chocolate doesn't seem like the greatest idea either. I've run out of ideas. Maybe Randolph's scheme is my last resort, that, and salvaging *Miranda*. I hope to mold the relationship with Irving into something long-term at Ardor Publishing. I have to get him to sign off on this book, authorize the next portion of the advance, and approve my idea for the next one. "I can do all things," I remind myself. Or at least God can.

Ho-Bee will stay with Kari and Clint as I can get a cheaper round-trip ticket and fly back into Chicago. Then with success on my trail, I'll hop the bus with Ho-Bee and head home. I'll miss my royal, loyal pal Ho-Bee while I'm gone. "At least wanting a bestseller brought you to me." I nuzzle his neck.

"John's less lonely here," Bette tells me when I call to let her know of my plans. She's taken John to her own apartment.

"People say cats are independent souls but I think they're closet romantics. They don't want to admit they need other people but they start acting strange when they're alone too long."

"I always left the radio on for him."

"I know, but it's hard to curl up with a radio. This way, if the power goes down, he'll be in a climate controlled environment with a radio, CD player, whatever a cat of his culture likes."

"Maybe I should have leased out my apartment for three months. I'd have saved some money," I say.

"You're certainly obsessed with money, these days," Bette says. "I remember when you lived to write. Now it seems like you write to live. That wasn't part of our bestseller goal."

"'I will not go there,' says the cat. 'I will not go there, that is that!'"

Bette laughs. "Ok, so don't think about it." I wish I could.

"Is John coughing up fewer bezoars?" I ask.

"Haven't seen any this week."

"Good. I've been so absorbed in all this, in the plight of my life and how broke I am that I haven't kept up well with you or John or anyone. I feel so self-centered. You know, I was a cellulite bump away from actually, maybe, if all worked out well, getting to meet Oprah. My oiled body betrayed me." I ended up with a huge black and blue bruise and my muscles tensed back up like I'd climbed Mt. Everest, but I don't tell Bette that. I don't want my pals to think me ungrateful for gifting me with the massage. "I have a lot of foot treatment stuff I bought. When I get back, we'll have a foot soaking party, a small thank you for paying for the massage. Meanwhile, I use it 'everyday' as I was told by the massage therapist. 'Don' wait. Every day,'" I say, as Croatian as I can.

"You could chuck it all and go back to Spain, Annie."

"I don't think Jaime really meant to suggest that we could somehow work things out. Nothing has changed from when I left. And besides, my translator was only eleven. She probably got it wrong."

"But Kari read it too and what he said wasn't just an offer, Annie. It's a promise."

"You're right. Publishers make offers. Agents make offers. Publicists make offers."

"They make promises, too. Just as lovers do. Along with commitments."

"He was never my lover," I say. "We never—"

"You know what I mean. He introduced you to his mother, for heaven's sake. And his sister. He's serious."

"I'm not."

"And the question is ... why not?"

I can't answer her. I think of the chameleon I made at the Children's Museum and I think I might be seeing with new eyes.

Bette sighs. "Well, try to keep in mind that if things don't go exactly the way you want in Denver that you still have other options."

"I'm not going back to Spain, Bette—"

"Other financial options. You have two bedrooms. You could always sublet your office to a roommate to help pay the bills. I know a couple of people at work who might be interested. Maybe the newlyweds your agent is uniting will need a place to live for awhile."

"Very funny. Subletting to a total stranger won't be my first choice for getting out of debt," I say, "but I appreciate your effort to strategize."

"You can always get clear about what matters—"

"—Have the courage to act on that."

"Bingo," she says and I can see her pointing her finger at me long distance.

We finish talking about the bills. She gets me up to date on the Sunday school kids. She's thinking of signing up for an art class at the college. "Oh, and your lawn mowing kid asked for a final payment. I guess you forgot about him." I had. "See you when you get back," she signs off cheerfully.

Ho-Bee has a supply of food and a new pillow in his kennel

where he'll stay while Clint and Kari work. Kari's agreed to take him for a walk twice a day and I've provided her with pooper-scooper items to finish up with. I'm set to go west and meet the maker—or breaker of my career.

"Maybe you should fly to Spain when you finish meeting with your editor," Kari suggests as she drives me to the airport. "To find out if you came home when maybe you should have remained. Maybe all this misery with your writing, something that used to give you so much joy, is really part of a larger plan. A divine intervention."

"It would take that kind of intervention for me to fly back to Spain," I say. "I made a choice. It's over for Jaime and me. It was then and still is. I have a book to finish and a career needing a major fire built beneath it. No more kindling and that's that."

On the plane, I sit next to a man who, after we exchange stories about airline travel and comment on our occupations, tells me that he's always wanted to write a book.

"Good for you," I say and mean it. "I think people doing research on bezoars would have interesting stories to tell." *Is it coincidence that I actually know what a bezoar is?* That bit of knowledge impresses him.

"It's quite a fascinating research project and I plan to work that in, what composes hair balls in cats and how to diminish them. It's all that licking that does it. All that self-indulgent grooming cats are known for makes their hair roll into a ball that can actually choke them."

"Imagine getting choked by self-absorption," I say. "I heard that's how people catch peacocks, too, by putting out a mirror. The peacocks can't pass by without preening in front of it. Gives their keepers time to throw a net over them. Vanity," I say. Then think, "Not unlike humans, I suppose." I suffer from a mental health disorder I've decided: It's either metaphormosis, seeing metaphors everywhere. Or maybe it's metamorphosis, a disease of the literary mind that is forever changing into something different. "Bezoars are mostly composed of fats, right?"

"Yes," he says, eyebrows lifting. "How is it that you're aware of the composition of bezoars?"

"It was in the University of Wisconsin Alumni magazine. That's where I read it. Might have been an article you wrote."

His enthusiasm increases. "Cat food companies are barking at our door, so they can configure new formulas that will decrease bezoar production."

"Have they thought of creating canine cuisine dishes? I know this chef who—"

"My story wouldn't really be about the hairballs so much as the cats we use for the research. Nothing harmful," he says aware that I might be an animal activist with so much inner knowledge of a fur ball. "Our cats get to eat food and have any bezoars dissected. But back to my book: I could create this character that doesn't like cats but gets involved in research with them," he continues. "The researcher studies the contents and writes it all down noting changes in the cat's behavior as well. I think it could be riveting."

"Riveting." I agree though what rivets me at that moment are engine sounds. We're seated right over the wing and after we'd taxied out and been given the all clear to take off, my knuckles grip the seat.

"First flight?" he says.

I shake my head, no. "Eighty percent of airplane accidents occur on take-off and landing," I say. "It's the most dangerous time."

"I suppose that's true in research too," he says. "Setting up the study and drawing conclusions are the hard parts. Plugging along in the middle, that takes perseverance and maybe a little bit of faith."

"Not unlike writing … and life," I venture and suck in a deep breath as the plane lifts into flight. To keep myself distracted during the climb out I say, "You could become the *Murder, She*

Wrote of the twenty-first century with a whole series of stories with your crime fighting researcher and his cat. Publishers like series works. Call it *Bezoars Galore*."

He laughs. "So tell me about the book you're reading." He points to the mock up I'm carrying, the one Misty had made.

"This is a promotional piece for my next book."

"How did you go about getting it published? Do I need an agent? I mean, can you get published without an agent?"

"With brute force and awkwardness," I say. "I'll give you the name of mine if you'd like. He's a good judge of ideas. If he likes yours, he might take you on."

He pushes his black-rimmed glasses up against his nose. "Do you mind my pumping you like this? I've never met a real author before."

"It's fine," I say. I write Randolph's name down.

"I know this is really personal, but what can I expect to make off of a book like I'm planning? Seventy, eighty-thousand?"

"Well, I shouldn't have quit my day job," I say. "I made about twenty-five cents an hour writing last year. I'm on my way right now to confer with my publisher, Ardor Publishing, about a pay raise."

"What sort of books ... are they?" He whispers the words as he presses his chair to recline. I think his eyes gleam just a bit.

"Light romantic novels. Kindling stories, the kind that might take off if the conditions are right and burn into a passionate frenzy. Entertaining stories. Passion isn't about lust, after all," I say. "It's about intensity, believing in something deeply that consumes and makes you forget about anything else. That's passion. It's the perfect name for a publisher of totally engaging, fiery stories. Ardor Press."

"I see."

"Authors get published when they're passionate about their stories, and they never let the impossibility of its being published or the likely outcome that their story will never be read by anyone else stop them from simply writing that story down. We assume the position of a writer, keep the commitments we make to ourselves and the story, and tell the harpies sitting behind us that we've gone deaf, that we can't hear them and then we write and write. As long as I can put down one word after the other, that's all the farther ahead I have to see. And then I make a list of ways to promote my book once it's published and —"

"Like getting on Oprah? I mean, that would really make it, wouldn't it? Have you considered that?"

I sigh. "I've done a number of things to get my book noticed," I say. "I've considered paying people on airplanes to hold my book like I am now. Not that they'd have to read it. They can put the real book they're reading inside it. Just having it 'seen' can help. I make my mother go in and buy a book so the book-store will be glad they stocked at least one copy. It isn't always the smartest author who gets known but the one who persists."

"Oh yes, I read a study about that. After a first test, half the students were praised for their brilliance and the other half for their effort. On the second test, the kids praised for their brains dropped 20 points while the effort kids raised theirs forty."

"You see what I mean."

"Have you tried to get Oprah interested? Seems like that's a natural way to go."

"I find it's more fruitful to expend energy on the writing," I tell him and realize it's true. I launch into my effort speech, the one I need to give myself. "Don't wait for inspiration because she might not show up. Start writing before you think you should. Ignore that dry scratchy cough and pay attention to your com-mitment. Don't even let yourself imagine that your cough can keep you from your calling. Think of it as hairballs in the morn-ing, that your body is telling you not to listen to your passion. It's your job to show up, not throw up, that's all; and to tell the story you've been given the best way you know how and to trust that you're not alone in the telling."

"These harpies, you say they're with you when you write? You co-author with them then?"

"No, with the muse, your guiding spirit, God. That's who writes with you. And readers, too. I'm always thinking about the readers."

The person in front of me arches his neck, looking at my seatmate while the person on the aisle side of him raises his eyes to the ceiling.

Perhaps I'm being a bit too passionate about my stories.

"Is everything all right?" A flight attendant approaches.

"Everything's fine," the researcher beside me says. "She's a writer and she's excited about her new book."

My face feels hot. "Yes. Everything's fine," I say. "We're discussing the publishing business." I hold up the mock-up. "I'm sorry I got carried away."

"You wrote that?" the flight attendant asks. "How exciting. Are you working on something? I've always wanted to write a book." She leans on the seat in front of me. "How did you go about getting published?"

I'm actually grateful for the turbulence that forces the "seat-belt" sign back on so the flight attendant has to scurry away.

I watch the world beneath me, the orderly plains, the mountains dusted with white. Everything looks organized which is what I want for my life, not a Spanish knight with promises they can't keep. *Spanish Knight. Might be a book title to consider.*

The researcher and I exchange cards and I add Randolph's number on the back of mine. "Tell him we talked," I say. "It might help." I stick the card in a copy of *The Long Bad Sentence* that I pull from my purse to give him.

"An appropriate name for a literary novel," he notes looking at the cover. "Is it about the academic world, grammar, sentence length, and all that? I see it has a few bars on windows of the institutional-looking building. Academia feels like a prison sometimes." He smiles.

"Not exactly," I say.

"Well, I'm happy with your suggestion of my book. *Bezoars Galore,*" my seatmate says. "I like that. If it ever gets written or published, I'll send you a copy." He looks at my card again. "Do you have a cat?" I nod. "And if a new cat food is developed as a result of the bezoar research, I'll send you a bag. Small payment for your writing consultation today." He smiles.

Give and you shall receive. It's a promise.

⑥

A little sweetheart from AP meets me at the airport surprising me. I thought I'd need to take the shuttle. This is promising. "Mr. Stellar would have come himself but he's in meetings all afternoon." She introduces herself as Miss Sweetheart and giggles when I give her a questioning look. "It's such a silly name, don't you think? But it's mine." She's dressed in a chic chocolate-colored suit with matching four-inch heels.

I want to vegetate, not have to relate, so I'm looking forward to a time to recover before meeting Mr. Stellar.

"Mr. Stellar, Irving he likes to be called, he's so nice, will pick you up for dinner about 6:00 p.m. That should give you enough time to rest and freshen up, don't you think?"

"Yes. Of course."

Miss Sweetheart chatters throughout the forty-minute drive from Denver International airport. She loves working at Ardor Publishing, enjoys all the people. "Will anyone from Sales or Marketing or Publicity be joining us for dinner?" I ask.

"I think it's only Mr. Stellar. Irving," she says and my heart sinks. The dinner partners, the time and place of the meal, all speak clearly where one stands within the publishing house. So does where they put an author up for the night or if they do. Dinner with my editor alone before the fashionable dinner hour of 8:00 p.m. has "gum on the bottom of a sneaker" written all over it. If the restaurant and accommodations are less than first class, so am I.

The motel looks like the ones where CSI victims appear, but it's inexpensive and I booked it myself. Still, a lovely basket of flowers and fruit await me on the dresser in my room with a card from the AP staff. How sweet! The rose offers a fragrant scent and is reminiscent of my first book with them, my one and only regional bestseller.

Irving calls me promptly at six. "I hope your flight went well," he says.

That cello voice. "It did. Thanks for asking."

"Excellent. There's been a slight change in plans, for which I apologize. A rep from New York has flown in unexpectedly and I've been called to a dinner meeting with him and the publisher and another author. I'm terribly sorry, but I've asked Miss Sweetheart, whom you've met, to arrange for your meal and anything else you'd like at our expense, of course. And we'll have the whole morning to work on the edits and come to final resolutions."

Someone flying in unexpectedly from New York could mean disaster. Could that be the high-powered female editor Randolph spoke of, the one whom Irving was involved with? If she wants to resume the relationship, he'll be distracted and if she doesn't, he'll be morose. Either way, he'll have a difficult time considering my dilemma—or Miranda's. If my sister were here she'd tell me to cool it, that my imagination is running away with me. Yes. Be calm.

"I'd hoped we could talk about the next book this evening. And about the decision to move *Miranda*—I still think of the book, as *Miranda of La Mancha*—to the later publication date. I want to understand what you have in mind. To talk about your wiggle room."

"I'm sure you're concerned," he says. "And we can address that in the morning."

He didn't say, "You've no reason to be concerned," just "we can address that in the morning."

Violins out of an English horror movie screech into my brain. All my imaging as I left Chicago sinks. The Greek harpies rip the duct tape from their mouths singing, "You're going under now! Bezoars galooooooooore."

Chapter 21

I stop my ruminating (that thing cows do, too) over my notes, then go to bed. I sleep well.

Just as I awake, I dream. I walk with a small child who has a shock of white hair—organically grown. The child, a little girl, holds my hand tight. At some predetermined time, no reason that I can see, I pull away, have somewhere else to go. She cries begging me to stay. "What would you like me to do?" I ask and she says, "I'm an orphan. Take me to a game show."

"You want something so meaningless?"

"It has value. All the choices are fun," she says.

"Stay a while," the child with the white shock of hair pleads. I'm ready to leave but the orphan child won't let me go, convinces me to stay but for what? Looking silly on a game show?

Thank goodness, I wake up but the feeling of the child being left behind stays with me.

I call Kari seeking solace and learn that Ho-Bee hates being alone in his kennel. "Last night he got out and nearly jumped over the side of the geranium ledge to a sure death. We'd left the balcony door open a ways. Clint says you should have named him Houdini. We may let him sleep on our bed if you don't mind." Kari waxes on about Chicago's weather, brisk and beautiful with all the oak and maple leaves in the park in their prime. It'd dropped nearly to freezing the night before, a sure sign of the season.

"Everything going okay there, hon?"

"Not really. I couldn't meet with Irving yesterday. He just

has this morning and I had this weird dream, about a child not wanting to let me go."

"I always suggest being things inside the dream, so you can see what it's trying to say. You know, be the little girl. What's she afraid of?"

"She's afraid of being left behind. That's what she said. That she's an orphan."

"We are all orphans in our way," Kari says, her voice soft and counselor-like. "Maybe you're afraid that you're being left behind from something you really want."

"You mean no husband, no children, maybe not even a future as a writer?"

"It's your dream, Annie. God still speaks through dreams, you know. Sometimes it's the only way he has to get our attention. Something to think about. Got to run," she chirps."Clint's taking the car in to be detailed. We can't seem to get a strange smell out of the carpet and we keep dragging in ground coffee on our shoes."

I want to ask her about the pregnancy test kit but if she wants to share that with me she will.

Bette sounds cheerful over the phone when I call her. She tells me my mother's called and she's told her where I was. "You ought to call her. She can't stop talking about your Jaime sending her that picture."

I'd forgotten.

My Jaime. My Jaime hasn't taken no for an answer it seems. Persistence or rather follow through in a man is as lovely as a paper-trained puppy and nearly as appealing. Maybe I should give him a second chance.

"I'll call her tonight. I hope to have good news to report," I say.

"And listen," Bette says."I met the father of the boy who mows your lawn. Nice man once he calmed down and realized you were gone or you'd otherwise have paid up on time. Why

226

didn't you tell me that dating material came along with tending the yard?"

"I didn't know," I say.

"You've been living way too long inside your stories, Annie, while real life has been living right down the street. He's an adorable man. I'm sorry you missed him. I just might get that happy ending you've been looking for."

⑥

I dress in a simple black dress. New Yorkers involved in publishing all dress in black, I've heard, and I want Irving to know that I, too, am "east coast savvy." I wear red Spanish Pliner pumps and a floppy brimmed red hat. I like hats and I want something visual for Irving to remember me by, not to mention that I like covering up my frizzy hair and the hat brim shadows my face, diminishing the dark worry circles. I pin a silver and amber dragonfly on my dress, a small but elegant accessory. Jaime gave it to me while we gazed at what remained of an old Roman bridge to watch pigeons taking a siesta in the Barcelona heat. My sister says such men who give personal gifts rather than vacuum cleaners are rare and I need to hang on to someone like that. I pat it once and whisper a prayer that I'll accept whatever the day brings.

I check out and await Miss Sweetheart who arrives on time and cheerily opens the door and reaches for my luggage.

"You're gorgeous," I say. Miss Sweetheart blushes nearly matching her tailored burgundy suit. I feel as dowdy as dust.

"Thank you," she says the first sentence without that up-lift. She perkily pulls the car door open and chattering, drives me to the offices of AP where I step inside as she holds the door for me. It's easy to confuse the publishing house with a paralegal space judging by the small rabbit warren cubicles that line an open meeting area. But the wall decorations give it away as literary over legal: Posters of best-selling book covers accessorize the pale blue walls while in between them, copies of AP's titles line floor to ceiling bookshelves. I look for some of my earlier titles with a quick read of the spines. Only their blockbuster bestsellers that I didn't write face with the covers out: *Passion's Delight* and *Hot Sauces for Home*. For the first time those titles sound more like cookbooks than steamy romances. My loyal friends and my mom, too, always face my titles out when they invade a bookstore. I still don't see *Sweet Charity's Rose* here, not even scrunched at the spine between *Mighty Excite* and *Total Eclipse*.

Maybe they've given all the copies of *Sweet Charity* away as gifts to visiting dignitaries. I'd heard some publishers do that. Or maybe they're letting them go out of print and haven't told me yet. I look for my latest on a counter near the sign "AP's Latest." *Sentence* isn't even there. What can that mean?

"I will not go there," says the cat. "I will not go there, that is that."

"This is our graphics area?" Miss Sweetheart says, pointing to a wider set of cubicles brightly lit. "Covers and ads and promotional materials are birthed here?" She points out the rights and revisions area as the wheels on my luggage squeak along behind us like a wayward grocery store cart. We maneuver along the plush carpet into the sales warrens where people with headsets and microphones hunch at computers convincing book distributors of the latest titles they won't want to miss. Each cubicle holds an LCD screen flashing at us even if no one's there to watch. Framed photos of family and other personal mementos affirm human inhabitants perch there. Soft music soothes the visitors but does nothing to reduce the pace of people moving between cubicles, asking, answering, nodding. They sell to bookstores and distributors and book clubs and I have a flash of regret that I haven't realized before how hard they work to convince a book buyer to risk their limited dollars on a particular author's book. They have less time than a television commercial to make their case.

"Deadlines," Miss Sweetheart explains of the intensive focus people have on their computers. "People are always working on deadlines. I'm sure you are too?"

Of course. And my struggle with deadlines sets their schedules into dithers. Or as Irving noted, since I haven't made my deadlines, the team and even other authors have to reorganize theirs.

Shame warms my face. I needed to face the reality of my predicament much earlier than this, but it's how I've always dealt with disappointment, pretending for as long as I can that it doesn't exist. If I hadn't, I would never have married Stuart.

A few employees nod recognition when Miss Sweetheart gives them my name; most smile with that glazed look that comes over people's eyes in elevators. They have so many authors to remember. Or maybe they know I'm on literary death row.

We round a corner and Miss Sweetheart puts her hand out as though we're making an abrupt stop and my seatbelt might not work. My floppy red hat flops. "That's Donna Mathews. I just loooove her books, don't you? She's an A author, you know."

We *are* graded!

Donna Mathews, a svelte woman in her early fifties who wears purple with red scarves that swirl near her chiseled chin, her rumored cheek implants high and pink with emotion, sweeps out of the office that has windows from floor to ceiling. With all those windows, I know the office must house one of the vice presidents. Editorial or production won't warrant such opulence. "Thank you soooo much," the woman says. "I'm so delighted. You are tooooo divine." She positively trills as she throws a kiss to someone I can't see standing inside the office door. "I knew we'd come to an understanding."

I want that to be me in three hours, trilling, coming to an understanding.

"Would you like to meet her?" Miss Sweetheart asks.

Donna Mathews starts down the hall and Miss Sweetheart moves forward introducing us. As Miss Mathews smiles, I notice a chicken coop full of pigeon toes fluttering at her eyes. "I've heard of you," she says before I can acknowledge her work. "All good, I might add. It's a pleasure to meet a fellow AP author. Aren't we fortunate to be part of this house?"

"We are," I tell her, surprised she even knows my name. She is after all, an A author while I linger at pass/fail.

"I wish I could chat," she says, "but I've an interview to make," and she strides off. I wait for Miss Sweetheart to restart the tour. Instead she says, "We're here" and knocks on the door Donna Mathew's just left with her swirling scarves.

I see his feet first. He wears cowboy boots, expensive, alligator hide. Gray boot cut pants with a crisp crease covers very long legs that my eyes move up and up. He stands three inches taller than me. Five foot ten or eleven, I guess. His black western cut suit coat drapes perfectly beside a flab-less waist. His shirt's a crisp white, and the tie is sophisticated swirls of tiny black and white stars, reminiscent of a New York mayor. When he stops smiling, nothing in his face sags.

He isn't sixty, nor fifty: not even close.

He's not old enough to have been in the business for as long as Randolph has implied.

"Prematurely gray," I say out loud as I take his outstretched hand wishing I could control my blurting habit when I'm nervous.

He laughs. "Since I was twenty-five."

His eyes, when I finally allow myself to meet them are a very engaging blue. He bears few pigeon toes.

"Miss Shaw," he says.

"I'm sorry I mentioned your gray hair."

"It began with one white section, just a streak of white but by the time I was thirty, it had all gone to gray. I recognize you from your publicity photo," the cello voice says, then. He still holds my hand.

"You mean I really do look like my pictures? That's not good news."

He smiles. He has kind eyes. "Thank you, Ursula." He nods

to Miss Sweetheart. "I appreciate your attention to Miss Shaw."
He releases my hand.

"I do too," I say. "Thank you."

She disappears down the hall and for a moment I wish she'd
stay. I almost call her back, like the child in my dream. There's
strength in numbers. Me alone at last with Irving. I feel like a
stuttering child.

Irving steps back into his office and invites me in to a spa-
cious area of wood and glass. It feels organized and open and
grown-up while my squeaking luggage makes me feel like a
three-year-old pulling a tardy wagon behind me.

My previous book titles are stacked on Irving Stellar's credenza including *Don't Kick Me*. The attractive woman on that
cover holds her red-skirted derrière seductively toward a large
foot, inviting a kick, even while she pronounces the title that
spews from her mouth. The book bombed though readers have
reported that they like my characters because they have desires
—we all do—but often behave in ways that get them the opposite of what they wish for. And they can't understand why. *Sweet
Charity's Rose* is in the room, too, with pink petals melting to
opaque as the petals dribble on the table at the book's edge. I
love that cover. I hope the one they've proposed for *Miranda*
will be as inviting. *The Long Bad Sentence* is on a shelf behind
him. At least there's one copy in the publishing house.

A few children's books are placed face out on Irving's bookshelf, too. I wasn't aware that AP publishes children's books.
Must be in a totally different division.

On the wall hangs a framed quote by the Himalayan explorer
W. H. Murray: "The moment one definitely commits oneself,
then Providence moves too." It's a quote I have in my office!
An oil painting of two children picking bluebonnets in a Texas
meadow dominates the opposite wall and picks up the tints of
gold and blue and browns running through the thick carpet. My
eye catches a Scripture printed on a paper weight on his desk:
"Commit to the Lord whatever you do, and your plans will

succeed." My Bible bookmark has that Scripture on it! We have more than writing in common perhaps. Irving works in a peaceful, classy office in the presence of children and inspiration. It's not at all what I pictured.

"Do you believe that?" I ask. "That Murray quote?"

"It's one of my favorites," he says, his eyes turning to it. "And yes, I do believe it. Of course the commitment must be authentic, genuine, something of the heart. It's a gift to Providence that way and Providence always gives back."

I thought of Bette's telling me to throw my wish for a bestseller to the universe and how lovingly it would come back.

Not this month.

As Irving removes his suit coat to hang it on the wooden holder near his desk I see my *Miranda* manuscript open to the pivotal scene, when Miranda knows at last whether she will accept Jaime's proposal or not. Irving's been reading it. Even more intriguing is what sits on the edited pages, weighing them down: a ceramic cat with wild colors, what I'd call a "Gaudi cat." The eyes are amber. It looks like the cat I've had Jaime buy for Miranda in Barcelona.

I am trilling already.

(6)

Miranda was unprepared for what happened at the Nautical Museum in Belém and yet it proved the turning point for how she would decide.

They'd taken the streetcar from Lisbon to the outlying city and arrived later than Miranda would have liked if they were to avoid the day's heat. Jaime's niece and nephew had come with them; his sister and mother rested at the air-conditioned apartment they'd rented in Lisbon for the week. With the two children in tow, Miranda and Jaime looked a bit like a family together, a husband and wife on an August holiday with their two school-aged children. They'd stopped at Casa Pasties de Belém and made their way to the back-room where tables like lily pads in a sunlit pool hunched helter-skelter on the pink tile mosaic floor.

Like a short snake weaving through grasses, Jaime led and Miranda put her hands on the shoulders of Paol, his nephew, while that boy put his hands on his sister's shoulders until they found an empty table against the blue tiled wall. The tiny pastries delighted her, but the sounds of people chattering in different languages didn't soothe Miranda as it had the night of the opening ceremonies. Now the voices sounded like old crows cawing. She felt alone, an outsider, orphaned.

With her limited Spanish, Miranda couldn't engage in the conversation between Jaime and his kin. He raised his eyebrows at her more than once, wiggling them in that way he had of including her. But they could be speaking of some childish game or the challenges of his work or even her melting make-up, right in front of her. She really had no idea.

"Ah ... is what we have?" he said when the children wiped their faces on the napkins, the fluff of sugar sifting down the front of their shirts.

"The pastries?" she asked to clarify.

Jaime shook his head. "These," he says spreading his hand to include the children. "Is what you have?"

"I don't have any children," Miranda said. Surely he knew that; she must have told him. She really had no idea who this man was. Maybe they were really his children and not his sister's at all. Could that be? Had she missed something in translation?

He shook his head. "What we have," he says.

"Will have? Do you mean what we will have?"

"Si," he said, beaming. "A ... mas. Mucho mas."

How many children did he want? She hadn't even said yes to his marriage proposal yet and he was counting offspring? Well, she'd said yes but she'd thought he was jesting. A marriage proposal after a single week of togetherness could only be doomed.

"The Nautical museum is open now," Miranda said. "Let's go ahead and go before it gets hotter."

Jaime took a little pause to translate, then nodded and told the children in Spanish. Obedient, they rose and he gestured for them to go out first. Miranda followed with Jaime pressing his hand against her lower back. She shivered.

They walked a block or so to the Museum housed in a former convent. Miranda kept hers eyes on the park across the street, on the children skipping ahead of them, on anything but the hand that felt warm against her back. Children? He wanted many children? This moved too quickly. She wasn't ready for this. What would it mean if she accepted his proposal and made her life in Spain? Not return to America? What about her commitments? Her heart pounded from more than the oppressive Portuguese heat.

A line for admissions already formed outside the ornate old building housing Portugal's artifacts from her naval history dating back to the 1400s. Miranda fanned herself in the morning heat with her black lace cathedral fan.

"We should have come earlier," Miranda said. "I always like to be early."

"Wait here," Jaime told her and the children.

He disappeared across the tile mosaic courtyard, then rounded a corner. She waited, smiling at others in the line, then stopped. She'd read somewhere Americans smiled too much at perfect strangers so Europeans thought them dolts. At least she ought to hold her smile until after she'd been properly introduced or had found a way to ask for help using the formal Señor or Señorita with eyes properly dropped. After that smiles were welcomed. Even flirting was expected. Miranda didn't flirt, and not smiling at strangers seemed rude.

Jaime returned, motioning them to join him.

"We'll lose our place in line," Miranda protested.

He pulled on her and the children ran ahead. "Ah ... side door, open."

"Is someone there to sell tickets?" Miranda pulled back.

"We go in free," Jaime said. He winked.

"They'll let you?" She looked around to see someone who had given consent. Perhaps another guard as a courtesy to Jaime, a police officer, was letting them in. The children had already gone inside, disappearing into the dark cool she could feel though she'd stopped outside. No one around looked official.

Jaime grinned at her, pointed with his chin. "Come."

"No," she said. She shook off his hand. "I won't go in there without paying. It's a pittance. They use the money to keep up the museum."

He shrugged. "The door is opened. The childrens go through. I go through. You ... stand out here in this heat. Is this not ... stupide?"

"No, it's not stupid. It's what's right." She crossed her arms over her chest. She tapped her toes. "You of all people should know that. We'd be breaking a law."

He shook his head at her, sarcasm coming from him for the first time. "You Americans, you are always so honest." She felt her cheeks grow warm and it wasn't from the hot sun.

"It's a bad example for the children," she said. "Your being a police officer makes it even worse."

A few others from the original line had followed them around and now they too were slipping in without paying, Jaime saying something to them in Spanish or Portuguese. Soon they'd have to send someone to this side of the building or half the line would make its way here entering illegally.

"I'm goings in," Jaime said. "If you go back to the line we will be all cooked before you're ready to leave."

"You mean finished," she said. "Not cooked."

He stood just inside for a moment letting others pass by him taking the cheating route. His dark eyes called to her.

It was her moment of truth. Could she spend the rest of her life with a cheater? Was this just the early sign of his true character coming out? Did his saving people's lives and risking his own each day outweigh this, this atrocity he committed against her sensibilities? No. They did not. She might be exaggerating; it wasn't exactly a serial killing she'd experienced, but what he did was wrong. How good that she discovered it now, before it was too late. Fate. Providence opened her eyes.

She turned her back on him and resigned herself to a longer wait in line under the hot sun, a righteous wait, to a longer life, alone.

Miranda never saw Jaime — nor any of the others — leave coins in the brass pot set in the darkened hallway farther inside the door.

⑥

"I see you've read the moment-of-truth scene," I say, nodding with my floppy hat toward the manuscript on Irving's desk.

"And so it is," Irving says. "And this, perhaps, is ours."

He hasn't asked me to sit. "Aren't we meeting to talk about *Miranda*?" I look toward his desk. Beside the manuscript, a red pen leers larger than a baseball bat ready to strike me out.

"I've scheduled us with production and editorial first."

"Excuse me?"

"I knew you'd want to talk about the title and the cover. Sales and marketing want to let you know what their plans are as well."

"So there still are plans to publish my book at the regular schedule?"

"There's a chance."

I let myself sigh inside.

"We'll have to do some hard talking about the text and timeline, right after lunch," Irving says. "For now, let's see how *Miranda* fares with the rest of the team."

"It must be a challenge to design a cover with the text and title not secure," I say, keeping my voice cheery. There's something to be said for putting on a cheery face. I need to thank my mom for the lessons.

"The designer went with the marketing information you provided last spring."

"The book's changed a lot since then," I say.

"Indeed," Irving says. "And it has those two endings." This time his warm smile sends a beam clear through me and I swallow.

"I've decided on one ending," I tell him. "My previous editor always made that final call but I've grown enough now that I need to do that myself." *Assume responsibility. Don't be an orphan.*

"And you'd choose?"

"The one that makes Miranda happy," I say.

"Indeed." He notices the squeaking luggage then as I move to follow him down the hallway.

"My flight leaves late tonight and I'll catch a cab from here so I had to bring my luggage with me. I can stay longer. If we need to, to finalize things." It will cost to change the flights but be worth it if I convince Irving to sign-off on the edits, accept the manuscript, release the advance payment, and maybe even return to the original release date.

Irving nods. "Let me store it behind my desk." He smiles and I notice that a strap from my lacy black bra hangs outside, looped around a luggage sticker reading *Recuerdo Barcelona* that I'd found in a little shop and stuck onto the carry on.

"Recuerdo Barcelona," I say under my breath.

"Memories of Barcelona. What you bring back along with the Gaudi posters and bullring ashtrays," Irving says.

"You've been in Barcelona!"

"Sailed there two years ago. One of the world's most beautiful harbors. I have some fond memories of that place, not unlike your Miranda's."

"Recuerdo Denver," I say at this happy coincidence. I unzip

the luggage pocket, then stash my bra inside. "I'm hoping to bring back fond memories of my first visit to Denver, too."

"I admire your optimism," he says in tones as sultry as the south. "Shall we proceed?"

Indeed!

Chapter 22

There is a proud undying thought in man,
that bids his soul still upward look
to fame's proud cliff!
Sam Houston

Irving motions me toward another office where several people wait with bagels, cream cheese, and juices on a side board. Papers spread before them on the shiny conference table. I wish I'd brought Randolph along with his agent's eye in case any of this discussion becomes contractual. They offer me sustenance but I'm too nervous to eat.

As people introduce themselves, I try to remember first names of people telling myself a little story to go with them, an idea suggested by a memory book I read (I can't remember the author). The author said that sheep can recall the faces of fifty individual sheep for up to two years which explains why as a child I'd watch our neighbor's sheep look longingly over the fence at each other. They acted as though they dreaded being apart.

As the memory book suggests, I concentrate on their first names giving them a visual story. Lively Louise, production. Sexy Suzanne, marketing. Big Bill, sales. Kind Ken, special markets. Gentle George, graphic arts. Chipper Chandra, copy editing. I once thought of Irving as Irksome as he made me transform all those *Miranda* scenes. But after witnessing his encouraging smiles he'd become Inspiring Irving.

And except for the absence of AP's CEO, this is an A level meeting. Long-term decisions can be made here today. Things are looking up.

"We're really looking forward to the publication of this book," Lively Louise says. She's angular, active, and twirling a pencil between her fingers, pencil over finger as she speaks, stopping suddenly to point it at someone or something she wants to particularly note. The movement and her positive introduction distracts so I almost miss the second half of what she's saying. "... fall-winter cycle next year will be so much better. I'm sure you can understand the climate for light romances isn't good right now. What do you call yours?"

"Miranda of —"

"Kindling, that's what it was. Irving said that was a sort of brand you'd included with one of your revisions as part of your cover name: 'Annie Shaw. Kindling stories to build a fire in your heart.' A lovely image of a small, romantic fire. Quite clever."

So she's read some of the revisions, too. Each specialist then gives their take on the book, what will make it marketable. The cover, back cover copy, catalog copy, sales, publicity. They all know about Miranda and the details of the opening ceremonies, even the colorful cat given as a gift from Jaime to Miranda. Irving must have kept them posted. Yet all I'd been thinking, all I'd really sent Irving, were little crumbs that like Hansel and Gretel he had to notice and pick up to find his way to the end.

"Sales of *The Long Bad Sentence* have been inconclusive," Big Bill of sales says. My ears perk up. "I think it's the ending that really doesn't tell us if the nurse and guard actually decide to get married. A good romance has to have at least an engagement at the end."

"We may have failed you in editorial," Irving says.

"Oh, no, editorial did everything it could," I say. "It was me, I'm the problem."

"I only bring it up," Big Bill says, "Because we don't want to repeat the same mistakes."

Lively Louise says, "We have a new editor. Irving's working well with Annie, aren't you? I can call you Annie?"

"Yes, please. All of you," I say. Familiarity breeds commitment I'm sure. "

Irving nods and so do I. I've never attended this sort of meeting with the other titles and I'm gazing at Irving's encouraging smile when Lively Louise says "I think this Miranda book has the same pizzazz as *Sweet Charity's Rose*."

Sexy Suzanne says, "I loved that book. Oh, it could have had a little more, you know, steam, but it was such a happy book. Boy gets girl! And in this one, I really want Jaime to get the girl."

I swallow. Girl gets boy, boy gets girl, that's what a romance is. Maybe that's why *Don't Kick Me* and now *The Long Bad Sentence* aren't selling. Reader letters express appreciation for the inspiration, for how relationships develop, but they never mention the romance part at all.

Maybe I'm writing the wrong kind of book. Maybe I have the wrong publisher! But I can't change now. I have to get *Miranda* published or I'll have to move back in with my parents. Discussion about the cover keeps me from hyperventilating at the thought of moving back home and hearing again my dad's many old jokes.

⑥

"Let's hear about the front cover, George," Lively Louise says.

Gentle George sighs. He has caterpillar eyebrows and an Eyore, turned down mouth. "It can be changed," he says of the artwork he passes out now. "This is just the concept. I have to find the right silk to photograph, to get that languid look I want and that the cover needs to give it texture. We've tried a number of designs but this is the best I think." He wipes at his jaws. This was an artist's agony, having to share his artistic creation for a committee. I can commiserate.

The colors are vibrant, reds and browns, earth tones that

make me think of Spain. But the models dominate the cover. They include a winnowed damsel dressed in magenta diaphanous silk leaving little to the imagination regardless of the quality of silk he might find to photograph the model in. She lies arched over the arms of a Conquistador alpha male, a Spanish knight, with dark eyes and a beard that looks so rough it could file down the chain mail he wears if not the vehicle ID number of the chariot in the background. *Chariot? Medieval?* The ancient Cathedral of Barcelona, my Miranda's city, looms out of a fog behind the models while dark and brooding faces of armed men glare over stone parapets in the distance.

It's a shocking cover for its suggestions of both hot steaminess and historical context. I'd written neither into my text. Nothing about this cover says "light contemporary kindling novel" except the new title emblazoned across the cover. My hands shake as I hand Gentle George back his masterpiece for a book now titled *Bilked in Barcelona.*

"Indeed," Irving says. "You've captured quite a lot here, George. But I think we still have a little work to do." His eyes are sympathetic. Irving's my lifeline here, the only one who really understands Miranda's needs, or mine. It's not their fault, I realize that now. I haven't met my deadlines or kept them abreast. What else could they do but imagine?

"The cover's never really finished until the print schedule is firmed," Gentle George says. "We can lighten it more and make the sunset a little rosier so it doesn't look quite so dark. The lighter silk should help with that too."

I smile at him. He's a professional, as are they all wanting to do their best. Could Gentle George see my upset stomach as though I'm stuck in a car surrounded with sweet raspberry scent?

"I wonder if we might emphasize contemporary Barcelona," I say. "A girl traveler, a handsome policeman, in uniform? Aren't uniforms happy attractions?" The team nods agreement. "And

I thought of a new title. I haven't told you yet, Mr. Stellar ... Irving, but what about *Spanish Knight*?"

"Has possibilities," Big Bill in sales says. Gentle George nods his head too.

"There's still time," Irving assures me. His eyes suggest we two are the only ones in the room and I wonder if this is how people taken hostage feel, clinging to one potential rescuer. "The story is a contemporary, though, George. I'm not sure you realized that." To me he says, "The catalog frequently displays a title and a cover that change before final publication. I'm sure you're aware of that, Miss Shaw. It's the ISBN number that provides advance sale orders to choose the correct book for a book buyer. They rarely even look at the cover at that point knowing it will likely change. The cover copy is what matters."

"Yes. No, I wasn't. Though I've never had the ... privilege of being at this stage of um ... development before. It's very kind of you to —"

"As soon as the manuscript is final, we can go ahead with final copy," Chipper Chandra says folding her hands over the text. "And when might that be, Irving?"

Irving looks at me. "About that," I say, "I wonder if —"

"Our plan is to try to get print media coverage several months before release, whenever that is," Sexy Suzanne interjects. "We're looking for a good marketing bang, something really big to bring us media attention." She looks at her Black-Berry notes and scrolls to find what she's looking for. "I was thinking a drop from a helicopter placing you into a signing at a mall, sort of like the rappelling policeman who lit the torch did?"

"It was a fireman, because that's what firemen do," I say.

"Well, what did Miranda's policeman do then?"

"He competed. In golf," I say.

"Oh. Well. Not too romantic, that."

"And he rescued his damsel from a band of thieves," Inspiring Irving says.

"So we could stage a mall robbery and have you rescued right in front of the cameras."

"I love it," Big Bill says. "With a stack of mock-up books and our would-be robbers knock them over. They run through the mall and we'd have an actor dressed as a Spanish policeman chase them and bring them to justice. The sound bite would be 'A read, good enough to steal for.' I like it."

"I know we're not supposed to discourage creative thinking," Lively Louise says, "but faking a robbery with people nervous about safety and all? I wouldn't want the book associated with crime."

"That might work for *The Long Bad Sentence*," says someone from marketing whose name I've totally lost.

"We don't want to stage fake things without people knowing they're fake," says Lively Louise. I think about Randolph's plan to bring a fake Jaime to Chicago for a fake marriage and I cringe.

The team nods, slightly sadder but they turn to me and ask if I've had any thoughts about marketing and publicity.

I clear my throat and open the folder I've kept with me. "I'm having these brochures made up. I thought I could —"

"We could have done that for you. Posters too, for signings," helpful Suzanne says.

"I didn't want to bother you."

"We appreciate cost cutting measures and authors who team with us," Lively Louise says.

"We need something really punchy," Suzanne says. "Something to make readers sit up and take notice."

Do I dare tell them about Randolph's plan?

"Well, my agent has this idea. Not to step on anyone's toes or anything. It's probably a long shot, but it involves the Oprah Winfrey show —"

"Your agent knows Oprah?" A universal gasp. Lively Louise turns her whole body toward me as I sit beside her. The rest of the tablemates perk up too as though choreographed by David Foster.

"Not ... exactly," I say.

"If you can get on Oprah's show we'd be able to move this title back into the earlier release date," Lively Louise says. "Is this for real now, or just fiction?"

"Oh, it's real," I say. "His plan is real. Whether he can pull it off or not, that's the question. I'd hate to have you count —"

"We'll be making final production decisions within the week. If your agent has a plan in place by then, we'll put you back into the spring lineup. Otherwise, I don't know ..."

Irving starts to rise. He motions me to join him. "I think we've accomplished what we can here. We'll have the manuscript completed by the end of the week. Won't we Annie"

I nod, I'd agree to whatever Invigorating Irving might suggest.

Chapter 23

"It really would be best if you rescheduled your flight," Irving says back in his office. "While I'm confident we can complete the revision discussion before midnight, I would like us to have some wiggle time. That meeting took a little more time than I intended."

Irving says wiggle like waggle and I'm not sure at first what he means. I'd do anything for him for giving me this last chance. Kari says her clients often ascribe qualities to her she really doesn't have just because they're grateful for the therapeutic insights they acquire in her presence. "It rubs off," she tells me, "but I never take it personal. I'm not the wise woman they think I am. They are. They've done all the work." Maybe Irving understands author adoration too.

I hadn't found a way to get us from that room with ease while Irving not only slipped me out without more details about Oprah but he did it with the promise of the issuance of the advance check when the book was accepted—if it was—within the week.

"Wiggle time is good," I say.

"I'll ask Ursula to see if she can rearrange your flight and get you accommodations for the night. We might even be able to squeeze in a photo shoot with marketing and publicity, to update your headshot. Will that be agreeable?"

"Indeed," I say. *Keep your editor happy, rule one.*

Irving punches the intercom and Miss Sweetheart sashays in. Irving gives her the particulars while he points me to a chair.

"So advise me about your agent's plan," Irving says after Miss Sweetheart's left to rearrange my life.

"Can you tell me about *Bilked in Barcelona* first? It's not really going to have that title, is it?" I sit down on a chair across from his desk.

"That title didn't make it on your list, then." He smiles. Warmth oozes.

"It sounds like some police novel with con artists roaming around taking advantage," I say. I remove my red hat, set it on the edge of Irving's desk and fluff my hair with my fingers.

"It's very misleading."

"Especially in a title," I say. "I've bought lots of books for their title and I'd be really irritated if the book wasn't about what the title suggested. And the cover ..."

"One doesn't want to annoy one's readers."

"Right. So can we get some of that changed? Can you do that?"

"Keep in mind that marketing really has been successful in placing books for us and sales have done fairly well with your titles, except for the last two. They seem to think they can sell this book with that title and that cover."

"But they aren't selling what I wrote."

He leans back in his chair and cocks his head. "Authenticity matters to you," Irving says.

"Yes. It does." I cross my arms over my chest in a non-negotiable position.

Irving picks up the Gaudi-like cat and runs his hands over it, petting the ceramic feline, his thumbs rubbing on the amber eyes. "The Oprah idea?"

"That's a long shot," I say, my shoulders slump. My finger-nails becoming suddenly more interesting than Irving's colorful porcelain sculptured cat. I don't even want to discuss Randolph's idea with the subject of authenticity having been broached. "It's worse than the mock robbery mentioned in that meeting."

He sets the cat down and folds his hands over my manuscript.

They're large hands with wide cuticles and well-manicured nails. He raises his eyebrows in anticipation of my explanation. *Gosh, he has kind eyes.* "We really are in this together, you know. So tell me about the Oprah ... thing."

"Randolph, my agent, has this person, acquaintance of his, who's willing to act as a Jaime, pretending to be my long lost lover from Spain who wants to be reunited with me on national television. On the Oprah show. You know she always does those reunion things for people, bringing them together, especially around the holidays."

"The Jaime from the book?"

"Not exactly. But in that vein. He'd pose as a policeman who met me in Barcelona. All that would follow the plot line of the book. It's embarrassing to even talk about," I say. "It's so improbable that against my better judgment I told him to go ahead and see what he could do but I really don't —"

"And is there a Jaime in Barcelona pining for you?"

I swallow and look away. "For his Miranda, yes, though I don't really know if he's pining, exactly —"

"You've written an autobiographical novel. That does explain some things."

"No! It's just a story. Well, all novels are somewhat autobiographical, aren't they?" I sit up, my hands resting on the chair arms, elbows out as though I'd take flight. *Calm down. He's on your side.*

"Frederick Buechner says both fiction and theology are autobiographic."

"Does he? I read his works but I never came across that quote." I like the works that appeal to Irving. It's reassuring. "I don't know about my theology, but I do know that the part about Miranda pining away for her lost Spanish lover isn't about me. It's fiction. A novel I'm willing to make better, with your help. But I don't actually think my agent can pull this off." I sigh. "The only way to make this book have any possibility of being a bestseller is to simply make it as good as I possibly can."

Irving gauges my answer. He rarely blinks I note, like some of those interviewees on cable who never seemed to need to, their passion so intense for their subject they can't afford the time loss that comes with a blink.

"Indeed," Irving says at last picking up the manuscript. "That can be rare in a writer, that willingness to revise time and again until both author and editor agree. It's been awhile since I've worked with someone so confident they'll consider every possibility of editorial change."

Confident? Me?

"And one who also has a connection to Oprah," he adds. "Well, the possibilities are endless indeed." He smiles, his full lips as inviting as a chocolate bar.

We work through lunch with Miss Sweetheart responding to Irving's request for sandwiches and herbal teas. We have a number of things in common now: that Gaudi cat, Chai Tea, Frederick Buechner, and that neither of us drinks coffee. I assume that producing a good book will be another.

Later in the afternoon, dark chocolate arrives courtesy of Kind Ken, Miss Sweetheart tells us. "This is good," Irving says. "Two hour blocks of time are really all one should devote to such intense mind work of seeing with new eyes without a break."

He sees revisions as seeing with new eyes too!

"We've been at it for," he looks at his Mickey Mouse watch and says, "five hours."

"I'm sorry it's taking so long," I say. "I realize it must be a wretched book to require so many red lines with revisions that are deeper than changing the color of Miranda's hair."

"A fair number of authors assume that's what revisions are, changing a chapter title or a tidbit of description." He stretches his arms over his head and the material pulses against well-toned abs. "But when I write, it's in the revisions where I find out what the story is trying to teach me."

"You write?" I say.

He nods toward the bookshelf and then he stops himself and

249

turns back to face me. "A little. Mostly I admire others who do," he adds, "and contribute as I can to richer story telling for them."

My eyes move toward the bookshelf. Perhaps he hasn't intended to reveal that writing part of himself. I notice the titles of the children's books then. "You like Marion Plush, too, I see. Have you met her?"

"Our paths have crossed."

"Well, I love the sound of her last name, Plush." I drag out the sh sound.

"It does carry happiness, that word," he says.

"Real writing."

"Excuse me?" Irving says.

"Children's books are real writing. Children won't let you take three hundred pages to make your point." He nods agreement. "And they won't let you preach or pound either. They just want the story. If it's any good, whatever message there is in it shines through. It's what we should all aspire to," I say, "that quick burn into meaning."

He raises an eyebrow. "You've done some thinking about children's writing."

"Doesn't every writer? Until they realize how hard it is." I munch on the piece of dark chocolate. "Wasn't it Cicero who apologized for writing his friend such a long letter saying he didn't have enough time to write a short one?"

"I'd like to see AP publish a few children's titles," he says.

"Really? Wouldn't that cloud your adult publishing waters?" I ask.

"Adults buy children's books," Irving says. "I certainly do. For nieces and nephews, friends' children. I'd be inclined to look at what else a favorite author published, in an adult line, if I liked their children's books." He taps his pencil lightly on the desk. "In fact, it's one of the reasons why I like your works. Your stories are the very kind of stories we could pair well with a children's market."

"Well. That's very kind. Anyway, I'd be lost without an editor to help me cut my words down to size. I could never write a children's book or even young adult. Marion Plush is so gifted."

Irving says, "Imagine how useless an editor would feel if the manuscript arrived as perfection. Yours isn't as difficult as some I've edited."

"There are worse writers than me?"

"Just writers who need more work than yours."

"But why would you publish them?" The chocolate's getting softer. The room or my hands are heating up.

"We don't." He clears his throat, shuffles papers, doesn't look at me, and then inhales a deep breath. Looking me straight in the eye he says, "Annie ..."

I lick my lips. Here it comes. He's getting ready to tell me that he's done all the salvaging we can do and there's no hope for Miranda or me. She isn't going to be bilked in Barcelona nor meet her match in La Mancha or have a Spanish knight in her life, either.

"Would you be interested in dinner?" Irving says instead. "Away from here. I realize there might be some trepidation on your part. And it isn't wise to mix business with pleasure, but it might make this process of finalizing ... things go more smoothly if we got to know the authentic side of one another."

His words melt like Barcelona chocolate, slowly, as though filling up my veins.

Is he flirting? Preparing me for the worst? What kind of a woman can't tell the difference? What business do I have writing romances anyway, a woman who's never really been romanced in her life except for Stuart, and I know how that turned out. Jaime? Well that's another chapter but I don't feel like turning any pages.

The room feels small. "Dinner?" I squeak. "Well, I, we could. Certainly." I flutter my fingers at my earrings, hold my throat, try to find a comfortable place for my hands. They rest on the silver and amber dragonfly, dart away as I fluff my fingers through my hair.

Irving appears to stifle a grin at the same time that I smell the good quality of Kind Ken's chocolate more powerful than before. I open my palms. Soft chocolate oozes. It must be all over my face too! I reach to pick up my red hat leaving dark fingerprints on the brim from the still melting chocolate. "I'll freshen up a bit first," I say, backing out into the hallway.

I make my way to the washroom outside Irving's office. At least it's unisex so I don't have to worry about wandering into the wrong one.

In the mirror I stare at a face that rivals the face paintings of a street fair artist or maybe an Aboriginal child. Chocolate streaks my cheeks, my jaw line, my neck. There are no paper towels so I use toilet paper pieces that dab and stick and the hot air dryer pastes them on tighter. I re-wash my face and hold it against the blow dryer. Calm. Stay calm. It's only a dinner, a working one at that. I take a deep breath and one last look in the mirror. There's nothing I can do about my hat hair sticking out over my ears and the blow dryer pushing my bangs upward into a stiff meringue twist. I'm just grateful there's no author photo shoot in my immediate future.

@

"Annie," Randolph says into my cell phone. "You're going to kiss me all across the continent when I tell you this! Where are you, by the way?"

"Denver. Having dinner. With my editor," I say. "It's my agent," I tell Irving. I give the I-have-to-take-this-call-look and Irving returns to his mescaline salad.

"She's going for it! Whole Hog!"

"Who? And what?"

"Oprah! And get this. The production manager says they not only want to fly your Jaime here, well, our Jaime, for the reunion, but they want to have the wedding on the air, the entire ceremony. Dr. Phil will do the pre-nuptial counseling and all Oprah's pals will help you find the perfect wedding dress, order the flowers. Her chef will do the cake and reception and you even get a pre-nuptial spa treatment. The dog, too."

"You told them I have a dog?"

"You do, don't you? Oprah loves dogs and they're springing for something at ..." he pauses as though reading. "Here it is. At Élan-Canine Salon for the dog. Everything filmed of course. And then the wedding and the honeymoon too. It'll be the biggest thing since Trista and Ryan's wedding a few years back. That Ryan was a policeman, too, wasn't he?"

"Fireman."

"Righto. What a tie in. Maybe they could be your best man and matron of honor. I'll propose that. People will know your name, Annie, and your sales will skyrocket!"

"But not as an author. Not as someone who wrote a good book —"

"No buts about it. This is the biggest thing I've put together since I got Barbara Walters to interview that Sumo wrestler who wrote a cook book."

"Randolph, I can't! I don't know this man you've hired. It isn't possible to marry him and Oprah will find out. I'll be blacklisted forever for misleading her public."

Irving looks up from his salad, puzzlement on his face.

"I really think —" I continued.

"Well," Randolph says, "we could bring the real Jaime here. Your Jaime."

"Who told you there's a real Jaime?" I whisper.

"Your mother. Your sister. Your friends. They all want your Jaime brought here and I've talked to him." I gasp. "He's willing. Shoot, kiddo, this is a marriage made in heaven. It was meant to be and it's all paid for. We bring your Jaime here and it'll be authentic. It really will be a long lost reunion and you'll be able to leverage it into a bestseller. Surely your publisher could work those angles in pre-sales. Let me talk with your editor."

"No! He's, he's busy. Randolph, what you're proposing, it isn't me," I say. "Don't ... don't involve Jaime in this, please. It wouldn't be right."

"Come on, Annie. Hand the phone over to your editor."

"He wants to talk to you," I say. "Oops, sorry, I guess I cut him off." I pick up the cell phone I've dropped into my salad. I wipe the phone down, then lay it beside my plate. I'm shaking.

"What did he want to talk with me about?" Irving says.

"You'll know soon enough. I'm sure he'll call back." I push the ringer to mute wishing I could do the same to my life.

⑥

"Bette, how could you?" I say into the phone in the ladies room. She's the only one I'm able to reach. Misty, Kari, and Darlien got frantic messages left on their phones while I ignored Randolph's attempts to call back.

"What?"

"How could you tell Randolph to bring the real Jaime here? Do you know what he's arranged? He's got Oprah's producers willing to produce a wedding! I'm not marrying Jaime, not on terror-vision or anywhere. Not. It's bad enough to have this total stranger come, but the real Jaime will confuse his life, make him think there's a possibility of our future when there isn't."

"I didn't think he'd actually pull it off," Bette says. "None of us did, but then we thought if he did get him here, even if Oprah didn't do a show related to it, that you'd face your fears and really decide what you want for Jaime and for your life."

"I know that I don't want Jaime in my life! You're my friends! You're supposed to help me reach my goal, not fly me off course."

"Speaking of flying," Misty says, "I read a story about geese and how a lead goose when it tires drops back and lets another goose break down the wind resistance. She'll let others help carry her. That's all we've done. You're still in charge, still flying toward that target of getting a bestseller, but you need to step

254

back a bit and let the rest of us carry on for you. We're birds of a feather flying together."

"I think you've cooked my goose. If Oprah finds out —"

"She'll understand that sometimes people change their minds. But at least you'll have him here to work things through and be able to part as friends if that's what you decide."

"This has nothing to do with getting a bestseller or having my name recognized as an author," I wail.

"Maybe getting a bestseller isn't your real goal anyway, just like going to the fridge doesn't fill you up. At least I'm guessing that's why you have that *IT'S NOT IN HERE* sign under the frig light. There's something in the back of your frig that I can't recognize at all."

"What would my true goal be?" I ask.

"Maybe you want to be happy and you think a bestseller will do it."

And maybe there's something in the back of my life I just need to throw out.

Chapter 24

📖

"Are you okay in there?"

"Yes. I mean no. I'll be out in a minute," I tell the female voice accompanying the knock on the restaurant bathroom door.

"You were gone so long," Irving explains as he stands when I return. "I was worried."

Irving's taken me to a four star restaurant marked by waiters hovering, wearing white towels over their arms (among other items of clothing). "I took another call," I say and change the subject to dessert.

The Crème Brule's a four star dessert, and it's all I can do to not lick my fingers and poke at the crystallized sugar pieces that like confetti are sprinkled around the gold ring on the dark blue plate. Chamber music plays in the background. I have no intention of telling Irving any of Randolph's gory details but somehow the music, the fine cuisine, and his cello voice, not to mention his gun-sight steady gaze, act as catalysts for confession and I tell him about Randolph and Jaime, about how in the book I added that Jaime had really paid to go into the museum so readers would like him when in fact he hadn't. And that was why Miranda refused his proposal.

"Marketing will be enchanted with the details," Irving says when I finally finish.

"So you can see I can't marry Jaime, not even if the whole affair is paid for. He wasn't really offering marriage anyway. He got caught up in the romance of the games and the beauty of Barcelona." I ignore the repeated proposal he's sent in his letter.

"Easy to do," Irving says.

"That's right, you've been there."

"A long time ago but I loved Barcelona, especially the Sagrada Familia Cathedral. Imagine designing a cathedral to honor the Holy Family knowing you wouldn't likely live to see its completion. It was only a quarter finished when he died in 1926. But he had a vision and pursued it despite the critics or his own mortality."

"It's still not finished. Not for twenty more years they figure. Is that where you bought your Gaudi-like cat? I bought mine there, too," I say. "We have something in common."

"Many things, it seems," Irving says with that gun-sight gaze.

My heart skips a beat.

Irving waits into the silence then says, "It doesn't really ring true in your story, Annie, the reason Miranda decides not to marry Jaime."

I clear my throat. "Doesn't it?"

"I really want us to find another scene, something with more drama to it, to create the case for Miranda's final decision, that pivotal event on which the whole story turns. What are the values of Miranda's life, and what causes her to do the things she does? It lacks ... causation that she wouldn't marry the man simply because he didn't pay to go into the museum. We need a cause that will make Annie's decision memorable."

"Miranda. It's Miranda's life. You said Annie."

"Did I?"

I nod. "Vanity maybe? She fears she'll disappear inside Jaime's family, inside Jaime's country, inside Jaime's job, and she'll lose herself."

"She couldn't write while in Spain?"

"Miranda teaches preschool," I remind him. "I'm the writer."

"Indeed. So she couldn't work with children in Spain, until they start their family?"

"I wonder if they have any more Crème Brule." Irving looks toward the waiter, raises his hand, and then asks for another dessert. Irving avoids my eyes and we're both silent until the dessert appears. The note inside my refrigerator—*IT'S NOT IN HERE*—passes before my eyes but doesn't stop me. With enough sugar to barricade my heart, I can hear Irving tell me anything.

Irving says. "So will you go through with it?"

"With what?"

"With the pre-nuptial counseling and the Oprah wedding? It sounds like your agent would be quite disappointed if you didn't and I know our team will find the publicity too much to resist."

"Will AP publish the book whether I do or not?" I ask.

"Whether you get married on national television is not the issue," Irving says. "But we'll have to come up with something pretty amazing if I'm to convince the editorial team that this book meets AP's expectations."

"Even with all the revisions?" I feel my hand shake as I lay down my spoon.

"I'm afraid so."

"But we've worked so hard."

"Indeed, but the truth is much of the book, though beautifully descriptive, is composed still of what most people skip over. They want to be involved in your story, Annie. They want to see themselves in Miranda's predicament. You've held yourself back from that and thus from authenticity, the very thing you were hoping to convey. I'm not sure we can rediscover that without a fair amount of additional work and time."

"I'll put the work in, I will," I say.

"Looks like there are two deadlines heading your way then." He folds his napkin. *Time's up.* "This book and your agent's plan for your future."

"Both twined together," I say.

"Fact and fiction often are. Take one last crack at that pivotal, life-changing scene. If it's strong enough with the revision,

I'll go back to the team and see if we can firm the final publication date. That's all I can promise."

I almost told him what the pivotal scene should be but I couldn't. Risking got me into trouble with Stuart; it got me into trouble with Jaime. Some things are just better left unsaid.

"And didn't you say you had another thought about a title?"

I nod. "What about *Spanish Knight*," I say.

Irving smiles. "I like it. I like it a lot."

I lick the spoon of the Crème Brule and look into eyes that could be someone's Spanish Knight, indeed.

⑥

Irving and I agree to meet first thing in the morning to make final attempts to have him happy about the manuscript. I fear that his decision is written in stone along with my ticket to debtor's prison. Irving drives me to the annex of the Brown Palace hotel where Miss Sweetheart has arranged a room. He gets my luggage from the trunk. A taste of winter's in the crisp mountain air.

"Thank you. For dinner, for driving me back."

"Annie ..." he says, his voice low. He clears his throat. "I want —"

"To assure me we can work this out, I know. I appreciate that. But you don't owe me any miracles."

"No," Irving says. "I want, I wasn't prepared to ... it's with some trepidation that I —"

"— Try to produce a decent book out of nothing? I believe it's where the phrase 'You can't make a silk purse out of a sow's ear' comes from. I under —"

"— Appreciate your hesitation about your agent's idea."

"You do?"

"Longfellow wrote that fame is like a footprint in the sand of time. It doesn't last long if it does arrive and how it arrives makes a difference, it seems to me. It takes courage to set a limit, to have a line beyond which you will not go. Some people will do anything for a moment of fame. I've often wondered how far I'd violate my principals in order to achieve what I think is satisfaction. That you have a limit is admirable, indeed."

He leans toward me. *For a kiss? I don't need this complication.*

It's a gentle hug held for a moment longer than expected. Still, it's a simple period in a long mostly bad sentence of an evening. I drop my red floppy hat I've been carrying.

"I'm sorry," he says as he steps away, both of us bending for the hat. "I had no right to confuse things. You looked so —"

"Pathetic," I say as he hands me the hat.

"Sad. And genuine," he adds as he steps away. "Please, forgive my intrusiveness."

"You were being kind," I say.

He clears his throat and sounds like an editor again. "See if you create a better reason for Miranda to say no," he says. "We'll look at it in the morning. Goodnight, Miss Shaw, Annie. Sleep well."

The squeak-squeak of my luggage wheels is the only sound to break my walk down novel death row to my room.

@

"It's midnight," Bette yawns into the phone.

"I was up anyway," Misty says.

The conference call feature on my phone actually works!

"Norton's got a stuffy nose," Misty continues. "It was time for his medicine. What's up?"

"This better be good," Darlien says. "I got an early shift." She doesn't sneeze.

"Are you on, Kari?" I hear an "hmmm" before I lay out the scenario. "It's really awful," I tell them. "First I thought, no, no! Then I was angry and then I tried to bargain and I really wanted to just cry."

"Sounds like the stages of grief," Kari says.

"Am I through them all?"

"Not until you reach acceptance," she says. "And then the grief can start again."

"Maybe I'm still back on bargaining. If I tell Randolph no, he'll probably drop me as a client. If I tell him yes, I'll be miserable having done something I don't believe in, not to mention hurting Jaime, letting him come all this way thinking I'm going to marry him."

"Won't the producers interview you first anyway?" Bette asks. "They'll never go along with it if they don't think you're really in love."

"That's what Dr. Phil is supposed to help us figure out, work out the love part, but I'm sure Randolph hasn't told them that Jaime wants to marry or that I don't."

"Take that out of your nose right now!"

"What?" We say in unison.

"I was talking to Norton," Misty says. "We planted beans in a bucket today and he tried to stuff one into his nose. Speaking of substances in the wrong places, I'm not going to send out any more cat nip mice to radio and television stations."

"Why not?" Darlien asks.

"Because I got a call from a radio station saying they weren't sure what was in them, that the filling looked suspicious and they were going to call Homeland Security."

Oh for heaven's sake!

"Maybe Mavis can do follow up calls to set up interviews and explain," I say.

"We'd all come to California to see you on Dr. Phil." Darlien gets us back on track and I'm grateful. I think.

"Randolph sent a fax to my hotel with the arrangements so far. They'll pre-interview in Chicago with Dr. Phil in LA, something preliminary, using Skype I suspect. Maybe it'll all end right there and I won't have to go through with anything more."

"What does your editor think of all this?" Darlien asks.

"He can't really pass up a possible Oprah link to the book; his team would bean him if they ever found out he discouraged an opportunity like that. But I think he doesn't want me to do it because ... it's not really me."

"He knows you that well?" Bette asks.

"He wants me to write a scene with a better reason for why Miranda didn't marry Jaime. He thinks Jaime's not paying to go into that carriage museum isn't enough."

"What do *you* want?" Kari asks. "That's what really matters."

I know what my editor wants; my agent; Jaime; my mom. I even know what my friends want for themselves and for me: to be happy. But what do I want? I think of the Proverb, the one I really love that reads: *Desire realized is sweet to the soul.* I don't know what will make me have that sweetness. I tell them that and they tell me that like good friends we'll stick together and that we should all pray about it, too. And we do.

I sit for the next few hours like a fat cat with my back against the headboard, legs straight out and David Letterman's tiny television face lying in between my toes. I barely hear his top ten and think I can give him numbers: Ten Things to Keep a Book from Becoming a Bestseller. Number Ten: Write a Book Composed of Parts People Skip Over. Number Nine: Write a Book Based on Your Life and Fudge the Ending. Number Eight: Let Your Editor Hug You Good-Night to Complicate the Plot.

I can go on? I'm a writer after all? Maybe I can get work writing for Letterman? Miss Sweetheart's uplift endings are contagious.

I'm letting my subconscious work on the final scene while I flip to an old movie. I anesthetize myself with its mindless car chases and explosions. My life is exploding too. I'm not going to get the acceptance or the advance. I'll probably have to pay back what I've already gotten if the book is rejected. The book won't get published. I have no visible means of support. If I do what Randolph wants, I'll probably be sued for deception or worse, ruin the life of a nice Taco True employee or a policeman from

Spain and never forgive myself for the deception. And if Oprah ever found out … well, I've seen her be upset with an author who claimed truth for fiction (I can't remember his name) but it wasn't pretty.

Thanksgiving Day commercials already pepper the airwaves. Soon it'll be Christmas and then the end of the year and the end of my career despite all the work of the team, all of the effort of Irving and Randolph, my friends and even my mother.

I wish Ho-Bee sat on my lap. I miss hearing John's purr of contentment.

The car chase in the movie rages on. Despite my numbed state, I notice a car parked on a certain corner that the protagonist frequents. The car is covered with an advertisement for an insurance firm. Not only a logo on the door, but all around the car, the roof, the sides, the hood and trunk, all covered like a biker with tattoos.

Visual. That's what people notice. Visual things. I sit up. I need one visual snapshot, one visual connection that can go viral on You Tube and if Oprah was in it too, my book would become a bestseller for sure. *Visual*! Of course! It's how children's books invite adult readers—all those lovely illustrations, whether flotsam or fields. Then later, the text weaves its way into a reader's heart and children create their own pictures in their imagination. Words are the wings of imagination, not the wings of destiny. But first, the pictures have to capture.

It's all about getting attention. That's what I have to do before Randolph makes any more U-turns in my life. If I can get Oprah interested in the actual book, we won't need the fake relationship. It's about the book, not me, not my name!

Authenticity, that's what Miranda wanted. It's what I want too, to be real and to feel as though the me I am is the me I'm presenting to the world in my stories and in my life.

I turn off the television. A plan forms on the wings of imagination and it inspires my revision of that final scene—let the Spirit help me do what I know how to do.

I hand Irving the new final ending the next morning in his office. I'm wearing a sapphire blue sweater and my Smith Travel pants, the one's I'd worn on the Barcelona trip so I'm feeling connected to my story. My lacy black bra is on me and thus not hanging out of my carry-on bag. While people walk by the tall glass windows looking out onto the hallway, Irving reads the manuscript changes. I chew on the sides of my nails; poke my toes into the plush carpet.

He looks up at me at last. "It smelleth of the midnight oil."

"You think it stinks?"

"No, no! It gives the impression of hard work and effort. It's something an old English professor of mine used to say."

I have worked half the night.

"Indeed. It's a surprise ending but one that makes sense, is congruent and consistent with the characters. I think we might have a chance with this. Especially if your agent's efforts bear fruit as well."

"About Randolph's plan … I have another idea that came to me last night," I tell him. "If it works, I won't have to go through with this Dr. Phil-Oprah-wedding-thing that really has nothing to do with the book or even my life. It really doesn't."

"Based on this new ending, I'm not so certain of that," Irving says.

His eyes are like lasers right into my soul.

I swallow. "Could you give me until after Thanksgiving to work out my other promotional plan? Maybe just before Christmas?" I'm back to the bargaining stage of grief. "Marketing and publicity will be happy with it, honestly they will. I'll even rework some of the other scenes and put a little bite into them. No sex, mind you, but some bite," I tell him.

"Ardor Publishing does like passion," Irving says. "Readers need a plot driven by desire. Passion and betrayal. Acceptance and forgiveness. The emotions of the human heart struggling against itself.

"On more than the cover you mean."

He laughs. "I'll work at that end, to get the cover to be more reflective of your story, and see if they'll hold off with their final decision until after Thanksgiving. Make it an early Christmas present if I can."

"If we can get the cover a little more contemporary and the title a bit more reflective of my book, with these changes, we'll be back on schedule, won't we?"

"There's a good chance of it. But Annie, if I'm not able to push this ..."

"I'll buy it back." The words pop out but it feels right. I have one more option to rescue *Miranda* even if these plans don't work out. I can publish it myself. It doesn't all depend on Ardor Publishing.

"Indeed. That's a major commitment," Irving says.

"It honors the story."

Once one makes a true commitment to something, then Providence moves. That's what the Himalayan adventurer, Murray, wrote, and Irving believes, too. I'll commit and the wings of destiny — or my friends' hopes and prayers — will carry me through.

From: Website Contact Form
To: Annie Shaw
Name: John Wilson
oldreader@librarynet.net

I have to say I'm quite surprised that I found your work, Miss Shaw. I was in my library looking for an old bestseller from 1948 titled *The Young Lions*. It's my goal in my retirement to read every New York Times Bestseller ever written or at least since they began keeping record. *The Young Lions* was checked out but there your book was next to where his titles would have been so I picked it up. Location, location, location, as they say. I likely would never have selected a book

by a young woman writing of romance but I have to say the book
was quite charming and I intend to buy a copy for my granddaughter
so I hope it is still in print. She's a hopeless romantic and I do like to
nourish that in an adolescent reader. Teenagers have such a hard
time as it is with all their ups and downs in life that if they can find
stories that celebrate family and faith, then truly, it is a gift given to
help them survive the travails of life. Have you considered writing for
young adults? They really do need good reading material. Anyway,
The Young Lions was written by Irwin Shaw. Is he a relative of yours?
If so, I'd certainly tout that on the back of my books if I were you. It
would surely help you become a bestseller. Not that I know about such
things you understand. I'm a retired lawyer. My wife died last year and
my only son and his family live hundreds of miles from me. Now that
I have more time for them they're off onto their own adventures so I
have lots of time to read. Thank you for giving me new authors to look
for and new stories to nurture my days.

Sincerely, John Wilson, Esquire

Chapter 25

For where your treasure is,
there will your heart be also.
Matthew 6:21 NKJV

"I need to buy an older model car," I tell Clint and Kari once I arrive back in Chicago. "A clunker." They've picked me up in the raspberry-smelling coffee car with Ho-Bee bouncing up and down in the back seat, plopping on my shoulders, then seconds later down on my lap, his white belly turned up for me to scratch. Kari's bought him little booties to keep his feet warm against the growing winter. He twists up then tugs at my red hat I've carried then shakes it like a snake stopping now and then to lick at the brim. "No, that's chocolate," I tell him and roll the hat up and stuff it in an outside pocket of my luggage. "Chocolate's bad for dogs. He missed me," I say to Kari and Clint.

"He did. We all did," Kari says.

"What do you need a car for?" Clint asks. I see his eyes in the rear-view mirror.

"I'm surprised that you're going to drive back to Milwaukee," Kari asks. "And invest in a car now, too."

"I'm not driving back. It's to help get myself a bestseller, visually," I say. "I don't want to spend too much." I have $5,000 remaining on one credit card and it has to get me through the next month and perhaps make a down payment on repaying the advance if I need to buy my book back. Randolph says Dr. Phil and Oprah will both pay $500 for my appearance but they'll spend thousands in wedding expenses. I can't stoop to that, I just can't. Maybe I could do the counseling with Dr. Phil but not the wedding. I'll see what Randolph thinks about that.

"Someone in my office always has a sign up on the bulletin board," Clint says, "trying to sell an older model car. Does it need to be an automatic?"

"It really doesn't matter. It only has to run about twenty miles and back."

Clint frowns. "What are you investing in, Annie?"

"An idea," I say. "Ideas are good investments, aren't they, as a rule?"

" 'Where your treasure is, there will your heart be also,' " Kari says.

I stroke my dog and try not to think about what I've been spending my money on if it suggests where my treasure is. If Kari's quote is accurate, my heart's on its way to the city's dump.

⑥

Kari comes home from work two days later to find me teaching Ho-Bee how to roll over on command and to get him comfortable doing it in a little Santa suit complete with hat. He'll be part of my "extravaganza" as I've named my last promotion in Chicago.

Kari sets the table leaving a cupboard door open as she often does. She's planned a big meal for Clint she says is the way to a man's heart.

"Speaking of a way to a man's heart, I read in the airplane magazine about new brain research where they showed men a picture of a bikini-clad woman to see what part of their brains lit up. Then they showed them other pictures and one kind of photograph lit up that same part of the brain. Guess what it was?"

"Cars," Clint says as he puts his backpack briefcase on the credenza.

"Nope. Your guess, Kari."

"Some piece of sporting equipment. A hockey stick or a football."

"Nope, both wrong," I tell them. "Pictures of hardware: drills, staple guns, screw drivers. Tools. Can you believe it?"

"The hardware store is as sexy as a bathing beauty model? That's hard to believe," Kari says. "But now that I think about it, I've watched you in the hardware store, Clint. There is that look of lusty anticipation."

"I rest my case," I say.

"Maybe you can wrap your manuscript around a hammer and send it to Stedman," Clint says.

I hadn't thought of that.

"I might be better off coming up with a fragrance that smelleth of hardware," I tell them, "and squirteth it on the manuscript sent Stedman's way."

"A client of mine has an old VW bug she's been trying to sell," Kari says putting me back on course. "I'll get you her number. Her son's gone off to college and didn't want to drive it across country. It runs good yet and you'd be surprised how much stuff you can stuff into those little cars."

"They'll start in cold weather too. Be good for you back in Wisconsin," Clint chimes in.

"I'm not driving it back there. I'm having it … wrapped," I tell them. "Decals with the name of my book all over it, like NASCAR sponsors. I'll be parking it where it'll be seen. On Oprah's street. And then I'll resell it."

They look at me as though I've slipped on a cement step and hit my head.

Maybe I have.

⑥

Bette calls later in the week as I'm making final arrangements for my wrap. "I'm having a newspaper delivered to my place," Bette says. "Arnold hand delivers it now." She giggles like a school girl in love.

"Who's Arnold?"

"He's the *lawn* boy's dad but he picks up a paper for me every morning and drops it by the center. He's taking me to meet his other children on Thanksgiving Day. He lost his wife a few years back. I think this could be the real thing," Bette says. "I can't begin to thank you for making this happen."

"I'm happy for you," I tell her, and I am. I'm a little wistful, too, that she's encountered someone in the everyday who might be a partner for her, every day of her life. I wish that had happened for me but it didn't. Rewriting the final scene helps me accept that.

"But I didn't make you and Arnold happen," I tell Bette. "You did. Just by being you and offering your kindness to me to look after my flat and John. You were in the right place at the right time. See what comes from your generosity? Give and you shall receive," I remind her.

"When are you coming home? John really does miss you. And his place, too. I miss having you pop over on my lunch break. And those Sunday school kids have started to ask me if you've died."

"That's awful. I'll text you during class next Sunday so they'll know I'm alive. But soon. I'm coming home soon. I have a few more things to do here. My extravaganza as I'm calling it, and then I'm gone."

"Do you need us to come?"

"No. You're doing good things where you are."

"We're trying. Misty's posting something nearly every day on Oprah's website about your books. She's got Darlien doing it too and your sister's found fellow officers willing to post. They read *The Long Bad Sentence* and liked it. And get this: Darlien's eating better. She says since the Neti pot thing, she hasn't sneezed and food tastes so much better. Isn't that great? She actually ate an apple with me last week."

"Really?"

"She also wrote a letter to her policemen's trade magazine

about your proposed book. You ought to write an article for them. Did you ever write something about your kids and the Reading Ready program?"

"I've been … occupied," I say.

"And we covered the book fair with Mavis, too. That was fun! So you worked on your final revisions with Irving?"

"I did. And Irving seems to like the big scene change. Now he has to convince the rest of the team to proceed."

"And when's the taping of the Dr. Phil show?"

"Right after Thanksgiving."

"We should come for that. Have you met the guy who'll play your Jaime? Or is the real one coming?"

"No. And if my extravaganza works, I won't have to do that show or Oprah's at all."

⑥

Kari and Clint invite a few friends over for Thanksgiving. I help with the stuffing, make the pear and sweet potato dessert. I notice that we've set the table for eleven but four empty places remain unfilled by the time the bird is bronzed and steaming and all the other guests have arrived. Kari gives no explanation as we sit down to eat and the conversation weaves itself around a dozen subjects. It's a nice gathering and Ho-Bee lies on his side in the living room, snoring, his favorite thing. I imagine Jaime at one of the empty chairs. No, he just wouldn't fit.

Eventually the subject finds its way to the fact of my writing. "She's quite accomplished," Kari says speaking of me. "She'll have her fourth book out in the spring. Tell them the title."

"They haven't decided yet," I say preparing for the inevitable, aghast you-don't-get-to-decide-the-title look on Kari's friends' faces.

"What's it about?" one of Kari's colleagues asks instead.

I give the usual response from my intention statement and then add, "It's about risk and desire and authenticity, what you're willing to do to stay real."

271

"You should get Oprah to read it," Clint's associate says. He chews on a dark piece of turkey meat. "Doesn't she like those 'musty' books?" I wrinkle my pigeon toes in confusion.

"I don't know what a musty book is."

"I must change. I must find my way. I must —"

"You must stop," his wife says pressing her hand on his sleeve but I can tell she isn't upset.

Maybe it is a musty book. I might suggest that to the back cover copy writers. Maybe a musty book is better than kindling.

"But Oprah would mean a lot of recognition, isn't that so?" Clint's colleague lifts his eyes to me over the top of his drumstick.

"Yes, but it isn't easy to get Oprah —" I begin to explain when the doorbell rings.

"Oh, here they are!" Kari says, rising quickly. "I didn't want to say unless they actually made it." She turns to me, winks, then she opens the door.

In walk my mother and father, my sister. And, the real Jaime.

Chapter 26

Of course, Randolph hasn't heard a word of my protest; he does what he thinks is best.

"You don't have to pay for plane fare," Jaime says after he kisses me swishing me off my feet. Introductions are made and I've closed my mouth from surprise both at his arrival and that his kiss left me empty, nothing like the "stay in this kiss forever" kind of Barcelona. "Oprah pays for plane. Is so American, the woman pays." He grins that infectious grin, and I detest Randolph for interfering and love him at the same time. Jaime is a good man to spend time with—just not for a lifetime.

"We knew you'd want to see us too but we didn't want to say for sure, in case something happened with his flight," Darlien says. "Mom and Pop and I can't stay but the weekend. How long Jaime stays is up to you."

"Did you quit your job?" I ask, alarmed.

"I takes next year's August vacation early," he says. "I have month's time only."

He has eyes the color of Ho-Bee's.

"You can be married by Christmas. Isn't that so lovely?" My mother says.

I gulp. "Mom ..."

"Oh, I know. You've lots of things to discuss. But a mother can dream, can't she?"

"They won't show the program until after the holidays, but it'll get taped right away, right?" Darlien asks.

"Randolph hasn't given me the details. Just the preliminaries with Dr. Phil."

"He is the best man?" Jaime asks.

"Best man? No. I mean he is a good man who can sort this all out. I wish you hadn't come —"

"Before the date was set," my mother interrupts. "It's hard to get excited about a wedding when you don't know the date, isn't it, son?" my mother says.

"He doesn't have a date?" my father asks. "Why does he need a date? I thought he came to get married to Annie." My mom pokes him in the shoulder, her signal for silence.

My head hurts. Now I'll have to work around Jaime in order to get my extravaganza in place and go through with the Dr. Phil portion to placate them all. Jaime reaches for my hand and holds it. *"Recuerdo Barcelona,"* he says kissing my fingertips.

My memories are becoming musty.

⑥

My pre-owned lime-green Volkswagen bug coughs and jerks me into the "We Wrap It" plant, the garage of Guido and Visconti down the street that I've found through the internet. They plaster pictures and logos around the sloped back, the hood, the doors, just like NASCAR sponsors, only I don't have any sponsors, only me, though Jaime's come with me. I feel guilty that he's using up future vacation plans for what I know will not be a happy result and find it difficult to talk with him about what really matters, instead focusing on my extravaganza.

Onto the hubcaps, Guido and Visconi tape small copies of the bright mock book cover that my friends brought with them the day of Oprah's show. I've made duplicates in various sizes and everywhere else the words *Spanish Knight* wrap the car with color. It's a risk going with the manuscript not yet finished with a title that isn't firmed, but it's the book connected to all the hullabaloo with Jaime and Dr. Phil, so I decided to go with that book, imagining it into being. Two sandwich boards like the kind that bookstores put out in front to announce an author visit are in the back. A reader board, printed on both sides, will ride the car top.

"Theze is for Oprah?" Jaime asks.

"Not the show," I tell him. "But otherwise, yes."

I pay the brothers, then drive the bug back to Kari and Clint's apartment amidst honks and cheers from fellow commuters as a light snow begins to fall. People point and stare. I'm drawing visual attention. It's not the Oscar Mayer Weiner mobile so familiar to Chicago, but I'm on the right track.

"You'll have to be careful it doesn't get ripped off," Clint says as we stand in the parking garage. "That Santa you've mounted near the reader board could attract would-be thieves. I can see a bunch of college kids finding it an added attraction for a holiday frat party."

"It's so big. And gaudy," Kari says.

"Gaudi," I comment. "That's how that term got its meaning, something big and raucous and filled with strange angles like Gaudi, of Spain."

"Si. Gaudi," Jaime says. "He design many things in my country."

I've sub-let the parking space from one of Kari's neighbors who's gone south for the winter. I try not to think about my expenses: parking costs to keep my moving ad safe; my flat rent in Milwaukee; all my expenses at home. And I contribute to Kari and Clint's grocery bills. I want to do something big for them before I leave but any helpful gift may have to wait. I'm on my final thousand dollars. The preliminary of the Doctor Phil show is Friday. I have to put my car to work this week or be forced to do the taping to stay financially afloat.

If I can put the Oscar Mayer Wiener song out of my head, it'll be better, I tell myself. Maybe I'll see the VW bug mobile for what it truly is—a shot in the dark of a marketing world. Instead I hum my little song as I dress Ho-Bee in his Santa outfit and me in Mrs. Clause's costume. We're doing a dry run in full costume.

"This is St. Nicolas?" Jaime asks.

"We call him Santa Claus," I say, "but yes, it's basically the same thing. The children love him. The parents will get a laugh seeing Ho-Bee, but they'll also see my book decal on the trunk and the reader board."

"But maybe you are too … open." He gropes for words, points to the car.

I look at the reader board. It reads:

I HOPE OPRAH LOVES *A SPANISH KNIGHT*

"It says what I wish," I say though it might suggest something other than a book title. Maybe I should put the title in quotes. "I was going to have them write 'Oprah Loves *A Spanish Knight*' but that would be false advertising. I don't know if she loves it because she hasn't read it yet. This is more … authentic."

"Will the Oprah want everyone to know she loves this Spanish knight? How will this sell your books?"

"What? No. It's my book. The cover is all over the car. I hope she likes the *book* I've written. That's what this is all about."

Everything works fine for the afternoon dry run around the block from Kari and Clint's condo. People stop and chat. I have an exceptionally fine day and talk about my book using my title, *Spanish Knight*, giving people a tiny Christmas bell I got at ten for a dollar at the bargain store. I hope it'll remind them of the final lines about the bells of Barcelona. Several people commend me for my creativity. "I'll bet she notices it," one says. "You know, if you get Oprah interested, you'll have a bestseller."

"I hope so," I say. I have my elevator sentence down flat and can tell people what the book's about. "It's about a woman trying to decide whether to settle or risk searching for something more," I tell them. The women got it right away. Most of the men have a sour stomach look on their face until I add, "And it's about the International Police and Fireman Games in Barcelona and a couple who meet there."

"Ah. Sounds interesting. I didn't know there were such games."

One woman suggests I should give away something to eat. Chocolate, maybe. I wish I had Barcelona chocolate pieces. That would be perfect.

Back in the condo, Jaime lies on the couch, his hands clasped behind his neck. It's his bunking place since he's arrived. He rolls the sheets and blankets up during the day. Ho-Bee sleeps more quietly in my bed perhaps protecting me from the deep breathing coming from the living room. I'm baking dog cookies to hand out using Chef Smith's recipe minus the fire and the okra. People like pet treats better than goodies for themselves. I'll serve hot flavored teas to humans.

"If Oprah likes your book," Jaime says, "then we gets married."

I drop a cookie sheet. "No. Really, nothing has changed from Barcelona. Nothing."

"I change for you," he says. His dark eyes twinkle at me. He stands up to kiss my nose. Ho-Bee hops beside us leaping tall enough to lick my cheek.

"You mean you've changed your mind about children?"

"Maybe that is a change I could make."

I look at him with new eyes. Could he really do that, change, just for me? No. I didn't believe he could in Spain and I don't believe it's so now. He'd have to make such a change for himself most of all, or when things got challenging—and they always do at times with kids—he'd resent me.

"'I will not go there,' says the cat. 'I will not go there, that is that.'"

"What you saying about cats?"

"Nothing. I've got too much on my mind right now. We'll talk about it after tomorrow when my bug-mobile's had a chance to do its work."

Jaime has a puppy-dog disappointed look on his face, and I realize he's taken a huge risk in coming here and I'm avoiding him, avoiding talking about what really matters.

"I change," he says. "Love changes."

I sigh and want to tell him that changing for another person is never the best answer. That's what Miranda learned and it's what I know for sure. I'd tell him, but I need to watch the cookies so they won't burn.

⊚

"To be honest," I tell the Dr. Phil producer who calls the next morning, "I'm pleased Dr. Phil will offer prenuptials as you should know that we have some concerns about the relationship between Jaime and me."

His voice blasts on the speaker phone sitting between Jaime and me. Jaime stares at me.

"Excellent," the producer says. "We want to talk about long distance relationships. That's the entire point of the programming. We'll be sending a film team to your home tomorrow, to assess your compatibility around issues. House arrangements, money, work—what kind of work do you do?"

"I'm a writer," I say. "I actually have a new book coming out—"

"And about sex—"

"Sex? You'll be asking about sex?" I squeak.

"Right. To see if there are areas of differences. It's part of what pre-nuptials are about. Levels of experience, differences in preferences, that sort of thing. Solving problems before they occur."

How do I tell him that there has been no sex? There's nothing to discuss in this regard at all. I'll be talking on television about things I haven't even shared with my dog. I don't want to embarrass Jaime or myself by discussing issues of such intimacy, especially when they require a translator. My ex-husband and I spoke the same language and we needed an interpreter to deal with intimate issues. Or rather to not deal with them.

"And children, how you'd want them to be disciplined, that sort of thing. You have pets? That's always a good indicator of

278

how you'll be with kids. Plan for say four hours. We might have you take a drive, talk in the car."

"I only have a very small VW bug," I tell them. "I'm pretty sure there isn't room for a camera."

"We'll post one on top that looks in as you drive. Not to worry. We'll get you covered."

⑥

November 30. I dress in my Mrs. Santa outfit and pull the little hat and sweater onto Santa Ho-Bee. I consider giving him the other half of a diet pill that I think might calm him down but I don't want anyone to think I mistreat him. A Jack Russell's supposed to be active and seeing one lying belly up, asleep, for more than a minute, might send off alarm bells. I grab the book brochures; hold the mock-up of the cover given me the day of our A-level meeting. It's got those steamy models but we just might end up with that cover. I mean, Irving can only negotiate so much and he's already gotten me a reprieve on the book's death sentence. I've photo-shopped my own title onto the front and blown it up and put the cover on the sandwich boards. It will stand at either end of the street my car is parked on. It's sure to attract attention. But the car is wrapped with the Misty-designed cover with my new title superimposed. The visual interests will slow people down so I can hand them my brochures, offer them a cup of Santa Tea, and if they have a pet, give them a cookie and wish them a happy holiday all the while advertising my new book. Of course, my target audience is one person: Oprah.

Snow falls in huge white flakes muting the dirt and the sounds of the city. Still, people drive faster through the accumulating slush than I'd imagine. Jaime insists on coming with me, "for protections" he says. We ease the bug mobile and park it just outside of Oprah's gated estate. Her neighbors will see me. Her personal assistants will see me. Her chef will see me. And when she leaves for the studio and when she returns in her limousine, she'll see me too. She'll see the blow up of the book, the cover with my name in big black letters and when I step out with dog in hand to hand her a brochure, I'll also ask if she'd like to see the manuscript. How could she turn down such an inventive way of reaching her? She might even be amused. Ho-Bee's a natural charmer and Jaime looks quite festive in his green elf suit and hat.

Bundled up in hoodies and a parka, we're in place early. A cloud-muted sun hovers over the horizon. I stand outside the car holding Santa Ho-Bee while Jaime pops Christmas carols into the cassette player. The windows are down so the neighborhood can hear them. There's little traffic this early on Oprah's street. No one slows down to read the car or accept dog treats.

But traffic increases and snow and slush work in our favor and eventually some cars slow and I step out then and use Ho-Bee as a pointer to my book title. A few people smile and wave back gesturing with their hands. I think they've waving. In between, I hand Jaime Ho-Bee to warm him in the heated car, then grab him again when someone approaches. Heat escapes and his little body shivers. I'd wrap him tighter but then his attracting presence can't be distinguished from a pillow all wrapped in white. No one will stop long enough to get a cup of tea from a pillow let alone accept a brochure about a book from one.

A couple of hardy pedestrians, dog walkers, stop to take tea I've heated with one of those pots that plug into the cigarette lighter. They ask to borrow a doggy pooper bag. When I say I don't have any extra, they accept one of my brochures and use it as a scooper. Something about that is rather depressing.

Three people shout out one car window that they don't have any change before I realize they must think I'm a panhandler staking out new space and that my doggie dish of treats is asking for money.

A flock of middle schoolers walks by with heads bowed into the snowflakes, but they stop when they hear Santa Ho-Bee bark. Maybe their mothers will see my brochure when they empty their children's pockets on washday. Maybe one of their mothers is Oprah's producer or manicurist and she'll remember the brochure and tell Oprah. It can happen. It's possible.

"I thinks this is not so good an idea," Jaime says as the day wanes and our stomachs growl. Ho-Bee's been fed but I didn't pack a lunch for Jaime or me.

"It's my last hope, it really is."

In the long gaps between cars or walkers, Jaime broaches the subject that brought him all this way but I avoid it. "I need a block of time without interruption to talk about this, Jaime," I tell him.

"You are frightened," he says.

"No, no, nothing like that. I need to concentrate on my extravaganza."

"You fear moving to Spain."

"No, that's not it. Truly. Let's talk about it later, please?"

"All peoples fear looking foolish, but love ... is like new design for foolish, like Gaudi, making new of something old. The cat someone makes to be like Gaudi."

I think of the Gaudi-like cat I bought for myself, the one I used in my manuscript; the one like Irving has. A cat designed and sculpted and painted with uniqueness. Maybe Jaime's right. Maybe a fear can be turned into something new and amazing.

"*I will not go there,*" *says the cat.* "*I will not go there, that is that.*"

By 4:00 p.m. our stomachs are growling in unison and I agree with Jaime we may as well call it quits. I'm removing the Santa from the top of the VW bug when a dark-windowed car approaches slowly.

"Quick, hand me Ho-Bee," I tell Jaime.

But it moves on leaving me to consider the failure of my day.

If Oprah's personal assistant or her chef or her personal trainer comes by, I fail to recognize them. I never see Oprah. We are splashed on, cursed, and have familiar gestures sent our way.

"Did you know that the middle finger gesture comes from medieval times," I tell Jaime. "Enemies used to cut off that finger to prevent them from pulling their bows and shooting arrows ever again. So they lifted that finger in triumph after a battle, to show that they still had it. Isn't that sweet?"

He looks at me, aghast.

A news helicopter flies above us on its way to some sad event somewhere. I can read the station's call letters on the side though it's almost dark. How much gas have I burned up keeping the car warm? How much time have I wasted on this venture? I think of Kari asking me what I treasure. I blow against my cold fingers. Jaime stamps from foot to foot.

"You're a good sport," I say and realize what a good man he really is and how foolish I've been to not pay him more attention, not address what truly matters instead of chasing fame. "Want one last cup of Santa Tea before we head home?" He nods and I fit the adapter into the cigarette lighter to heat the pot yet again while we pick up the sandwich boards at the end of the block.

"Something smells of funny," Jaime says as we meet back at the bug and stick the boards in the back seat with my manuscript. It never even made it out of the box.

I sniff.

"Did that tea spill?" I stick my head through the front seat window as the cigarette lighter adapter puffs and sparks and catches fire to a box of tissues I've left between the seats. I reach for them but Ho-Bee gets there first hopping up onto the dash, an act that bumps the brochures I've left on the dash into the flame. Instead of suffocating it, it fuels it. I swat and cough and Jaime yells for the fire extinguisher which of course I do not have. I grab the dog looking for something to suffocate the fire while Jaime attempts to extinguish the now licking flames swatting at the burning brochures with his gloves.

"Fire! Fire!" I scream batting now at the flames with my Santa hat in one hand and holding onto Ho-Bee with the other.

The dog's high-pitched bark pierces my ears, and I can't tell if he's in pain from a burn or from my squeezing his chest to keep him from jumping down or back into the car.

The upholstery's on fire and Jaime yells to "stay back!" while he scoops up hands-full of road slush to toss at the car but to no avail. Black smoke billows up as I follow it into the sky. I see that sky-cam chopper heading back toward its station. It circles, then hovers overhead as we stand helpless watching the burning car. I hear the squeal of tires as a TV van roars to a stop spilling out a cameraman bearing long cables that tangle like discarded licorice strings. The cameraman isn't zooming in on my wrapped car but instead on the dog whose little ear tips like my eyebrows are singed. Ho-Bee yaps his displeasure at the cameraman through the smoke. He leaps from my arms yanking the leash from my hand.

"Ho-Bee, come back."

Ho-Bee circles the TV cameraman's leg while I lunge for the leash and the dog wraps it and himself like a tee-ball swimming ever tighter around the cameraman who slips. And slides and tumbles into slushy snow.

I let go of the leash too late and Ho-Bee stands triumphant on top of the cameraman while smoke billows around us.

Now there are enough cars in the vicinity, it looks like a parking lot. Drivers gawk and point and then a police car swings in followed by the "Animal Control Unit" and the fire department truck. The firemen spray foam over my bug covering the scorched reader board on the top of the car with the title of my book. The recovered cameraman pans the foam but not my book title.

"I'm afraid I'll have to cite you," the police officer says when the fire is out and the firemen wrap up their hoses. A tow truck arrives. I want to ask if any of the officers have been to the International games in Barcelona but somehow, it doesn't seem the right time.

"What law did I break?" I hold the dog who lays his head over my forearm. He smells like smoky wet fur.

"Laws," the policeman says. "For starters, interference with traffic flows on a public roadway. Endangerment of an animal. That could get you real jail time in this PETA precious neighborhood. Health department violations. You were serving food and drink. Do you have a food handler's license?" I shake my head no.

Jaime approaches and offers to help, tells them he's a policeman in Spain. The officer is pleasant but continues to write. "Were you panhandling on a public street?"

"I was giving things away. I wasn't asking for anything," I say.

"In that outfit, I can see why."

My Mrs. Santa dress is dark with soot and will never make the Runway Project finals.

"And finally, you're in violation of this neighborhood's homeowners covenant related to advertising and bill boards. You've got three of those fines coming. The two sandwich boards at the corners and the car itself all wrapped up to look like what, a book?" He looks at the hubcaps. "Spanish Knight? Is that you?" He looks at Jaime.

"No. It's a character in the book I've written. I didn't realize there was a law against parking a car in a street."

"Can't have a billboard," the police officer says. "And the tow's required. Got to get this car out of here. You'll have to come down and pay the fines and the towing charge to get it out. You can ride with me," he says. He wiggles his nose at the scent of smoke clinging to our clothes, my dog.

"I wanted Oprah to see the name of my book and let me give her a copy of the manuscript." Tears well up and Ho-Bee licks them from my soot cheeks.

"Yeah," the police officer says as he folds his pad and hands me my citations. "Somebody last week tried the same thing.

Wrapped a van, though. But they didn't burn up their car to do it. I forget what the title of their book was."

We clamber into the back seat of his cruiser.

Someone else has already thought of wrapping a car to promote their book? I'm not even uniquely bizarre.

I look at the back of the policeman's head through the bars. It's as though we've committed a terrible crime sitting in the back seat separated from the police officer when he was just being kind giving us a ride to the station where I can call Kari and Clint to come pick us up. The cameraman gets a shot of that.

"There's Oprah now," the policemen says. He nods with his chin to a large black limousine easing its way out through the gate. "She's the one who called. Someone told her there was a street person hanging outside her gate again, someone with another book."

"Oprah was at home all day?" *So close, so very close!*

"Yeah, but she didn't tape today," the officer says. "Likely heading off to a party, she is."

I watch as the long car moves past us. The tinted windows make it impossible to see if Oprah's really in there. If she is, and she looks toward my car with its reader board now pitched at a mountain climbing angle and covered with extinguishing foam, she'll have to twist her neck to read my book title along the side of the still smoking car.

"A writer, huh?" the officer says as we pull in behind the tow truck. His eyes meet mine through the rear view mirror. "I've always wanted to write a book. How'd you get yours published?"

Chapter 27

You ask and do not receive,
because you ask amiss,
that you may spend it on your pleasures.
James 4:3 NKJV

Clint and Kari rescue us from the police precinct. Ho-Bee now bears blobs of almond-butter cream on the tips of his ears, evidence he survived the extravaganza. Kari's clients swear almond-butter heals burns quickly so I have some on my former eyebrows as well. Jaime's hands are wrapped in cream-filled gauze too. I've lost my eyebrows and look ... blanched. We all still cough up upholstery smoke.

"Thanks for picking us up," I tell Kari back at their condo. Clint and Jaime are in the television room watching football so we're alone.

"I'm sorry we didn't get your call earlier. I worked late. Maybe you can deduct the cost of your fines as research for your books," Kari says.

"That might have worked for my *Long Bad Sentence* book but not for Miranda. Besides, I have to have an income in order to deduct anything. I have my fines and accumulating legal bills from spas to city ordinances and I doubt they'll be deductible either. At least the Humane Society released Ho-Bee to me so he didn't have to spend the night in jail."

"Did any good come from this scheme?"

I consider. "We met some interesting people waiting for you."

"Possible characters in a future novel?" Kari asks.

"Maybe. But I'm not sure I'll write another novel." My admission surprises even me.

"I'm sorry I didn't say out loud that this latest scheme seemed over the top, even for you."

"It might have worked. Oprah called us in to the police or probably one of her bodyguards did. I guess we looked dangerous out there. And she probably does have to worry about stalkers."

"Or cookie-giving-marketing-maniacs."

"I know, it was crazy. It's all been crazy." I'm close to tears.

We turn on the 11:00 p.m. news and there I am, soot-stained, looking out through the windows of the police car.

"Notoriety is not the same as fame."

⑥

"I'm sorry," Irving says to me on the phone the next morning. "Without the Oprah connection, the decision's been made to forego the publishing of your book." His voice strums across the strings of my heart.

"I did make the evening news," I tell him. "And the jury is still out about getting on Oprah. That might still happen. It's not Christmas yet. I still have time."

"You did what I asked. The drama that announces Miranda's reason for not staying with Jaime is much stronger. But in the end ... it lacks the passion necessary for Ardor Publishing. I wish it were different. They'll push the book forward only if there is some remarkable notice from an Oprah or an Angelina."

"So my agent's scheme is our last hope."

"I'm afraid so."

Spanish Knight sandwich boards are stowed behind police barriers until I either go to court or pay the fine for my unauthorized billboard. I can't pay the towing charge unless I borrow from my parents. How embarrassing is that? My eyebrows are missing and I've already received hate emails from people who saw the news clip and twittered my name. They think I was negligent with my dog. And maybe I was but he's gained weight, at least that's what the veterinarian's scale records. She tells me I'm still a good mom and to take Ho-Bee home and enjoy him. Except for Ho-Bee, all my investments have been for naught.

"I appreciate your efforts, Irving, I truly do."

"Well, let me know the outcome of your taping tomorrow," Irving says. "We can proceed from there."

I don't think there's anywhere to proceed.

"Jaime," I say later as we sit with our feet up on the cassock in Clint and Kari's living room. We're alone. My cousin and her husband are asleep in their beds but I can't put yesterday aside. "What you said yesterday, about my being afraid, well, you're right. I am."

"Theze is not necessary," he tells me. He looks sleepy but I'm sitting on the couch, his bed. He squeezes my shoulder. "I take good cares of you in Spain. My family will love my American bride."

"But see, I'm not ready for marriage," I tell him. "I wasn't when I was in Spain and I'm not now."

"It will be organized by Oprah, the American way. You will have a wedding planner. I hear of them. They do everything, every day."

"No, it's not the wedding I'm not ready for, it's marriage," I tell him. "It's, there's so much between us that we haven't even talked about. We really don't know each other and we're so different."

"I can change for you."

"I can't ask you to do that," I tell him. I touch his face, his stubbled dark beard. "People who try to change for the wrong reasons end up in trouble. Gaudi wasn't creating a cathedral to please someone else when he gave us his singular designs. They came from his heart. And my heart just isn't where yours is."

"We will discuss with Dr. Phillip, tomorrow," he says and pats my hand. "It will be a good thing to talk about as Americans do, spilling our colons on television."

"I think you mean spilling our guts," I say wishing that I had enough courage to stop what will happen the next day.

⊙

Dr. Phil's film crew arrives for the pre-taping. By phone, Misty's advised me to be myself. Bette tells me to let Dr. Phil lead. She must not watch his program because he's always in charge. Darlien says to be careful I don't say something that I can be sued for. Randolph reminds me that the future of Miranda — and his daughter's next tuition payment — rest on my shoulders.

A translator is part of the crew.

Perhaps when I left Jaime in Europe without explanation, it was like allowing someone else to choose the ending for my stories. Now I have the chance to write a new ending. Dr. Phil will surely be able to help me say what I need to.

"So how long have you known each other?" Dr. Phil asks. We can see him on a television screen though he's in California while Jaime and I sit together on Kari and Clint's couch in Chicago. Depending on the results of this pre-taping, the program will either air or not. It will be out of my hands after today. I'm still letting someone else write my endings.

Dr. Phil has the kindest eyes and with the high definition technology I can see that without the make-up, his face would be overrun with pigeon toes.

"We met last summer, in Barcelona," I say.

"It was love at first sighting," Jaime says. He grins at me, his white teeth gleaming as he reaches for my hand and holds it.

"You're soul mates," Dr. Phil says. "Maybe you don't need prenuptial discussion."

A translator says something to Jaime in Spanish and Jaime smiles. "Si," he says.

"I take it you concur Mr. Garcia?" Dr. Phil says, then bends that now-famous pate toward me, piercing my eyes with his. "Mr. Garcia looks rub-it-in-your-hair-happy, but you, not so much. Am I right Miss Shaw?"

"I'm happy but maybe not as certain of things as Jaime is. He flew all this way from Barcelona, surprising me, but I wouldn't describe us as soul mates."

"Do I detect pre-marital jitters?"

"More like pre-marital seizures." Ho-Bee hops onto my lap and I release Jaime's hand to stroke the dog.

"So what have you done about that? Have the two of you talked?"

"I've been ... preoccupied," I say. I pet Ho-Bee who is fidgeting on my lap. "I have ... a book, this deadline, so I haven't had time to explore my feelings."

The translator hums into Jaime's ear.

"Work?"

"I'm a writer," I say.

Is this an opening? Can my book come into the conversation so easily? Can this be the moment I'd been waiting for? I sit straighter on Kari's couch. Ho-Bee sits up too, almond-buttered ears alert.

"She comes to America to finish her books," Jaime says. "Then I follows her."

That part is true.

"Work has taken precedence over relationship," Dr. Phil says. I nod, yes.

"It's how I do things," I tell him. "I'm pretty passionate about my writing."

The producer says something I can't hear but Dr. Phil touches his ear piece.

"How's that working for you?" The famous Dr. Phil line. I knew it'd be coming sometime.

"I've finished the book, titled *Miranda of La Mancha*. No, it might be *Spanish Knight* or maybe *Bilked in Barcelona* and —"

"This isn't a commercial for your writing, Miss Shaw," the

producer in the living room says to me. His eyes are sharp as obsidian.

"I'm sorry. The story grew out of my time in Spain with Jaime and it's been my life these past months, getting it down on paper, revising it, being true to it."

"I detect animation when it comes to your writing but you seem pretty docile when it comes to love. So how's *that* working for you, your preoccupation with work rather than pre-marital bliss."

"Not very well," I whisper. I drop my eyes, embarrassed by my earlier boldness.

"We've done a little checking on you, Miss Shaw," Dr. Phil says then. "You've had recent encounters with the legal system I see. Made the nightly news a couple of times. Just last evening."

Their researchers are good!

"I was being inventive, promoting my book, and I had a few complications. A writer's got to do what a writer's got to do. Commit. Persevere. Succeed." *Surrender.* I try to sound cheery. Ho-Bee looks at me and cocks his head: he knows I'm faking my confidence.

Dr. Phil asks, "You're willing to make yourself look foolish for your book but not for love?"

"I begs her to stay but she leaves me behind," Jaime says. His voice catches. He's rescuing me again. I turn to look at him. He has tears in his eyes. He truly does care deeply for me.

But I've known that. That isn't why I left him. Ho-Bee jumps from my lap to his, the ultimate comforting dog.

"So is it true that your career forced you back to America, away from this idyllic, romantic encounter, this new phase of a commitment begun in Spain, Annie? I can call you that, all right? It helps the audience become more familiar with you if I use your first name. It lessens the wedge between you and them." If he'd been in the room he'd have patted my knee like a friendly father.

"I can call you Phil?"

"Not likely," the producer interrupts. "Let's stay on track."

"Yes, call me Annie, that's fine."

Dr. Phil takes no notes but has a memory like an unhappy wife. He won't be distracted. "Your fiancé is quite moved," Dr. Phil says. "He doesn't care whether you're a published writer or not." Jaime nods. "Have you considered that you could write while in Spain?"

Dr. Phil sounds like Kari now wondering about the reasons why I didn't stay in Spain, the Sous chef of emotions preparing to shred excuses as though they're last week's lettuce leaves and just as limp.

"Yes, but it would be more complicated from Spain. I don't like complications."

"Yet you've put yourself in compromising positions these past weeks." Now he looks at his notes. "Some sort of ruckus at a dog salon, a restaurant, a spa. Let's tell ourselves the truth here, Annie. What's the real reason you didn't remain behind to find out if this is the relationship you say you always wanted?"

I look at Jaime. He deserves honesty. My moment of truth. It's not all about profession; that's not the only reason I didn't risk it all and stay in Spain.

"Because he doesn't want children," I whisper.

"You don't like children, Mr. Garcia?" When Dr. Phil asks a question it's like an IRS auditor making statements masquerading as questions that are more like accusations than requests.

"I have many nieces and nephews," Jaime says. "I loves children."

"Is there a misunderstanding here?" Dr. Phil says. "Something lost in translation?"

"Jaime loves his sister's children," I say. "But he doesn't want any of his own. He said as much."

"Mr. Garcia, is her dog barking up the right tree?

Jaime nods his head in agreement. "Is true."

"And your organic clock is ticking," Dr. Phil says to me. *Has my mother been talking to everyone I know?*

"Biological clock." I say and swallow. I really don't want to get any more intimate than that.

Jaime leans forward, his forearms against his thighs. Ho-Bee squeezes through his arms, and licks his gauze-less hands. He holds the dog's fat belly.

"Why is that Mr. Garcia? Jaime. I can call you Jaime, right?"

Jaime nods. "It is not right to bring childrens into a world where a father must leaves and maybe not come home as he is shots by a thief. My profession, it gives me reasons to not have childrens."

Why, he's worried about leaving a family behind should something happen to him! I had no idea that's how he feels. He's only told me that children are needy, that they need much. Maybe what he meant has been lost in translation.

"You could give up being a police officer, change your profession," Dr. Phil says. "Lessen the risk of leaving your family behind though there's risk in all we do."

"I come here to tell her I will give up being a policeman," Jaime says. "But today I know I cannot. I miss even being away from my Barcelona when I know I could help. Being with police yesterday, here in America, reminds me of good work they do. We do. Important work. I will always be a policeman. My father was. My grandfather. It is what we do." He turns to me. "I am sorry. I say I can change for you but I cannot. How I feel about childrens, that is same, too." Ho-Bee jumps down and trots over to the camera man, lifts his leg and—

"NO!" I shout and Ho-Bee stops.

Jaime looks at me. "Is what I do," Jaime confirms.

"It wasn't what you said. It's Ho-Bee. He was about to ... never mind."

"I don't want to bring sadness into children's lives," Jaime continues. "No childrens. I remember my father." I reach to comfort him but he resists with a flicker of skin, the way a horse shivers off a fly.

"So, Annie," Dr. Phil says, "that's a deal breaker for you?"

I nod. "With your biological clock marking off the numbers it's pretty clear that you have a couple of very hard choices to make. You could marry Jaime who obviously loves you and hope you can convince him to maybe have children one day. He obviously does value children and the quality of their lives, greatly. Or get him to change professions. But being a police officer appears to be in his DNA. Or don't marry him and hope to meet the man of your dreams one day who does want children. But you might find him too late, assuming that you ever do. Perhaps you'll live a life without bearing children of your own. How you accept that choice is up to you. These are important questions for you both. "

I nod. "On the clock face of intelligence, really, really smart is right next to really, really dumb," I tell him. "But sometimes you can't tell the difference until you're looking back over time. I'm just not sure if I'm at 11:59 a.m. or at high noon."

"Aptly noted," he says. "Jaime sees you as his soul mate and with you could be rub-it-in-your-hair-happy. But I don't get the same sensation from you, Annie. For you, his love is not enough. You want children in your life, children of your own. That's my opinion and that's what you wanted, right?"

I nod yes.

At least I've told the truth and didn't have to say it to Randolph's fake Jaime sitting beside me.

"It's a good issue to explore, this fast love, long distance relationship with unresolved issues around children. Our discussion will help a lot of people make up their mind about challenges, that and the role of work in their lives. We'll likely fly you out." To the producer Dr. Phil says, "Gene, I think you'd best suggest to Miss Winfrey's producers they hold on taping that supposed wedding show though. After listening to these two, I think that's a dog that won't hunt."

⑥

We are actually going to fly to California unless I stop it. I'll be admitting in front of the world how important children are to my life and that I may not ever have the chance to fulfill that dream. Maybe we'd help someone else, telling what happened to us. But I'd be sharing an intimate story. I've avoided telling even my friends the reason I didn't stay in Spain.

Jaime and I go for a walk after the taping. The sun's come out and the snow looks like glitter on a child's birthday cake. We can see our breaths in the air.

Jaime holds me close to him with one arm. "There might be a thiefs," he says and gives me a wistful smile. Thieves brought us together in Barcelona.

His arm is warm and comforting, like that of a friend. But the tingling excitement felt in Barcelona during a summer love is missing. It's not only that he doesn't want children, it's that the spark of passion every marriage needs just isn't there. It's what I need to tell him.

"Can we stops someplace warm? Talk, without the cameras?" Jaime asks.

"Sure," I say. "Sure. There's a little bookstore around the block. Let's go there for a cup of coffee. I need to say some things I didn't say in Spain."

A west wind rips across Lake Michigan. I pull my coat collar up around my neck and burrow inside as we walk. Hundreds of people come and go along the street, so many in couples walking hand in hand. I may not ever have someone to share my hand for a lifetime. It's a possibility I'd better get used to. Somehow, it doesn't seem so bad.

In the entry way of the mall bookstore, I glance at the "coming events." Authors always do, honoring unknown colleagues, hoping to find their own picture there and savor a brief moment of satisfaction. My picture isn't there but what I do see causes me to pause.

"Look at that," I tell Jaime. "Marion Plush is coming here next week for a reading of her newest children's book *Tibidabo: To Thee I Will Give*. That's the name of Barcelona's highest mountain peak, right? The tour guide said so. It's what the devil promised Christ when he tempted him. Pretty lofty subject for a children's book."

"Is a Spanish writer?" Jaime asks. "Marion Plush. This is someone you know?"

"I didn't know I did, but now that I see the publicity shot, I see that I do." I point to a photograph I thought was the illustrator's photo. It's an author shot. "That's Irving Stellar, my editor. Former editor, actually. He's also Marion Plush the writer of that book."

Chapter 28

"…fame.
If it comes at all it will come because it is deserved,
not because it is sought after."
Henry Wadsworth Longfellow

I've taken Ho-Bee for his walk and sit now in Kari and Clint's living room. Jaime's at a hotel making arrangements to fly home. Randolph has yet to call me though I've uploaded the Dr. Phil tape to him. I know as soon as he watches it he'll be ready to strangle me that the Oprah wedding is off. I have to tell him that I want to buy back Miranda's story but he'll figure that out too. Without the Oprah connection, Ardor Publishing isn't going to publish my book anyway.

Ho-Bee jumps on his imaginary trampoline up and down, doing the same thing but never getting any closer to the frog collection. Does he expect different results?

At least Jaime and I are truthful now. I feel no pitter patter of my heart when I'm with him. Even if he insists on staying in America to let events unfold between us, I know that as children are in my heart, law enforcement is in his and never the two shall meet. *Miranda* knew it too. That's what the new ending I gave Irving was all about. My story knew the right ending before I did.

"I had no idea," Kari says when I tell her what Dr. Phil labeled "the deal breaker" for our relationship. "You've never said much about wanting kids."

"Neither have you," I say. "But your car talked."

She looks puzzled.

"I found the pregnancy test the day I fumigated your car."

She frowns. "It's a client's. We … my biological clock blew its alarm when I was twenty-five. We thought we'd live our lives happily without having children. Lots of people do. It's something we learned to live with. But then you came to stay." Kari smiles. "And we went to the Children's Museum. After that trip and watching you struggle these past weeks to find what you want, Clint and I had another serious talk. We're thinking about adoption." She blushes and I can see her as a beautiful mom.

I high five her. "I didn't know," I say. "I mean, you don't even have a dog."

"Dogs aren't a pre-requisite for kids, Hon." I get up and turn on the gas fireplace as Kari says, "You and Jaime would have each other too, you know."

"But it wouldn't be enough. I know that our love isn't enough or I'd have risked and remained in Spain. Truth is, I just don't love him in the way a future wife should. I was whipped off my feet, just like with Stuart, only this time I did admit to myself that it wouldn't work with Jaime even before I knew I didn't love him."

"So Oprah isn't going to know your name or make you a bestseller after all."

"I read once where Oprah said that if you don't know yourself before you achieve fame then fame will define you. I don't have to worry about fame defining me … but I almost did."

Kari lifts her glasses from their dangle cord around her neck, perches them on her nose, then looks over the top of them at me and says in her best counselor voice: "Está aquí. A wise place to travel to."

"I'll have to get a job to pay everything off, pay you back, and buy *Miranda* back, the works. I have lots to get done."

"Will you publish your book yourself?"

"I don't know. It might be that AP is right and it's not the great American novel. I mean in a good romance, the boy gets the girl, so I don't think Miranda's life qualifies. Maybe I could self-publish it but I'd hire an editor. I need editing like Ho-Bee needs his walks. I think I'll let it sit awhile and then reread it and revise it yet again before I decide to save up enough to self-publish."

"People who do self-publish have to do a lot of self-promotion, I've heard."

"Yeah. And we see how well I've done with that!"

"Your eyebrows will grow back."

"But not before my first job interview. When I get back to Milwaukee I'm going to see if my preschool teaching position is available, but I'll take whatever I can get that'll give me more time for my Reading Ready program kids. Maybe I'll work for a doggy day care place. Ho-Bee would love that."

"You've found your treasure, Annie, and reached the final stage of grief. Acceptance."

"But didn't you say that the cycle can begin again? That it's just part of living?"

"We have to keep renewing what truly matters or the grief can take us back, that's true."

I nod. "I just hope I don't make a fool of myself hanging on to a fleeting treasure."

(6)

"I actually feel ... serene," I tell Misty over the phone. "I've re-energized myself with daily devotionals."

"That's good," Misty says. I can hear Norton's television program rattling in the background when I call. Misty's come to the phone breathing hard. She'd been exercising, getting back into her original pre-Norton weight so she can Walk for The Cure with her friend. She's got us planning to do that too, as a team.

"The thing I feel sad about is that I didn't meet my bestseller goal, that I failed ... us. Even if we went on Oprah's show as

Randolph planned, she wouldn't know me as an author and that was what it was all about, promoting the story."

"I've been thinking it was about something more," Misty says. I can hear her chomping a carrot now. "Maybe we failed you by not better refining the goal. People accomplish their desires because they're certain of their destination, where they'll end up. You didn't really want to get Oprah to know your name. You wanted to be famous, right, so the books would sell?"

"I had mixed goals."

"Right. Becoming famous is dependent on someone else. Fame doesn't mean fulfillment. A real goal is one you can work toward making happen and it doesn't require another person's doing something. A satisfying goal is one that can make a difference in the lives of others as well as your own, don't you think? We came up with schemes to get attention for you but attention wasn't really it. I mean, you got attention. You made the evening news."

"Twice."

"You had fifteen seconds of fame."

"As a soot-stained alien whose eyebrows were eaten by moths."

"They'll grow back."

"I now have the attention of several lawyers and insurance companies and the local police and maybe the EPA and Homeland Security. At least Ho-Bee wasn't taken from me."

"See, there's always a silver lining."

Bette has a different take on my treasure as we have another conference call. "I think you wanted to find a way to know that the work you do is worthy. You gave Oprah the power to do that for you and that's silly, really. You're the only one who can decide if the work is worthy and it's worthy if you're staying close to the true Provider of a satisfying life. Fame has nothing to do with it. If only one person reads it and says, this mattered to me, you've done worthy work, don't you think? Even if it's a child you encourage with your Reading Ready program. That makes writing worthwhile."

"You could be right."

"You just want to make a living, like the rest of us, and if you can do that while doing something you love, well that's wealth. That's fulfillment. I think that's what you were really after. But if you have to take a part-time job or a full-time one and still pursue your dream, that's all right. You'll have more gruel to feed your story."

"Sometimes I wonder if I wrote that book not just to make sense of what was happening between Jaime and me, but to forgive myself for making such a big mistake in marrying Stuart."

"It wasn't a total mistake," Darlien says. "You learned from it and didn't repeat it with Jaime. I'm working on why my marriages have ended as they did. Maybe some time we'll talk about that, Annie." Darlien offers another insight from her cell. "You have to have a good time," she says. "I love to win when I compete in golf but what matters is letting yourself take in the good things we've been given and caring about the people you're with and what they bring to your life. You should frame those emails from happy readers. They'll remind you why you write."

"Then why was I so discombobulated after seeing that my editor is the author of a successful children's book? Am I jealous?"

"Maybe you're still not certain that *Miranda of La Mancha*, or what did you change it to? Never mind. Maybe that isn't the right book for you to write," Misty says. "Maybe those green eyes are telling you to look at something else. Your editor is doing what he loves. Maybe that's what you envy."

"Here's another way to look at this, Annie." It's Bette. "When geese are in the V formation, the lead goose takes all the hits, like you did. But while she's flying, she creates a vortex that lets the other geese travel along behind her with less energy. The lead goose sort of brings the other geese along, pulls them into that vortex. Look what seeking your goal did do: I've met Arnold and a terrific bunch of kids. Darlien's eating better than she ever has."

"That's true. I ate sushi last week!"

"Misty, Misty's going to Walk for the Cure helping other people and getting herself back in shape, right Misty."

Misty concurs.

"And Kari?"

"Clint wanted a dog," Kari says. "And we'll get one now. But we're also going to start the adoption process for a child. Bette's right. You've pulled us along with you and we've all discovered new things. Our prayers for your success were answered. Just not as we imagined."

⑥

I'd often wondered why Marion Plush's pictures didn't appear in his/her books; only the illustrator's photo graced the jacket. Maybe Irving wants people to think it's a female author writing his children's book. John Wayne's real name was Marion. A lot of men were called that in earlier days. Women can be seen as more nurturing, better with young children than men. But he might have told me. I was right there, asking about Marion Plush, for heaven's sake, gushing over her work. He'd deceived me while we talked about authenticity.

On the other hand, he seems perfectly happy to write without having everyone know who he is. Fame isn't part of his promotional pattern. I wish I could talk to him about that.

What am I thinking?

Our relationship is severed, or at least will be once Randolph tells them I want to pay the advance back and control the work once again. I'll make it into something I want to write, wanted to write in the first place and see what other new insights the story might tell me. Hopefully AP will find another title to slip into that spring slot, another new author joining that splash down the publishing water slide. *Miranda* will have to wait but I'll return to her with a clear head. What was it Thoreau wrote? "Rather than love, than money, than fame, give me truth."

⑥

Both Bette and Darlien are on the line. "I can drive down and get you," Darlien says. "But not this weekend. There's a Packer game."

"I'll take the bus back. Jaime's returning to Spain. We're still friends. He says we can stay with him whenever we venture to Europe again."

"I'm sad for you," Bette says.

"Don't be. This is really better."

"I still feel badly that we didn't help you reach your goal."

"You guys have set me straight. I accomplished all kinds of things, including now having a great dog to share my time with. I learned how far I'm willing to go to reach for fame and the cost of that. I'll have great stories to tell people the next time they say, 'You know what you should do? You should get Oprah to pick your book.'"

"Let me know your schedule," Bette says. "Arnold and I will come by and pick you up at the bus station."

"You and Arnold are quite an item," I say.

Bette giggles.

⑥

I see Jaime off at the airport.

"I enjoys America," he says. "Good peoples live here. I make it on television news program my first visit," he grins. "It will be hard to top that."

"Maybe the next time don't wear an elf suit."

I watch until his British Airways plane lifts from the tarmac, waving Jaime into the future as well as my past.

Back at the condo I pack my collection of goodies accumulated while in Chicago, mostly related to Ho-Bee's needs. I contact the bus about bringing the dog with me, how large a kennel I can have. Luggage filled and accounted for; Clint hugs me and tells me to invest wisely. He scratches Ho-Bee's head and I think he might be a little sad to see his canine cohort leaving.

"Can we stop at the bookstore on the way?" Kari says. "I'd

like to pick up Marion Plush's new book for one of Clint's nieces, for Christmas."

"*Tibidabo*. Sure. I need a copy for myself. Maybe I'll send one to Jaime's niece and nephew." When was Irving's signing? I can't remember. Learning who the author was that day with Jaime so distracted me I didn't take note of the date. "Maybe the bookstore will have signed copies left."

"I'll see," Kari says as she parks the car.

"I'll wait here," I tell Kari. "I'm a mess. But pick up two other copies, all right? I'll pay you back, I will."

"Oh come on in. Ho-Bee will be fine for a couple of minutes. You love bookstores."

"My absent eyebrows will scare little children," I say.

"They'll think you're a character out of *Where the Wild Things Are*."

I slide out, make sure Ho-Bee has a window cracked, and follow her into the store. A small cluster of readers sit in a semi-circle in the author area. A white-haired man in cowboy boots bends over his books, signing his name. *Irving*. My heart does a little skippy beat.

"Just pick up the books from the side table. They have the 'author signed' stickers on them," I whisper to Kari, push her forward. I crouch behind the book shelves. Lemony Snicket and Madeleine L' Engle look over my shoulder from the shelf.

Kari decides to wait in line to speak to him!

No! Just pick up the books.

Irving looks up when Kari reaches him. He stands and shakes her hand, his eyes soon searching over her shoulder. He doesn't offer to sign the books Kari holds. He acts as though he doesn't realize she's there anymore; that anyone is. Eyes glued to mine, he leaves people waiting as he walks toward me.

My palms feel sweaty. I steady myself by clinging to the bookshelf that's not nearly as sturdy as it looks. I long for chocolate. Good, Barcelona chocolate.

"Annie. Miss Shaw. I'm so glad you came. So pleased." He

takes my hands in his. His touch feels hot. His forehead wrinkles as he looks at my missing eyebrows but only for a moment. Then his eyes are back to mine.

"*Tibidabo*," I say.

"Excuse me?"

"Your book. The Barcelona title. Congratulations. I didn't know. I didn't realize."

"I meant to tell you in the office that day but things got convoluted. I meant to say that I had an idea for a different publisher for your *Miranda*, that any more changes would have diluted the spark that's you, which your readers have come to expect. But I didn't. An editor always has to be wary, especially one who is also a writer and not only an avid reader, not to impose their voice onto another author. We run the risk of imposing."

"I needed imposing. Especially with *Miranda*," I say. He's still holding my hand. "But buying the book back will be better for me. I've decided to put my Miranda on the back burner, where she'll simmer rather than take over my stove, my kitchen, my life." I've been rattling along and he's let me. I lean closer into the book shelf.

He smiles. He does have the most engaging smile. "I'm occupied here, for a little while yet. Could you wait? Perhaps we could have dinner together? We could get a cab back to your cousin's."

"My cousin —"

"Won't mind, do you think? But I'll ask," Irving says. He turns to wave at Kari but I know the answer to his question, not her.

"'I will not go there,' says the cat. 'I will not go there, that is that.'"

"Excuse me?" Irving says.

"Just a phrase from a children's story that's been living in my head," I say. "I'm on my way to the bus station," I tell him. "I'm heading back to Milwaukee."

"Would you consider delaying for a day? Please?"

My hesitation is shorter than my eyebrows.

"I have commitments to keep so no. But you can write me if you wish. I promise I'll answer more quickly than I did before."

He looks disappointed but he accepts. "You know how to write your own story," he says. "I'll call you. Will that be all right?"

"I'd like that."

"I will go there," said the cat. "I will go there, that is that."

⊚

This is your story speaking. I thought you'd lost your way but you're back on track. All of us are afraid of being humiliated, looking foolish. It's part of our story. You think Oprah doesn't have her trials? Of course she does. You think Oprah never felt foolish, made a choice she regretted? She wakes up like you do everyday asking herself what kind of day to make it. Like her, you can ask how you'll bring a lift to another person's life, hoping to have the courage to face whatever trial will come your way. Take a little time to pat a dog or stroke a cat. Even famous people have to get up each day and write their story. It's what living looks like.

Reading a good truthfully told story does fill people up. Your job is to listen to the next story calling your name and write it down. That's me of course. If you don't write me down, I'll find someone else to do it, I will. If you don't write me down the way your heart tells you to, you'll miss the lesson and the blessing every story promises even when you're the only one who knows my name. And for the record, fame is a door best opened without pushing.

Your friend, Story.

⊚

Randolph hasn't spoken to me, but Irving tells me that he's being very professional in my efforts to buy back *Miranda*. Soon, she'll belong to me again and Randolph might handle my next writing venture whatever that may be. Clint has a lawyer friend who is taking care of my letter writing to Élan-Canine Salon, the chef's restaurant, the spa's window damage, my fines to the City of Chicago, and will go with me to the interview with Homeland Security about the catnip mice we sent to reviewers. I'm not on anyone's most wanted list. No sheep are walking around bleating at me as a "Baaaad woman, baaad woman." I've placated the animal rights people by sending them photos of Ho-Bee's perfectly healed ears.

I've signed up to be a substitute teacher back in Milwaukee. The school's just a block away here in Shorewood. I can walk to work and while I won't get rich financially, creative thinking will surround me as little wings of destiny flutter through my days drowning out the sound of the ticking of my organic clock. Buster from the Reading Ready program has welcomed me back and I've signed up for a few more kids to read to, too. I'll volunteer for another Sunday school class next year; the kids are in love with Bette, just as Arnold is.

I finished the cat picture book just before Christmas. I've started a young adult novel about a young American girl forced to move to Spain with her family and how she overcomes her loneliness. It's good work, engaging and much harder than I thought it'd be. And I've already decided that when I finish it, I'll use a pen name and not my real name. So I can keep who I am separate from who I am when I write. Something with a unisex name like Billi or Robin but not Marion.

Last week, I wrote the grant to fund an afterschool writing project in the mall. I call it "Treasure Shopping with Words" because that's what we'll be doing. It's what I'm doing now with my life.

Irving signed a copy of his book *Tibidabo* to me and brought it to me for a Valentine's Day gift when he flew in to meet my parents. The book is a reminder of what I won't ever do again: to try to have it all in return for something that doesn't fill me up.

One Year Later

📖

"*Bezoars Galore.* However did you come up with a title like that?" Oprah asks her guest, a studious looking man sitting across from her at her Harpo Studios in Chicago where she tapes for her new cable channel.

"On a plane, if you can believe that. A fellow author suggested it. Very encouraging young woman. I've got her card here somewhere." The man tugs at his sport coat pocket, pulls out a bent card. "It's my lucky charm," he says tapping the card. "I don't know much about her. She was on her way to Denver and gave me the encouragement I needed to write this book. Even referred me to her agent and gave me a copy of her book *The Long Bad Sentence.* She was working on another. As an afterthought, she suggested the title to my bestseller *Bezoars Galore.*"

"People can be so kind, can't they?" Oprah says.

"She certainly was."

Oprah turns the card over. "Annie Shaw. That name sounds familiar. Doesn't it Carol?" She looks off to the side to one of the producers. "From the website posts?"

"I think most of her books were published by Ardor Publishing," her guest continues.

"I'm intrigued by the title of this book, *Miranda of La Mancha.* I can't tell if it's a campy title on purpose or just literary pulp. I'd like to find out more."

"Her agent said it never got published. She writes children's books now. She's living in Denver, I believe. But I'll ask when I send her the newly developed bag of cat food designed to reduce bezoars. I'd be pleased to introduce you to her," her guest says. "It's what we authors all dream about, you know, getting Oprah to know our names."

Book Group Discussion Questions

By prior arrangement, Jane can visit with your book group via speaker phone. To arrange a time, contact her at www.jkbooks.com.

1. What did Annie desire? Did she know what she wanted in the beginning of the book? How did she come to recognize what truly mattered in her life or did she? Does fame lead to fulfillment?

2. Can you name a current desire in your life? What strategies are in place to move toward your goal? Is desire the longing for a past pleasure or does the Proverb 13:19 that Annie references, "Desire realized is sweet to the soul," say it best? Did Annie find her sweetness to the soul?

3. "Honesty without sensitivity is just plain rude. A person can be rude, even to herself, you know." What does Kari hope to accomplish by telling this to her cousin, Annie? Have you ever been rude to yourself, saying things you wouldn't say even to your worst enemy? What kind of harm can that bring to our spirits? How did Annie's lack of confidence affect her efforts to build a bestseller? Does the study Annie mentions about how praise for effort versus skill affected children's grades speak to how we can encourage each other?

4. Annie says: "They're my best friends. They've prayed and stayed with me through whines and dines. Maybe Bette's right. Maybe this idea came as divine intervention just when I needed it to stop those harpies." Do you have negative voices like harpies suggesting there are dreams you can't pursue or shouldn't? How do you silence them? How do your friends help you silence them? Do you think the ideas to help Annie's book become a bestseller were Divinely inspired? Why or why not?

5. Kari recounts a way to evaluate decisions using a clock face. Some decisions are really, really smart (at 12 o'clock) but some are really, really dumb (at 11:59). We can't always know until we look back through time whether a decision was a wise one or not. Have you ever done something your friends/family thought was 11:59 but it turned out to be a 12 o'clock? What made the difference?

6. Throughout the book Annie receives emails from reading fans. What did the emails say about Annie's writing that Annie overlooked as she worked on her revisions for Irving? Was she writing the wrong kinds of books or was she truly with the wrong publisher?

7. How well did Annie deal with her ex-husband's demands? Could having a clearer understanding of her desires have kept her from marrying him in the first place? Did she learn anything that helped her resolve her issues with Jaime? With Irving?

8. How well did Annie deal with Jaime's request? Was she right in saying that if he changed for her—or vice versa—that when their marriage faced challenges they would not have the resources to sustain it? What do individuals need for accommodation to be healthy and not where someone gives up much of who they are to please the other?

9. Bette says that Annie's friends will be like midwives working together against the "Pharaohs." What does she mean? Do we all have pharaohs in our lives? Later Bette tells a woman that we should all be midwives, that "midwives start cheering for the mother long before the delivery." How can we cheer our friends (or our own efforts) on long before the final goal is reached?

10. Annie mentions the phrase learned in Barcelona, *Está Aquí*: You are here. How does accepting that phrase help the characters in this story or does it? Do we need to know where we are before we can find our way to where we want to go next or where God wants to take us?

11. Who achieved fulfillment in this story? Are any of the characters not on their way toward building a happier more productive life? Does this book meet Annie's criteria for a romance novel? Why or why not?

Acknowledgments

This little labor of love grew from a seed planted by Don Pape and Dudley Delffs years ago and has been watered through the years by my agent Joyce Hart of Hartline Literary Services in Pittsburgh and now my editors at Zondervan, Sue Brower and Becky Philpott. I thank them all and especially Sue for helping me find the story. Darlien France of Sonrise Academy in The Dalles, Oregon, won the auction fundraising bid to have a character named for her and she let me take liberty with it. She bears no other resemblance to the bossy older sister. Retired police officer and friend, Donna Stoner of Arizona, allowed several of us to join her competition in Spain and other venues since, and I am grateful. She's nothing like the bossy older sister, either. The official name of the event held every other year around the world is the trademark World Police and Fire Games and not the name used in this story. Judy Schumacher, friend and prayer partner of Adquest Inc. in Wisconsin sent me the *Almost Famous* pin that made me smile and helped define Annie's story. Several writing colleagues offered memories from their exposure to celebrity television show experiences. My own friends cheered me on during the writing; my husband Jerry cheered loudest at "the end." But the errors and omissions, the characters and their insights or lack thereof are all from my own head. What treasures readers take away are gifts that *Story* gave. I'm grateful to have written them down.

View Jane's monthly words of encouragement at www.jkbooks .com where reader groups can also arrange for speaker phone visits with her. Please sign up for her monthly *Story Sparks* newsletter at that site as well. Track her at www.Zondervan.com, The Author Jane Kirkpatrick on Facebook, follow her on Twitter or on her blog www.jkbooks.com, and her dog Bo's blog at www .BodaciousBothedog.blogspot.com. Help her have more followers than her dog has!